THE CACKLING OF THE CROWS

NEAL SELLERS

THE CACKLING OF THE CROWS

THE CACKLING OF THE CROWS

ACKNOWLEDGMENTS

I started this journey on March 27, 1997. Because life happens, ironically, I completed the story, on March 26, 2017, 20 years later almost to the day. The journey continues … Thank you …

- Leslie Sellers, my loving and supportive wife
- Lisa Pitts
- Wynnette Lee
- Jason Davis
- Tracey Washington
- Carmela Capalad

If this book can provide enjoyment, touch, inspire, or help someone, then I'm fulfilled.

Blessings.

PROLOGUE #1

Winnie stood up and walked toward me, and sat down on the floor in front of where I was sitting. She grabbed my hand and held it.

"Wow. I didn't think we would end like this! We had a great run! But you know we can't be together anymore, right, Que?"

"What are you talking about, Winnie?"

"I don't belong anymore ..."

"I've got to see you. We've got to talk. We can work this out, Kiyy," I pleaded.

Man, I went out in the name of love trying to salvage our relationship, but you women can be cruel.

"I don't want to see you. You're not gonna change my mind," she challenged.

"Oh … you gonna see me, Kiyy. And you gonna tell me to my face that we're over! You gonna look me in my eyes, and tell me you don't love me anymore!"

"Wow, she's pretty, Uncle Que," Karen gushed.

"Yuuuup," Aaron chimed in, as they both just stood there and gawked.

Out of the corner of my eye, I marveled at the fact that K.P. was blushing. Now that doesn't happen too often.

"Is she your new girlfriend?" Karen threw out boldly.

K.P. playing along for as long as she could, busted out laughing and grabbed the kids in for a bear hug.

"No, I am not the new girlfriend, you rug rats, and you know this too, 'cause I've known you both since doo doo diapers," K.P. said laughing.

"She ought to be!" Suzie Que mumbled through a perfect smile for Steven's and my ears only.

"If I could have gotten your older sister to come, we could have had a foursome!"

Jinx looked puzzled.

"We don't have an older sister, Que."

K.P. laughed and filled Jinx in on the joke. "He means Mom, Jinx."

Our desserts came and we dug in. You know that age old saying that you know that food is good when everyone is quiet? It applied here. After savoring our first few bites, we offered each other samples.

"Que? Want a *piece of my apple pie?*" (How many of you thought what I thought? Raise your hand … Good. So it wasn't just me!)

"Is it still hot?"

"I say it's steaming, but you have a taste and tell me if you like?"

"Would you two dogs in heat cut it out?" K.P. groans.

"She started it," I protest.

"And I'll finish it too," Jinx coos as she plays with some pie on her fork with her tongue.

Four women. Each a part of my life, each a part of my heart. Be patient and re-live what I've lived through. Would I do it the same if I had the chance to do different?

PROLOGUE #2

They know something I don't and they revel in the knowledge that I can't decipher their language. I've missed the signs, even when I expect the unexpected. The future remains a mystery to me. The past remains a mystery to me. The present remains a mystery to me. They used to caw. They just cackle now. The cackling of the crows.

IMPRESSIONS

Riddle me this:
What is the most feared species on the face of this earth?
And in the same breath, the rarest of
species in this day and age?

Every morning, and I do mean every morning, and subsequently throughout the day and night, it's the same damn thing. "Caw … Caw … Caw." Other mornings and afternoons, it's "Caw … Cackle … Cackle … Caw," and still some mornings and evenings, it's just "Cackle … Cackle … Cackle," and then I wake up from the same dream. I'm falling, I see flashes of people and I hear crows. Then everything is black, but I still hear the crows, but the sounds are different, not the same cawing. That's all I ever remember, and then I wake up hearing these crows outside my bedroom window. It's got me perplexed. What? Come on now, are you gonna be one of those readers that talks to the book? No need to hide now, I done peeped your style. You're not gonna let me tell my story, right? I suppose you have a better one, too. So, then why ain't I reading your book? In the future, I'd appreciate it if you'd keep your comments to a whisper under your breath. That's right, I hear you. No, I'm not bugging out. In fact, I see you right now. In fact, I see you all the time … If you're not me … then you wouldn't understand what the hell I'm going through. Comprende … Capisce … Kaputt … Understand? (Apologies to UTFO).

Everybody ought to listen to rap! Great! That sentence alone has eliminated about half-a-million potential readers. Don't all y'all stampede to the door at once. :-) … Stop smirking. Yeah, I'm on the damn Internet too. So now you "know-it-alls" are trying to put a profile to me … Hmmm … likes rap … appears confrontational … got to be a black man. Yep, I'll bet my stock quotients on that … yes, siree. Well, Joe Suntan, tell them what they've won!!!

Warning!!! If you continue to read this book, you may turn out like me, which ain't a bad thing if you ask me. But of course that depends on who you're asking. I drip with sarcasm, so if you can't swim, stay outta my pool. Funny thing is … I used to be a lifeguard. So I could save you both ways, if I wanted to. I suppose you think I forgot what I was talking about, huh? Well, I didn't. Just putting it off, you know how we do! Besides, I gotta get a few things off my chest this morning, so either step or put an "H" on your chest and "Handle It." It's my book, right? So, my pace. :-) …

This style is identical to none. It reads like music, it's conversational, flowing with peaks and valleys, non-stop with awkward pauses. It's liquid. It's uninhibited. While it appears to be constrained in lieu of conventional grammar, this technique goes outside the box, beyond the pages of this book. The pages lead to a road that has no end, your mind. If you can allow yourself to not become constrained with traditional grammar's finite ellipses and embrace new structure and new direction, with thoughts within three dots that represent presence, wisdom, and direction, expressed or not, you might find your own creative road that will never end. Enjoy the journey.

The manner in which this is written, reflects that aforementioned road with ellipsis (…) denoting a void or omission in our lives. The three dots represent God's presence, God's wisdom and God's direction, those ellipses missing in our lives more times than not.

I share this simple daily prayer:

God … I pray for your presence in my life … I pray for wisdom to recognize your presence … I pray for direction to follow your presence … I pray for understanding to receive your presence … And I pray to give grace to all as you have given grace to me. Amen.

God's presence is all around us. Take a look around you. Go ahead, do it. The sky, the ocean, the stars … the beauty of flowers, animals, people. God's wisdom is all around us. Not man's wisdom. God's wisdom. Not only does it come forth in the Bible, but innately we feel it … we know right from wrong, good vs. evil. Yet we reject this wisdom because we have been given the ability to choose. Who do you think gave you this ability? God's direction is clear as well. You want Heaven or Hell? The path is clear to either destination.

And unto man he said, Behold, the fear of the LORD, that is wisdom, and to depart from evil is understanding— Job 28-28.

God's grace allows us forgiveness for our sins and the opportunity to confess those sins, and do better. A gift from God that we all take for granted. Accept God's gift before it is too late.

Three dots have now entered your psyche, and you have no choice but to associate them henceforth forever more with God's presence, God's wisdom, and God's direction. You're welcome sinners and saints. So if you get to parts of this book where you find it hard to push through and continue reading, remember the ellipses and see it through. It'll be worth it. Feel free to cop the prayer for your own, and may it motivate you as it has for me. Back to those things I need to get off my chest.

This is a how to book … how to succeed in life … how to fail in life … how to get the girl … or guy (for the ladies and the honey boys!) … how to do whatever the hell I feel like talking about, until or if I decide to speak on what this book is really all about. *What makes me an authority?* I'd appreciate it if you'd stop interrupting me. As my mother and every other mother who passed the line down would say, "Don't make me have to say it again!" And if your mom was the type to sprinkle in some profanity every now and then … somebody say, "Hooooo!" … I'm a hip hop junkie (Apologies to Nice & Smooth) … sue me!

I am an authority because I have a damn opinion, whether or not it is right or wrong. Either way, that's not for you to say. If you can defend your position, and here's the key word: *intelligently*, then you too can be an authority. Can you guess what I do for a living? When you get constipated … backed up for the uneducated … and you finally let it out … and the shit hits the fan? I'm the one that cleans that shit up. Never mind that you could have taken a laxative and made it easier on your damn self and everyone else around you. Now if you haven't figured out what I do yet, then there's still hope for you. If you have, God be with you, 'cause there's no turning back. You need help!

I should have been a damn psychiatrist or a psychologist (still haven't figured out which one yet). I'm not gonna insult your intelligence, even though half of y'all don't know the difference between the two anyway. In fact, I was just like you. Stop fronting, because if I said "Pop Quiz" right now, you couldn't tell me what each does nor the difference between the two. But alas, do not fret. Never let it be said that Gregory Que (pronounced "Q" for those who appreciate proper pronunciation), did not help those in need. As a public service, I'm gonna stop writing and give you one minute to go and look up the two words. I'm not playing. That's the problem today, all this knowledge out there and everybody's too lazy to grab it. And to show you that I'm serious, the next page will be blank, so you won't feel like you're missing anything. If I could look it up, and I consider myself to be intelligent, so can you …

The Jeopardy timer starts now …

The World Book Dictionary defines psychiatry as "the study and treatment of mental disorders," and the same book defines psychology as "the science of the mind." Psychology examines the reasons why people act, think, and feel as they do. So a psychiatrist is a doctor who treats mental disorders, and a psychologist is a doctor who is trained to explain why we (people), do the things that we do. Now those that just realized that they've been played … pick up your faces and peep the rationale. And those who don't know what the fuck just happened … just pick up your faces.

A little intellectual stimulation never hurt anyone except an idiot. For those that actually went and looked up the words, I thank you. You appreciate learning, and it's always a good habit to look up words if you're not sure of their meaning. Ain't nothing worse than someone who thinks that they're intelligent because they're using words not in everyday vocabulary, and then use those words out of context. And I ain't gonna embarrass you by blowin' up your spot, but you know who you are, and everybody else knows who you are too. For the rest of y'all lazy asses, I knew you would just turn the page, mumbling something along the lines of, "Fuck that, I ain't looking up shit!" So your lazy asses still benefited because I thought about you. But in the long run, if you don't join the bandwagon, you're the one that's gonna lose out. Because while everyone else is increasing their vocab, and becoming more intelligent, yo' ass ain't gonna know what no one's talking about because you're still talking, "Fuck that shit."

Don't get mad at me, I'm trying to help you. And just in case some wise-ass (_Ô v Ô_) is out there thinking, "Why he didn't use *Webster's Dictionary?*" 'Cause in my house, we didn't have *Webster's*. He didn't come to my neighborhood. *World Book* did. So my parents bought the whole set, the children's books, the dictionaries, the encyclopedias … what is an encyclopedia anyway? Just kidding … look it up for the real meaning at your leisure. By the way, the plan is to take care of them with the millions I make from this book and the movie rights … trudat. So spread the word about this book, so I can give my parents what they deserve. Support the black man! Damn … I just lost another hundred thousand readers! Y'all hate to hear that term, don't ya? I wonder why? Could it be that no one ever does? Just ask my man Spike Lee!

Of course, me and my brother and my two sisters just let it all collect dust for the longest until

Mom said, "Your father does not put in the hours he does for y'all to be some dummies. Educate yo'self before I start holding class with this belt!" So … some readers were born. :-) There's some truth to the statement, "Reading is Fundamental," so dust off the cobwebs and take a look see at a book near you.

Excuse me, phone's ringing …

"Que Quarters."

"What up, Ho'?"

"Now all the way live from New York City…"

"It's your girl K.P. Grab the mic and get busy…"

"Can I kick it?"

"Yes, ya can!"

"So gimme them drawers so I can tell your man …"

" … Check the panties that I left in your coat, and while you're sniffing them there … let me clear my throat! De Ni Ni Ni Ni Ni Nirrrr Ni Ni…"

"Ohhhh! … Have mercy, baby … I hope ya don't mind …"

"Let me clear my throat!" (Apologies to DJ Kool).

"What up with you, Ho'?"

"Nothing, Ho'. What's on the menu today?"

"You, if you'll let me!"

"Que, you're so good for my ego …"

"Uh oh. I know that tone. What's the matter with you?"

"Nothing."

"K.P., you know I'm not a dentist, so I'm not pulling any teeth. I'm gonna ask you one more time. What's the matter?"

"You know it's Jinx, again."

"What happened now? I thought she got her shit together ever since Snow got killed."

"I don't know if she's still grieving or what, but she's just let herself go again. Work slacking, bumming around."

"It's been five years!"

"I know, but look how long it took you to get over Kiyy…"

"Why you gotta go there!?!"

"Sorrrry! Didn't know it was still such a sore spot. Anyway, Jinx adores you, then again who doesn't … ?"

"I can name a few."

"Me too. Anyway, why don't you come by and take us out today?"

"What? You don't trust me with Jinx alone?"

"Hell no! You're always talking about how you gonna get in this family. My mama ain't even safe!"

"I know that's right. Yo' mama is fiiiinnnne!"

"I'm not laughing, Que..."

"What? Are you afraid she's gonna give it up before you do?"

She laughed at the apparent absurdity. Or was it? Hmmm.

"I knew you had to laugh at that!"

"You're a fool! What if I went after your dad?"

"My mama would whip that ass! You know Pat don't play that. I don't care if she does love you to death!"

"You know Que, you better stop flirting about my mama..."

"Where the hell is that coming from?"

"She's always talking about how if she was younger, she would give you a run for your money."

"*Your moms* says that? Awww, shit! It's on now!"

"You know if I didn't kill you, Darren would, and Jinx would kill you just because you didn't get with her!"

"I'll whip your brother's ass, and who said I can't have Jinx too?"

"Boy ... it's a good thing we're best friends, 'cause I'd be all in that ass ..."

"I didn't know you was into that! Is that what the Krappa's getting?"

"You better stop calling him the Krappa, 'cause you gonna have me calling the Kappas that one day. Besides, why do the frats diss each other like that? I thought it was all about unity?"

"See, now you're letting the Operator know that you're a GDI ..."

"What!?! And what is? ... Never mind. And how do you know that the Operator is even Greek?"

"Operator? ... Operator?"

"Que, you're a fool ... Stop it."

"Operator ... if you're Greek, let us know. Give us one of those Operator sayings."

"The operator ain't even listenin', Que ..."

"Operator ... please?"

PLEASE DEPOSIT TEN CENTS TO CONTINUE.

"Ohhhh shit!"

"Told ya, K.P. Now Operator, I'm a Que 'til the day I die. What are you? Are you a Krap ... I mean Kappa? Naw, can't be, you would have cut the connection."

PLEASE DEPOSIT TEN CENTS TO CONTINUE.

"Knew ya couldn't be. Are ya in a fraternity?"

THE NUMBER YOU HAVE DIALED IS NOT IN SERVICE RIGHT NOW.

"Yo, K.P., this shit is wild. She's in a sorority."

"How do you know?"

"There you go showing that GDI ass again. Didn't you just hear the number is not in service now? Think, woman."

"Shut up."

"Okay Operator, I'm going out on a limb for Greek solidarity here. Respect due to all the sororities, but if you're in the sorority that I think you're in, you know it's close to my heart. And I'm gonna ask you to go out on a limb too. Are you my sister?"

"Oo oop!"

"Que! That's that Delta call, ain't it? That's what your mother and sisters do!"

"Thank you, Operator! You've made my day! And we'll just keep this on the down low."

PLEASE TRY YOUR CALL AGAIN LATER.

"Operator, are you flirting with me?"

"If I wasn't on the phone with your ass Que, I would never believe this."

"Operator, here's my number. But wait … you already know it! (lol) … So I tell you what, feel free to give me a call anytime, and I'll make sure K.P. is nowhere to be found!"

"Oh hell no, I'm blowing up your spot! Operator, he's got a girl already!"

"I am as free as the wind, Operator. She's just jealous, so please call if you'd like."

THANK YOU FOR CALLING.

"I bet she doesn't call."

"You mean you hope she doesn't call."

"No, I mean I bet she doesn't call. Wanna bet?"

"Nope. If she calls, I'll be happy. And if she doesn't, I was happy that she acknowledged my questions."

"You're just saying that 'cause you know she's listening now."

"She was listening before, so her mind was made up then."

"Such a damned charmer."

"How do you think I've been your friend since childhood? Remember I seen ya fat ass (_!_) before the Krappa or any other brother for that matter. I said it then that you would have a big ol' butt."

"Uh huh, in the bath tub with your inch worm …"

K.P. busted out laughing at her character assassination shot … to the dismay of every man.

"Whoa! All righty then, let's clear that up right now! … Hey! … *Hey!* Ain't nothing funny, K.P.!"

"Oh, now it ain't funny? I connect you with inch worm, and you get all sensitive. What's that all about?"

"Cause you know that shit ain't true ..."

"What? Proof is in the pudding, right? You saw my fat ass ... I saw your inch worm ..."

"How old were we, K.P.?"

"Didn't this just happen last night!?!" (Raucous laughter).

"Are you finished laughing, Ho'?"

"Don't get 'Michael' on me now! ... Tito ... give me some tissue ... Jermaine ... stop teasing! (Apologies to Eddie Murphy). I know the Operator is dying laughing now! ... Okay ... okay ... we were babies."

"Ya know, if you think about it, an inch long at that time could be saying something. Who knows? Your ass definitely remembers!"

"'Cause the shit was so small."

"Well, ain't nobody complaining about Floyd and the Crew now! Matter of fact ... I hear that Busch Gardens has been closed for some time. What's up with that?"

"Fuck you, Que!"

"That's why Busch Gardens has been closed, 'cause certain people can't operate the rides!"

"That's not what I told you, and you know it. But I ain't telling you shit no more."

"Who loves ya, K.P.?"

"Are you coming by or what?"

"Is your mama gonna be there?"

"Goodbye ..."

"Aight ... I'll be by later, Ho'."

"Later, Ho'."

That was my girl, K.P., but to you, she's Katrina Parker. We've known each other since we were born. Her mom and my mom grew up together, so our families are pretty tight. K.P.'s father was killed by a drug dealer about fifteen years ago. Without going into too much of the details, Jinx used to go out with this dealer named Snow. His real name was Luther, but only, and I mean *only* Mr. & Mrs. Parker could call him that. Jinx and Snow had been together since Junior High. Luther's father had died during that time and he took it pretty hard. Soon after, he took to the streets and started slinging. Now understand, every street kid ain't bad. I was a street kid and look how I turned out. Don't say a damn word! Anyway, Snow was a nice guy who had no one to turn to. The streets showed him love, and he took it. I'm not saying that his choices were right. Remember what I said earlier about who's to say what's right or wrong?

Spare me the legalisms, I hear them all day, everyday … I'm saying though …

Mr. Parker took an interest in Snow, but by then he was so far into the game, if he had walked away, enemies would have still been gunning for a brother. Tough situation for a father to be in. I can't even say what I would have done if it was my daughter in the exact same circumstance. Tough as it was, Mr. Parker was making some head way with Snow, you know, telling him to think about the future, especially as it concerned his daughter, Jinx. Mr. Parker let Snow know that he didn't approve of what he was doing, but they had an understanding that if anything ever happened to Jinx … well, let's just say Snow might as well just put the gun to his own head. I think Snow respected Mr. Parker more because he didn't forbid him to see Jinx. Personally, I never understood it, and I used to ask K.P. all the time why her father allowed it. She just said that Snow was a different person when he entered their house, like night and day.

Next to Biggie Smalls, I was probably Bk's biggest booster, always biggin' up the city of Brooklyn. I know it's a damn borough, but it might as well be a city. Back in the days, I used to live a thug type life, of course now I'm into smug life. But back then I ran with what today you'd call a sick type clique. Yo, if I come clean now with some of the stuff I did back in the day, my moms is gonna have a heart attack. But remember, I'm trusting you the reader to spread the word about this book, so I can take care of *mi* parents. Anyway, since I took a step away from that lifestyle, I kept a good rapport with a lot of shady peeps. Word got back to me through the tunnel (on the down low for the uneducated), that a crew was gonna make a move on Snow's operation. So, without me being the messenger (that's how you stay alive, son), I made sure that Snow got the message through the grapevine. So when these cats made their move, Snow was ready for them, and basically he brought in da noise and da funk. When it was over, brothers was being sized up for caskets. In this game, there are no rules except an eye for an eye, so brothers was plottin' and schemin'. On the day shit hit the fan (it's funny how terms come back, and are used differently conceptually), I was in school. More on that at a later date.

Mr. Parker had taken Jinx to the movies, they did stuff like that … Father/Daughter day, Mother/ Son, Mother/Daughter(s), Father/Son … I thought that was cool. In fact, I wished we had done that more in my family. Mrs. Parker's car was parked in the driveway and not in the garage. I know because she blamed herself for not putting the car in the garage. It really wouldn't have mattered, because they would have got them either way, the street or the driveway. Well, Mr. Parker parked across the street from the house, and as he and Jinx were crossing the street, a car passed by slowly, then stopped with both tinted windows on the passenger side coming down when someone yelled, "Hey, Jinx!?!"

Jinx stopped and turned toward the car. Mr. Parker stopped and turned as well. Someone from the car called out, "*Meda* Jinx, is that you?"

She called out back to the car, "Yeah … who … ?"

Before she could finish her sentence, shots had rung out. When it was all said and done, Mr. Parker had jumped in front of Jinx, and had shielded her with his body. He caught all the bullets meant for Jinx. The funeral was one of the saddest things I've ever experienced. Snow paid for everything, and I think he took it harder than the family if that's possible. Of course he blamed himself, and I guess rightfully so. If the family blamed him, you'd never know it publicly.

During the months that followed, Snow kept a low profile. Then one day, I saw him huddled up in the house with Darren, K.P. and Jinx's brother.

Darren had changed, and I can't say for the better. He had become bitter, and who's to blame him? I can only empathize because my father is still alive. Snow knew a little about my rep back in the days and he asked me for advice. That's all I needed now, the weight of someone else's world on my shoulders. He asked me if I'd retaliate. I asked what would it accomplish? Mr. Parker wouldn't be coming back.

Then he asked the question that always provokes a response, and nine times out of ten that response is emotional… "What if it was your father?"

He went on to explain that Darren wanted revenge and had approached him for help. How could he say no? Once again, a position that I was not envious of. He continued to say that his father was dead and Mr. Parker had been like a father to him. He loved Jinx, and she looked at him at times like he should have done something by now, but of course she never actually said it. I think maybe it was just the way that Snow looked at it that made him feel that way.

"I know you're in school now Que, and I wouldn't ask you for help 'cause I know you don't do that now."

You and I both know that when someone says something in that way, they're looking for help.

"What do you want me to do?"

You had to let me reminisce, huh? Although, maybe that's one of my problems. I haven't really dealt with some of the demons of my past. And maybe I never will. But hey, I may thank you one day on the street for helping me confront my past … ya never know.

I didn't even listen to my messages last night, actually, never got the chance … got a booty call … and well, you know … booty … I mean … duty calls! :-) Remember how you used to hear stories from your boys? Or for that matter, ladies, your girls? About all the wild stuff that would happen to them? And you'd be sitting there agreeing, like it was routine and it happened all the time to you, but you were actually thinking, "Damn … why that shit don't happen to me!?!" And now that you're older, you realize that it didn't happen to them either. Well hell, I didn't front, none of those erotic, off-the-wall encounters ever happened to me when I was younger, and I had no problem saying so. Although I did lose my virginity at eleven, and I did have an "in your dreams" encounter before I went to college. But the scandalous stuff has happened as an adult. Is everyone else making up for lost time too!?!

My "in your dreams" encounter and my booty call last night involved the same girl. I've known her now for about fourteen years, since the night of our first encounter. Guess you wanna hear details, huh? I suppose that if I tell it, you'd be more than happy to listen (or read). :-/ Well, you need some background first. I'ma say this now, 'cause you're forming your own impressions about me, yet you don't know jack about me except for what I'm telling you, of course. But still, you may never catch the essence of who I be. I'm a gentleman by nature … and a hooker by choice. What does that mean? Let's just let it marinate for a while. I have never cheated when I've been in a committed relationship. You can believe whatcha want, but that's the truth. And I know some of you ladies are sucking your teeth, 'cause I said a committed relationship. What does that mean, you say with an eye roll? To me, commitment and monogamy go hand in hand. It's a conscious decision and effort to effectuate a relationship to a level of stability where two people can become one. So when I'm in a committed relationship, it's all about me and the young lady that I'm with … point blank … period … the end. I'm a "romantic." You do know that they're a dying breed nowadays? Just like the educated black man with street smarts, add extremely handsome (hey, if you don't believe it, no one else will … love thyself, people!), no kids, good job, nice car, and own place to the equation. You've got the most feared, and the rarest of species in this day and age! Yes ladies … I am a grrrrreat catch! :-) Though in this day and age, I am more of a cynic. I still hold my "romantic" values, but you'd be lucky to catch the vapors. This is a thinly veiled plea for the lady of my dreams to find and rescue me!

Anyway, I had a high school sweetheart named Kiyler (Kīy-ler), Kiyy, for short. I can only say that we were in love at the time, well, I can say now that *I* was in love (sorry, some bitterness seems to seep out when I talk about this). You'll have to ask *her* about her feelings. Yo fellas, you know how you're reluctant to let any feelings show for whatever reasons? Maybe it's a male intuition or something. Women say that it's because we don't want to appear soft or feminine? Whatever. I've figured it out, and I'm gonna help you ladies with something that's not rocket science. We've all heard the stories about men being told it's wack to cry and "to be a man" (feel free to interpret as you see fit). Contrary to popular belief, men do have feelings. Women, you've experienced them on rare, and for some of you, I do mean *rare* occasions. It usually ends with the woman saying to herself, "Why doesn't he do that more often!?!"

Drum roll please! … … … … … … … Because more times than not, you take a man's kindness for weakness! Sure, you talk about wanting a nice, sensitive guy, but who do you run to? A bad boy. (Puffy, you marketing genius, or whoever deserves the credit for making everybody want to be down with this term). A guy treats you with respect and dignity and y'all don't know how to act, 'cause you're not used to being treated like … like a queen. So what do you do? Take the kindness for weakness. Of course not all of you, right? But enough to say something about it. See, now I done gone off on a tangent, mixing apples and oranges and stories. We'll save that one for another day.

Back to Kiyy. We were inseparable. We did everything together and never seemed to tire of the other's presence. It was said that if ever two people belonged together, it was us. Of course, hearing that now just makes me shake my head, but back then I believed it too. Now everyone had their cliques and crews in high school, and we were no exception. Kiyy was best friends with Pamela and Simone … They had been together since Grade School. Pamela went out with this Panamanian guy named Sammy and Simone went out with this guy named Alex. Ironically, while everyone was marrying me and Kiyy off, they were frowning on Alex and Simone's relationship and saying that it wouldn't last. The common complaint seemed to be that Alex was too domineering, and didn't give Simone any room to breathe. Ironic, huh? Especially when you find out that Alex and Simone are now both doctors and married with children.

Well, we all meshed together by default. The girls bonded with this kid named Carlos that they met during Freshman Orientation, and had been friends with since, and they brought him into the mix. The rumor going around about Carlos was that he was hanging out in the closet. I'm not one to knock nobody's hustle, your lifestyle and choices are your own, just as long as you respect mine. Every once in a while, he would try and downplay the rumors by displaying some signs of manhood, but he didn't try too hard. Carlos never confirmed nor denied the rumors and we accepted him as part of our little family. It got to the point that I actually would defend Carlos to my friends when they got on my back about our friendship and how it looked to everyone else. I suppose, in hindsight, I tolerated him a little more because of Kiyy, Pamela, and

Simone. The truth is that over time I did come to accept him for who he was, and trusted him because of the closeness of our group.

It was my senior year, so I was preparing to do the college tour thing. Kiyy wanted me to stay in the city and go to college, I wanted to go away. Never did I dream that this difference of opinion would be the beginning of the end. I guess I never really understood her despair until well after our relationship had ended, and I'm not so sure that I could really see it then. In our high school, we had a program that allowed students that had finished up their credits to graduate early a chance to live away on a college campus for a few months. Sort of a college prep course thing, to get used to college life. I jumped at the chance, but Kiyy begged me not to go.

"What am I going to do without you!?!" she pleaded.

"I'm only going to be gone a semester. Besides, you can visit me on weekends."

"Don't you love me!?!"

"Of course I do! How can you question whether I love you or not!?! This isn't about that, I'm trying to establish a foundation for our future ... can't you see that?"

"You can establish a foundation here."

"I think that I can establish a better future and foundation for us if I check out my options for education out-of-state as well."

"I don't want you to go."

Suffice it to say that you know I went, right? Kiyy did visit me on weekends, but I noticed a cool tolerance toward me. I reasoned that maybe it was her way of gradually becoming less attached to me because she began to realize that my going away to college was becoming less of a dream and more of a reality. I accepted that because I reasoned that everyone dealt with things in their own way. At the time, I didn't feel that she loved me any less, nor did I love her any less. I had heard from my boys back at school that she was hanging out with Carlos a lot, and they cautioned me that it didn't look right. I told them that there was nothing to worry about, that he was keeping her company while I was away. Besides, she was hanging out with the crew and he happened to be a part of it. I told them that they hadn't noticed him because I was always around, and besides, he wasn't into girls like that, y'all know what time it was. Basically I got cursed out and was told to wake up and smell the coffee, he was trying to push up on her.

"Yo … the boy is hotter than July," I reasoned (Apologies to Stevie Wonder).

"Yeah, we know, but something ain't right," they said.

So you know what I did, right? I did what I thought a man should do. I confronted Carlos. I had come home for a weekend and the crew had gotten together. At the time I wasn't sure, but I am now. It seemed that there was tension within the group. I noticed that Carlos had an attitude with Pamela and vice versa. In fact, Carlos tried to snap at me, and we nipped that shit in the bud quick fast. And although Kiyy seemed to take his side, I just attributed Carlos' mood to PMS. Well, the next night, it seemed that things had calmed down and I pulled Carlos to the side.

"There's something I want to ask you, Carlos, and I'm coming to you man to man." :o|

"Yeah, Greg. What is it?"

"How do you feel about Kiyler?"

"Huh?"

"How do you feel about Kiyler?"

"What do you mean, Gregory?"

I hated it when he called me Gregory, just the way he would say it!

I see how we gonna play this, I thought. *Play dumb ... but it's written all over your face.*

"Do you have any feelings for Kiyler?"

"Of course I do! I have feelings for all of you guys, you know that."

"All right, my bad. Let me get straight to the point. Do you like Kiyler? Are there any emotional feelings toward her? Do you want her as more than a friend? Are you trying to get with my girl!?!"

"Oh Gregory! I look at Kiyy as a sister, just as I do Pam and Monie. I look at you as an older brother. I wouldn't do anything to harm you guys! The truth is, Kiyy has been a wreck since you left her ..."

"Hold up ... I did not leave Kiyy ..."

"That's not how she sees it, and I've tried to get her to see that too. She's been lonely and I've just been there for her as a friend would be in a time of need."

"She hasn't said anything to me about that."

"And she won't, either, because she doesn't want you to stay on her account. She wants you to stay because you want to be with her."

"We've talked about that, and my decision to go away has nothing to do with how I feel about Kiyy, and she knows that."

"She cried every night the first two weeks you were gone. She didn't want anyone to know what she was going through, but I overheard her and Pam talking. I called her one night to see how she was doing, and she sounded horrible. She said she missed you, and I suggested that we go hang out to get her mind on other things besides the misery that she was going through. She seemed to brighten up a little, so I suggested that we hang out some more. One day, some of your friends saw us and approached us, and asked how you were doing. Kiyy said that she assumed that you were fine. I asked her later why she said that, and if everything was all right between you two. She just said that she needed a friend and she was glad I was around ..."

"All right, enough of that. Kiyy and I will handle it. But back to you. So you're telling me that there is nothing going on between you and Kiyy? You haven't developed any feelings toward her?"

"I can't believe that you're asking me that!"

"Yeah, but you ain't answering the question either. Look me in my face and tell me there's nothing going on with Kiyy, and that you don't have any feelings toward her."

For as long as I live, I'll never forget that moment. He looked me dead in my face and said, "I am not trying to get with Kiyler. I view Kiyy as a sister and nothing else, and I am hurt by your lack of faith in me because I consider you my older brother."

"First of all, you should not be hurt if nothing's going on, and second, you know that if I want to know something, I don't speculate, I go straight to the source. I've heard rumors and that's why I came straight to you, so you could tell me the truth."

"Who said that?"

"It's not important who said what. But what is important is what you confirm or deny. You denied, so that's that … it's squashed. I just hope you're not lying to me."

"Gregory, I can't believe that you would think that I would lie to you …"

"I can't believe it either, so that's why I asked."

About two weeks later, I got a call from Kiyy, and she dropped a bomb on me (Apologies to the Gap Band).

"I don't think we should be together anymore. I want to break up!"

"What!!?!!"

"I don't want to be with you anymore!"

"Where the hell is this coming from!?!"

"I don't feel the same about you as I did."

Who is this cold mechanical fish that I'm talking to? I asked myself. *This is not the girl that I fell in love with. What happened to my girlfriend? Somebody call the cops because my girl has been kidnapped, and this girl here is holding her for ransom!*

"While I've been by myself, I've had time to think about things. You've changed ..."

"I've changed!?! Is this about me leaving? That don't even sound right. You don't even sound like yourself, Kiyy! We've got to talk so we can get to the bottom of this ..."

"There's nothing to talk about. My mind's made up."

"Hold up ... You smash me in the face with a brick, and you just gonna leave me on the floor bleeding!?! You're willing to give up our relationship just like that? Without a fight? You're telling me you don't love me anymore?"

She paused, but didn't say anything. Then it hit me!

"Is there someone else?"

Time seemed to stand still as my heart began the trip out of my body, stopping in my throat. Again, she said nothing.

"Who is it?" I whispered.

"It doesn't matter ..."

"Who is it!?!" I said a little more forcefully than I intended.

The silence was deafening, until she whispered, "Carlos."

To this day I still get chills from my blood boiling when I think of that moment!

"But I love you," I stammered, going out like a little biiiiitch!

More silence.

"I've got to see you. We've got to talk. We can work this out, Kiyy," I pleaded.

Man, I went out in the name of love trying to salvage our relationship, but you women can be cruel.

"I don't want to see you. You're not gonna change my mind," she challenged.

"Oh … you gonna see me, Kiyy. And you gonna tell me to my face that we're over! You gonna look me in my eyes, and tell me you don't love me anymore!"

I hung up the phone and immediately made two calls. The first was the airport. Remember this was back in the days when the airlines were having fare wars, and flights were dirt cheap … I'm talking People's Express like cheap. The second call was to my boy, Kenny b.k.a., Dexter St. Jock, to pick me up at the airport.

"Don't tell nobody you're coming down!?! Que, what the hell's going on?"

"Just pick me up, please. I got a stop to make, and handle some business."

I stepped off the airplane the next day and headed for the front of the terminal where I was to be picked up. Kenny is waiting for me, and as I get into the car, I hear my name being called. I turn around and I see Kiyler.

"What the hell are you doing here!?!" I growled.

Kenny looked at me as if I were crazy, he knew how I adored Kiyy.

"We should talk."

"Not now … but we will."

"Where are you going, Gregory?"

"Home," I said, not being completely truthful, because I was determined to make a stop before I made it home.

"Then I'll follow you …"

"No, you won't … And how did you get out here anyway?"

"Pam is in the car over there."

I looked over and Pam gave me a cautious wave and smile. I walked over to the car. Pam and I had always been cool with each other. She got out of the car, gave me a hug, and whispered, "I'm sorry, Que. I don't like the way this is going down."

"We'll talk," I promised.

"Que, she knows you like a book. She called last night begging me to meet you at the airport. She said you were way too calm and that you were going to sneak into town."

I had to smirk. :-/

"I didn't believe it until I saw you getting into that car."

"What was I sneaking into town for?" I asked, tongue-in-cheek.

"It may seem that I'm lost in the mustard but I do ketchup! You're looking for Carlos! Between me and you, you won't find him. Kiyler told me she strongly suggested he go home to Bolivia for spring break."

"Well, I'll be damned! … Fuckin' Kiyler!"

"Que, you two need to talk. Kiyy is confused … We'll talk later, go with her. Take my car, drop me home, then drop the car back and we'll talk."

"Aight."

When I explained to Kenny that I was going to take Pam's car, and I told Kiyy to come with me, Kenny looked at me with a "What the fuck is going on?" look. Pam said that we needed to work some things out, and I nodded. Kenny offered to drop Pam off, with his agenda being, no doubt, to find out what was going on and to try to kick it to Pam at the same time. Pam looked at me, and I nodded my approval that he wouldn't attack her or nothing. We drove in silence to Brooklyn, and I decided to pull into a Dunkin' Donuts … don't ask me why!

We sat at a table and I broke the ice.

"So, how you know I was coming down? … You call the airport or something?"

"No," she managed with a weak smile. "I know you."

"Well, Kiyy, if you know me so well, how can you give up on us like this?"

"Things have changed, Que."

"At least now you sound like the woman I've been with for two years."

"What do you mean?"

"I couldn't name the last time you called me Gregory. You starting to sound like … like …"

"Carlos?"

"Why him, Kiyy? I don't get it. What the hell do you see in *him*? You've heard the rumors."

"He's misunderstood. Besides, he's been there for me …"

"And I haven't? ... Misunderstood? What the hell does that mean!?! What has he been saying to poison your mind against me?"

"He hasn't said anything., he's just been there for me and he's told me to listen to my heart."

"And your heart is telling you to leave me and be with *him*!?!"

"We have fun together, and he hasn't deserted me."

"You think I deserted you!?! That's what this is about, me leaving you to go away to school?"

"When you left, it made me realize that you weren't there for me one hundred percent."

Whhhat!!!!!!! I could not believe that she could even form her lips to utter those words. I was sitting across looking at her, and she looked the same, but this was definitely not the woman that I knew. It's like she had been brainwashed or something.

"I'm not trying to hurt you, Que."

Well what the fuck! You could have fooled me! Why do women always say that!?! Especially when it's a triangle that's involved. Somebody's gonna get hurt, but they never mean it to be you! Kiss my ass with that! (_x_)

"Really, Kiyy? Well, you've got a funny way of showing it, huh?"

"You can have all of your stuff back."

"Oh … bless your heart … thank you, thank you … but *no* thank you … I don't want it. You keep it all so that you can remember the mistake you're making. You will never in your life find *anyone* that will love you the way that I do, or treat you the way that I do. You remember that!" (Typical "ego" driven statement, huh ladies?).

"I need to go … You're making this too hard for me."

"We can leave when you look me in my eyes, and tell me it's over … and you don't love me anymore!"

She looked into my eyes and looked away. Then she started to get up. I grabbed her wrist and asked her to sit down.

"You owe me that much Kiyy," I said.

Tears formed in her eyes as she looked me in my eyes and finally said, "It's over."

It's funny, but after she said that, I felt an eerie calm come over me … like it didn't even register or affect me. She got up to leave again, and again I grabbed her arm.

"Tell me you don't love me anymore," I demanded.

Again, time stood still as I'm sure our whole relationship flashed before both of our minds. Then she said something. Her lips spoke words, but I couldn't understand what she had said, so I asked her to repeat herself.

"I don't love you anymore."

I still believe to this day that I had an out-of-body experience, that I died for an instant, looking down upon us sitting at that table in Dunkin' Donuts, and then jumped back into my body. My heart burned as if I'd been to hell and back! She jumped up from the table crying as she ran out of the donut shop. I wanted to go after her, but I couldn't move. To this day, I believe that she still loved me at that moment that she told me that she didn't. Call it foolish pride or whatever, but my romantic side just wouldn't let me believe that she could turn her love for me on and off like a faucet. Not the way we shared each other's lives. Just call me Boo Boo the fool. I don't know how long I actually sat there, but I do remember the trickling of a single tear down the left side of my cheek.

Pam opened the door and my face told her that the news would not be good. I handed her the keys and she told me to come in. I spoke to Pam's mother and then we retreated to Pam's bedroom.

"Say it ain't so."

"I wish I could, but it seems that we are no longer together."

"I can't believe her! She is making the biggest mistake of her life!"

I had to admit that it felt good hearing that coming from Pam, another cutie with a head on her shoulders. Pam went on to become a doctor herself. I sat on her bed and she sat next to me. Then she began telling me all that I had been missing.

"This is between you and me, Que … Kiyy has been seeing a doctor …"

"What! … Wait … What!?! What happened? … Is she pregnant!?!"

"No, no, no. She … um … she, ah … she lost it."

"She had a fuckin' abortion!?!"

"No … no … no … That's not what I mean, she's not pregnant. I mean, she lost it … She had like a nervous breakdown. She's seeing a psychiatrist or psychologist or something … a doctor!"

"A nervous breakdown!?!"

"Your leaving had some kind of traumatic effect on her and she couldn't handle it."

I got off the bed and walked to the window and just stared out into empty space.

"So it is my fault!"

"No, Que, it isn't your fault. The doctor explained to Kiyler that as a child she went through certain experiences at home that drained her of her self-esteem. Then along comes Prince Charming, who builds her confidence level back up, albeit unknowingly. But now it seems to her that he is about to leave … and she can't handle it."

"She always told me for the longest that she had something to tell me, but she never did. I wonder, is that it?"

"I don't know, Que. But she told me that in confidence, all right? But I feel you need to know."

"Don't worry, I got you, Pam."

Pam breathed a sigh of relief.

"Okay."

"So she's shutting me out?" I asked.

"She thinks that she'll be riding a roller coaster if she stays with you."

"But I don't understand, this just came out of the blue!"

"Not really … "

Pam seemed reluctant to continue.

"Don't bite your tongue now, Pam. Tell me."

"Carlos planted a bug in her ear. He said with you being a good looking guy and all, that those college girls would take you away, eventually. He talked about stuff he heard."

"Kiyler's too smart to fall for that dumb shit ..."

"I thought so too, and I told her that you weren't that way. Carlos and I got into it, and I cursed his ass out good fashioned. But that's not all. Carlos views this as an opportunity. If he can make it seem that he took the most popular guy's girl in the school, it will kill all those rumors about him being gay."

"What did I do to him?"

"That's what I asked him. All he could do was shrug his shoulders and say that he actually liked Kiyy, and wanted her for himself. I told him that I was going straight to you with all of this."

"How long ago was this?"

"That was the last weekend that you came down."

"Hmmph ... It all makes sense now. I thought you guys had some kind of fight. But why didn't you tell me then?"

"Because Kiyy begged me not to, said she was going to tell you on her own. Of course she doesn't believe that he's using her. The night you asked him if anything was going on with Kiyy, he nearly had a cow. He ran to her and told her that maybe they were moving too fast ..."

"Oh ... he didn't think it was such a good idea anymore, huh?"

"You spooked him with that 'look me dead in my eyes shit.' By that time it was too late, Kiyy was willing to end her relationship with you for that piece of shit."

"That 'honey boy' snaked me! I'ma see him one day ... that's my word!"

Pam motioned for me to sit back down beside her on the bed. She placed her hand on my leg. Yo, now I already told you that Pam was a cutie, and when she placed her hand on my leg ... I felt a spark (you know ... like electricity). She must have felt it too because she abruptly pulled her hand back and gave me a sheepish smile, and I noticed her cute little dimples.

"I better be going, Pam."

"All right. Hey, are you okay?"

"Yeah man, you know me ... I'm a trooper ... I be aight."

I stood up and then she followed suit. Pam is tiny and I kind of towered over her. She had to look up at me and I had to look down at her. She held out her arms for a hug and then we embraced. We loosened our embrace but still we clung to one another. I looked into her eyes and she looked into mine. Then after a pause, I lowered my head and I kissed her ... Yep ... I kissed her on her forehead. Damn! Y'all actually thought I was gonna go out like that! :-/ Shame on all of y'all. Don't even play me like it wasn't you either. All of y'all thought that I was gonna kiss Pam and we was gonna get busy in her bedroom. Face it ... y'all thought Pam was the 'booty call' girl, didn't ya? I mean, I know you don't know me, but damn, give me the benefit of the doubt. I just finished telling you how much in love I was and how much of a romantic I am, and y'all throw me to the dogs (no pun intended). But that's all right, I should expect that mentality from society today ... after all, sex and violence is what sells, right?

The phone's ringing brings me back from that trip down memory lane, and I let the answering machine do its thing. I listen to the voice fuss at me for not picking up.

"I know you're there, bum!"

She ends her call with a laugh and a directive.

"Call me back!"

That was my baby sister, Nina ... The family and close friends call her Ni Ni. And if I hear that any of you bustas has tried to kick it to her after this, watch your back. If I don't get cha, her husband Peter will, and if he don't, the twins will be crawling all over that ass. I'd like to publicly thank my parents for producing some fine looking children. You know who looks the best, right? :-) ... Don't even play yourself. Fine, go ahead and play yourself. Anyway, Ni Ni is a professor at NYU, but peep this, she's only twenty-five. Hey, you may not be impressed, but I am ... Dr. Nina Que-Anderson, you suckas. While Dexter St. Jock boasts about having his Ph.D. in pimpology, and Puffy and Mase hand out Playa Hater Degrees, Ni Ni has gotten her Ph.D. in Sociology.

You know how when you see someone and say she's fine, but when she opens her mouth, she doesn't sound how she should look? Feel free to jump in and explain that one anytime, you psych types. Look let's get one thing straight ... if ya wanna be down with me, ya gotta pick from my Appletree (Apologies to Erykah Badu). Again ... for the wise-ass (_Ô v Ô_) out there, I know how the song goes, it's my favorite, but for my purposes I changed it a little. Damn, don't be a tight ass (!) ... Calm your nerves. Point is, I'm the type that speaks what he thinks, so if you didn't want to know, ya shouldn't have asked me. While this attitude has caused me to live a somewhat stress free life, I have been accused of being too blunt. Again, sue me. So if I choose to talk about things that make you uncomfortable, or speak on things that you feel are better discussed behind closed doors, or suddenly go off on a tangent that might have absolutely nothing to do with the topic at hand ... oh, well! Did I lose some more readers?

Getting back to Ni Ni ... Ni Ni is petite, she gives the appearance that she's soft spoken ... don't be fooled ... she'll let ya know ... and the girl is more intelligent than I am by far, and I think I'm intelligent. She's about five-two, a hundred and fifteen pounds, with brown eyes, shoulder length hair, and a kool-aid smile. Ya know, I was the originator of the kool-aid smile, and the one-hundred watter (the smile that lights up a room), but then again, Ni Ni and I look like twins, even though we're not, so there. Where Ni Ni gives the appearance that she's soft spoken, my other sister Sharon, we call her Ronnie, makes no bones about being outspoken.

Ronnie was sort of rebellious in a mild sort of way. Never got into any trouble that we know of, but we all have some skeletons in our closet ... I know I do! She made it known early on that she would test authority. I guess she didn't want to live off the fame of my name in the neighborhood, so she built her own rep. Ronnie was the classy version of the 'Around the Way Girl' (Apologies to L.L.). Early on she was referred to as Que's little sister, but after a while I became known as Ronnie's big brother. Ronnie hung out in the park playin' handball. Brothers in the park knew she was my sister and wasn't trying to go *there*, 'cause they knew I wasn't having it. Now I knew the crowd that I ran with when I was younger was scandalous, so you know I wasn't trying to have my sister rolling with them. But she had other ideas. Of course we clashed on these views much times, but she wasn't tryin' to hear me. So you know what I did, right? I put everybody on alert about my sister. She may be cool with y'all, but don't get any ideas! Nope, not even one!

So I let Ronnie be, keeping an eye on her from afar, but not crowding her space. Ronnie's about five feet five inches, one hundred twenty-five pounds, brown eyes, shoulder length hair, with the family kool-aid smile. She's married to Sticky Fingers ... yeah that Sticky Fingers (if you lived in East Flatbush, hell maybe other parts of Brooklyn too, you've undoubtedly heard of him), a.k.a. Keith "the Thief" Robinson who plays for the Atlanta Hawks. Oh, now you wanna be my friend, huh? Ronnie favors my mother, Ni Ni favors my father and my grandmother, I'm a combo of Mom & Dad (Duh!), and my older brother is my father's twin.

Dr. Sharon Que-Robinson is a twenty-seven-year-old Physical Therapy Specialist. You can see where this is going right? Doctors are running in this family, and if you're really perceptive, you might anticipate that that's how Sharon and Keith met. You know with Keith playin' ball and all, the potential for knee injuries … then therapy? Nice little scenario, huh? Haven't you heard the saying that "nothing is ever as it appears to be?" What appears to be the obvious is never the case?

I know I know … you're still trying to get used to my style of writing. You're used to being spoon fed, and what is written down is usually what the author meant to convey to you. Throw that reasoning out the window, here. You *will* be doing some thinking … double meanings … hidden meanings … some obvious meanings :-) … and not so obvious too. Stop groaning! This way, you'll be on your toes and you may even develop some analytical skills. Look it up!

Ronnie runs her practice out of Atlanta, and I'm almost embarrassed to say that she has twins too, Lisa and Keisha. Only because you probably don't believe me, hell, I'd find it hard to believe too, as rare as identical twins are. Forgot to mention that Ni Ni's twins are boys, Kevin and Revin. Keith and Ronnie have been together since high school, Samuel J. Tilden, affectionately called "Killden High." Actually, they went to Meyer Levin Junior High too.

Mom and Dad wanted Ronnie to go to private school like I did. Yeah right, Ronnie wasn't trying to hear that. She had friends in Junior High that she wanted to be with. And to this day, I believe that Ronnie did bad on purpose for those standardized tests to get into the "so called" specialty schools, Bronx High of Science, Crooklyn, ah … Brooklyn Tech (hey, that's what I heard), and Stuyvesant (where you learn computer hacking skills on the down low, but you ain't heard that from me, that's what the papers have said), and I think she tanked the tests for the ABC Schools (A Better Chance, whom I'm a product of), also.

Well, Keith lived in the neighborhood, East Flatbush, and the saying goes, "If you couldn't find it, Keith's got it." Keith was the resident "Klepto" (Kleptomaniac). Now that I think about it, he was always complaining about how he never got nothing when he was little. And you know all kids complain about not getting things, but that really, and I mean *really* was the case with Keith. I think I actually witnessed history when I saw him boost his first piece, it was some penny candy. Don't laugh!!! Who hasn't taken candy when they were little? Of course not you, oh sanctimonious one! Well, then good for you, I'm impressed by your honesty. Well, Keith's career was off and running, he graduated from penny candy to toys to clothes at the Gap to electronics and appliances to cars. Legend has it that he stole a ring off the Principal's hand while shaking it, and hid it in a bottle of glue, hence the name Sticky Fingers. The rumor has legs, but I heard it like this:

He was in Art class, and he was bragging about how he could boost anything. He was challenged to break into the Principal's office and get something. Apparently they had all been to the Principal's office so many times they all knew it like the back of their hand, so if Keith got something from out of there, everybody would know where it came from. Keith deemed that too easy, so he told them like Robin Harris used to say, "Make it easy on yerself," referring to the bet.

When nobody could come up with anything, my sister Ronnie, who was not at the table with them, but could hear the conversation from the table where she sat, leaned over and sarcastically said,

"Why don't you take Mr. Margolis' ring off his finger?"

As everybody turned to hit her with the "What the hell you doing in our conversation" look, Keith had said,

"Bet. And if I do it and don't get caught, you gotta go out with me! Aight?"

She smirked, "Not a problem, 'cause you can't do it!"

As fate would have it, like right on cue (no pun intended), Mr. Margolis walks into the room. Keith proclaimed that he would have the ring by the end of the week. Now this is where shit gets kinda hazy … one thing is sure … Keith grabbed a bottle of glue in his left hand, and poured some into his right. They say it was that clear glue that's thin and you can brush on.

He walked up to the Principal and said fervently,

"Mr. Margolis, how ya been?" as he extended his right hand.

Mr. Margolis proceeded to shake Keith's hand, at the same time sayin',

"Now Keith, I hope we won't be seeing you in my …"

He never got to finish his sentence. Keith reacted as if he forgot that he had glue on his hands.

"Oh! Mr. Margolis, I'm so sorry. I got glue on my hands, let me get you a towel!"

Now Michael Douglas won the Oscar for Best Actor that year for the movie Wall Street, but word is, if you had been in that classroom that day, you would have sworn that Keith had stolen the Oscar for Best Actor because of the performance he put on. He looked around hurriedly as if looking for a towel, at the same time exclaiming to the Art Teacher that there was glue on Mr. Margolis' hands, and where could he find a towel. You would have thought that the class would have laughed, especially those that knew of the conversation that had just taken place, but nobody laughed. Ronnie said because everyone got distracted when Keith started acting frantic to find a towel for the Principal.

Again, it gets hazy … some say after the fact that he used two hands to shake Mr. Margolis' hand like you would shake with the right and cup the hand that you're shaking with your left. Others swear that he used one hand and that was his right hand. Nobody can remember if he had the jar of glue in his hand or not, that would've explained the hand thing. And nobody can remember if Mr. Margolis was even wearing the ring that he usually wore on his right ring finger that day, although we have to assume that he was, if humans are generally creatures of habit. Right, psych types? And to this day Keith won't confirm or deny any details, not even to Ronnie. He just said that he was trying to impress her, and that at the time, that was the only way he knew how. Well, what we do know is that Keith showed everybody involved the ring in class at the end of the week, and thus the legend of Sticky Fingers was born! And by the time the stupid Principal realized that his ring was gone (rumor has it that it took about a week), nobody suspected Keith and those in the know wasn't dropping dime. Rumor also has it that after Keith and Ronnie had been going out a year, Keith gave Ronnie the ring as an anniversary gift, although to this day, neither Keith nor Ronnie will confirm that it happened, or that they still have the ring.

Anyway, so you know Ronnie had to go out with Keith, right? Well, they set some date and Keith comes ringing our bell and my brother Steven answered the door. Steven is the oldest. Steven didn't know Keith, but he had heard the name Sticky Fingers circulating around the neighborhood now, as everybody started calling Keith that, and I guess Keith kind of liked it too because when my brother opened the door and asked who it was that was coming to see his sister, Keith said,

"Sticky Fingers."

Now Keith's lucky that I didn't answer the door, because his ass never would have gotten in the door, bet or no bet. Steven wasn't as strict with guys and my sisters as I was.

Steven smirked and said,

"Sticky Fingers, huh? Come in and have a seat. Is that what your mama calls you?"

Keith said, and I kid you not,

"Not yet, but I'm working on it!"

Steven cautioned, "Well, Sticky Fingers, if *my* mother comes in here and asks you what your name is … you would want to tell her what yo' mama named you, comprende?"

"True … true," Keith agreed.

"True indeed," Steven assured him.

Well, neither Mom nor Dad was home, and I wasn't either, so basically Ronnie and Keith went out. The rest may be told at a later date. After they got married, Keith, Steven and I were talking at the Reception and Keith observed,

"Ya know, it's funny how things turn out. Who would have thought I'd be playin' pro ball, and have all these stars at my wedding? Remember back in the day?"

Steven nodded.

"I remember when you first came to the house," Steven said.

We all laughed.

"Yo Steven, I never thanked you," Keith added.

He proceeded to shake Steven's hand and bring him in for a hug. My brother looked sideways and said,

"For what?"

Keith laughed.

"For answering that door, because if Que had answered the door, we wouldn't be here today!"

Rowdy laughter ensued.

"Ain't that the damn truth!" I assured them, cutting through the laughter.

Ah … impressions … my reputation precedes me!

2

OH ... BOTHER!

A mind is a terrible thing to waste!

"You are a sex starved kitten!"
"Meeeeeeeeeooooowwww!"
I had to laugh at Winnie. She stretched her feline body and suggestively pawed toward 'Floyd and the Crew,' at the same time putting Eartha Kitt to shame with her purring!
"Easy! ... easy star! Can I get a minute!?!"
The three previous times, I think it was three, that's when I started counting ... hell I done lost count. Anyway, every time I thought I was spent, Winnie would coax another round out of me. The woman has developed skills. But that's not the most important thing. Of course it helps, but I think that

the ladies will agree with me here, that variety is the spice of life. What do I mean? Do you want it the same way, every time, all the time? Well, me neither. Winnie credits me for opening her up. Meaning, I brought her out of her sexually reclusive shell. That's not the first time that I've heard that, but you won't see me patting myself on the back or saying that brothers ought to be thanking me for the pleasures that they're now receiving … that's not my steelo (at least not publicly). :-/

"I remember a day when I was the teacher and you were the student."

"Well, what marks do I get for this? …"

"Oh … damn!"

This is one of those times where Floyd has a mind of his own! Besides, I can't let Winnie think that she is now out doing the teacher. Excuse me while my tongue elicits Rachelle Ferrell notes from Winnie.

Well, it seems that Winnie's insatiable appetite has been tamed for the moment. Sorry I took so long, but satisfaction is guaranteed. I got to keep going until *you* say enough!

"I'm gonna wear your ass out one day, Que!"

"Sorry fair lady ... that's not likely to be
'Cause I'm the Sexual
Intellectual G. Q-u-e, ya see
I'm smokin' boots, so stay away from me
The Surgeon General warns that
I may complicate pregnancy
'Cause the rules of seduction
don't apply to me
I bring agony when tongue meets anatomy
... Ask the beauty 'bout the beast
that's never been tamed Janet
Jackson's pleasure principles
have never been the same
I leave a Body of Evidence,
Madonna knows my name
Like Nine Inch Nails, she felt the
Pleasure of Pain Simp-ly scandalous,
step back, you can't handle this
An amateur, I'll damage ya ...
then seal it with a kiss
I'm all this, I'm all that, you
can't diss, you can't rap
So play the back Sadsack, 'cause
ya gets no dap
Zap the rhythm of a dancer,
drop ya like Cancer
What!?! You think you set me
out!?! ... Wrong answer
Come one, come all if you dare

And if I get to Shanice, she'll sing
more than a Silent Prayer
... Snap, Crackle, Pop, props that I got
Just like Naughty by Nature, I say
Hooray for Hip Hop! Hoooo!"

"You *still* rapping, you hip hop junkie!"

"Some things will never change."

"Then that means that Janet Jackson is still Number One on your list, huh? With her non-singing ass!"

"Aaaay ... Watch that! I'll whip ya ass over Janet. Don't talk about my girl, yo!"

"She could sing the alphabet and you'd be clappin' your hands like a fool!"

"And dare anybody to boo her too!"

"So, has the top five changed any?"

"Funny you should ask. As a matter of fact, it has. Janet is still Number One, but she almost lost her ranking."

"Naw ... no way. I don't think she's gonna be too happy to hear that!"

"Forget you, Winnie. :-) There's rumors going around about Janet having a baby ..."

"With the Spanish guy she's with?"

"I assume so!"

"Damn ... listen to that tone."

"Anyway … Toni Braxton is right there now."

"Toni Braxton? Hmmph … I guess you can say what you want about Toni Braxton, but girlfriend be wearing them dresses!"

"Ya think she don't!?!"

"So you're saying that if the rumors are true about Janet and the baby, she's out of the top spot?"

"I may just have to concede to the Spanish guy."

"Like you had a chance anyway."

"All I want to do is meet anyone in my top five, and we'll see what happens from there."

"So does Toni have the Number Two position locked down right now?"

"Right now, but all of my top five have the potential to be Number One."

"So continue."

"Ananda Lewis is Number Three …"

"Who?"

"The co-host of that BET show 'Teen Summit.'"

"Yeah … she's pretty."

"Not only that, but she's opinionated and intelligent … definitely 3B's material."

"Wait … don't tell me … I remember … the 3B's are: body … brains … and beauty."

"You got the order wrong. It's brains, beauty, and then body. And quiet is kept, if I could get with her? … My single days might be over. Assuming that we clicked on all cylinders, and she had the same values that I had."

"And those would be?"

"Trust, honesty, commitment, communication? You know … the foundations for any lasting relationship."

"Uh huh."

"What you mean, uh huh? Sounds like you don't believe me?"

"Let's just say I've heard it before."

"Maybe you have, but you haven't heard it from me before."

"Is that supposed to mean that it's the gospel? … Like, the truth?"

"Have I ever lied to you before?"

"Not that I know of, but all that means is that your ass ain't been caught yet!"

"See, that's what I'm talking about. I don't need the drama. Most women think like you do. A brother starts out with a strike or two right off the bat, without even earning it first. That mentality says prove to me that you're not a liar instead of giving me the benefit of the doubt."

"The benefit of the doubt? … I'm sorry, Que, but in this day and age, you got to earn the benefit of the doubt! Sisters are tired of the games, the lies, the lines, the lack of attention to their needs. It's like a rap I remember you saying talking about what women of today want …"

"'Girls Of Today.'"

"Yeah, yeah … How did the chorus go again?"

"You remember some of my raps?"

"You've got some talent, Que. Yeah, I remember some titles and bits and pieces. Can't give you too much props though, don't want your head to grow … the one on your shoulders that is! The other one is big enough!"

"Give me some of them covers!"

"Your feet are cold!"

"What?" I laughed.

I purposely placed the balls of my feet against Winnie's thigh and she jumped, pulling the covers with her.

"I repeat. Your feet are cold!"

"You know what they say, cold feet … warm heart!"

"*No* one says that, Que … Hands … Cold hands, warm heart."

I got up to go to the bathroom.

"You can't please everyone."

"So now you're a walking cliché?" Winnie smirked.

"Hey … if the shoe fits …"

Winnie threw her pillow at the bathroom door just as I closed it behind me. After handling my business, I got back into the bed with the pillow Winnie threw at me.

"I think this is yours."

Whack! I slugged Winnie with the pillow and it was on! Naked Pillow Fight! Have you ever indulged? I highly recommend it! Fellas, make sure your partner has ample attributes. Ladies, feel free to do the same. :-/ Not only is it pleasing to the eye, it also evokes sexual arousal. Excuse us as this mood swing triggers endorphins which stirs the call of the wild within us, leading to the production of oxytocin, leading to more endorphins, ending with happy happy, joy joy! Was it as good for you as it was for me!?!

We slumped down together on respective sides of the bed, sweaty and content.

"Bet you want these cold feet on you now," I teased.

"Let's take a cold shower, Que!"

"My, my, my … the freaks *do* come out at night, don't they?" (Apologies to Whodini, and to Johnny Gill … ha ha).

"Yes. And they shower too … let's go."

"No, Winnie!"

"Come on. After all, it's your fault I do it now."

"Please, don't remind me."

What started as a dare turned into a daily way of life. Winnie and I spent New Year's Eve together one year, and as we lounged around after parties and too much liquor, we watched the annual Polar Bear swim. Now, if you're unfamiliar with the Coney Island Polar Bear Club, it is the oldest winter swimming organization in the United States. They do an annual swim on New Year's day in the Atlantic Ocean at Coney Island every year. If you need more of that in your life, they swim every Sunday from November to April. Then they give way to the wimps of summer. (lol)

Well, I jokingly dared Winnie to do it the following year, and she countered my dare by saying if she did it, I had to do it the following year. This is why you shouldn't drink, people. Still coming down off the effects of my alcoholic state I agreed, never once thinking that Winnie was actually serious. The next year I found out, as she brought me to the beach, and I watched her and about forty others run into the Atlantic Ocean on a 15°F day.

The way Winnie described it, it was the most electrifying thing she's ever done. She couldn't describe the feeling initially, but she told me later she felt freedom, exhilaration, and an awareness she'd never experienced before. And fellas, the way she put it on me when we got back to her place … let's just say I became a believer.

So fast forward another year, we come upon the New Year, and Winnie reminds me that I am supposed to take the plunge.

"Oh helllllllll no!" I told her.

"Two years ago, you looked at me and told me you would do it. I did it last year, and now it is your turn, Mister!"

"I was drunk!"

"You were sober enough to make conscious decisions."

"You've been hanging around me too much. I'm revoking your access!"

"You can do whatever you want after you take that plunge."

"I didn't think you were going to do it, let alone expect me to do it too."

"Duh, that's what a dare is. Are you going to do the honorable thing and honor your commitment, or am I going to have to get grimy, questioning your manhood?"

"Ouch, Winnie! I'm kind of backed up into a corner, now aren't I?"

"Through no one's fault but your own!"

So on New Year's Day of that year I, Gregory Que, took the plunge with the Coney Island Polar Bear Club, with Winnie by my side, doing it again. It was an experience. Once I got past the mental and physical shock, it was all good. What did you think? I was gonna tell you I was screaming and carrying on like a bitch? Picture that! On my Kodak, that would be wack! (Apologies to UTFO).

So, I grudgingly took the cold shower with Winnie because there really wasn't a good reason not to. It wasn't going to kill me, it made her happy, and eventually I will reap the benefits from it. Fellas, the goal is to win win win. And it's okay to take one for the team (the team being you, of course), to get to a greater good, whatever that might be. It's always a plus to have good will in your back pocket. Remember that. We're back in the bed, loungin' ('cause we lazy like that). :-/

"Okay, Que, do you remember what we were talking about before you used a pillow fight as an excuse to get another natural high out of me?"

"I just want you for your neurotransmissions, Winnie."

"You are so weird! … Yet so addicting!"

"And you speak my language," I reminded her. She shook her head.

"I really don't know what that says about me!" she laughed.

"Aight, we were talking about one of my raps that you remembered."

"Yeah! 'Girls Of Today'."

"I was surprised you remembered it."

"How does that chorus go?"

"Girls of today want more than Mercedes Benz, the diamond ring or just having babies. Girls of today want more than material things, just simple pleasures and the joys that life can bring."

"Exactly … that's what I'm talking about, Que. Sure, the material things are nice, don't get me wrong, but the little things are just as important, if not more. You always talk about being a romantic, so you should know what I'm talking about."

"Oh, now you gonna act like you don't know, Winnie?"

"Like a certain person we both know says, 'What have you done for me late-ly?'"

"Is your name Janet Jackson?"

"No."

"Then you would want *not* to go there!"

"Yeah … yeah … yeah … you know I'm right. But I ain't mad at ya though, I'm just sayin'. You used to send cards for no reason at all …"

"Or surprise you with a pint of your favorite ice cream …"

"That's right, or just a pack of gum because you thought I had run out, or a phone call saying that I had crossed your mind. Que, you used to call them 'simple pleasures.' Those kind of simple, thoughtful things will make a sister go the extra mile. You know, find the strength and desire to give a brother some when she ain't really feeling it. Surprise you with a gift, a nice gift too, or cook a gourmet meal."

Winnie's right. I've been slacking, and I know better too, 'cause that's what separates me from the next man. Winnie's not my girl, but I would still do those things, because that's just me. I derive my pleasure from seeing and knowing that you're pleasured. Of course, you do have to earn that right. OK … she may have been right about that other point too … "earning the benefit of the doubt" … ya happy now!?! You fellas have just been given one of my secrets, and I didn't give it to you. I hope that you don't believe that it works, 'cause it doesn't. Nope … it doesn't work.

"I'm grooming you for some lucky young lady, ya know!"

"Is that right?"

"I know that you and I can't be together 'cause you want kids and I don't, so I might as well look out for a good sister for my 'stink!' You know I got final say, right?"

"Huh?"

"Anybody that wants to be with you, got to come through me. And if I don't think her ass is right for you, she out the door!"

"God help her! 'Cause after Moms, my sisters, K.P., you, and God knows who else that feels they have some say in my future get through with her … she's gonna be running for the hills!"

"If she's a good woman, though, she'll suck it up initially, but if it gets out of hand, she'll kindly but sternly tell us to back off because she has your best interests at heart as well. And if it's done the right way, she'll get props."

"So now I know why I don't have a girlfriend! Y'all done scared everybody off!"

"Don't you be putting the blame on us, you know good and well that if you wanted a girlfriend, you'd have a girlfriend! These poor girls out here are dying to have your baby!"

"Don't even put the whammy on me, Winnie. I ain't trying to have no kids right now. You know that. When my foundation is set and I feel that I can comfortably support a wife and kids, you'll be the first to know, Godmomma!"

"Speaking of which, you probably would have had some by now if it wasn't for dumb ass Kiyy. After I heard what happened, *I* wanted to whip her ass. Then again, I guess I owe her because we might not have met. But you know … there's something I've always wondered about that whole situation, and I'm gonna finally ask you today because one, I have the courage right now, and two, I believe we're close enough that I can ask you."

"Damn, Winnie, after all that, I don't know if I wanna let you ask your question. Shit."

"I know. I should have just asked it, right? Instead of prefacing …"

"What's the question, Winnie?"

"Did … did you feel a certain way about the situation and the guy who Kiyy ended up with? I mean the kind of guy … I mean …"

"That he came across as gay?"

"Yeah … I mean, how did that make you feel? How did your boys, whoever, react to you after what went down?"

"Wow. That's a piercing question. Can't say I saw that one coming."

"I'm sorry, Que … I didn't mean to overstep …"

"Naw, you good, Winnie. As close as we are, you've earned that right …"

"Still, Que, saying it out loud, I'm thinking I should have deaded that question …"

"The short answer is that my ego took a hit, but my manhood stayed intact, if that makes any sense to you?"

"I get it …"

"Do you really? Because this is a one time opp … The box has been opened, and I'll explain if you don't get it, or don't want to go in now because you think it's embarrassing."

"I think you're some kind of special …"

"Really, Winnie, I'm just a man. A man who loved a woman, and got hurt by a woman. It's as simple as that. The other dynamics, the optics, they don't hurt like that. The world sees a girl leave a guy for an effeminate guy … That's reality. That guy who it happened to, me … just sees the girl leave for someone else. The pain of that is what I feel."

"But how did you get past how others saw it?"

"I didn't. That's the ego. But to their credit, my boys … they realized that I was hurting … They let it be. If they talked amongst themselves, I never knew it. The only time it was brought up was when my boys asked if I wanted him to disappear. I said no. That was the manhood."

"I repeat … you are some kind of special."

"I don't see it, and I guess I'm glad I don't …"

"Man … I remember that night we met, you was on a hunt …"

I laughed at her shifting gears.

"We done with that? I can close the box, and we shall never speak of this again?" I chuckled.

She snuggled up to me and put her head against my chest. Then suddenly, she grabbed Floyd and the Crew in a firm but gentle grasp, startling me!

"I get this anytime I want … my lips shall never speak of this again!"

"You are a fool," I laughed.

"Just for you, Mr. Que … just for you."

"A hunt, huh? What you mean by that?"

"I mean … You were actually looking for someone to get with. It was written all over your face. Women know the look. Let's just say most women know the look. Your eyes spoke words without saying a word … But finish your top five."

"What? No, no, no, no. You know I hate that … don't start something and not finish it."

"Did I say that I wasn't gonna finish it? You got somewhere to go? You need to check in? Somebody else's bed waiting for you?"

"Damn … where's this coming from?"

"This doesn't happen often, but I'm being selfish tonight! You got a problem with that!?!"

"Actually, that forceful, definitive tone is kinda sexy … you turning a brother on right about now!"

"Good, 'cause I'm not letting you leave tonight. You're spending the night, got it?"

"Whatever you like," I said, in my pleasing "Coming to America" voice.

She started laughing, but a brother did kind of find that arousing! Especially when he's not used to hearing it. See the point?

"Would you finish, please, who's Number Four?"

"Veronica Webb."

"The model?"

"Uh huh. I've been into Veronica Webb since that 'You're Ugly' video …"

"The one that went, *You're ugly! You're, You're, You're, You're … You're … You're Ugly?*"

"Yep. Double O and Velour …"

"Daaaaaaammmmnn! You going back in the day, son!"

"Veronica Webb is what the 3B's are all about. When she opens her mouth, something intelligent comes out. Of course, I wouldn't mind reversing that …"

"You are such a dog!"

"No … for real … I'm joking … *I'm joking!* Nothing but respect for her and all women that respect themselves, hell, even the ones that don't. Come on … Stop looking at me like that! Y'all do it too, and you're worse than men! Oh … Oh, y'all don't do that?"

"Yeah, we do, but it was funny seeing you try to clean it up!"

"You ain't shit, Winnie!"

"Thank you!"

"You know she's a B-Girl underneath the polished diamond, right?"

"Why you say that?"

"She's on Funk Master Flex's 60 Minutes of Funk, Volume Two tape …"

"Tape? Don't you have any CD's?"

"What's a CD?"

"Dinosaur!"

"Your whole famn damily, futha mucka!"

"Yuck fou to you too!"

"Like I was saying … she's on his *album* talking 'bout she got the 'premium' kit kat … I'm euphemizing here!" :-/

I know, I know … He's such a nerd! Winnie gives me side eye, but ignores the nerdy portion of my comment.

"Veronica Webb, you better go, girl! Tell the *world* that your stuff is da bomb! I'm feelin' her now!"

"Well, I definitely got a taste for chocolate! My kind of woman … the kind that can roll with the bourgie crowd when she has to and still roll wit' the big dogs and the downright grimy and gritty if she wants to. Honey is straight up chameleon!"

"Sounds to me like your three and four should springboard your one and two!"

"You may be right if you look beyond the surface and analyze."

"Isn't that what we're doing?"

"Look, I didn't say that my list had to be politically correct."

"But it should at least be logical!"

"I'm ignoring you …"

"'Cause you know I'm right again … Not in the debating mood tonight, huh, Que?"

"*I am about … to proceed … with the Number Five selection …*"

"Please, not the Bill Cosby voice, okay? … You have absolutely no sense! Who's Number Five?"

"Pam Grier."

"Pam Grier!?! You cannot be serious!"

"Many brothers had their first wet dream over some Pam Grier!"

Brothers understand where I'm coming from. Look at any of her movies. She was sexxxy, outspoken, loyal, smart, did I say sexxxy and fiiiiiiiiine, she was the original B-Girl.

"Hello … how old is she?"

"Precisely the point, Watson! And she's still fine … and she can still get it!"

I don't drink coffee, but I do drink beer

I don't do windows, but I'd do Pam Grier!

"You're reaching with Pam Grier."

"It's a guy thing … you wouldn't understand! Oh! And honorable mention goes to Tatyana Ali!"

"Oh … you losing me now! You done went from the nursing home to robbing the cradle! Besides, she looks just like the Teen Summit girl."

"Shoot, she's over eighteen now! And Ananda and Tatyana don't look anything alike. They've both got their *own* identities. Don't get it twisted!"

"*You* don't get it twisted! I didn't say that they couldn't have their own identities, I just said that they look alike. Tatyana Ali! How old are you!?!"

"Wait … Pam Grier's too old for me and Tatyana's too young? I don't *think* so! What happened to 'Age is just a number?'"

"Ask Aaliyah!"

"Aw … You cold, Winnie, weren't those just rumors!?! And she's a cutie too."

"Whatever! The fact remains that brothers always want to trade in the older model for the newer one. What did your boy KRS ONE say?:

Girls look sooooo good, but their brain is not ready, I don't knooooww …

I'd rather talk to a woman, 'cause her mind is so steady, so here we gooooo!'

"Ain't that some shit … look who's throwin' rhymes in *my* face, and the 'Teacha's' rhymes at that! I am impressed."

"Sometimes hip hop seems to be the only language that gets through to that thick skull!"

"Hip hop is the culture, rap is the language, okay? Got it? Well, another very honorable mention goes to Karen Alexander. She was up in that 'Ugly' video too. She's got such an innocent, yet seductive look about her ... and a smile that could melt ice cubes!"

"I don't know much about Karen Alexander, but she is pretty."

"You don't know much about any of them!"

"You know what I mean, smart-ass."

"And a most honorable mention goes out to Lana Ogilvie."

"Trailblazer ..."

"And I can't forget about Dominique Dawes!"

"I wish she had won that individual gold medal ... but Que, she's young too!"

"About twenty ... but she's a little cutie though ... and I love those bow legs of hers!"

"Damn, stop drooling, you St. Bernard!"

"Ummph ... ummph ... ummph!"

"You need help, Mister!"

The phone rings and it startles Winnie as she wonders aloud who is calling her at such a late hour. She looks at me for a reaction, but you'll get none from the kid. She answers it and walks to another room, and I half-whisper to her that she doesn't have to leave on my account. She gives me the finger. I hear her in the background telling some kid that he spun the wheel and it came up on her name tonight. He must have offered some explanation because she countered that her wheel did not have his name on it. Oww! Conversation over!

"Kindly inform your stable that when I'm here, they need not call!"

"Hey, a girl has got to have backup, right? … But mind you … I don't deal in booty calls like that. I decide if you're worthy, you don't decide that *I'm* worthy … like you're doing me a favor!"

"Handle yo' bidness, gurl!"

"I'm for real, Que! Besides it's your fault. You schooled me too well!"

"Man, if guys found out somehow that I schooled you on the do's and don'ts, they'd revoke my membership! You are in very exclusive company with my sisters, although Ronnie wasn't trying to hear me, and K.P."

"Have you ever slept with K.P.?"

Usually I'm unflappable, but even I can be caught off-guard once in a while. For just a minute, I got that squirmy feeling that guys get when they've cum pre-maturely. Whether it was yesterday or ten years ago, all you fellas know where I'm coming from. And if ya deny it, you're lying. It's either a yes or no answer, but why do I feel the need to get more info before I can answer? Paranoia? Curiosity? Survival? I need to know the M-O (motive), behind the question. Blame my profession? ... Not buying it, huh?

"Have I ever slept with K.P.? ... Why are you asking me that?"

"It's a simple yes or no answer, Que. When you answer the question, I'll tell you why I asked."

Damn! Straight to the futha muckin' point! Winnie has definitely been around me too long, she's turning the tables on me. I'm usually the seducer, not the seductee! My definition of seducer here is one who is able to get information from someone without giving up any. I pride myself on being a master of seduction, and I'm getting played like Lotto! Have I underestimated Winnie? She gets props, 'cause she's learned her lessons well!

"What's up with the cross examination, Jonetta Cochran?"

"I'm prosecution, thank you very much! Your Honor? ... Permission to view Mr. Que as a hostile witness?"

"Permission granted ... Proceed."

"Oh, you little hooker! You gonna be attorney, judge *and* jury!?!"

"Objection! Request to have those last comments stricken from the record, your Honor?"

"Sustained! Watch your mouth, Mr. Que! Homey don't play that in my court! Continue prosecution."

"So you did sleep with K.P., huh? Didn't cha!?! … Didn't cha!?!"

"Objection! Your Honor, the prosecution is leading … the prosecution is leading the witness, plus she's being argumentative!"

"Defense counsel, I didn't get your name?"

"Mark Clark, your Honor."

"Well, Mr. Clark, if you had *bothered* to go to your evidence class? … in law school? … you would have learned that there are certain latitudes granted for hostile witnesses! Objection overruled! Now answer the question, Mr. Que."

Well, all righty then! How the hell does she know that!?! It seems that I'm in a no-win situation here, so much to my chagrin, I must wear the "H."

"All right, all right! I'll answer the damn question!"

"Let me remind you, Mr. Que, that the penalties for perjury are stiff fist and swift, almost Caligula-like!"

"Damn … it's like that, your Honor!?!"

"It's like that ... and that's the way it is ... huah!" (Apologies to Run DMC).

"Hmmph ... I have not slept with K.P."

"What was so hard about saying that?"

"Why did you ask?"

"No reason."

The look on my face is saying, "Don't even play me like that!" But I'm secretly pleading within, "Please tell me ... don't play me."

"Stop playing with me, Winnie."

"I'm not. I was just curious, that's all."

"I'm gonna ask you one more time, Winnie ... Why did you ask that?"

"You always mention us in the same breath, and I know that you and I are sleeping with each other, so I wondered about her and the relationship that you have with her."

Warning signals have now overloaded within my brain. Do I pass go and get two hundred dollars, or do I go straight to jail? In jail without no bail ... In jail because I failed (Apologies to the Fat Boys). We proceed gingerly, but smoothly, looking for an out.

"Because I hold you both in such high esteem, besides I've known K.P. all of my life ..."

"You know, I bet you think you could sweet talk your way into Fort Knox. I know that already, and don't insult my intelligence and say she's just like a sister to you either. She *is* your type of woman."

Here's out try Number One:

"My type of woman? I don't have a type of woman."

Even I had to admit, that was weak!

"Does brains, beauty, and body ring a bell!?! Okay, then … answer this …"

"Whoa! What's up with twenty questions?"

"Are you feeling uncomfortable? Correct me if I'm wrong … but who says, 'If you got the nerve to ask it, I got the nerve to answer it!?!'"

"What's the question?"

"Does she know that you and I are more than friends? … That we're sleeping together?"

"Who, K.P.?"

"No, Janet Jackson, Mr. Selective Amnesia!"

What the hell is going on here? There are lessons to be learned here! How did I get into this position!?!

"She's never asked, and I've never volunteered any information."

"She knows. Just like I knew that you hadn't slept with her or that you've never told her about us. It's written all over your face."

That's the second time she's referred to that, and I'm not liking it.

"And you say that to say … ?"

"You like her, Que … but I don't expect you to admit it."

If I didn't know better, I'd swear I was in Vietnam, 'cause the bombs are just dropping!

"There's nothing to admit … and how do *you* know that anyway?"

"It's elementary, Watson … simple deduction really."

"Well, you're wrong."

"Am I? You don't seem to have a problem with Kenny knowing that we slept together, do you? Unfortunately, and I mean unfortunately, I slept with him also before I knew you. But you two are good friends."

Here's out try Number Two:

"Winnie, the circumstances are totally different. Kenny was in the room with us. And since you brought that up, you can answer a question that I asked earlier about me being on a hunt."

"You were on a hunt. I noticed that the minute you walked in the house with that girl. And I decided right then and there that I wanted to get with you.

You were so sexy in a nonchalant sort of way. What was that girl's name again?"

"Nicole. Is that what women do? Decide on the spot if they're gonna give a guy some play?"

"Sometimes, if you don't mess it up by opening your mouth. A girl could be set to get with a guy, and he'll mess it up for himself, by offering information that nobody asked for. If I didn't ask what kind of car you drive, or what you do for a living, don't volunteer the information! It's as simple as that. That does not impress me. If I didn't ask you if you've traveled around the world, or what stars you quote, unquote 'hang out with,' don't give me the 411."

"So I got lucky because I didn't say anything?"

"No. With you, it was a little different. When you walked into the room, I felt the aura that surrounded you. I know it sounds corny, but you have a powerful presence. And you give off a nonchalant arrogance that can drive some people crazy, yet it draws them in. It's hard to explain, but it *can* be interpreted as being anti-social or stuck up. But once someone gets to know you, they see that it's neither ..."

"Is this how Jordan felt when Van Gundy likened him to a 'con artist?'"

"You know, I'm giving you a compliment, Que. Van Gundy was giving Jordan a compliment also, and Jordan took it out of context on purpose. Jordan knew good and well that Van Gundy was not saying anything derogatory about him. He wasn't saying anything that the rest of the league or any real basketball fan didn't already know. Van Gundy just said publicly what everybody else was saying privately."

"You are a Knicks fan, huh, Winnie?"

"For life, and don't you forget it too. But like I was saying. Your aura is not flashy, it's quiet. You guys use the term 'hooker' to describe yourselves. Well, to me you're two different hookers. One of the differences that I noticed between you and Kenny, and there are a few … but when Kenny walks into a room, he has to let everyone know it. He'll walk to the center of the room, like he's on display and he's giving all the ladies a chance to see him, and consciously, although he probably thinks it's unconsciously, makes an effort to draw attention to himself. And obviously some women like that or else he'd have flipped the script a long time ago. You, on the other hand, play the background and silently take in everything that's going on. And I don't know if you know it or not, but you have one of the sexiest voices that I've ever heard. It just fits your personality."

"C'mon, stop playing with me …"

"And that's another thing, it is so cute how you don't take well to compliments. You're very humble at times. It's like you're not used to hearing them. Combine that humbleness with that quiet arrogance and you've got the makings of something very sexy. You don't try, you just are. And that's *your* hooker. I remember complimenting you on your cologne that night and you seemed almost embarrassed to accept the compliment. Don't get me wrong, you were polite, but your expression showed uncomfortableness."

"Can we change the subject, Winnie?"

"See what I mean? Look at you."

"Can we get back to the hunt, please?"

"Even though your demeanor said cool, calm, and collected, your eyes said 'wild.' They had this glow about them, and like I said before, most women know the look. I told Angie about you."

"I always thought she was pulling my leg with that 'look' talk. And what did this 'look' say?"

"Whoever you got to was gonna get their world rocked! And I wanted it to be me!"

"Yeah, right! … Has Angie ever seen this 'look' in my eyes?"

Winnie laughed. "If she hasn't, after I told her about us, she'll probably say she has, just 'cause she wants to get with you."

"You *told* her about us?"

"Yes, I broke rules. It was so good, I had to tell *someone.* I hope you're not upset about that, Que."

"Upset? You want to send girls my way, that's on you, Winnie."

"I know, Que. She's the only person I told, but I didn't think she was gonna get with you anyway. You met her and immediately saw warning signs, and I knew you'd keep her at bay."

"I should do her just to get back at you!"

"You hear yourself, right, Que?"

"Do you hear yourself, Winnie?"

"I already said it was my bad."

"So Angie's on me because of what you told her about a 'look' you saw in my eyes, and that same 'look' she may or may not have seen from me?"

"Yeah, I think that about sums it up. But Angie had already heard of 'the look.' She just didn't know anyone that had seen 'the look' or met a guy that had expressed 'the look.'"

"Not about details of what you and I actually did? Just this legend of 'look' thing?"

"I wouldn't use the term 'legend,' but yeah, the 'look' has something to do with it. Only she can tell you how much it is driving her to get with you."

"Sounds like legend to me. Does every woman know about it?"

"I don't know about every woman. But *women* know about it. Men don't."

"Maybe women just want to believe it."

"Maybe, but there are women who have experienced it, like myself. So there's that."

"You're dripping, Winnie."

"Maybe I am being sarcastic, but you're being an ass right now, dismissing what *I've* experienced! And that's why 'the look' is safe because even when men find out about it, they don't believe it. I am really surprised about you, though!"

"I didn't say I didn't believe it, Winnie."

"You're not saying you believe it either, Que."

"Did you know about it before someone shared it with you?"

"I had heard about it. But then I got the details about it."

"And what you saw from me was a description of what you were told?"

"It really sounds like you don't believe me."

"I don't believe this 'look' stuff."

"You don't believe *me*? Ask a woman about 'the look' … Ask your girl *K.P.* about 'the look.' I bet she asks you what women have you been talking to! Why do you think Angie's on you?"

So what's up with this "look" thing, ladies? Is that how it goes down? Never mind that I don't know what it looks like. Betcha won't be seeing the "look" on this face no more!

"Sounds to me like this 'look' thing is a polite way to say that some guy is horny."

"Typical guy response. It's a girl thing, you wouldn't understand! Horny has a different look altogether!"

Well, if that ain't some "Secret Squirrel" shit, I don't know what is! Just when you think you're on the road to learning something about women, you come to a sign in the road that says you haven't even scratched the surface yet! But this is good, because the more knowledge you pick up, the more situations you'll be able to handle.

"Did Nicole say something to you when I sat down on the couch and started talking to you?"

"Yeah. She asked why you did it. Like I'm a mind reader or something."

"You didn't even know what was going on, did you?"

"If you're referring to you pushing up on me … nope, I wasn't on that page."

"Well, we sure finished the chapter together, didn't we?"

"Sounds to me like you were the one that was on the hunt, Winnie!"

"Don't even try it. I just gave you the opportunity to get what you were seeking!"

"Bull! Then why did you ask me if Nicole was my girlfriend?"

"'Cause I wasn't trying to be disrespectful. Once you told me that she wasn't your girl, and that y'all were just friends … hey, it was on. Kenny told me the same thing. He also wanted to know why I wanted to know, but I guess he found out."

"You cold …"

"Kenny is the last person I'd be feeling sorry for, as big a ho' as he is!"

"I cannot let you disparage my friend Kenny."

"When I say something that *ain't* true, you're more than welcome to defend him."

"He's generous, good hearted, and …"

"A ho'! A straight ho'! You know good and well, Kenny is the type to smile in your face, but be thinking, 'Yeah, but I did your girl!'"

I had to laugh at that. Not because it was true about Kenny, but that it's true about any guy! Guys are just cruel like dat (Apologies to Digable Planets, lol). Do you ladies do that too? I know you do. Somehow you get invited to a wedding, and you're sitting there while the bride and the groom are exchanging vows with a smirk on your face thinking, "Yeah, but I did your man!" or "I had him before you did." I know a lot of y'all can't even look in a mirror right now because you'd see yourself, and just bust out laughing … 'cause you know it's true! Yeah, you can call us Petty Roosevelt, but I'll just call you ladies Petty White.

Winnie continued in on Kenny,

"After things happened with us, he thought he was hurting me by telling me that he was fooling around on me anyway. He got pissed when I told him that if you ever held classes on the art of making love, he should be the first person in line!"

"See, that's why he had an attitude with me for a while, Winnie. You saying stuff like that!"

"Hey, I'm sorry if the truth hurt … No, I'm not! I know he was trying to kick it to that other girl that came with you, Nicole, and those other two guys."

"If I didn't know better, I swear you sound a little bitter, Winnie."

"I can admit my mistake. I got hoodwinked, bamboozled, went for the okey doke! I took an 'L.' How do you say it? 'Put an "H" on your chest and "Handle it"!?!' That's me!"

"How did you two meet?"

"Through a girlfriend whom I found out later had slept with him too!"

"Before or after y'all met?"

"After."

"Damn, she wasn't a friend at all."

"All I can say is that I was a different person back then. More trusting, more oblivious, more naïve. I thought I could change a leopard's spots."

"Oh no! You thought you could be the one!?!"

She shook her head and let out a deep sigh.

"Yeah, I was one of *them*. But I learned. Thank you."

"Are you thanking *me*?"

"Yes, I am. I'm thanking you for letting me inside the mind of a guy. Straight up too, no chaser, no watered down liquor, straight hundred proof."

"You should be thanking Kenny. If not for him, we'd have never met."

"I'd like to believe we would have met. Six degrees of separation."

"I don't know nothing about that, I was in another world. Secretly wallowing in my own pain."

"I knew something was bothering you, but of course I didn't find out until weeks later that it was your break up with Kiyy. Do you believe in karma?"

"I guess. Why do you ask?"

"Because it was the craziest thing. When I went into Kenny's room to lie down on the bed, I secretly hoped that you would come and lie down on the bed with me. Mind you, I didn't know you from Adam, hadn't said but a few words to you, but yet I'm hoping for this crazy ass act to happen."

"As crazy as it sounds, when I came into the room and laid down next to you, I wanted something to happen too, but I wasn't about to initiate anything. That's why I was on the edge of the bed, teetering off the edge like a stiff board, staying as far from you as the bed allowed."

"Why did you come into the room anyway?"

"To lie down. I didn't even know you were in there. But when I got in there and saw you, I decided that I would just lie down as far away from you as I could. So if somebody walked in, as Kenny did, they wouldn't think nothing."

"And I wanted to say to you that I wasn't going to bite … unless you wanted me to! Did you honestly think that nobody would think anything?"

"I actually did. As I told Nicole, what was the big deal? I was tired, you were tired, there was a bed, we were on it, we had our clothes on, we weren't doing anything, you were with Kenny, I was chilling."

"That's scandalous, because that room had pure unadulterated lust all up in it! Anybody could feel it!"

"So Nicole got an attitude for the rest of the night, and I told her that she didn't have to take me home. That's how I ended up sleeping on the couch after everyone left."

"I asked Kenny about that, but he never said what happened."

"So when y'all went to the bedroom and left me on the couch, I was pissed. It hit me that I had nobody to be with. I was even more pissed when I heard sounds coming from the bedroom."

"Believe me, you had nothing to be pissed about, it was all an act. I was not feeling him then, I was thinking about you."

"Tell me anything, why don't you!"

"I'm telling you the truth, Que."

"At any rate, I couldn't take it, so I yelled at y'all to keep it down so I could go to sleep. I guess nobody heard me, 'cause nothing changed… That rikkity-ass bed kept moving."

"Oh, I heard you, and I told Kenny that we should stop, but he said, 'Fuck Que, it ain't my fault that he's alone tonight!'"

"And I ain't mad at him, either. I probably would have said the same thing. Brothers have no compassion for others when they're getting theirs!"

"Yeah, but I had other ideas. I knew what I wanted to do, but I didn't know if I'd have the guts to say it. But I did say to myself that if you told us to keep it down again, I'd say it … and you did … and I said it!"

"You know … there must be something to that karma thing, because I told y'all to keep it down, hoping that something would happen, but not ever dreaming that it would actually happen. A fantasy, ya know? And when you invited me to come in and join you two, I knew I was hearing things!"

"I could see Kenny's expression in the dark, and it was like, 'What did you just say?' By that time it was too late, the words were already uttered, and you were already at the door wondering if you had heard correctly."

"When you said it again and Kenny told me that I had heard correct and then got off the bed, I jumped from the doorway back to the couch, ripped off my clothes, got some condoms, jumped back to the doorway and onto the bed in one motion! Brother wasn't playing. I thought I was dreaming and I had to take advantage of this opportunity before I woke up. But you assured me that it was not a dream!"

"I could not believe that the words actually came out of my mouth. It was what I wanted to do, but I didn't think that I could actually say the words. I had never done anything like that in my life before. And it hit me too after it was over, but not until Kenny brought it up. Kenny turned on the light after you left the room and I had the biggest smile on my face. I was in another world … it was called fulfillment! And he just kept saying over and over that he couldn't believe I had done that. He also mentioned that he had never heard me yell like that before. What could I say, Que?"

"Well, he was sitting in the corner, Winnie."

"Oh, you don't know? He got up and left the room! I thought I had told you that."

"He left the room!?! I kept waiting for him to join in, but he never did."

"He left the room and came back later to see if we were finished, left again, and then came back to watch the finale. I was so embarrassed when he threw that back in my face. That's why I avoided you after. I didn't know what you would think of me after the fact."

"We couldn't help it if we were enjoying ourselves! And you know how it turned out, 'cause we've reminisced about this many times. I respected you, and here we are today. By the way, I just wanted to let you know that I know what you did, and you're not off the hook with K.P.!"

Winnie removed the covers from herself, got up, and went out of the room. I made a note of the fact that she didn't make a move to cover herself up. Yep, she has come a long way. I remember when she was bashful about letting me see her body. No matter how many times I would tell her that her body was something fierce, she never believed me. And make no mistake about it, Winter Summer has a hellacious body! You trippin' off her name too, huh. She's immune to all the jokes, so don't waste your time. Still … you can't resist though, right? I know, 'cause every once in a while I'll drop a one-liner and she'll give me the "duh" look. I tease her and ask her if she's related to Donna Summer, the Disco Diva?

She says no, and I say to her that her mama must have been getting busy listening to "Spring Affair" by Donna Summer in the dead of winter, and she got her name because there was nothing else to fall back on.

"Do you want something to drink?" she calls from the kitchen.

"What do you have?" I respond back.

"Milk."

There's silence and then she laughs,

"Among other things like juice and soda."

Not playing into her hands I respond, "Juice is fine."

She returns with my juice and gives it to me. Pow! And then Pow! The pillow comes down hard on me again. Feeling the effects of her sneak attack, I pull the covers over my head.

"So my milk ain't good enough for you, huh!?!" she laughs.

I peek from under the covers.

"Are you finished, Psycho Woman!?!"

She extends the glass of juice to me and I tentatively reach for it. She raises the pillow again.

"You're gonna make me spill the juice on the bed, Winnie!"

"And?"

"And the sheets will be wet."

"It'll just mix with all the juices that are already there. A nice cocktail, if you will."

"You just nasty."

"The sheets will be changed anyway … Okay, look … I'm putting the pillow down."

She does just that, and I take the juice from her, as she settles back into the bed.

"So how's the practice going?" Winnie inquires.

I shrug my shoulders, warming up for an answer to the question.

"It goes. There are good days and there are bad days. Right now, I'm just trying to stay afloat."

"Well, it takes time to establish a business. I think that it's great that you even went there."

"Believe me, it wasn't my choice. It came out of necessity. Nobody was trying to hire a brother, know what I'm sayin? Bill collectors and those damn student loans' people wasn't tryin' to hear that I couldn't find a job!"

"That's the scary part, because your resume is pretty impressive."

"You've seen it in the gutter of the street too? Everybody and their grandmother has a copy! But what's even more scary is that there are people out there just like me with even more impressive resumes and they can't find a decent job either … let alone a job doing what they actually went to school for. Why is that? I'll tell you why …"

"I didn't mean to stir up a hornet's nest!"

"Naw it's not that … I just gotta get some of this bitterness out."

"Why are you bitter? Do you feel that the world owes you something?"

"You mean 'cause I'm black? … Naw that's too easy, and that's the excuse that everybody jumps on the bandwagon with. I have never had anything come easy for me. Grades in school, money, even women …"

"Women? Forgive me if I find that hard to believe!"

"You're forgiven, but yes, even women. I've become gun shy. Ain't tryin' to catch another broken heart. But getting back to what I was saying … Compared to how things seem to fall into the lap of some people without them even trying, I have had to scratch and claw. Don't get me wrong, I don't have a problem with hard work, it's all I've ever known. But hard work doesn't seem to get you props anymore … Maybe it's just me."

"What do you mean?"

"I mean ... I can't speak for other professions ... but in mine, everything seems to have given way to greed and treachery! Maybe that's too harsh an assessment?"

Winnie shakes her head.

"Naw, I didn't think so either. What ever happened to the good old fashion values of merit? I look at my resume and I'm impressed, and I'm my own worst critic! Sure, I may have lacked experience, but it's the age old question, 'How do you get experience when nobody gives you the chance to get experience?' Now I'm out here on my own doing trial and error ..."

"But you're surviving ..."

"Yes, I am ... but that's not the point. I wanted the chance to work and gain experience, make mistakes, and know that I could make them and the job would be there to guide me. Now, if I make a mistake, I may not know I made it until it's too late ... and that's my ass. I wanted my own but I didn't want it without the proper know how. I wasn't ready."

"It is the point, Que. In spite of all that hasn't happened the way you saw it or wanted it to happen, you are surviving. Are you ready now?"

"Winnie, I've got no choice but to be ready."

"Then you will soon be thriving. The hard work will pay off. You know that."

"Doesn't ease the bitterness, Winnie."

"Que, why do you think nobody has hired you?"

"Hmmph! Where can I begin? For starters, nowadays, it's not what you know, but who you know, and more than that, it's who knows you! The fact that I'm a young intelligent black man doesn't help matters because, say what you want, the powers that be are not trying to let me have but so much power and my experience has been that we as a people don't help and support each other as other ethnic groups do."

Yeah, I've probably lost some more readers, but c'est la vie! We're too busy cutting each other's throats. Don't get me wrong, every race does it. I guess I just notice it a little more here among my own, huh? Tommy Chin keeps it in the family. Sal hires his cousin Tony. When Bob's job is looking to hire, he brings in his own to interview. When Tyrone's job is hiring, well, you fill in the blank. When the guy Bob brought in to interview starts to excel and exceed Bob's performance, Bob may get mad, but he'll step up his performance because he accepts the competitiveness and feeds off of it ... turning a negative into a positive. But when somebody comes in outdoing Tyrone or Tanisha, they get ostracized (you know what to do), :-) and talked about because Tyrone and Tanisha now feel threatened … or they've been lazy and now they've got to step up their performance and they resent that. Meanwhile, you're not trying to show nobody up, that's just how you've always done things.

And God forbid that you try and infiltrate Bob's job, he'll always tell you that they're looking for someone with just a little more experience than you actually have. Meaning, more times than not, that your skin tone doesn't go with the office furniture. So if I say that I'm bitter, it's not because I'm expecting something, it's because I'm not even getting the opportunity to earn my props. Add that to the unwritten stress that I as a black man go through every day (we're not even going to get into that!), and we're talking el grande frustration. Hey… but I'm definitely not asking for your pity, I just want my opportunity. It just amazes me how some people take things for granted.

"Those people taking things for granted probably never met hard times, and cannot appreciate them as you will when your blessings rain down on you. Then I'll be Ralph singing to you, '*Can you stand the rain?*'"

"I thought you were gonna say Johnny. Now that would have been scary! You singing Johnny Gill's part!"

"I'm not singing in his voice, silly! My *female* voice!"

She elbowed me and then pinched me, mumbling,

"I'll sound better than you! They let anyone sing in the church choir!"

"You would scare the blessings away, singing Johnny's part. There's a drought over in these parts!"

"Well, I believe that your time is coming. This is all happening for a reason. Just don't forget us little people, okay, Que?"

"Ummph."

"Hey, I know things about you that the tabloids would be dying to get their hands on, so you better be nice to me!"

Winnie laughs, but I don't find the shit funny at all and I tell her so.

"Oh no, you're not insulting me in my bed!?! You know damn well that I was joking with you, and if this is the beginning of one of your legendary mood swings, you should leave and take it home with you, Gregory!"

Now normally I don't take that kind of talk from nooooobody. I'm quick to exit "stage 'left'," or better yet, ignore you. Of course I knew Winnie was joking, but she didn't have to know that. This is one of my exercises to keep people on their toes, so they don't get complacent with themselves around me. Yeah, maybe I'm wrong, and I can't even begin to tell you why I do it. Well, maybe I can, but I won't. Figure it out for yourself.

Sometimes I cross the line (but you know that already), and I might have done it this time because Winnie only calls me Gregory when she's heated, just as I call her Winter when I'm thoroughly pissed off. Winnie has an edge over you guys though, and she calls my bluff. She has me figured out better than anyone ever has except maybe for one person. Of course my complexity is such that you will never truly understand the man behind the kool-aid smile, but that doesn't stop people from trying.

"So you think you got me figured out, huh?"

"No, Que. I'd never make that mistake. It's useless trying to figure you out, right?"

"Don't patronize me."

"I am really upset with you! I can't believe that you would *go* there. You of all people know that I would never do anything to hurt you ... *AND YOU*

KNOW THAT TOO! But you decided to see how far you could go. When are you gonna realize that I'm not your enemy, I'm your friend. *I-Just-Want-To-Be-Your-Friend!* I don't want your money. Heck, I could live without your love. I do want your respect. I do want your companionship and friendship. And maybe even one day, I'll *deserve* your precious trust!"

It's not hard for me to apologize. I mean, I really can admit when I'm wrong, but sometimes, I just don't do it. I call it the "Whateva's Cleva" paradox. But if anybody deserves an apology here, it's Winnie. Don't ask me why, I know I should apologize, but I'm still hesitant. And Winnie knows this about me too. Am I just being stubborn? Hell, I make no apologies about who I be. This comes with the territory if you decide to accept who I am. I don't force you. Many have tried, some are still trying, and some will make the attempt in the future. It's a callous way of looking at things, but then again, I never told you that my world was peaches and cream.

Winnie continues, "I can understand your bitterness, but if you're going to take it out on the rest of the world, I wish you'd leave me out of it. And don't use it as an excuse to say what you feel and hide behind it to hurt somebody else because your world isn't the way you want it to be! I don't appreciate it, and I damn sure don't deserve it!"

Leave it to Winnie to pull no punches. You're probably enjoying this too … and yeah, I deserve it, so I'll stay quiet and just put that "H" on my chest. Winnie knows that I'll listen to her, but I ain't gonna hear this all night. She knows how I feel about harping on stuff and refusing to let it go. I hate nagging and I hate it when every time you do something, everything that you've ever done in life is thrown back in your face. That's a crumb in my knapsack! What has the past got to do with here and now? Everything, you might say. And you know exactly what I'm talking about.

But here's your typical example: You're arguing with your significant other about … oh, let's say, leaving one dish in the sink (another crumb in my knapsack). Stick to the issue at hand. Don't use this argument to bring up past idiosyncrasies like, "Why did you speak to Jasmine at the mall that time, when you know I don't like her?" Forget the fact that Jasmine spoke to you and common courtesy calls for you to return in kind … or you didn't even know that she wasn't liked. What has *that* got to do with the tea in China? Translation: What does that have to do with what we're talking about now? Unfortunately for guys, this is just something that you're supposed to know. Well, good luck. That's like asking a guy what the difference is between a Panty Liner and a Panty Shield! Stop smiling, ladies!

"You're right, Winnie. I shouldn't have done that to you. I apologize."

It's Winnie's turn to give me the much deserved cold shoulder … and believe me … I'm catching frostbite! Do unto others as you would have them do unto you … Sound familiar? Like I said before, I can wear the "H," but don't try to "out stubborn" me … You'll lose. Meaning, give me what I gave you, but don't try and take it to another level and add on an extra layer. I don't play that. Either accept my apology and we move on, or don't accept it and we move on. Don't leave me hanging. Nobody ignores you better than I do, so don't even go there. If I apologize, and you try to play games and make me squirm by giving me the silent treatment, or the extended cold shoulder after an acceptable amount of time (we all know what an acceptable amount of time is, so spare me the semantics), you'll be the one to regret it. Trust me on this one.

You get two strikes. I'll ask you a question twice, and if you don't give me an answer … then it's on, and if it's on, then it's on and I'm gone! My body may be there with you, but my mind and spirit will suddenly take a vacation. And they bothered to tell no one where they were going, or if and when they'd be back! It's always interesting to see who makes the cut and who gets kicked to the curb. Winnie, and K.P. for that matter, haven't experienced this wrath first hand, but they've witnessed others go through this, and 'twas not a pretty sight. So they know that I'm serious with this, and although they've both been to the max many times, neither has ever gone over it. Just the same, they've let me know that the same rules apply to me, and I respect that. See ... so do unto others ...

"Hey you ... I'm sorry, okay ... ?"

No response ... and to tell you the truth, I expected it. I offer another attempt because after all, I am the reason for her silence.

"I'm sorry, Winnie."

Still no response, but again, it's not unexpected. But I've got an ace in the hole. If there is one thing that Winnie loves about me, it's my ability to put a smile on her face. I'm a very spontaneous person, which can lead to unpredictability, and in my case, it can be madcap, zany unpredictability. I jump out of bed and strike a Superman pose. Mind you, I am "butt naked Willie" right about now. So I'm swingin' in the wind, ya know? 'Cause I got a little blood flow going (Warning! This maneuver is to be performed only by a professional). Those in the know get what I'm sayin' about the blood flow, this is not to be attempted by amateurs. You won't get the desired effect!

The conversation flows like this:

"Floyd … it seems that Winnie is upset with me."

I move my hips slightly, causing Floyd to sway, and Floyd answers in Winnie's favorite Disney-animated voice,

"Oh bother, Que … Whatever have you done now?"

Winnie nearly erupts, but she's quick to catch herself. I'm sure she wants to see how this is going to play out.

"I have caused shame and pain upon my good friend, Winnie."

"Oh bother, Que … you silly Willie … don't you know that I am ever so fond of Winter. Truly, if not for her, I should not have a place to hibernate! Apologize at once!"

Winnie cannot help but to explode with laughter at that.

"I've tried, Floyd, but I don't think she's trying to hear me."

"Oh dddee deea dee dear … oh dear … what are we to do, Que?" the Crew responds, panic-ridden.

"Now don't panic, Crew … I'm sure Floyd will think of something."

Winnie is laughing hard.

"Winter?" Floyd asks. "Is there anything that I can do to make up for Que's inexcusable blunder?"

Winnie smirks at my attempt for peace and positions herself in a thinking pose.

"I don't know," Winnie allows. "Your boy really fucked up … I mean … I don't know!"

"Winnie … Winnie … Winnie … talk to me … you know I'm the brains of this operation …"

"Ain't that the truth! And it's been proven once again too!" Winnie laughs.

"Hey, I resent that!" I protest, but Floyd silences me with a hard smack to my left leg.

"Quiet Fool! This is an A-B conversation, so C your way out!"

"Well, I never! …"

"And ya never will again if ya don't let me handle this, Que!"

"You go, Floyd!" Winnie cheers on.

"Now, Winter," Floyd continues. "Whatever may I do to ensure your good graces again?"

"I don't know, Floyd, but I'm sure you'll think of something … "

"That's it!" Floyd trumpets.

"What?" Winnie asks, genuinely confused.

"If I think of something really big, will you forgive Que?" Floyd questions.

"Perhaps," Winnie says, not giving in. "But you better come up with something really big to make up for this!"

"Think … think … think," Floyd begins. "Think … think … think … Oh, bother … all of this thinking is starting to give me a headache!"

Winnie lets out a shriek of amazement and pure delight as she busts out laughing, clapping her hands and bouncing up and down on the bed like a little school girl. In Floyd's quest to think of something big, he has begun to grow before Winnie's eyes! And he keeps growing and growing.

"I cannot believe you … I was not thinking big like *that*, Que," Winnie cries with laughter.

"How do you come up with this stuff!?! … Forget I said that!!!"

"A mind is a terrible thing to waste!"

"Come here, you silly ol' bear! Winter is here and it's hibernating season!"

Just call me Que ... Bear!

3

MUSICAL CHAIRS

If you were a Smurf ... which one would you be?

I finally checked my messages and I almost forgot that it's my night to host "Off the Hook."

"Off the Hook" came about because a group of us got bored. There's only so much clubbing one can do. I've been a club head since I was a teenager, and basically for me it was "Been there, done that!" We got tired of the norm too, going out to dinner, movies, etc. You get the drift. This is the second year that we've done "Off the Hook," and I look forward to it. There are seven of us, four girls and three guys. There's K.P. and Kenny, who I've mentioned earlier, Gillian, Maxine, my cousin Temple, my frat brother Casino, and moi. Every other Saturday of the month, we get together at somebody's crib and vibe. In our case, we do something out of the ordinary. We decide at the beginning of the year on twelve themes, one for each month. The themes are geared toward the outrageous and scandalous, thus the name "Off the Hook."

This month's theme just happens to be sexual connotations … go figure! :-) Hey, you gotta be an open-minded person to attend our sets, that's basically the only criteria. Give the event a chance. Each of us can invite up to two people. At first, we didn't give notice to people about what they could expect. You know that caused problems. Some people were too stuffy in my opinion, and thought some of our antics bordered on derogatory. Basically, to avoid the crab ass people now, the host communicates with the other five members on the Wednesday before the set, and kind of outlines what he or she intends to do. The members have the discretion to decide who to bring for that particular set, and can tell the people only what the host tells the members, along with what the theme for the month is. If you're with it, show up and have a good time. If not, hey … maybe next time. Nobody rains on our parade. If we get the vibe that someone is trying to act brand new, they gets ta' steppin'.

Just to get a feel for our perverted way of looking at life, this month we've watched and critiqued a porno movie while eating erotic chocolates … know what I'm sayin'? Just think anatomical. I wonder why no one left with who they came with? :-) That's a joke, people! Our sets are not politically correct booty calls! That night was isolated. I'm sayin', though, there was a full moon. Nobody anticipated that.

… Anyway. In the past, we've listened to an opera sipping daiquiris; karaoke with Bon Jovi, Wu Tang Clan, and Tom Jones (talk about cultural diversity!); a Leggo my Eggo chicken, waffles and ice cream affair where the only way you got to eat was to beat somebody to the toaster and literally grab your waffles; water gun fights against some senior citizens; and discussions on everything from whether Luther and Oprah look better with the weight or without the weight, to what's better, flame broiled or fried. I prefer flame broiled, but when I eat fried, I hit one spot (shout out to Dave Thomas).

As I prepare myself a little breakfast, oh, I didn't mention cooking skills, huh? Add that to the resume. Although today's breakfast is simple (bacon, cheese grits, and cheese eggs), do not sleep. Mama did not raise no fool! She was adamant about her sons knowing how to cook. We know all about Mom's persuasive skills, don't we? She told us not to be dependent on some woman to put a meal on the table. Good advice, too. A girl had offered to cook dinner for me once. I told her that I would buy the food and wine. But she insisted on doing everything, told me to just show up. Something about saving my energy. :-/

Anyway, I gets to her house and I'm chillin'. My pager starts to blow up. I forgot that my pager was on beep for the first page, so of course she heard it. After that, though, I put everything on vibrate. Now fellas, I don't know how you do it, but I give code numbers to everybody that has my numeric pager number (if you have my alpha-numeric number, then you know you're special). So when you page me, you put in the number where you're at, then hit the * button, put in your code number, then hit the # sign or hang up. Simple. If you don't put in your code number, I'm not calling you back. Of course, there have been times when I've bent the rules because I've recognized the number, but you need not be concerned with that. It used to be that if I was with a female and another paged me, I would give the one that I was with respect and not return the page until later. That was how it used to be. Now, no secrets. If I get paged, and I feel like returning the page, I do. Family gets returned with no hesitation. My fellas, K.P., and Winnie get top priority, and everybody else gets blessed when I get the chance. So my pager is getting blown up. I don't have a clue who it is because there's no code and I don't recognize the number.

Huh? *Who just asked why I didn't turn it off? ...* Because the next page could have been an emergency! Fool! Always one jackass in the crowd, huh? What!?! So step up! Make yourself known! We can handle this how *you* want to handle this! I'll be damned if you think you can act up in my book and get away with it!

Big up your chest and you might get rest

'Cause I ain't the other brother you wanna go and test!

Sorry about that. Gotta handle my business. As I was sayin', though ... honey keeps hearing the pager, 'cause I don't have that subtle vibration, I got that jack hammer action. She asks me if I want to use her phone. I decline because I don't recognize the number. Finally, the page comes through again and the number is followed by Kenny's code.

Okay, now I know who's paging me, so I ask to use her phone. I call the number and Kenny picks up the phone, asking me why I haven't returned the previous pages. I kindly explain the reason to *my* satisfaction and ask him what the deal is? He's at some girl's house and she's got a friend. Basically he needs me to run interference so he can get his. I told him I'd get back to him. Mind you, while you just got both ends of the convo, this honey only got my end. So she heard me explain why I didn't get the page and that I'd get back to Kenny, although I said, "I'll get back to you."

After I sat back down to watch TV, honey comes in five minutes later asking me why I called another woman's number in her house. Can you see where this is going? At first I didn't know what she was talking about. I told her that I called one of my boys back. She called me a liar. My right eyebrow goes up, the first sign that you done fucked up. So I asked her what the hell she was talking about. You know what she did, right? After I hung up the phone, she *69ed the number! And didn't even try to conceal it, either!

So I'm bugging over the fact that this honey has got the gumption to call me out when there ain't a damn thing going on with us! But to my credit, I didn't blow up. I kind of laughed it off. I told Ms. Nosy Ass to call the number back and ask for Kenny. She told me there was no need because an answering machine came on with a woman's voice on it. Don't you know that during that time, Kenny and those girls went out to get something to eat. Now she's going on and on about the fact that I done lied to her. Y'all know how I feel about nagging, and I'm not taking no crap from nobody, especially when I'm actually telling the truth! I told her that there was nothing going on with us so why was she tripping? She threw that "it's a matter of respect" thing in my face. I'm damned if I do and damned if I don't tell the truth!

She goes into her room and closes the door! What's that all about? I stopped playing "run, catch, and kiss" (and all those other variations), a long time ago. I let ten minutes go by and finally after a half hour, I went to the door and turned the knob. Locked! She informed me from the other side of the door that she wasn't coming out to cook, until I apologized for calling another woman's house. I was not feelin' this and I damn sure wasn't apologizing, for what!?!

So I walked into the kitchen and started cooking the food. I don't know if she fell asleep, or if she figured that I didn't know how to cook lobster and shrimp. Or that she thought I was trying to make it up to her by trying to start the cooking process, and she would eventually come and take over. Well, anyway, by the time she came out of seclusion, I was pouring my sweetened butter over the remainder of the second lobster! Damn right I ate the first, and the shrimp!

But wait! Before you accuse me of being totally out of control, I did think of her. I left her a plate with two shrimp on it. As I walked out the door, I told her next time to find out first whether someone can cook or not before you give ultimatums and *tries* to play someone for a sucka.

I smirked and told her before I closed the door that, "Mama didn't raise no fool!"

A few days later, Connie, the girl that introduced us, called me and told me that honey was so impressed that I knew how to cook, and that the two shrimp that she was fortunate enough to get were the bomb (like I didn't know, it's all about the seasoning). :-/ Connie asked me for my version of what happened. I told her, and she laughed. Apparently, this wasn't the first time that the *69 thing had gone down, so Connie said that honey just had to learn the hard way. I told Connie to relay to her that I wasn't calling her back, and not to waste her time 'cause I wasn't interested in her apologies.

I also screamed on Connie for hooking me up with someone that's got issues.

So fellas, let that be a lesson to ya. You may think you got it going on now, but imagine how much more attractive you'd be to women (think fringe benefits, my friend), ;-) (wink) if you knew how to cook and cook well. Tell you what, start off small. Cook breakfast for a lady and see the rewards that you reap. You may see it right then and there, or you may see it later, but trust me, you will see it. Remember my simple pleasures?

My brother, Steven? He knows the basics. He can survive. But he didn't take to it like I did. I guess he didn't have to because his wife loves to cook. I'm amazed that Steven is in the shape that he is in, 'cause "sister girlfriend" can burn! Suzanne (we call her "Suzie Que"), works magic in the kitchen. Y'all don't know my mother, but when Pat starts throwing out props in the kitchen, you know you got it going on. Speaking of which, Steven left a message, let me call him back.

"Hello?"

"Suzie Que? What would it take to get you to leave your husband and run off with me?"

"Today, not much. How are you, Que?"

"Oooo, did I call at a bad time?"

"No, your brother promised the kids that he'd take them to the circus, and now he's trying to front."

"But we both know he's gonna take 'em, right?"

"Oh yeah, he will, but Steven is so stubborn sometimes. But your mother always told me that it runs in the family."

"Unfortunately, stubbornness does run in the family. And when we ask Mom and Dad who we get it from, they always point to each other!"

"I know that's right! You eating okay? You know we have plenty food and I can send some over to you."

"Suzie Que, I'm not worthy! You know I ain't never gonna turn down *your* cooking …"

"Guess what, Que? I'm making beef ribs tomorrow …"

I sucked my teeth.

"Awww woman! C'mon, you know you're not playin' fair!"

"Soooorrry, you know the rules, sweetie. So who ya bringing?"

Steven and Suzie Que are on this mission to get me married. They've established these rules that during the week, and Saturdays, I'm allowed in the house to visit, bug out with the kids, vibe, whatever. But on Sundays, I can't step foot in their house unless I have a female companion for dinner. Suzie Que is not playing fair, because she knows I love her ribs (the sauce should be patented), and the only way I'm gonna get them is to bring someone to dinner. They've even got the twins in on this. Yeah, yeah, yeah! Steven and Suzie Que have a set of twins too, a boy and a girl, Aaron and Karen.

"I don't wanna talk to you anymore, Suzie Que. Where's my kids?"

She laughs and says, "Hold on."

Suzie Que tells one of the kids to pick up the phone downstairs, and I hear a little female voice.

"Hello?"

"Who dat is?"

There are giggles on the other end of the phone, and I repeat myself.

"I said … Who dat is!?!"

"That's jus' my baby daddy!"

"Who dat is?"

"That's jus' my baby daddy!"

I guess Suzie Que hadn't hung up the phone yet 'cause she said,

" … Excuse me? What did you say, young lady?"

Uh oh … damage control. I tell Karen to explain what we've talked about.

"Mommy, Uncle Que heard me singing that one day and he asked me why I was singing it. I told him because I liked it. He asked me if I knew what the song was talking about. I told him what I thought the song was about. He told me in order to listen to songs like that I had to be able to separate real life and entertainment from a song."

"And?" I coached.

"And if I want to know the real meaning behind songs I hear on the radio if I don't know it already, to ask you or call Uncle Que."

"So now you've got a little protégé, huh, you hip hop junkie?"

"Now, Suzie Que, you know ..."

"Steven's gonna get ya, bad enough I like it."

In the background, I hear Steven, and I tell Suzie Que to put him on the phone. I tell Karen to say it to her Daddy.

"Uh uh. I'ma get in trouble, Uncle Que."

"No, you won't, sweetheart. I promise."

"Who dat is, Daddy?"

"What? ... Karen?"

I laughed.

"Que?"

"Say it again, Karen," I coaxed.

"Who dat is?"

Finally, Steven catches on and replies on cue, "Dat's jus' my baby daddy!"

Karen, hearing this, squealed with delight. "Daddy, you know that song!?!"

"Your daddy's kind of cool, ain't he?" I chimed in. "Okay, let me talk to your father. I'll talk to you later, sweetie."

"Bye, Uncle Que!"

Before she could hang up, she's yelling to Aaron that their daddy knew a rap song. Aaron runs to the phone in the basement.

"Hey, Uncle Que! Hi Dad! … Dad, who dat is?"

Steven, feeling his oats, replies more confidently.

"Dat's jus' my baby daddy. You 'bout to get fired gurl, shut up and be quiet, gurl … Now y'all both get off this phone," Steven says laughing.

Karen squealed with more delight, then they hung up the phone and ran to tell their mother.

"See, now you done made their day, Steven. They think their Daddy is real cool. Of course, we both know different!"

"So you say, but everyone knows I'm down for whatever! (Apologies to Ice Cube). Guess Suzanne told you about dinner tomorrow, huh?"

"Why do you do this to me?"

"Just brotherly love. So who ya bringing? 'Cause I know you're not missing those ribs!"

"I don't know."

"Steelers play the Cowboys tomorrow too! So if I was you, I'd be bringing someone that is a football fan!"

"Yaaaa … that's right!"

"Well, I gotta go. Off to the circus. Until tomorrow then. Later, Que."

"Peace."

Steven is thirty-four years old, about five-eight, a hundred and sixty-five pounds, mustache, brown eyes. He's my father's twin. He was always dissecting stuff when he was little and shoving the remains in my face. So it's no wonder that he's a surgeon. I know, I know, another doctor. He met Suzie Que in med school. She's a pediatrician. The twins came during his first year of interning and her last year of med school. They got married two years later, and have been happily married for five years now. They live out in Dix Hills, Long Island. Yes! They're makin' chedda'!

Listen. Did you hear that? There it is again. I actually thought that I might make it through the morning and not hear it. Guess not. Remember the sounds I told you about earlier, the cawing? Well, I just heard them again. Upon going to the window I see six crows on a tree branch. Six, and they all stop cawing when they see me. They're all looking directly at me. What the hell is that about? I pull the window shade down, and I swear the cawing now sounds like cackling. Some days, I'm so busy that I don't get to dwell on this. But the weekends are different because I don't have as much to do. And I have no choice but to think about it.

"I found out who it was. I've actually known for a minute now, but they don't know that I know who it is."

"So what do you want me to do, Snow?"

"Que, I need people that I can trust. I know that you're close to the family. Darren is too emotional right now. He's a ticking time bomb waiting to explode, but I can't blame him. I'm trying to get him to understand the art of war, strategy … patience. That ponder, deliberate … wise warrior thing. But I need people that understand how the game is played."

"You read *The Art of War?*"

"Damn, son. Don't sound so surprised!"

"Naw, naw, that's not it. I mean, I read it too."

"I know that. What? You thought I was joking when I would always say that we looked up to you guys? That's why I need people that understand how the game is played."

"And I understand the game?"

"Yeah, you do. I heard the stories about you, son … running with the Wolfpack. When we was growing up, *we looked up* to you guys."

Damn, back in the days, it would have been cool to hear something like that. But today, I cringed to know the effect that we had on those kids. Is this what they call maturity?

While we were huddled in the corner of K.P.'s house, Mrs. Parker stumbled upon us and immediately her antennas went up.

"Excuse me, you two. Is everything all right?"

Snow looked at me as if I was the fast thinker, and even though I was, I didn't appreciate being put in this situation.

"Yes, Mrs. Parker. Luth—I mean, Snow asked me a question, and you know since I'm in school now, everybody thinks I can answer their questions."

I *hated* lying to Mrs. Parker, but I didn't think it was such a good idea to tell her that we were actually considering avenging her husband's death! That would have went over real well.

"Luther?"

"Yes ma'am?"

"You're not in any trouble, are you?"

"No ma'am!"

"You do remember what we discussed and what you promised me, right?"

"I do, ma'am, and I intend to keep it. That's why I'm talking to Que."

"Really? Well, I'm certainly glad to hear that."

Mrs. Parker was beaming now.

"Moms?"

"Yes, Luther?"

"Can we keep this just between us? I kinda want it to be a surprise, okay?"

"Sure, Luther. It's safe with me."

"Thanks."

With that, she left the room. And I'm sitting there wondering what the hell just went on. So I asked him.

"Yo, what was that all about? The promise and all that?"

"I told Mrs. P. I was gonna get out the game and go back to school."

"What!?!"

My mouth was wide open. I couldn't believe what I just heard. But that explained why Mrs. Parker was beaming.

"But not until I take care of this. That'll be my last hurrah!"

How prophetic those words turned out to be!

Met up with K.P. and Jinx around two o'clock in front of Junior's in downtown Brooklyn. Junior's is famous for their cheesecake, and I had a sweet tooth. Not to mention that I had special ordered some cheesecakes for tonight's "Off the Hook" and I had to pick them up. I got there before them so I waited outside.

A guy who didn't look homeless to me asked me for some change. But then again, how is homeless supposed to look? Now I used to give change to people when they asked for it, because to me, they looked like they needed it. But I'll be damned if I'll support some rock star's habit. For the impaired, a rock star is slang for a crack addict. A lot of these cats have made panhandling a lucrative career, and have actually messed it up for those that truly need it.

So I gives nothing to no one anymore, especially since a girl I know told me the story of how she used to give this guy change because he looked the part. Clothes torn, shoes with holes in them, basically "tore up from the floor up." She went to this restaurant one night (she said it was upscale), and saw the guy she had been giving change to "dressed to the nines" with a lady playin' mack daddy, daddy mack, sipping Cristal at a table for two. I told her she should have taken the bottle since she probably helped pay for it! Most of 'em out here are playin' folks like Lotto. I'm not sayin' *don't give*, but beware and use your own discretion. Just don't come back to me sayin' you didn't know when I done schooled you on the haps.

"S'cuse me, Mister ... but you sho' is one fine hunk of specimen ..."

I turned toward the voice of K.P.

"Check this out? I don't know if I wanna get with you yet, but who da Shorty next to you?"

"Shorty!?!" Jinx exclaimed. "I don't think that you can handle this package with lines like that! Besides we talkin' two for one, and you don't look like you swingin'."

"I'll wear yo' little ass out, and then take care of her for dessert."

"So why we standin' here talking, Slim? Put out for the hotel, a little wine and dine, and we'll see whether you get to back up or whether you has to pack up."

"Why don't I just cut to the chase, and drop my pants now?"

"Oh, you got it like that, huh?"

"I drop my pants, I get both of y'all, right?"

"If we like what we see, we'll take care of thee!"

"Stand back, 'cause this whole place 'bout to get dark!" (Apologies to Bernie Mac! I miss that "futha mucka!").

So I unbuckled my belt and pants, and prepared to give Floyd and the Crew a little air. Just as I'm at the point of no return, Jinx rushes me and hugs my waist, preventing my pants from coming down.

"You fool!" she screams, laughing, "What are we gonna do with you!?!"

"If that's all I got to do to get both of y'all … hey! … Notice, K.P. ain't move a muscle, right?"

"Damn right! I wanted to see what I was getting and whether or not you was gonna punk out, but Jinx saved your ass."

"Yeah, I saved him! I don't want the world going dark or sharing the sight of my stuff, and you either for that matter!"

"Jinx? You wasn't gonna share me with K.P.?"

"Hell no!"

On that note, we entered the restaurant as yet another person seeking spare change opened the door for us. Had the nerve to curse us when all he received for his efforts was a thank you. I started to reach in my back pocket for a can of ass whippin', but K.P. and Jinx preached peace, and I decided at least for the time being to keep hope alive. Anybody else miss Robin Harris?

The host seated us in the non-smoking section and the waiter assigned to our section brought over menus. I wasn't hungry, thanks to my late breakfast, but I told the girls to feel free to order. I did want dessert, and I had my mind set on the double chocolate layer cake. The girls wanted dessert also. K.P. ordered cheesecake even though I told her that we would have some tonight. She just said that she would have some then too. Jinx ordered hot apple pie with ice cream.

"So why did you want to see us, Que?" Jinx asked.

"Do I need a reason to want to spend time with two of my favorite girls?"

K.P. smiled. Obviously Jinx knew nothing of our purpose for gathering, and we planned on keeping it that way.

"If I could have gotten your older sister to come, we could have had a foursome!"

Jinx looked puzzled.

"We don't have an older sister, Que."

K.P. laughed and filled Jinx in on the joke.

"He means Mom, Jinx."

Our desserts came and we dug in. You know that age old saying that you know that food is good when everyone is quiet? It applied here. After savoring our first few bites, we offered each other samples.

"Que? Want a *piece of my apple pie?*"

How many of you thought what I thought? Raise your hand. Good, so it wasn't just me!

"Is it still hot?"

"I say it's steaming, but you have a taste and tell me if you like?"

"Would you two dogs in heat cut it out?" K.P. groans.

"She started it," I protest.

"And I'll finish it too," Jinx coos as she plays with some pie on her fork with her tongue.

"I thought we'd check out Coney Island today, go by the N.Y. Aquarium. You guys game?"

"Changing the subject, Que?"

"K.P.'s getting jealous, Jinx."

"Look, just do her and get it over with, okay?" K.P. gripes.

"But I want both of you. My fantasy of sisters, ya know?"

The waiter brought the check and I asked him to get the host so that I could get the cheesecakes that I had ordered. While we sat there waiting for my cheesecakes and making small talk, something Jinx said triggered a reaction that actually had nothing to do with what she said. Has that ever happened to you? Someone says or does something that reminds you of something else, and the two are totally unconnected? Anyway, I asked the question that was suddenly on my mind.

"Hey, I wanted to ask you guys a question, okay?"

"What's the question?" K.P. asked.

"What do you two know about 'the look'?"

K.P.'s face, which had a smirk on it before the question, suddenly went expressionless. And Jinx's mouth opened slightly and closed just as quick. I caught the quick eye contact between the two and said to myself, "Well, I'll be damned. It is true!"

"What are you talking about?" Jinx replied coyly.

"Look, I know y'all know what I'm talking about. I saw the way you looked at each other."

"Who have you been talking to?" K.P. asked.

"Somebody who I thought was pulling my leg, but I guess they were telling the truth. But I won't know for sure unless you guys come clean with me."

"How she gonna play us like that?" Jinx spat.

"I didn't say it was a 'she'."

"You didn't have to, Que. Ain't too many guys who know about that. She must like you an awful lot!" K.P. concluded.

"So who is she?" Jinx demanded.

"Oh hell no, I ain't tellin'. Not after the way y'all done reacted. Besides, K.P., we've shared things before about guys and girls."

"I didn't say that we haven't."

You know what I think? I think that Winnie set me up. She knew the reaction that I'd get. And you women out there knew it too. Aight. I see how ya livin' (like a turkey on Thanksgiving … fowl! … 'foul' for the uneducated). Y'all really do stick together, huh? Now I just have to figure out what her reason was. I have an idea, but I'm not sharing it with you.

"So you gonna tell me what it is?"

"It's a look that guys get when they want to be with someone and their eyes say, 'I'm gonna rock your world.' Guys always tell you that they're gonna rock your world, but you can always tell if it's actually going to happen by the look in their eyes."

"Don't confuse it with 'horny' either, that has a different look all together," Jinx chimes in.

"This friend of yours must have seen the look in your eyes to comment about it," K.P. drones.

"Yo, what's up with the tone of voice?"

"You don't get it, do you? Whoever she is wanted it known that she had seen the look in your eyes. She calls herself sending out a message that she's claiming you, and probably most important, that the look was for her. Therefore I can only conclude that we know her or know of her, or she knows us or knows of us."

Yo ... I felt very played! The unsuspecting messenger! Everything K.P. said made sense. Why else would someone want to make something like that known? It wouldn't mean anything or be satisfying if the recipient of the information didn't know of the provider of the info. At least that's how I see it. Do you agree?

"Yo ... I'm on my way over!"

"Que, I've got company right now."

"Get rid of him, Winter. I'm on my way over!"

I hung up the pay phone, got in my car, and stopped by my house to put the cheesecakes in my refrigerator. I guess you may have figured out that we didn't hit Coney Island or the Aquarium. Not because K.P. and Jinx didn't want to. I asked for a rain check. I wasn't in the best of moods, and they didn't deserve that. Somebody else did.

"What's the matter with you, Que?"

"You want to know what's the matter with me? Number one, I don't appreciate you using our friendship to send a message. Number two, I don't like being made a fool. Number three, I'm fuckin' pissed off at you, Winter!"

"What the hell are you talking about, Que!?! First of all, you need to count to ten and walk your ass back in here and try again. Second of all, I don't need to send any messages to nobody through you … What are you talking about? And third, I never want you to look like a fool. What is this about?"

"It's about that 'look' shit. I asked K.P. about it, and she nearly went bananas!"

"Stop exaggerating. So she reacted, huh? Good. That's what I wanted."

"What!?!"

"You should know by now that I don't do things just to do them. You know there's a reason. And when it comes to you, your best interest is always the best reason."

"Well, your warped-ass mind better come up with a good reason, today!"

"Now how did she really react? What I know of K.P., she's a cool cucumber."

"She basically said that whoever told me wanted her to know that they'd seen 'the look' in my eyes, and that this person must like me an awful lot."

"Damn! She's better than I gave her credit for. I'm impressed. You didn't tell her who I was, did you? Or that we slept together?"

"Hell, no. But her sister asked who it was that told me."

"What's her name, Jinx? The one that adores you?"

"Yeah."

"That's my bad. I thought that you'd ask her when you were alone. Now you definitely can't tell her that we slept together."

"Your bad? I look like a fool and it's 'your bad'!??!"

"Que, had you been by yourself, you would have seen that K.P. likes you. That was the reason I suggested you ask her."

"Oh, so you knew that I would, huh?"

"That's right. Of course you won't answer it for me, but ask yourself this question: If you don't like K.P., then why haven't you slept with Jinx?"

I looked at Winnie with admirable disgust. Sometimes I don't like Winnie because it's almost like looking in the damn mirror!

"Whatever."

"And don't think I didn't notice how you didn't believe me the other night, but K.P.'s confirmation today is the gospel. *I-am-offended, Mister!*"

"But Winnie, I—"

"'But Winnie I' nothing. It's okay. I'll get over it. I still love you, but it's just more proof on how you feel about K.P. You need to stop fronting with me, and more importantly, yourself!"

She approached me and hugged me, and I hugged her back. Sometimes you take for granted good people that have your back. I try not to do that but I am but a man. An egotistical, mistake-making, blow-your-back-out, fine ass looking man! (lol)

"Winnie, I didn't mean to offend you."

"But yo' arrogant, 'I made a mistake,' 'orgasm-giving,' 'sexy ass self' *did*."

Is there an echo in the room? Is this the universe's way of proving Winnie's point that she knows me? I just said remnants of that same 'ish to myself. You read it!

"At least we know why you tolerate me now?"

Winnie laughed.

"Yeah, you keep me laughing, you give me orgasms, you give me orgasms, and … you give me orgasms!"

She spread her hands out, palms facing up, and said, "Yo' arrogant ass (left hand) versus orgasms (right hand)!"

"Oh! It just got real in here."

"Think it didn't!?!"

She dropped her left hand down, and raised her right hand upward, turning it so her palm was facing the sky.

"Raising the roof on orgasms! Orgasms outweigh yo' arrogant ass all day, every day! And I'm gonna get them from you as long as I can. Until one day you're gonna wake up and realize you keep denying how you feel about K.P."

"Because you know me so well, don't you, Winnie?"

"Stop 'dripping,' Que. It kills you that somebody could actually know you, doesn't it? News flash! I'm not the only one. There-are-other-primitive-earthlings-besides-moi," Winnie laughed. "Anyways, who knows you better than I do? Maybe one or two people outside of family. No more than three. If I had told you what I was doing, you would have never went for it. Now the ball is in K.P.'s court, and if I'm as good as I think I am, she'll make a move."

"You damn right, I never would have gone for this. Who made your ass 'Chuck Woolery' all of a sudden?"

"The person that loves you and wants the best woman for you, and believe me, it's K.P.!"

<hr>

Kenny is always the first person at my house when I host, and he always shows up with two honeys as his guests. He's never brought one of his boys or any other guy. His rationale is why bring sand to the beach. That's Dexter St. Jock, as we affectionately and sarcastically call him. He's a showboat, but he's got a good heart. Since sisters declared it okay to be a dark-skinned brother again (thanks in part to Wesley Snipes, who I've run into a couple of times in the street, and I have to admit that the brother is down to earth, not full of himself), my man is like a kid in a candy store. He introduced me to his guests, Callie and Valerie. I guess Callie and I made eye contact a second too long, 'cause Kenny mumbled under his breath to not even think about it, he was trying to get with her. Not a problem to me. You know my style … I play the background. :-)

I excused myself and went to answer the door. Gillian and Maxine greeted me with hugs and introductions to their guests. We affectionately call them "the odd couple." Rarely are those two apart. They've been the best of friends since pre-school, it seems to me. Gillian is barely five feet, and Maxine is "modelesque" (yeah I made it up), at six feet one. Both of them are sexy in their own way. Gillian walks like a black panther, just struts, and has the prettiest lips, and Maxine has a "mousey" high pitched voice that you overlook when you see those "bedroom eyes" (fellas, think "Terry" from En Vogue).

Our whole group, with the exception of Temple, met during our heyday at the Garage. Need I say anymore? All real club heads swore allegiance to the Garage and Larry Levan, and if you were really down, The Shelter and Life. But y'all don't hear me, though! And the hip hop spots? Simply love, love, son. If you know, you know! Who remembers

Harlem World? The Red Parrot? Broadway International? China Club? Nell's? Kilimanjaro's? The Tunnel? Before Funk Master Flex put it back on the map now that he controls the one and two's. Or the FunHouse? Or Roxy?

In Brooklyn, peeps may remember The President Chateau on Utica Avenue or Colonial Mansion on Church Avenue, where Run DMC made one of their very first appearances doing "It's Like That" and "Sucker MC's." I like to think that I had a small hand in helping them achieve superstardom. I hosted the show and let Run rock my mic (an MC sin, back in the day), because his shorted out. Otherwise, heads up in that place would have wrecked shop for "perpetrating the fraud." :-/ Can't forget the roller rinks, Utica, Empire, Park Circle.

And don't even get me started on the spots in Queens. I didn't hang out in the Bronx too often back then, but I can say that I've been to the Fever and some jams that Fashion spun at. Back then, Brooklyn didn't go to the Bronx too often and the Bronx didn't come to Brooklyn too often, unless you was rolling mad deep. Neutral ground was Manhattan … Union Square, The Latin Quarters, when they were around. Ah, memories … but back to reality. Gillian usually comes with her boyfriend, Trevor, and tonight was no exception.

"What the deal is, son?" I say to Trevor.

"I'm on the rocks, yo," he responds back, with a pound.

Translation: he chillin'. :-)

Gillian introduces me to her other guest, Beverly, and Maxine introduces me to her guests, Torry and Kelly (both guys). They enter my living room where already Kenny is taking center stage as he greets Gillian, Max, and company. If you didn't know better, you'd think it was Kenny's pad. :-) The bell rings again and I answer it.

I swear, if I hadn't invited Winnie to "Off the Hook" already, her ass would not be here! Of course it makes perfect sense that she and K.P. would show up at the same time. Paranoia? Is this universal? Do women get these feelings too? It must be just me, because as I opened the door, they were in conversation, smiling and laughing. Wonder what was so funny?

I immediately notice three things:

1. K.P. has Jinx with her.
2. K.P. does not have the Krappa with her.
3. Winnie has Angie with her.

As the data banks are analyzing these developments, Angie has already taken it upon herself to be the first to hug me. Out of the corner of my eye, I see Winnie, K.P., and Jinx exchange glances. After I peel Angie off of me, I hug Jinx (who gives me the evil eye), K.P. (who has her trademark smirk in place), and Winnie (who tries to look as if she has a halo on).

When I told Winnie she could bring a friend as my second guest, I did not mean Angie. If you haven't peeped it yet, Angie wants to jump my bones in the worst way. She's a good looking girl, a slim goodie, but the attraction is one sided. Basically, Angie is a pest! She tries to give off the impression that we're closer than we really are. I have to admit though, in the beginning, she was almost a victim. But a little voice kept screaming, "Fatal Attraction! Fatal Attraction!"

"So where's Marlon?" I ask K.P.

"Wherever he's at," Jinx sniffs.

Okay, moving right along. I don't even dare look in the direction of Winnie, but I can feel her looking at me and smiling. This is not good. Jinx is here and in battle mode.

"Is everything all right?" I ask.

"Yep. So introduce us to your friend, Que. Winnie says that she's a guest of yours."

"Actually, she's Winnie's friend. Angie, this is K.P. and her sister, Jinx."

I glare at Winnie, but of course, she doesn't meet my gaze. She hasn't made actual eye contact with me yet.

"Que's my baby," Angie gushes.

"Oh, is he now?" Jinx challenges.

"Hey, people … let's go mingle with the others," I interject.

I put my arm around Jinx and lead her and the others into the living room. The small talk ends when the girls enter the room, at least for the guys. Now I already told you that Winnie is a winner, and K.P. and Jinx are dime pieces, and even though Angie is bringing up the rear, she's no slouch either. Personally, I think that at that moment, each and every brother was starring in his own mini X-rated flick! If you could have seen the looks on their faces. Even my frat brother Casino, who came in right after they did, had the gaze as he walked over and gripped me.

"Yo, Dog, who the slim goodies that came with K.P.? I recognize yours, Winnie, but who are the others?"

"Chill with that, dog. No mention of Winnie, aight?" I whispered as we gripped.

"I hear you, Team. So yo, introduce me."

We walked toward the group. Casino and K.P. hugged, and I introduced him to everyone. He had his eye on Angie. Meanwhile, Dexter St. Jock, smelling new fragrance in the air, saunters over. He and Winnie grunt at each other and he introduces himself to Angie by kissing her hand. Jinx and Winnie roll their eyes up yonder toward the ceiling. Across the room, Callie's face showed displeasure for just an instant, while Valerie sucked her teeth. Torry, who smells opportunity (something must be in the air), :-/ moves from his spot by Kelly to Kenny's former spot between Callie and Valerie on the leather sectional. Beverly is sitting to the right of Callie and is checking Casino out. Max, talking with Gillian and Trevor, sees Kelly by himself and casually starts to make her way toward him. But Kelly has already made his way toward our group with eyes locked in the direction of Winnie, K.P., and Jinx. Got that? I'm talking musical chairs here. Angie, maybe not accustomed to the kind of greeting that Kenny delivers, grabs my arm.

Ding dong! Saved by the bell! Pun intended!

I remove Angie's arm and head toward the door. I open the door and behind me I hear Max greet Temple with a loud, "What's up, girl?" as she walks toward her at the door and they hugged. Played off nicely, I might add. :-)

"Hey, I get first dibbs on Temple," I kidded.

I hugged my favorite cousin and she introduced me to her guests, Dell and Hester. She motioned for Max and introduced her to Hester and then to Dell, telling Dell that Max was the person she wanted him to meet. If the smile on Dell's face was any indication, brother man must have felt like he won the lottery. Max was trying to play cool, but she seemed to have that smile thing going on too. I ushered them into the living room and let everyone get familiar.

Winnie is purposely, but subtly avoiding me, making small talk with everyone. I leave the room and go into my den where the cheesecake and other goodies are, making sure that everything is the way I want it before I start. I don't think that I was in the room thirty seconds before I feel arms go around my waist. I didn't need to turn around because I already knew who it was. There was no use removing the arms. Besides, it took more energy than I was willing to exert at that moment, so I just let it be.

"Hey, sexy. I just wanted to steal a private moment with you now. Hopefully, I'll get to build on this after everyone leaves."

"Got to clean up, Angie."

Now I'm sure that most of y'all would agree that if I was feelin' Angie, cleaning up after everyone left would have been the last thing on my mind. Can I get an Amen from the Amen Corner? Now if things go the way *I* want, somebody else is gonna be up in this piece!

"I'll help you clean up, and I guarantee you that it'll be fun."

The only thing guaranteed in this lifetime is death, higher taxes, and Don King's hair never flopping in Phoenix! Only the sanctimonious are taking this literally and chastising me. *Uh huh, uh huh.* Well, be my guest. I was saved from answering as K.P. appeared in the doorway with an amused look on her face, asking when we were gonna start.

"Right now," I said, breaking the chains around my waist.

I brushed past K.P. and as I entered the living room, I caught Winnie smirking at me. Angie, in hot pursuit, walked past K.P. and rolled her eyes.

Damn, I was not in the mood for drama, as I heard K.P., loud enough for all to hear.

"Ms. Thang, please don't get it twisted. I *will* bust yo' ass!"

"Excuse me? I *know* I didn't hear you correctly!" Angie said, perfectly rolling her neck.

"I don't stutter!" K.P. fired right back.

I swung around. K.P. usually doesn't let petty stuff like that get to her, but like they say, catch anybody at the wrong time and … hey.

"Battlecat," formerly known as Jinx, wasted no time adding fuel to the fire, stepping to her sister's back.

"Oh yes, heifer! We can set it off tonight, up in this piece! Trust me, you do not want to go there!"

Angie didn't stand a chance against K.P., and adding tag team partner Jinx to the mix just meant that the ass whipping wouldn't end no time soon.

Winnie, making it known whose side she was on, jumps in.

"Damn Angie, I told you that she was his best friend! Why you tripping?"

I did a double take! And I know that no one understood the gesture, except Winnie. What the hell was she doing? I told you that no one rains on our parade, and if one member says that you get ta' steppin', you gets ta' steppin'. Angie did not know how close she actually came to getting the boot, but cooler heads prevailed, with K.P. of all people coming to her defense. But that's K.P. for you. Was I wrong because I secretly had hoped that Angie would get kicked out?

Well, seeing the need for a cooling off period, I announced that refreshments were in the den and for everyone to help themselves. That wasn't the way I had planned it, but it seemed like the smartest thing to do right now.

"There's Smurfberry cheesecake along with Smurfberry punch. Warning! The punch will sneak up on you. Don't let the smurf taste fool ya. You have been smurfed! Or should I say warned!"

Everybody just looked at me. Finally, Casino spoke what everybody was probably thinking.

"Ah, yo, bruh? You okay? Sounds like you didn't take your own advice, there! Smurfberry cheesecake? Smurfberry punch? What's up with that?"

I sighed because I hadn't planned on dropping it on them like this, but I had to explain.

"Well, as everybody knows, our theme this month is sexual connotations. Everybody knew that they'd be watching cartoons tonight, but you probably thought they'd be X-rated ..."

"They're not?" Maxine asked.

"Tonight, we look at the world through sex-colored glasses … and what color is sex tonight?"

I let the question linger as I had everybody's attention. I know they were wondering what the hell I was talking about. I then answered my own question.

"Tonight, sex is blue … Smurf blue. We're gonna look at cartoons, but I decided that we would look at a tape I compiled of different episodes of the Smurfs from a sexual vantage point. I got some questions too that I want y'all to marinate on while you're watching the cartoons. Things that'll make ya go, 'Hmmmm.' Have you ever wondered where 'Mama' Smurf is? Or whether Papa Smurf gets his? And where did those little kid Smurfs come from anyway? And who's tagging Smurfette up?"

I'm bugging, right!?! Hey! Don't shake your head. We're all perverts to some degree. Some of us share it with the rest of the world, others hide it better, and do it secretly within their own mind. Well, I explore. That's how it is within our group anyway. I don't expect y'all to admit to anything. Anyway …

I almost busted out laughing because everyone (especially those who knew me), was looking at me like, yep … this kid needs to be committed!

Finally, after it all began to sink in, a voice booms out.

"Oh you on some next shit, Que," Trevor busts out laughing. "Yo, I'm feelin' this!"

Now Trevor had not spoken another word to no one besides Gillian and myself all night. I secretly thanked him in my mind, because his outburst set the tone for the evening as he caught everybody off guard … including me! Once my peoples showed love by agreeing with Trevor, the guests followed suit, and suddenly everyone was in a Smurfy mood. :-)

"I only have one ground rule. In order to feel the Smurfs, we have to be the Smurfs. So when you speak tonight, I want you to talk like a Smurf would, of course adding your own flavor to suit your personality. Oh, and one other thing. I want you to give thought to this also. If you were a Smurf, which one would you be? All righty then. Is that Smurfy with everybody?"

"Smurfs for me," Temple quips, giggling.

"Yeah, I'm kinda smurfin' this too, and I already know who I'd be," Casino allows.

Hester, one of the guests, was the first guest to speak openly, and who by the way, I was actually leery of. C'mon … with a name like Hester, well, I'm thinking stuffy. I know, who am I to judge, right? But I was wrong. :-)

"Temple told me that I had to be open-minded, but I was totally unprepared for this. You smurfed the script! I'm glad I came because I think I'm going to have a smurfin' good time!"

She must have been tickled with herself because she busted out laughing and started singing the Smurf song.

"*La la, la la la laa, la la la la laaa ...*"

"Now *we* can hang out!" I said as I joined her in chorus, and everyone else joined in.

After that little rendition, I sent everyone to the refreshments. Blueberry, ah, excuse me, Smurfberry cheesecake. Well, you get the idea. All the refreshments were either colored blue or had something themed blue about them, including the Smurfberry punch, which everyone was raving about.

Once everyone had their initial fill, we began to settle back down and watch the cartoons. In between the laughs and wisecracks, there were plenty of interesting observations, no doubt focusing on the sexual connotations that the Smurfs presented to the naked eye :-/ (or should I say the perverted eye). :-) Everyone agreed that Grouchy Smurf was that way because he was backed up (we're not talking constipation either, we're talking "lack of"). We had comments on all the Smurfs we saw: Papa Smurf, Handy (we concluded that "fixing things" wasn't the only thing he was good at), Brainy, Smurfette, Hefty, Baby Smurf, the two little kid Smurfs (and we still don't know the girl and boy's names), Greedy, Jokey, Clumsy, Lazy, Vanity, and Grandpa Smurf. Soon after, we got around to which Smurf everyone would be. We went around the room and Valerie started things off.

"I guess I'd be Smurfette," she said.

Torry was sitting next to Valerie and he smiled.

"Well, if she's gonna be Smurfette, I guess I gotta be Baby Smurf…"

"Baby Smurf? What for?" Valerie gushed.

"Simple," Torry began. "Number one, she's the only adult female Smurf I saw, and two, from what I've smurfed of Valerie, I would never go hungry again!"

"Oh, no, you didn't!" Valerie laughed.

"He did!" we all responded in unison.

The room howled with laughter! Valerie elbowed Torry, and Callie came to her friend's defense and popped him with a little round sofa cushion.

"Hey," Kelly said, coming to Torry's defense. "Makes sense to me. Y'all saw the cartoon too. The Smurfs had a famine. Nobody had any food, they was starving to death! My man's just being practical. Hell, I might want to be that little kid Smurf. Society may smurf me a break in a time of need and say it was acceptable for me to be breastfed. Ah, Smurf fed too! But naw, for real, if I was a Smurf, I'd probably be Jokey Smurf because I like the practical jokes."

"I couldn't be none of those Smurfs," Trevor concluded. "Smurf that! I'd step on the scene as Ghetto Smurf! That's how we smurfin'!"

The room howled with more laughter in between refills of Smurfberry juice and cheesecake.

"Since my man has obviously smurfed his mind, I have no choice but to bend the gender gap and become Brainy Smurf," Gillian laughed.

"Just as well," Max smirked. "Makes it easier to toss your little smurf ass!"

"Smurf you!" Gillian giggled.

"I would be Sweet Brown Sugar Smurf," Max said, "because when you mix me in, it always smurfs better!"

"Well, just call me Sweet Tooth Smurf," Dell allowed. "Cause I'll be your taster!"

"Ohhh … it's getting hot in here!" Temple said. "Look at Max blushing! You go, Dell! Okay Dexter St. Smurf, who would you be?"

Kenny smirked at the play on his nickname, while everyone in the room answered Temple's question in unison, "Vanity Smurf!"

"Hey, who am I to argue with the consensus!" Kenny shrugged. "But you'll know where to smurf up for that ride, a.k.a. Bronco Buck Wild Smurf!"

Out of the corner of my eye, I saw Winnie looking in my direction with a "duh" look on her face. I just shook my head and laughed. Temple proclaimed that she would be Big Momma Smurf (with her tiny ass self), whereas Kelly wanted to change and become Big Poppa Smurf. Her response brought more laughter.

"He really is Jokey Smurf, isn't he?"

All eyes were suddenly on me, as I hadn't noticed it was my turn. Duh! I was sitting next to Temple.

"I would be Hefty Smurf because my Uzi smurfs a ton!'"

"Oh Lord! My prayers have been smurfed!" K.P. feigned, putting the back of her hand to her forehead and suddenly fainting.

After the laughter, all the girls started fanning K.P. on the floor and then themselves, and the laughter started up again.

Once order was restored and everybody refueled again, Jinx said that she would be Customs Smurf, inspecting all the import/export that Smurf village had to offer, putting emphasis on assault weapons. :-/ Beverly and Callie asked Jinx if they could go into business together, forming Smurf S.E.X. Customs, Inc. (Strictly Erotic Examinations & Customs, Incorporated). Jinx advised her new partners that she would need no help with assault weapons.

"My first order of business is making sure Public Enemy Number One over there has the proper permits, and know how, to smurf that Uzi!"

She looked at me and winked, which of course led to more laughter.

"Am I gonna need an Attorney, Jinx?"

"Depends, Mr. Attorney ... Stop and frisk, search and seizure ... I won't violate you ... too much!" Jinx teased.

Winnie and I thought the same thing, as we looked toward Angie, who had a frown on her face. We shared a silent laugh.

"My sister will be leaving the import/export business immediately after this session, because she clearly wants to be a fugitive!" K.P. announced to more laughter.

Casino was next, and we really had no idea who he would be, especially since he knew right from the start. He began, "If I was a Smurf, no doubt, I'd be Greedy Smurf!"

This didn't seem to make much sense to Angie, as she stated what most of us had observed of Casino to that point.

"Excuse me, Casino? But you haven't eaten or had anything to drink tonight, as far as I know. Maybe I'm wrong?"

She looked around the room for approval, and it was true, I had noticed it too. There was still plenty to eat, so if he wanted something he could get it. But he knew that already. Heads nodded in agreement with Angie.

"You're right," Casino said.

"Then how the smurf are you gonna be Greedy Smurf?" Angie declared.

Casino looked at her, took a deep breath, and a big smile suddenly turned very mischievous.

"CAUSE I'LL EAT CHA OOOUUUTTT!!!!" Casino bellowed, sticking his tongue out, as we Que

Dogs are known to do, and finally flicking it for emphasis!

The room broke down! Everybody was on the floor! Casino went into step mode and started kicking a step. I jumped on the floor barking, hooks up, and joined him mid-step.

Even Angie had to laugh and she rose to the occasion.

"Well, I guess I'll just have to be 'All you can eat Smurf,' where we make sure even the greediest of Smurfs is smurfed!"

The fellas liked that answer as our barks mixed in with the rest of the fellas doing that Arsenio Hall "woof" thing. Winnie decided that she was gonna be Funky Diva Smurf, but her nickname would be Pepsi Smurf because even Ray Charles could see that she had the right one, baby! Couldn't argue with that, now could I? K.P. announced that she had to be Hip Hop Smurf, so we could get the 411, and keep up to date on the latest music and fashion. Finally, Hester completed the circle by declaring that she was gonna be Law and Order Smurf.

"Because somebody's gotta keep you outta control Smurfs in check!"

To top off the evening, we played Musical Chairs in my basement. Music provided by Yours

Truly. We locked arm-in-arm and skipped around those chairs to the Smurf theme song. The evening ended with laughter and fun. Beverly and Hester were the finalists, with Hester taking home the crown.

With refreshments still left, I told everyone to please take something home with them because I wasn't going to be able to eat it all anyway (nor did I really want it). I thanked everyone for coming and they in turn told me how much fun they had, especially the guests. They all hoped that they'd be invited back at a later date to another function. Upon leaving, the most common thought shared was that the Smurfs would never be looked at the same way again!

"We have got to be invited to another set!" Valerie gushed. "Who knew them Smurfs were some little freaks! I had a great time, please invite us again."

"I'm sure you two will be invited again," I offered.

Callie smiled at me and gave me a hug, whispering, "I'd love an invite back to Smurf Village."

Down boy! Down boy! Back to the accolades.

"You did your thing, Que!" Kenny acknowledged. "That Smurfberry punch was bangin'. I need that … I need that in my life, yo! Get me those ingredients."

"This was really 'Off the Hook,'" Beverly said. "You're the reason why I'm gonna be talking like Smurfs for about a week, you should know that."

As he and Beverly left me to continue talking, Kenny turned to give me the "Somebody getting done tonight look" and muttered, "She gon' be moanin' like a Smurf tonight!"

I laughed and left him to continue his maneuver.

"Oh my God, Que!" Gillian began. "Every time I see anything to do with Smurfs, I'm gonna think of this set!"

Trevor nodded. "This was one of my favorites so far, yo!"

That made me feel good to hear that. Mission accomplished. :-)

Angie tried to linger around, hinting not too discreetly that she wanted to spend the night. Guess who came to the rescue, and guess who had a smirk on their face? K.P. offered to stay and help clean up.

"Que, you want me to help you clean up?" K.P. called from across the room as she started picking up cups and plates.

Angie, not to be outdone, calls to K.P., "That's okay, K.P., I can help him. You don't have to stay."

K.P. just looked at her. You know the sound of a record screeching from the needle running over it? That's how it sounded in the room. And then the chatter stopped, and there was nothing but quiet as everyone froze. (lol) I'm exaggerating, but you get the drift. Upon seeing the look from K.P., Angie, with a moment of reflection, decided different.

"You know what? I think you and Que got this."

After hearing that, Winnie gave me the smirk. Remember, everything is not always as it appears to be! It seemed that no one was leaving with who they showed up with either. Dell left with Maxine, Temple, and Hester. Callie, who discreetly slipped me her number, and whom I would have let spend the night had K.P. not volunteered with the cleanup, left with Valerie, Torry and Kelly.

Kenny and Beverly got acquainted during the night and he offered her a ride home. Jinx took K.P.'s car because she had plans. I kidded her and told her she was kicking me to the curb, and she replied that I was always Plan A, but she had Plans B, C, and D on the back burner if she so chose.

Angie, maybe in part to get back at me, or maybe because she wanted to, accepted a ride home from

Casino. What an ego he has, huh? (lol) Winnie was going home alone, but you expected that, right? She basically chilled the whole night. Before she left, she casually asked K.P. what she was doing tomorrow. K.P. didn't have plans. She then asked me what I was doing, and I told them about dinner over at my brother's (and of course, the rules). Don't you know that K.P. asked if I wanted her to go with me, since the rules simply specified "female companion!" I was just outdone! Winnie threw in her two cents and said it was an excellent idea, smirking all the time.

Sometimes, I can't stand Winnie! :-)

4

———

GENTLEMAN BY NATURE
... HOOKER BY CHOICE

I be the Sexual Intellectual

I am phat, I am all of that, I can rock
a hype track. Knick Knack Patty
Whack, give this dog a kit kat.
Pass her off to frat, oh yeah,
don't forget the jimmy hat.
While you're there, wash her hair,
parlay round the underwear.
Double time the rhyme if I feel like
it, but then again I can handle the
Flo Jo, so act like ya know, ho'.
Girls come up to me and tell
me I got a pretty smile.
But they don't play me like Janet no more,
they don't say, "Let's wait a while."

My verbal skills are second to
none, but then so is my tongue
I'll play with kitty like a ball of
yarn and have ya, strung-out
With-out-a-doubt, the weather gets
warmer when I go-down-south.
I gets around and I've been seen Uptown.
But if S-S-Double-Double
U-V (SWV) calls,
I pause for the cause, then I
heads Downtoowwn.
I'm a Gentleman by Nature
and a Hooker by Choice.
My language has been known to
make a young lady moist.
But let it be known I can change up
like a Chameleon, Be intellectual,
then poof, Sexual Healing.
But lately girls don't want to
hear nothing about intellect.
A Gentleman's aim is to please,
so who am I to object?
I don't fess when it comes to the dress
And I'm never on sabbatical
when it comes to the vaginal.
My appetite just might be
hazardous to your health.
Remember FDS is best, so check yo' self.
So come on Hunny Bunny, give
the word, we can do this.
I'll fill your stockings, and
it's not even Christmas!

Gentleman by Nature ... Hooker by Choice. Another phrase coined by Yours Truly. Whatever does it mean? My frat brothers and I use this terminology as well, in reference to our fraternity, but the "Hooker by Choice" part is different. Don't even think about sayin' that there's nothing "gentlemanly" about the "bruhs." The consequences could result in grievous, bodily harm! :-/

What is a Hooker? Oh, I mean, sure ... everybody knows the so called universal meaning: streetwalker, lady of the night, or the quintessential term "ho" (I know I ain't right). :-/ But in the realm of Gregory Que and Company, a whole new meaning is attached. Within the "Off the Hook" bunch, we have our own little slang which we use quite fluently, I might add. Remember when Winnie and I were talking and she was in a sense describing how I am perceived to others? Well, she kinda hit it right on the head (her analysis about me after my "out" tries regarding K.P., middle of Chapter Two, if you're not fierce on the recall ... or simply continue to read into this chapter). :-/ There within lies your definition of a Hooker. A positive brother who has it going on in a whole host of areas (a chameleon), and he knows what he wants and how to get it. He draws you in

… he hooks you … he hooks you in, thus the term Hooker.

A Hooker makes you want to be around him, coincidentally, subtly, or even purposely (in my case, subtly, of course). Women, do not fret. There *is* equal opportunity up in this piece, and you definitely haven't been left out. You're called Hookees. Hooker? Hookee? "Off the Hook"? Get it? It's definitely deeper than Jerry Springer's "Final Thought!" :-/ If you still need help, remember when K.P. and I greeted each other over the phone with a "What up, Ho"? And we ended our call with "Later, Ho"? Right! Now you get it? Ho' is short for Hooker and Hookee. I knew you could do it! Sort of a reclamation of a negative term and flipping it into a term of endearment (just one of the many reasons I be the Sexual Intellectual). :-/ I did lift the pleasure, pleasing aspect of the word for my own purposes.

How do you *please* a woman? The easy answer is "you can't!" Ha ha ha ha ha ha ha ha! I thought it was funny, you didn't think it was funny? :-) Wait a minute. Do I have to explain the context of what I mean by "please" here? The easy answer referred to "in general". But I'm being specific, now. Oh, okay. I'm not trying to insult everybody's intelligence, but I do believe in equal opportunity, here. For those whose motor skills may be a little slow today, or you just got up and it takes a while for you to function (by the way … thanks for starting your day off with my book … I am flattered), or you're one of those people who needs something explained three different ways … TOUGH! Midterms are in a few weeks, and I'm gonna skip a few chapters. However, you will be responsible for the material that I haven't covered in class … ah, I mean this book. Damn, sorry. Had a flashback to a time back in school.

Didn't you hate your professors or teachers for that matter, when they did that? See, I have compassion. I realize that some of my readers may not have been fortunate enough to go to college, for whatever reason. Of course, why did they always tell us two weeks before the exam that we'd be responsible for the whole damn book when we spent practically the whole damn semester on two friggin' chapters! And we barely read *those* two chapters. Never mind that if we had taken the time to look at the syllabus anytime during the semester, we would have had this information at our finger tips. Who reads the fuckin' syllabus anyway? Joe and Jane "I gotta get an A," that's who!

Listen, there's something I wanna share with you, but I didn't want everybody to know. That's why I've been weeding readers out. Those that are still reading the book at this point have some substance about them, and you guys are the ones that I want to know about this. And I'm gonna tell ya. Here it is: I haven't always been the person that you've come to adore thus far. What? :-/ Were you expecting something else? Involving closet doors or something? Sorry honey boys, I DON'T THINK SO! Strictly for the ladies. You'll just have to dream about me, or beg some lucky young lady to put you on to the lowdown. My life is an open book (no pun intended). You know the motto, "If you got the nerve to ask it, I got the nerve to answer it." (Sorry, Wendy Williams, no "Down Low" segments here! :-)

I already told you that I was popular in high school. Well, it carried over into college. You gotta know how to assimilate, son! Now I went to predominantly white schools to get my education. Hey, sue me! If I had to do it all over again, knowing what I know now, I'd have done it differently. But I will say this, I was, and I say *was,* guilty of a prevalent view within some of the black community. Call it naivety, but I call it straight up intrinsic brainwashing. I wish I hadn't been so close minded back then. Perhaps ignorant would be the better word. I had this notion that I could get a better education at a white school as opposed to a black school.

My rationale was that in order for me to function in this world as we know it (in terms of black and white), I'd have a better shot at competing with an education from a white school. Think "…to beat the man, you have to first learn the ways of the man." (Are you following me?) The back side of my twisted rationale was that I dismissed black schools as nothing but "party" schools. But throw that rationale out the window because all I did my first two years at my "white" school was party. I know good and damn well I am not the only person that had this view, but once again, I don't expect any support.

My point? And you know there is one! Young black kids need reinforcement that black schools offer quality educations. Too often we hear about the Ivy League schools, the Harvards, Yales, etc., in the mainstream as the standards of excellence. Life is about choices, and you need the information to be able to make them. And I understand your thinking when you say, "Well, what did you expect? You went to predominantly white schools, what would they know about black schools?" Nothing. But had I had access to the info as I did the Harvards and Yales, my thought process wouldn't have been so biased and one sided. Maybe the information needs to be better circulated within the populace. Then again, maybe it is circulated and I just didn't know about it, because of where I went to school. And you'd probably say, "You're being naïve. Do you honestly expect predominantly white schools to give out information about black schools?" And I couldn't argue with you. But don't you see that's the point.

You cannot make the assumption that because you go to a white school, you're an Oreo, thus there is no hope for that person and he/she doesn't need to receive the information. So we as black college administrators (or white too … you're not off the hook, although I shouldn't expect as much from you as I would your black counterparts), just assume that the student wouldn't be interested in a black school. Yeah, I went to these schools, but I never lost my identity. My parents made sure of that, and my environment made sure of that. Now that I think about it, Mom tried to school me on black colleges and their worth. She did not force it on me though, allowing me to make my own decisions. I'll take the "L" on that, in retrospection.

That's one thing about this skin color, it always lets you know who you are (ask Mike Tyson, Michael Jackson, Michael Jordan, especially O.J. Simpson, and even Tiger Woods). Don't ever question my ethnicity. The good thing about going to those schools was that I was subjected to inherent racism. Every time I allowed my mind to think that I was actually accepted, an episode would occur to put me back in the proper perspective. And unfortunately, that perspective to *most* whites, no matter how cool you seem to be with them, is that behind closed doors you're still just another black person (substitute slur of choice).

You're probably saying to yourself, "You had to go to a white school to figure that shit out?" All I can say is that hindsight is 20-20. Some families have tradition on their side when it comes to colleges. The mother or father went to a black college so the children are exposed. But what about the parents who didn't go to college? How are their children to be exposed to the potential riches of a black education? By the way, my mother went to FAMU, so I just fucked up. Point blank, period, the end.

Now that I done pissed some more readers off, I can move on. Side note: in college and graduate school, I was considered a rebel rouser ... too black, too strong (Apologies to Malcolm X and Public Enemy). Hey, I just figured that I'd try and make it easier on future blacks that go to these institutions, so they wouldn't have to deal with the bullshit that I had to deal with! I was opinionated about the conditions that concerned black students, yet was still popular to the campus as a whole. Those administrations were glad to see my ass go … "And good riddance to you too, dammit!" Call it good people skills. I could curse you out with a smile on my face, or you could catch the wrath of a mad man. Say, you don't mind my tangents and side stories, right? If you do, tough … my book, remember? :-)

What I wanted to tell you was that … oh, you thought that white school/black school thing was what I wanted to tell you? Naw, that wasn't it, although I hope it is useful for someone out there. Now everybody gather 'round in a circle here so I can tell you. C'mon, tighten up that circle so I can share this with you. I told you this wasn't for everybody to know. You ought to feel special that you're even included in this little discussion. This story is something that you can share with your kids, something like, "Gregory Que was in that predicament and he overcame obstacles to be successful, and so can you."

Remember how I told you earlier that nothing has ever come easy for me? I used to think I was pretty intelligent (at least I was told that, and I got top grades in J.H.S. and H.S.), then I got to college. For most, it is their first true experience away from home, and even though I did that prep course thing, being away from home for four years was still foreign to me. I got my first "D" in college and I got my first "F" in college. Coming from parents that had high academic expectations for their children, this was just unacceptable. I was embarrassed and felt like a failure, but I had to accept ninety-five percent of the blame (all right, all of the blame). I did nothing but party for my first couple of years in college.

I did enough studying just to get by. My grades came home after freshman year, and my GPA (Grade Point Average) was 2.7, a B- average. My parents attributed my decline in grades to me adjusting to college and life away from home. Sounded good to me, so we rolled with that! During my sophomore year I continued my East Coast tour, partying here and there, until I began pledging my fraternity and of course the tour came to a screeching halt. I also made the mistake of taking some demanding courses during my pledge period.

The only thing that I'll say about my pledge period is that I was above for fourteen weeks. If you don't get it, ask somebody who you know pledged a black fraternity or sorority back in the days before lawsuits and weak ass pledges dictated how pledge processes would become (that's a whole chapter all to itself, for those who know like I know). Anyway, after my sophomore year and becoming a brother of my beloved fraternity, I found my ass on academic probation. Yep. Mr. Intellectual himself, on academic probation. This was definitely new to a brother! I need to make one thing perfectly clear. Pledging my fraternity was *not* the cause of my academic probation. People use that as a crutch and it gives pledge programs a bad name. Those that are "Greek" know what I'm talking about.

The reason I was on academic probation was that I did not adjust my study habits. I assumed that because I busted out high school, college would be a piece of cake. I also assumed (like Fred Sanford's son Lamont… "You big dummy"), that everyone else who was partying with me wasn't studying either. I learned the hard way that my priorities were ass backwards. Unlike today, I didn't have anybody who would share their experiences with me and prevent me from making the same mistakes that they made. But now that I'm sharing this choice info with a few good men and women out there, you can pass it on. Those kids gave off the impression that they didn't study, but behind closed doors, they were as cut throat as anybody! Stealing library books, ripping pages out of text books, not sharing all of their materials in study groups, but taking everything offered to the group by the other students. You get it. I also became rudely awakened to the fact that I wasn't as smart (double entendre alert), as I thought I was. I had to re-read sentences to understand them. I couldn't cram the night before and get a good grade. I finally learned that the system was gaming me, I wasn't gaming the system!

The point I'm trying to make is that I actually had to learn how to study in college! Of course in graduate school, I had to learn how to study all over again. Thus, you have just been given one of the keys to success, assessing situations and adapting to them. In college, professors are obsessed with details and the key is dedication, memorization and regurgitation. In graduate school, the key is discipline and the professors are obsessed with analyzation. I won't bore you with any more details, but I turned my last two years around, hitting the Dean's list each semester. I have learned that I *must* work hard and that I can't be unfocused or lazy, because I know the results. I made myself the intellect that I am today, and if my ass can do it, emphasize to your kids that they can definitely do it too.

Okay, class is over. Let me go back to the subject I started this chapter with. You do remember, don't ya? Don't turn the page back. The tangents were on purpose to test your memory skills. When you finish this book, I hope you'll be able to say to yourself, that Que kid is all right! He stimulated my mind, had me thinking, analyzing n' shit, kept my interest too. Definitely hit me off with some food for thought (I know, I know, too much Baduism). :-)

The one thing that brothers don't like is another brother telling them how to please a woman! We all know how to handle our business, don't we, fellas? Well, quiet is kept, that's not what your girlfriend is telling me. I've taken a survey, and based on the women I've talked to, the smiles of satisfaction directed my way, the number of women that keep coming back for more no matter how long the last time has been, and the overall demand of my body (yes, I am feeling myself once again), :-) I have come up with a list of do's and don'ts catered to the art of pleasing a woman (and yes, it is an art). My mens, I understand that you'll be reluctant to take this advice, but the one or two of you that put that ego aside will reap the benefits. By now, you've tried that breakfast thing on the DL, right? So I'm just trying to help the brother that wants to improve his skill set, the rest of y'all … play on, Playa. But remember this, don't get mad at me when your girl, your wife, or significant other leaves this book open to this section on your side of the bed (hint and a half for that ass), or better yet, steps to me after you've ignored her hints. She will have no choice but to compare us, and when the smoke clears … Well, you know what I'm sayin'. :-/

A woman wants confidence in a man, not necessarily arrogance. There is a difference, you know. Find out what it is and walk on the side that's appropriate for the situation that you're in. Do you want to know how a woman knows when a man is confident? It's so simple, you're gonna smack your boy! BECAUSE HE TAKES HIS TIME. It has to be understood that women achieve satisfaction that they rave about when they are put in the mood. Remember, fellas, you want to be set apart from the rest, so you have to do things that are not of the ordinary. And even if they are ordinary, they can be done in a way that still sets them apart if you just take your time. Every gesture is deliberate, every caress lingers, as you talk to her softly, mentally massaging her mind, preparing her for stimulation. Once she is mentally stimulated, the rest becomes easier. The mind is the key, and if you don't believe me, ask the women who just read that last descriptive sentence (a few lines up), if they let their minds wander for just an instance to picture that. Ladies? Do I get back up on that point? … And I hope I had a cameo in your flash video, too. :-) For those that don't know, now ya know. It's called foreplay! Mentally and physically.

Arrogance, on the other hand, is a young lady stepping out of the shower and opening the bathroom door and seeing you standing there smiling with your hands on your hips, nothing on but your white tube socks (in my case purple), and your "Jonson" saluting her at attention. Some women don't go for the socks, but I say if it works for you, roll with it. Just don't overkill. There was a time when I was known for the purple socks. But beware! Women will mention this as an aside when talking to their girlfriends if you've taken care of business. But if you haven't, the socks will be the focal point of your weak ass delivery. The point? Do not draw unnecessary attention to yourself if you can't back it up.

Remember when I was with Winnie earlier and I said that my pleasure is derived from knowing that the woman is pleasured, and I won't stop until she says when? That's the attitude I think men have to have in bed. This does two things and it bears repeating again. It lets her know that you are attentive to her needs, and she'll want to do the same for you and then some. If you have a vivid imagination, you can be a vivid lover.

Those that have had the pleasure of knowing me know that I have pet names for the various parts of the female anatomy. The two I'll share with you, although I'm somewhat reluctant because somebody is gonna bite. But let me set the record straight right now. These are my creations, and if you hear them anywhere else, somebody has seen this book or heard somebody who's seen this book, or knows somebody who has been called this by me. So don't let nobody con you into believing that they coined these terms, 'cause they playin' themselves. This is a world premiere. The general public has access to this information for the very first time. I repeat. *This is a world premiere!* Maybe I'm being a bit too emote, but ask me if I care? :-) Anyway, the affectionate edible terms are "Double Stuff" and "Juicy Fruit." Right, this is the time when you're supposed to take your imagination and decipher what each refers to. Okay, is everybody straight with that? Any stragglers? So I can continue? Cool.

If you want to be imaginative, think of something you would want done to you. You still need help? If you're not too prudish, and either of you don't mind getting messy, think of your favorite flavor and turn each other into sundaes. Or if you're a tantalizer like myself (*I bring agony when tongue meets anatomy ...*), draw pictures with your tongue, send tingles up her spine by actually licking up her spine, or put a piece of ice in your mouth and play connect the dots. You are as confined as your imagination, so allow your mind to create. Does that sound freaky or what? Don't worry, your secrets are safe with me. And unless requested, that sadism/masochism stuff (dripping hot candle wax on the body), is strictly a no no. :-) Fellas, if you just got to know whether she *could* be interested in something kinky in the future, smack that ass (gently) when you're in the appropriate position, of course, and see what her reaction will be! :-/ The prissiest sister may be the freakiest behind closed doors. Ladies, look me in the eye and tell me I'm wrong! Even if you're not freaky, variety and the opportunity to do something you've never experienced before could be the aphrodisiac that you're looking for!

One of the things I like to do is to sensuously suck on the bottom lip of a woman while I am kissing her. Don't ask me why, I couldn't tell you. It brings me joy! Kissing is something that a lot of people take for granted, in my opinion. I'm not talking about slobbin' somebody down either. But fellas, women like to kiss, and they like to be kissed with passion. Kiss her on her head, her nose, her shoulders, the parts of the body that most men seem to ignore. And if she's the type of girl that takes care of herself (regular manicures and pedicures), and you really want to make an impression, kiss the hands and the feet. I was gonna say suck on those fingers and toes, but that might be a bit too much for you to handle right about now. What do you think, ladies?

For those men that can reach a woman's G spot, ;-) do some homework and really take that woman to cloud nine! Did you know that a woman has more than one G spot? ... Did you know that a woman *has* a G spot? Fellas, for whatever reason, women seem comfortable talking to me about your short comings :-/ (multiple innuendos, huh?). Imagine what they're telling their girlfriends! But don't worry, Victor, I'm not gonna tell nobody about your, ah, deficiencies, and you don't have to worry either, Mark (I know ... I'm not right). But I'm here to help, so I have compiled a list of the more common complaints that I have been privy to from women about the male species. Men take comfort in the fact that I too had to learn at some point in my life. But one of the many differences between me and you is that I learned!

Here they are, THE TEN DEMANDMENTS (ya like that, don't ya ladies!?!):

1. *Knoweth thy woman* - encompasses everything from knowing what turns her on to whether she spits or swallows, or if she does either one at all! :-)

2. *Knoweth thy bra* - know how to take a women's bra off, whether it be Grandma's type with the hooks or snaps in the back to Vicki Secrets snaps in the front.

3. *Cumeth not too soon* - need I say more? ... You're on your own here. You don't expect me to give away all of my secrets, do you? Besides, if you're keen, you'd be cognizant of the fact that I already told you! :-/

4. *Do not taketh all day to cum* - you may think this makes you the man, but steady humpin' gets to be monotonous without variation, so know when to say when, reload ... round two ... then cum another one, and another one and another one! (Apologies to Lil' Kim) ... (that's if you gots stamina!) :-/ P.S. It's better to have too much stamina than not enough at all. Nothing worse than a woman ready to go some more rounds and you can't hang.

Bottom line ... manage your stamina or those that need to ... develop some!

5. *Ask not if thou hast cum* - you shouldn't even have to go there, you should know if you've handled your business. :-/ But if you can't tell, just put an "H" on your chest and handle it ... Swallow your pride.

6. *Shaveth thy stubble* - the "scruff" stings.

7. *Be not afraid of the vaginal*—the '90's woman's rally cry.

8. *Knoweth thy breast* - be gentle with the nipples ... be gentle with the breast. Do not do the shopping thing where you squeeze the breast for ripeness like honeydew melon, grapefruits, oranges, or strawberries. Did I cover the whole spectrum? :-) If she wants them rubbed or sucked hard, she'll let you know. Trust me! :-)

9. *Experiment not thy porno fantasies* - don't watch "Rasheeda does 125th St." or "Dirty Knees Alice's U.S. tour—From Figueroa Ave. to Fulton Street" and then expect her to be that woman. It's offensive to be likened to a porno episode and worse to

find your woman after viewing one to "get your rocks off." Women feel cheapened.

10. *Leaveth not in thy temptation* - if you know that you went in with something on and didn't come out with it, show a little bit of respect, dude ... RETRIEVE THE CONDOM!!!

Honorable mention:

- Don't blow in her ear like you're blowing out your thirtieth birthday candles.
- Nipples are not radio dials, so stop the twiddling and twisting.
- On your marks ... get set ... go! The Indy 500 she is not ... Know how and when to accelerate.
- Sneaking in the back door ... Anal sex is not for everyone.
- This one's two for one ... (a) If you want oral sex, try asking cleverly and seductively if she doesn't go there on her own first, instead of nudging her head toward the "Jonson." (b) If she blesses you by giving you oral sex, show your consideration by at least warning her before you cum. I've been told that the taste of sperm is not for

all. Here's a secret that I'll share with you … know the saying, "You are what you eat?" I'll just say this, when I eat a lot of spicy foods, I've been told that my sperm has a spicy taste to it, and when I eat a lot of pineapples and peaches, I've been told that there is a sweet taste. And check this out, I've even made hair grow because I take a lot of vitamins. Surely, you know that sperm is pure protein, and well, when mixed with the vitamins I take … hey. If you need your hair to grow, or clear skin, come see me and I'm sure that we can work something out! :-/

P.S. Ladies, if you see that you're gaining weight, yet you're not eating like a pig, consider this: Cut back on your sperm intake. Of course those that are looking to gain a few pounds … :-/

You're probably saying to yourself right about now, "No, no he didn't go there!" … I did. And whether you know it or not, most of you will be better off because I went there. So send those "thank you's" to my publisher. I will accept all gratuities. Just kidding! … (????)

"Angie is not for you."

"What?"

Guess who's going to dinner with me? We're on the Belt Parkway heading toward the Southern State Parkway and traffic is moving steady at about one o'clock in the afternoon, Eastern Standard time. Don't you hate when people do that? Give you information that you have no damn use for. Of course it's Eastern Standard time ... duh! I'm on the East Coast. You know that and I know that, so why do I have to say it, right? :-) Because some anal personality type out there (not *you*, of course), will actually get their jollies off by reading that sentence. That might be the first reader that I actually held onto. :-/

Dinner is usually between 3 p.m. and 5 p.m. When I go to dinner out there, I usually show up between 12 p.m. and 3 p.m. to unwind, if the twins will let me. If they're not snatching me up to show me the latest dances, they're trying to whip that ass at Sony PlayStation. And Suzie Que doesn't just make dinner. I've been designated as her official food taster. She's constantly trying to come up with new ideas for hors d'oeuvres. She trusts me to give my honest opinion and I do. For the most part, they're slamming. I'd be lying if I said that I liked everything, but more times than not, I ask for dinner time to be extended because I done ate a full course meal of appetizers! Sorry, can't share any details about recipes or ingredients. You wouldn't want me to be sleeping with one eye open looking out for Suzie Que, would you? … Why did I even ask you? You guys are too violent for me.

"I said Angie is not for you, Que."

"What are you talking about, K.P.?"

"I can't see you with her."

"Where's this coming from?"

Of course I knew where it was coming from. We were talking about the residue from the fallout at my house from "Off the Hook." Got that?

"I just don't think that she's your type."

There goes that "type" shit again! What's that all about? Is my type that obvious? "Mi tinks mi" may be becoming just a bit too predictable! Mental note: Flip the script!

"And before you even attempt to open your mouth and tell me I don't know your type, remember we grew up together, so I'm a little closer to you than the next ho'. Comprende?"

"Does your mother know that you talk like this?"

"No. Just my best friend … and ah, my sister and most recently Marlon, who's seeing a different side of me lately."

"Yeah, what's going on with that? Why wasn't the Krappa with you?"

"I'll tell you about it. But I just wanna be around somebody that knows and appreciates me."

"Now you know, I don't like the sound of that. A Krappa ass whipping is always in my back pocket … you *know* this, Miss!?!"

"Calm down, 'Rambro.'" K.P. smiles. "I know, I know."

"I'm just sayin', though. Put a cap in that ass!"

"*You could take the homie out the street … But you can't take the street out the homie!*"

"Ah Homie, K.P.? That's not it! It goes a little something like this:

You can take the boy out the hood, but you can't take the hood out the home boy!" (Apologies to the Comrads).

"Thank you so much for the clarification, Homie Gee!"

"Not a problem, Booty Brown. Wouldn't want you going out West and Ice Cube and company roll up on you, and ask you what your set is? … And you reply that you got a Magnavox 35-inch!"

"Very funny! And ya know, you're always talking about my butt. I know you want this! And maybe one day if you're nice to me, I'll let you touch it."

"Oh, but please, Janet? I mean, ah … What's your name again? … K.P.? … Could I? … Just, just maybe once?"

"You're dripping, Que! :-/ But you know I was serious about you and Angie."

"There's nothing to us."

"Uh huh, ok … if you say so. Now Winnie, on the other hand, is more your speed."

"Say what?"

"I could see you with Winnie."

"We're good friends."

"You're talking to me, sweetie. I know about your 'good friends.'"

"Naw. Angie and Winnie are good friends."

"She's the one that told you about 'the look,' right?"

Oh damn! I'm getting that squirmy feeling again!

"Huh?"

"You heard me clearly, Que."

Why is it that when guys get caught up in an awkward situation, the most eloquent answer they can muster is usually, "Huh?" I think I picked it up from hanging around Kenny who's always getting in trouble with some woman. Because you women always help us out by clarifying yourselves. Don't ever change because we guys really appreciate that! :-) I guess I will now have to obtain body armor because fellas are gonna be looking for a brother for blowing up the spot … but I can always hide out at your house, right, ladies?

"Angie. She's the one that told you about 'the look.' She probably figured that you would ask somebody. Maybe Winnie because you guys are 'good' friends or me because I'm your best friend. She probably called herself sending out her little message to Winnie because she didn't want her to get any ideas and to me when she found out from Winnie that I was your best friend. She called herself, staking out her territory. That's why she hugged you first at the door, followed you into your dining room, and rolled her eyes at me."

"Damn, so tell me, who was watching you?"

"Forget you. It's not like it wasn't noticeable."

Well, I'll be damned! Is that how it's going down? Is that how it's being perceived? Lucky ass, manipulating Winnie. Wow, I guess you could look at it like that, 'cause K.P. ain't no dummy! Unless she's trying to play me for the real 411?

"So tell me, Que. You always mention Winnie. How did you two meet?"

"Huh?"

"Really, Que?"

I think I'm getting a headache. This is what happens when two worlds collide, no? I knew this day was coming, but I didn't expect it today! Has that ever happened to you? It's really just a convenient way to put things off until tomorrow that you should have dealt with yesterday and are now presently a pain in your ass, today. Now I have a dilemma. What should I do? Should I tell the truth? Or should I not tell the truth? That is the question. Mind you, I don't want to tell you to throw everything that I said earlier out the window, but this is a sticky situation. I need a favor. I know, I know. I've got nerve asking you guys for help, but tell me … what should I do? Oh … What? … Nobody's gonna help me? It's that misery loves company syndrome, isn't it? What was that? … Thank you, sweetheart, thank you very much! What was your name, please? Thank you again for the advice. It is truly appreciated! Well, at least I know, I have one fan! … Huh? Is that so? *You say you're the anal personality type that got her jollies off by reading the Eastern Standard Time sentence?* Ooookay!! You do understand that anal personality type was used in jest, don't ya? (Hee hee) Whew! Can't be alienating my only fan! *Oh, you say you would have helped me ... oh, look ... and now you too?* Everybody's coming out the woodworks now, I see. Well, thanks. As for the rest of y'all, aight then. Not a problem because I was gonna tell the truth anyway. I just wanted to see if you guys would help me. So I stick my tongue out at you! :-}

"Que, you know I believe that we're still close, but I remember a time when we were closer. We talked about any and everything, and we didn't hesitate to call on the other when something was bothering us. We had no secrets. I think I'm to blame for the distance that's come between us. I've neglected our friendship, and I miss my best friend. It started when I began going out with Marlon ..."

"You were starting a brand new relationship, you had your priorities ..."

"That's not what I'm talking about and you know it. You and I had issues that were just brought to the surface and they were never resolved. I should have never sprung Marlon on you like that. I think we need to talk about them."

If you're one of those readers that always talks about an author's style (and I know you may still be trying to get used to mine), :-/ this may be one of those times where you'd expect me (or hope for me), to sidetrack into my past and bless you with details. That's riiiight … you know where this is going, don't ya? Guess what? We don't always get everything we want in life when we want it, so I'm not speaking on this. But I do reserve the right to revisit this, if I so choose, at a later date. Ya like that? An attorney told me to say that. :-) Wha'cha say? I'm gonna lose some more readers? *What? My peoples, if you wit' me … where the fuck you at?* (Apologies to Meth). For all those who didn't hear what my faithful few readers said, I'll ask them to repeat themselves. All right now, all in together now: "*PUT AN 'H' ON YOUR CHEST AND HANDLE IT!*" Thank you to those who joined in, and to those who didn't.

I don't care if you don't like it. No. I don't feel like getting into this right now, maybe later. If you're lucky!

The door opened and suddenly we were greeted with nothing but teeth in the form of a gigantic smile.

"K.P.!" Steven exclaimed. "What a great surprise!"

Hearing Steven's enthusiasm naturally made everyone in the house curious. Suzie Que made her way from the kitchen and looked down the foyer. Her eyebrows went up in surprise as she made her way toward us.

"Ms. K.P.! It really is a great surprise," Suzie Que said as she hugged K.P. after Steven.

The twins came to investigate and stopped in their tracks.

"Wow, she's pretty, Uncle Que," Karen gushed.

"Yuuuup," Aaron chimed in, as they both just stood there and gawked.

Out of the corner of my eye, I marveled at the fact that K.P. was blushing. Now that doesn't happen too often.

"Is she your new girlfriend?" Karen threw out boldly.

K.P. playing along for as long as she could, busted out laughing and grabbed the kids in for a bear hug.

"No, I am not the new girlfriend, you rug rats, and you know this too, 'cause I've known you both since doo doo diapers," K.P. said laughing.

"She ought to be!" Suzie Que mumbled through a perfect smile for Steven's and my ears only.

I turned around quick with a "Don't start with me look."

Suzie Que just continued to smile, lowered her head slightly, and raised her eyebrows with the "You know I'm right look" in response.

You think 'Everybody loves Raymond'? Everybody really loves K.P.! At least in this family, at least for me. It seems to me that they've been rooting for her for years, and if I didn't know any better, I'd swear that Steven and Suzie Que have some kind of side bet going. And knowing both of their know-it-all asses, I'd say the bet isn't if I'll be with K.P., but when I'll be with K.P.! I hope it doesn't appear to you that I'm in denial or something, 'cause I'm not. Didn't I say that if I wanted your opinion, I'd ask for it. Simon did not say! And all of y'all are about to be O-u-t, as in ass out in the cold! (_brr_) And stop looking at me like that! I ain't in denial and I ain't paranoid. She's my best friend! Now all of you think you're psychiatrists or psychologists or something?

Ah … which one is appropriate here? Do *you* know? :-/

Suzie Que excused herself and went back to the kitchen, and we made our way toward the den, after I extracted hugs from the twins. The nerve of them, forgetting me. How dare they! :-) Today, *K.P.* will be dragged to learn the latest dances and play video games, and I ain't mad at her. It's Ben Roethlisberger's first year as quarterback of the Pittsburgh Steelers. The QB job is now officially his. He's the man now! What makes it better is that the game is at the Cowboys' Texas Stadium, and because the Steelers have lost the last four games to them, their fans think a win is in the bag.

Now if you know anything about football, you know that when God created the heaven and earth and the Pittsburgh Steelers, you could not like the Dallas Cowboys and vice versa. It's against the laws of nature, physics, gravity, whatever. It's just not humanly possible! Guess who's a Dallas Cowboy fan? … The whole damn house! I'm in enemy territory!!!! Since we were little, I've liked the Steelers and he's liked the Cowboys. The trash talk for these games gets down right personal. Cowboys fans throw the current losing streak in Steelers fan's faces, and Steelers fans just hold up 5 fingers! So everybody is kinda pumped up for this game. Suzie Que likes the Cowboys because she's from Texas. Is the ribs picture thing starting to become clear? And the twins just like the colors of the uniform! K.P. is a Cowboys fan because her cousin is Emmitt Smith ... duh!

Ladies? Piece of advice. Men view women who like sports, who actually understand sports, and can talk about sports intelligently, as a rare commodity. Fellas, if you're lucky enough to have a gem like that, I applaud you and hope you're appreciating her. And another thing, fellas, if a lady who happens to be a little sports deficient tries to show a little interest in the things that interest you (football, basketball, baseball, etc.), show a little patience. 'Cause her timing in asking a question about the game is not always gonna be appropriate. It's gonna come with the Knicks up by two against the Bulls with 1.5 seconds on the clock and everyone and their grandma knowing that Michael Jordan is gonna get the ball. She's gonna ask why MJ has to take the last shot when three Knicks are mugging him to prevent the shot. Or she'll ask you why a football is elliptical (look it up), :-) when the Jets are finding a way to lose another game in the last two minutes. Mind you, intelligent questions, just not the best time to ask them. And ladies, you may want to show your man that you indeed know a little something, something … but wait until there's a commercial or a break in the action before asking your question or making your comment. You guys always say that we men can only do so many things at one time, so stop tripping us up. What do you think the commercials are for? They give us men the chance to unload our mental capacities so that we can reload them again when the sports action starts up again. See … and you ladies say that we're primitive … neanderthal even! :-/

Uh oh, the tasting festivities have begun. Suzie Que has brought out the first tray which has Swedish meatballs dipped in some fancy red wine sauce. Excuse me for a moment, I'm about to taste these … Oh, hell yeah! Deez be da bomb! I've got about three toothpicks hanging from my mouth, because I'm still savoring the sauce which has soaked into the wood. Now you know that's good! The aroma has attracted the masses as the twins lead K.P. into the room. Suzie Que offers the treats to her, and as the tray passes toward her, I grab some more.

"Damn, you'd think some people don't eat," K.P. snickers. "I know you're a bachelor and all …"

"No. I know that once your greedy paws get to them, ain't gonna be nothing left but toothpicks running for cover!"

The twins laughed along with Steven and Suzie Que, and with that said, K.P. put the first meatball into her mouth. She tried hard not to react, but after the third meatball, she was a victim too!

"Is this what I've been missing all these years? Oh Que, we gonna talk, I'ma …"

She told the kids to cover their ears and turn their backs, and then she mouthed to me that she was gonna bust my ass. Suzie Que said that she would help, and Steven just nodded like he was the Godfather or something. While the kid's backs were still turned, I pointed to my butt and blew them all a kiss. (_x_) I know a conspiracy when I see one! Suzie Que eventually brought out three more trays of different edibles. All I can say is that we ate, and we ate, and we ate. During this time, I picked up on a honeymoon vibe between Suzie Que and Steven. I took notice that their fire still burned as if they hadn't been married a week. I know it sounds like something farfetched that you get out of a romance novel, but these two oozed love. She sat on his lap and hugged him even though there was an empty chair next to Steven. He periodically kissed her forehead, cheeks and lips for no reason at all, just because. I looked at the twins, Suzie Que, Steven, their whole situation. Steven was indeed a lucky guy, and I hoped that one day I could have the same thing in a family.

K.P. noticed me "lost in space" and came and sat on the floor next to me.

"They have something special, don't they?" she said.

"What do you mean?"

"I noticed you looking at them, and you know what? I want that too."

Hint? … Naw couldn't be. Or could it?

"Want what?"

"Oh, is this 'I can't let anybody know what I'm really thinking mode'?"

Sometimes I really want to let K.P. back into that realm of my world. Sometimes I wonder if it was a mistake to give her a glimpse at all. Sometimes I wonder if I'm in a sense punishing her for the past. Sometimes I wonder if we should just leave everything the way it is. Hey! … *Hey!* Don't think that I'm having a vulnerable moment here, 'cause I'm not, okay!?! And don't think that K.P. has my number, either, 'cause she doesn't. And y'all can kiss my ass too, (_x_) 'cause I can tell by those silly ass smirks, that y'all don't believe me! *Whateva!*

"Huh? You thought I was thinking about them? I wasn't thinking about that."

"Don't lie to me. I could see the longing in your eyes. Do you forget who I am?"

Sometimes K.P. is a bit too observant for me. But then again, that's one of the things that I like about her. She thinks, and not only that, she thinks for two. We think alike. I remember times when we could finish each other's sentences. She knows that I kinda withdrew a little after I got hurt by Kiyy (among other things), but she continues to fight to bring me back to the good ol' days. And you know what? I appreciate the fact that she continues to try even if I'm being a stubborn jerk. But if any of you tell her I said any of this, I'll deny it and I'll come a'lookin' fo' that ass!

In a nutshell and in no particular order, we had drinks (and in case you're wondering, the kids had fruit punch), the Steelers won (my silence and giant smile did all the bragging), we played Twister, we ate dinner, we played Hearts and then Spades (K.P. and myself vs. Steven and Suzie Que), we had dessert. All in all, a good time was had by all. Suzie Que insisted that we both take food home with us, and me being the bachelor that I am, graciously accepted. :-) I tried to boost K.P.'s portions, but I was sent straight to jail by the twins, not passing "Go" and not collecting two hundred dollars. If you can't tell, we also played Monopoly.

If I told you that I dropped K.P. off and went home, would you buy it? Of course if I hadn't prefaced it like that, you wouldn't have had any choice but to buy it. Then again, I could just be baiting you guys. Why would I do that? Just because I could, I guess. But I'm not gonna be like that this time. That conversation between K.P. and myself that I didn't want to talk about earlier took place in my house after we got back from Long Island.

You know how some people get home and unwind with a little jazz, maybe some ballads? Not us. We unwound to the Wu, a little Biggie (the first album, we had to let "Life after Death" rest in peace for a while), and then we got started on my Prince collection. Yeah Prince. Music or life does not have to go in some kind of order, or make sense. I know he's the Artist now, but I'll be damned if I'll ever get used to calling him that. I like to brag about the fact that I have every album that the Artist (see I'm trying), has ever made, even some bootlegs. There's two concerts that I must attend every time these artists go out on tour, or my year has been thrown off track, and they're Prince and Janet Jackson. So, I'm being overdramatic. The point has been made, hasn't it? In my opinion, Prince was the innovator behind the notion that the B-side on a record could be released as an A-side. Look at songs like "Raspberry Beret" and the B-side being "She's Always In My Hair" (one of my all-time favorites), or classic B-sides like "Erotic City" (another favorite), or "Another Lonely Christmas." Don't tell anyone, but one of my fantasies is to cover one of Prince's, I mean the Artist's, songs. Hell no, I'm not telling you which one, as if!

We sat there absorbing the music, content with the notion that we were going to talk and it was going to lead somewhere, but perfectly willing to leave things as they were, if the ice wasn't broken. At least, I was. Of course, K.P. wasn't. After I broke up with Kiyy, the world was not a happy place for me. I withdrew from everyone and everything. I remember spending many a night just staring at the four walls in my room listening to "Suddenly" by Billy Ocean. Sometimes I cried, sometimes I didn't. For those that have been lucky enough, or unlucky enough (depends on your perspective), to have had your heart broken, you probably know that there are usually three stages: the "why me" stage, where all your emotions come pouring out; the "what could *I* have done to make it better" stage, where you indirectly or sometimes directly blame yourself for the breakup even if the other person was dead wrong; and finally the "kiss my ass" (_x_) stage, where you've hit rock bottom and there's nowhere else to go but up, and you get angry that you've allowed yourself to go through these stages, when you should have correctly rationalized that the other person whom you're agonizing over at that very moment, is not even thinking about you!

"You know we should have talked about this years ago," K.P. started out, "instead of letting it drag on for all this time."

"Maybe we really didn't want this day to come about."

"Maybe, Que, but I think that we both need to know this. At least, I do."

As I said before, after my breakup with Kiyy, I basically kept to myself. I didn't want to see anybody, and initially that included K.P. My mother and K.P. conversed often since I wouldn't see anyone, and my mother would keep K.P. abreast of what was going on with me. K.P. would call, but I didn't want to talk to anyone. K.P. would come by to visit, but I didn't want to see anybody. At first my mother went along with my wishes because she knew how hurt I was, but when she noticed that K.P. was the only one of my so-called friends that was consistently showing some concern over me, she let me know. And I'm sure that my mother developed some new found r-e-s-p-e-c-t (Apologies to Aretha), when K.P. forced the issue and asked my mother if she had a problem with her going up to my room to see me. Although my mother jokes with K.P. that K.P. actually told her she was going to see me and if Mom had a problem with it … tough!

Needless to say that when K.P. walked into my room, I wasn't happy. She froze, because she saw something that she had never seen before. I was sitting on the floor facing the door and I had my head lowered. When I lifted my head, I expected to see my mom, not K.P. She saw tears coming down my face. My mother had caught me teary-eyed before over my breakup with Kiyy, but I had refused to let a tear drop in front of her … at least until she'd held me in her arms, and I couldn't hold back any longer. After that, I kinda didn't care much about my mom seeing me in ruins. But K.P. was another matter. Not even when we were little had K.P. ever seen me cry, even though I'd certainly had reasons to. I guess knowing that, coupled with the fact of what she was witnessing at that moment, pressed upon her the magnitude of my pain. And as she stood there looking at me, she became overwhelmed and began to cry silent tears as well. The next thing I knew she was on the floor cradling me in her arms as we wept silently. We must have been on the floor for at least an hour, and she never said a word to me, she just held me. To this day I appreciated that, because it was like we were connected. She knew I was in pain, and because I was in pain, she was in pain. She felt me (that's kinda deep I think). After some time, she kissed my forehead, told me she'd be back tomorrow, and got up and left.

She came back every day too, and that's how she crept into my inner sanctum. She came in the door, I said it before, I wasn't tryin' to get hurt after Kiyy, no more (Apologies to Rakim). :-/ No, for real though, it didn't even go down like that. This was what friendship is supposed to be about. She lifted me up out of the doldrums and motivated me to move on, which I eventually did, and she deserves credit for that. For the next few months we hung out every day, and although we were already best friends, we really became *best friends*. We opened up to each other, and to this day we both know things about the other that no one else knows. Well, except for one thing.

"… And that's how Winnie and I met, K.P."

She looked at me for a few seconds, and I grew uncomfortable waiting for her to respond to me. Finally, after some more expressionless seconds, she broke out into her trademark smirk.

"Que, I'm so glad that you told me the truth. That's why we're best friends. You still have never lied to me, and I'm grateful for that."

"What are you talking about, K.P.?"

"I already knew how you and Winnie met."

"How the hell could you know that?"

"Kenny. Kenny told me the whole story."

I couldn't even get mad at that. Let that be a lesson to all you peeps. Imagine if I hadn't decided to tell the truth. I'da been caught up in a phat lie and I'da been lookin' real stupid. That's why I'm stress free and you're not. In the long run, honesty really is the best policy (sorry about the corny cliché).

"Why would he … ? When did he tell you?"

"When you and I weren't speaking for that stretch."

"Ummph. When I found out from you that you had slept with Marlon."

"And you had slept with Shannon."

"I keep telling you that I never slept with her."

"You know Kenny told me that he had heard that about Shannon, too."

"I guess Kenny called himself getting back at me by telling you about Winnie and spreading some rumor about me at the same time, huh?"

"I guess. Are you upset, Que? Are you gonna say something to him?"

"I ain't upset, but I can't promise you that I won't say something one day. Tell me this, though. What was your reaction when you found out?"

"My first reaction was that you needed Jesus, son! No, no … seriously … I had no reaction in front of Kenny, but within, I was a bit upset with you."

The phone rang and on the second ring I answered it, as K.P. went into the kitchen to get something to drink. You'll never guess who it was. Take a few seconds. All right, time's up. It was Angie. She wanted to come over and talk. Yeah, right! Before I could tell her that I had company, K.P. called out from the kitchen to ask me if I wanted something to drink. Of course, Angie heard a female voice in the background, and she let me know that she had heard it too. So futhermuckin' what! I ain't got to explain shit to Angie. I told her that K.P. was over and we were chillin'. She tried to drop some hints that she was still gonna drop by. Basically, I told her to not even play herself. *"Baby girl, just stop, stop, stop! Check yourself, uhn!"* (Apologies to L.L.). K.P. came back into the room and I told her who it was and what had been said. She chuckled.

"I guess I better leave, 'cause *I will* bust her ass this time!"

"Angie ain't thinking about coming over here, K.P She don't want none."

"Well, she better act like she know, 'cause my tolerance level for B.S. now is dangerously low!"

"Yeah, wassup with you, star? What has Marlon done to tick you off?"

"Well, that's why I kind of invited myself over to talk to you, because you're sort of involved indirectly. I wanted to tell you that and also something else that I've wanted to tell you for a while and I finally got the nerve."

"Sounds to me like you're trying to find the right words to say. Spit it out, woman."

"Promise me you won't move until you hear the whole story, Que."

"C'mon," I laughed. "It can't be that bad."

"Promise me!"

"Aight, aight I promise, K.P."

She struggled to gain her composure back, looked down at the floor for a few seconds and then looked me straight in the eyes as if there was no turning back. I picked up my glass and started to bring it to my lips, and then she spoke.

"Marlon raped me."

The next thing I knew, broken glass was everywhere. Apparently, I had dropped the glass.

"I'ma kill him," I said as I got up and went to my bedroom.

"Sit down, Que."

You know I ignored her, right? I found my keys and headed for the door. K.P. ran to the door and threw herself against it. I calmly picked her up and moved her to the side, but she threw herself back against the door.

"You promised, Que … Sit down! … Que, you promised … Sit down!"

I was eerily calm as I told her to move.

"K.P., I'll be right back. Move away from the door."

Suddenly, K.P. lost it.

"Sit down!" she screamed, "Sit down, sit down, sit down, sit down …"

She had sank to the floor and was crying hysterically as the same words became mumbled. I dropped to the floor immediately and held her right there until her sobs subsided.

<hr>

During the months that K.P. and I had hung out after my breakup with Kiyy, she had confided to me that she was a virgin. And to make a long story short, she also confided in me that she had decided that she wanted me to be her first. In retrospect, I can look back at that time and can now consider it an honor that she wanted me to be her first. And looking back on it, I did treat it as such, albeit unconsciously. But I'd be lying if I said an ego thing didn't play a big role, too. K.P. was my best friend, and I tried not to treat this lightly. But at the age of youth, we don't think logically all the time. In fact, my hormones were in overdrive. To deflower a virgin (as I've crudely put it), at that time, was definitely a notch on the belt. I'm not too proud of the fact that I put K.P. in that category back then.

Anyway, we were at her house in her room talking, and the talking eventually led to kissing, and the kissing eventually led to something else, and the something else led to etc., etc. Mind you, this wasn't the first time that we had kissed. It was the second. The first time was on the boardwalk of Coney Island.

We had actually joked about who had initiated the kiss. She said I did, and I say that she did. To tell you the truth, that's the only detail that I cannot remember. Now what I'm about to tell you better not leave this page. I mean it. I care a lot about K.P. and I don't want her to be embarrassed, or teased, you got that? If everybody's cool with that then raise your hand. I'm not playing. Raise your damn hand. That's right … you too … and you too!

All right now, check it, K.P.'s "juicy fruit" is the best that I've ever tasted! :-/ Mind you now, Kiyy's was very, very good (it was the second that I'd ever tasted), and Winnie's is just as good, but K.P.'s … Ummph. That's all I can say! Fellas, *you* know! Those that have gone down on somebody remember smells and tastes. K.P. smelled faintly of crushed roses. Guys may have a tough go of identifying the smell of crushed roses, but women know what I'm talking about. A delicious fruity aroma, not overpowering, but pleasingly pleasant. But fellas, I ain't leaving you out, just think of the sweetest, most pleasurable fruit that you've ever tasted. Well, just imagine that, and waa laa … you've just tasted K.P. And when we were alone, I'd call her by the nickname that I had given her … Sweetness … and she would blush every time! :-) I hadn't called her that in years … until tonight.

So things elevated and escalated, and before you knew it, K.P. asked me to make love to her. Now most guys would have just dove right in, and although I wanted to, this was my best friend we were talking about and I wanted to make sure that she was really ready, and that this was what she really wanted to do. In retrospect (and when you read further, you'll understand why I said this), maybe I should have just gone ahead without inquiring when she asked me to make love to her, because by asking her if she was ready, it gave her time to think about it. Now ladies, I don't know what you go through when you're about to lose your virginity, but I would imagine that it's a pretty emotional time. Yes? Help me out here. As I began to enter her ever so gently (yes, safe sex was in effect), I felt her cringe and I stopped. I looked at her face and I saw tears running down her cheeks. She told me that she was sorry and wanted me to continue. I tried, but she began to cry again and I knew that she wasn't ready yet. Then she asked me if we could stop. Being the Gentleman by Nature that I am, I did just that.

We never mentioned it again. Now during this time, Marlon (who lived in the neighborhood), had been throwing the full court press at K.P. every chance that he got. She liked him, but she knew that

I didn't particularly care for him because I felt that he was just trying to get between her legs. Especially since he knew that she was a virgin. She felt otherwise, and who's to say who was right because they'd been together steady since.

⸻

"Hey, Sweetness," I whispered as I wiped the tears from her face with my thumb. "You okay? Talk to me, are you okay?"

She nodded her head slightly as she shifted in my arms. We were still on the floor by the door, and I had no intentions of moving her. However, she wanted to go back to the couch. So we went back to the couch, and I sat down and placed her head in my lap as she lay across the rest of the leather sectional. I began to caress the side of her head when she turned to face me.

"You haven't called me that in years," she smiled weakly.

"I know ... Sorry ... I, ah, didn't keep my promise. But I'm still gonna buss' his ass!"

"No. I want you to hear the whole story, and then maybe I'll let you get to him." :-/

"Nice to see you smirkin', but you can't keep me from bustin' his ass."

"If I ask you not to, you'll do it."

"Well, don't ask that of me, because I don't think that I can do it."

"For me, you would."

"Don't do that. Why would you want to protect him anyway? … Never mind, I don't even want to know. When you're ready to tell me the rest, go ahead."

She did.

Apparently, about a week and a half after the episode between K.P. and myself, she had an interesting talk with Marlon. He told her that he wanted her to be his girl. K.P. told Marlon that she liked him, but she needed time to think. What she needed to think about were the feelings that she had developed for me. Her intentions were to talk to me and find out how I felt about her. Coincidentally (believe this, if you want), Marlon mentioned that he had seen me at the movies the previous week with this girl named Shannon, and that we appeared to be rather cozy. He asked K.P. if Shannon and I were going out. She told him that she didn't know of it. Do you know how Spin Doctors operate? They make things seem like they happened, but they actually didn't. Bootleg liars. After Marlon was finished, the insinuation was that I had slept with Shannon in the theater, and it was broadcasting. Incidentally, when she was always confronted with this, Shannon neither confirmed nor denied the rumors. K.P. told me that she never would have believed this normally, because it's not my style to publicly kiss and tell like *that*, but Marlon told her to call his sister who was with him at the time (the same sister who had nothing to gain by telling K.P. the truth, as he put it), and ask her. So she did, and his sister, Drew, told K.P. the same thing that he had told her. K.P. later found out from me that Drew wanted to get with me, herself. Are you following me, here? I'm not saying this reeks of conspiracy, but clearly those two had their own agenda. With that, Drew left the house.

Needless to say that after hearing this from Drew, K.P. was outdone. Seizing the opportunity, Marlon began kissing up on K.P. Considering what she had just heard, she eventually began to respond to Marlon. After all, she did like him, right? And it did seem that my affections were elsewhere, right? Before you could say guacamole, she found herself in the same position that she had been in with me, the previous week and a half ago. She told Marlon that she wasn't ready to go there yet, but he kept insisting that the time was right, and that he would be gentle. K.P. figured that it was nerves again, and allowed herself to believe him. He began penetration, and she said that nerves hit her again, and she asked him to stop. He told her not to worry and continued. She told him to stop again, this time a little more forcibly because she wasn't ready. At this point, she was crying, and upon him noticing her tears, he told her that it was natural to be nervous, but that once he was inside of her, she would relax. She told him that she didn't want him to do this, and he responded that she would thank him one day. With that, he was inside her, and she laid there like a stiff corpse looking at the ceiling as the tears flowed endlessly.

I sat there with my fist clenched and my teeth gritted as she told of her ordeal. I don't care what K.P. says, that motherfucker is gonna pay!

Back at that time, K.P. felt that she had been violated, but she didn't fit the classic "rape" scenario (i.e. violent abduction by stranger). She didn't think that anyone would believe her, and she even struggled with the notion of whether what Marlon did actually constituted rape. She had since learned about date rape, and had lived with this for years.

She went on to explain that she tried to move, and although it didn't actually look like she was pinned down, with him being on top of her and clasping her hands (fingers intertwined), the leverage that he achieved could actually disguise the fact that she was actually pinned down.

And just when I thought that she couldn't add any more grief to the situation, she did. She told me the reason that Marlon wasn't with her for "Off the Hook." I guess recently K.P. had reached her boiling point because although she had talked to Marlon about this before, she hadn't gotten it out of her system. Marlon had grown weary of it and didn't want to talk about it anymore. He felt like she was beating a dead horse. She wanted him to understand what he had done and what he had put her through, and he didn't seem to think he had done anything wrong. My personal opinion is that he would never admit that he had done anything wrong even if he did realize that he had violated K.P. (of course, I may be a bit biased). Anyway, they began to argue, and the argument grew nasty. Marlon called K.P. a bitch (definite no no, huh ladies?), and K.P. opened the flood gates. She told him that he wasn't as good as he thought in bed.

Now understand this. K.P. has technically only been with Marlon, so what did she have to compare him to? Are you feeling me here? She compared it to the time we had been together, noting the foreplay that I had given her, and although we hadn't actually had intercourse (I know, it sounds so un-benign, but I have to illustrate the point), she felt that we had made love. She told him about being with me, how she wished that I had been her first, and even though in the eyes of society, Marlon would be considered her first, she considered me her first. Ouch! She got kinda raw, huh? This hit Marlon like a ton of bricks. K.P. said that he stood there looking at her with his mouth wide open, and then suddenly, he charged her. He slapped her in the face, punched her in the shoulder, all within a matter of seconds, and then he picked her up and threw her across the room.

Here's something else that you have to understand about K.P.

I mentioned before that K.P. is a thinker. She thinks for two. I believe that K.P. knew that something would transpire if she ever got pushed far enough to expose her true feelings, and that she was prepared for the consequences in order to exorcise the demons that pervaded her inner soul. That said, you can now understand the next sentence. K.P. pulled a container of mace from her pocket, and when Marlon approached her again, she maced him! When Marlon fell to the ground in agony, she maced him again, and then went to get the bat that Marlon keeps by his door, and beat the shit out of him. She left him conscious, bloodied, and battered on the floor, shaking like a newborn baby.

However, before she left, she informed him that if he wanted to treat her like a man, she had to even up the odds, and if he wanted to get shady and go to the cops or think about touching her again, she'd tell the cops that he hit her and that he had raped her. Finally, she told him that if he ever thought about putting his hands on her again, she'd have him killed! *That's my peoples!!!* ... I'm not advocating murder here, but you gotta let 'em know that you're not having it! And just to highlight and underline what kind of woman K.P. is, she dialed 911! She told me that she also took a towel and wiped the bat handle clean of any fingerprints. I told her that either she had been hanging around me much too long, or the O.J. trials definitely had an impact on her. I also couldn't resist (tongue-in-cheek), asking her if she had left a bloody footprint. :-/ Probably bad taste, but hey, you get the good, the bad, and the ugly here!

I must say that even though I still wanted to empty a clip all up in his "cabbage," I was a little more subdued just knowing that K.P. had damaged his whole area (so if she asks me to back off, at least now I'll consider it). :-/ I was a little numb after absorbing all of this, but K.P. seemed at ease. I guess those demons had been excised.

"Que? Are you okay?"

"Yep," I exhaled.

"Are you sure, Que?"

"Yeah, Sweetness … I'm cool."

"Copacetic, even?" she giggled.

"K.P., I am fine," I laughed. "What the dilly, yo?"

Translation: "What's the deal? … What's up with you?" … I thought some of you may have needed some help :-) … You're welcome! :-)

"Give me the gun."

"Huh?"

"C'mon, Que … don't 'huh' me. I know you got it."

"I don't know what you're talking about."

"So you're telling me that if I reach around and feel between the small of your back, I'm not gonna feel .45 ways to 'heat' another?"

"Damn K.P. ... So! ... I mean ... I wasn't gonna 'burn em' ... I'm sayin' though ... I was just ... I ... But he damn sure was catching a pistol whipping!"

She laughed as she reached around my back and pulled the 1911 from its hiding place. In a swift series of motions, she removed the clip and "chambered" my piece. She removed the bullet from the chamber. I mean, hey, she remembered that I always keep one in the chamber. Call me twisted, but there is something inherently sexy about a woman deftly handling a piece (It's a guy thing, ladies. I doubt if you'd understand ... but then again, you may).

Then, as if from out of nowhere, an overwhelming feeling of desire suddenly engulfed me, and as I looked at her and she looked back at me, I was sure that I got the impression that her eyes spoke words without saying a word to me! Never mind that polarization thing where opposites attract and like sides repel. Our like minds told our faces to draw closer, so that our lips would meet. Throw the laws of physics out the window, here. I'd been here before, it was a familiar feeling that had not been truly felt since ... *Because you haven't allowed it to ...* It's always been there ... *Stop fighting it and succumb again* ... I won't get hurt again ... *You feel the same way for her that you did for ...*

We became slaves of this passion, and our lips were so close that we could both feel the heat emanating from them. And just when I felt the tingle of our lips beginning to meet … the doorbell rang! I mean … damn! Reality set in and poof. We were back.

We lost eye contact as the bell rang again. At first, I started not to answer the door, but K.P. convinced me otherwise. I reluctantly got up to open the door. As I got up, we both sucked our teeth at the same time as we both had an idea of who it might be.

I open the door, and I see …

5

MEMORIES CAN BE PAINFUL

Oh … agony! … Aaa … go … ny!

"Que? … Que?"

The voice was mesmerizing … even as a whisper … even though it had been years since I last heard it. She remained beautiful, and her voice could still calm the most savage of beasts. Yes, Kiyy still had that effect on me, even in a dream, a simple fantasy (Apologies to DeBarge). And every morning, I wake up to the same thing, except this morning, I was spared. I wonder why?

I know that I've been putting this off for a while now, and if you've forgotten what I'm referring to, or you just don't care anymore, I don't blame you.

The majority of you right now are going, "What the #%@! is he talking about now?" But there are one or two of you out there that have made this a personal quest … a challenge, to keep up with my style and sudden tangents. And I bet that they know what I'm getting ready to jump into. Now that I've alerted everyone to this, others no doubt will jump on the bandwagon and will begin to wake up out of their coma. While the antagonists and the protagonists may take this as a sign that my book is not "John Blaze" … i.e. hot, slammin', phat, the truth, bangin', or simply … da bomb (non-hip hoppers read: great, enjoyable, sensational, the cat's meow), because my thoughts and writing style are not cohesively coordinated. The thinkers are the ones I'm really concerned about anyway … everyone else is just along for the ride! I hope, I have challenged and entertained at the same time.

I mean, I never really understood how Kiyy fit in the puzzle. I always wondered how she got involved, why she was even around.

The call came in at 10:35 p.m. on a lonely Friday night (Prince fans know). :-) Forgive my attempt at humor, it's the only way that I can deal with this right now. Actually, it was Tuesday night when Jinx called my house, frantic. Darren had gotten himself shot. I wasn't surprised, in fact, I was a little amazed that it hadn't happened sooner. Darren had become obsessed with finding his father's killers. The cops had closed the case about a year ago, stamping it "unsolved." Of course, this didn't sit well with the Parker family, none more so than Darren. I made it to the hospital, and Jinx was the first to run crying into my arms. Jinx and I shared a secret, and it seemed to be rearing its ugly head again.

"You know who did it, Snow?"

"Yes, son. But that's not it. They know of you."

"They know me? Who's they? And from where?"

"Somebody in they outfit, but peep this, the boss man is not from here … tryin' to muscle his way into the NYC. He's out to get a rep. Tryin' to take out 'Big Willies,' but he done crossed the line, targeting innocents. He tried to get to me, but when I got word … and oh, yo … thanks for the DL tip …"

"What?"

"I know it was you, Que … sending info down the tunnel."

"Damn … if you know … then that means that he knows, too. That's how they know of me!"

"I doubt it, Que. My sources don't snitch."

"How you gonna say your sources don't snitch, and they told you about me?"

"They don't snitch to nobody else. Don't worry, I got ya back."

"I don't need you to have my back, but I do need to know who this new crew is!"

"On the real, I ain't never seen him out, Que. But I hear that one of his top lieutenants goes by the name of 'Chico Caliente,' or something like that. What kind of punk ass name is that? Pushin' product called 'honey boy' that you drink, taggin' it, the 'nectar that mortals seek.'"

"Seems to me, don't matter what he's called or what he push, they done tried to take you out, son!"

"True … true, and then he stepped to my girl, and her father is dead because of it. We gon' find out where the Honey Comb Hideout is, believe that!"

I sat in the hospital lounge recalling that conversation with Snow. And to this day, I still didn't know who this "Hot Boy" was. But his rep did grow, and now he controls, or has his hand dipped in, most of the dirt circulating in East Flatbush and other parts of town. Jinx was still shaking uncontrollably, and rightfully so. She had pulled me to the side and given me a no return envelope addressed to herself she received in the mail that day, which simply read, "It's gonna SNOW again." Of course that night, Darren gets shot.

Mrs. Parker sat in a chair holding herself as my mother held her. My father stood above them with Ni Ni next to him. Ni Ni's husband sent his prayers and wanted to come with her, but she convinced him to stay with the kids. Steven and Suzie Que were gonna drive in from Long Island, but Mrs. Parker convinced them otherwise. K.P. stood by a window just looking out into nowhere. This whole scene seemed eerily reminiscent of something I had been through. Then the elevator doors opened and reality hit hard again. Jinx and I reacted at the same time, but she reached him first. Marlon didn't know what hit him, or who hit him for that matter! The force of our forward momentum caused all three of us to crash to the hard hospital floor. I must admit that Jinx got more quality punches in, as I tried to make sure that he didn't swing on her by pinning his arms. But I did land a few before it was broken up (not how I wanted to, though).

As Marlon was being taken to be cleaned up, he had a bloody nose, bloody lip and a cut above his right eye. Jinx, who had not been calmed yet, yelled at him.

"You bitch! I hope you need stitches. Don't you ever put your hands on my sister again!"

Needless to say, this stunned everyone within earshot! All eyes went from Marlon being escorted somewhere to be patched up—to K.P.—to us as we were being sat down.

"What is going on here!?!" Mrs. Parker yelled at everyone, but no one in particular.

I wasn't sayin' "jack," and nobody dared say anything to Jinx because when she got in this state, it was best to leave her alone. Jinx is fierce when it comes to family. I remember a Christmas party that we all went to. Everybody was there: Mr. Parker, Snow, Ronnie had brought Keith, I was still with Kiyy. K.P. brought this kid named Shelton (Marlon wasn't in the picture yet).

It all started on the dance floor. Ronnie and Keith had been on the floor dancing, and some girls who were guests of a co-worker of Mrs. Parker were seated at a nearby table. Ronnie is like me. We don't like disrespect, and we will not tolerate blatant disrespect. Don't even go there, yo! We know blatant disrespect when we see *blatant disrespect.* And if yo' ass don't stop interrupting, I'ma show *you* blatant disrespect. And that's my word, son! It's the same kid that keeps doing it, too … I'm sayin' though …

Anyway, if it's plain to see that someone is with somebody else, show some respect. That's all I'm sayin'. And these girls knew that we were pretty much "coupled off" because they saw us all walk into the place holding hands, which you would think would mean "hands off." Not then, nor now, I guess, huh? The girls started with that "Psst" and hissing stuff, you know, that "cat calling" dribble.

Before I go on, I gotta say this. Keith has to take some of the blame here. Before they hit the dance floor, Keith had gone to the bathroom. When he came back, he told Ronnie that some girl had felt his butt. But when Ronnie asked him to show her who it was, he wouldn't. Said he had handled it. Duh! Then why tell her? I mean, you know her … you know how she is. You gonna tell her something like that, and *not* expect her to react? Keith got his own lesson in Academy Award performances. Ronnie shook it off and smiled at Keith. Needless to say that she did what I think most of you women out there would have done. She scanned the room and looked for candidates (done silently, of course). :-/ Then, after the allotted time period and some small talk with the rest of our table, Ronnie announced that she was going to the bathroom and asked casually if anyone else had to go … I'm dropping dime here.

Fellas, check it. Whenever there's a cattle call for the bathroom, plannin' and schemin' most def' is going on. I don't know if it's the tone of voice that a woman uses or if it's just custom. Women know. Maybe it's just been passed down from generations of women. I don't care if it's just two women. Think about it. How often do you see one woman among a group of women go to the bathroom in public alone? Yeah, yeah, yeah … y'all gonna give that "security reason" (some guy or somebody could be in the bathroom), as the alibi. Valid point, perhaps. But fellas, they bankin' on you to go for that … hook, line, and sinker! I'm telling you, mad info is passed off in there. I *know* that if you could be a fly on the wall of a woman's bathroom … ummph, ummph, ummph!

Back to Ronnie's bathroom call. Ni Ni got up to go with her, along with K.P. and Kiyy.

Eventually, they came back from the bathroom (I guess there was a line), :-/ and sat back down. No sooner had they done that, the DJ decided to go back in the day and play Brooklyn's basement party anthem, "Love is the Message." Nobody sits down to

"Love is the Message," so the party people that be got up to dance.

Ronnie grabbed Keith and headed toward the dance floor. Instinct (or should I say women's intuition or just plain old common sense), led Ronnie toward a table where only girls sat. Here's where Keith played himself. He tried to maneuver Ronnie toward another section of the dance floor. Big mistake! This just confirmed Ronnie's suspicions. There are lessons to be learned here, fellas … pick up what I'm sayin'? Like I said before, the girls started "cat calling," and I think that Ronnie was willing to let it go when it was low, but as it got louder and more persistent, she had had enough. So she turned and walked toward the table. With Keith in hot pursuit, she asked the girls if there was a problem. One of the girls wanted to be a "wise-ass" (_Ô v Ô_) and told her that *she* was the problem because she was blocking her view of Keith's ass. She then calmly proceeded to add a "bitch" to the end of her sentence.

Ronnie, just as calmly, smacked her in the face.

"Maybe you can see a little better now!" (Alrighty then!)

Kiyy and I had been dancing, as were K.P. and Ni Ni. Unbeknownst to me, Kiyy had been monitoring the situation. When she saw the smack, she left me and raced over there, intercepting one girl with a hard push. Like Kamikaze pilots, Ni Ni and K.P. swooped down from the North and South sides, daring somebody to raise up. I had to admit, they had they shit together! The girls, who must have forgotten that Ronnie wasn't by herself with Keith, were quickly reminded otherwise. Things got squashed quickly before more serious blows could be thrown when some adults near the table sent everyone in opposite directions. Good thing too! You would have lost your money if you had bet against the "Kamikaze 4" that night!

When we all got back to our section, Mom immediately asked Ronnie what had happened because she could see the commotion from where she and Dad had been seated. Keith, trying to play "peacemaker" (as he put it), had gone back over to the girls' table and was (as he put it), "squashing the beef." Ronnie didn't like this at all, and got up to get Keith, against Mom's wishes. Can't say I blamed Ronnie. What business did Keith have over there apologizing for Ronnie's actions, when incidentally it was his fault for the whole damn episode? Fellas, again … there are lessons to be learned here.

What Keith should have done is left well enough alone. The last thing a woman is trying to hear is her man trying to justify her actions to another woman … in public, no less! Trust me, Keith got an earful after everything was said and done. Not only from Ronnie, but my mother and Ni Ni too. Not to mention exasperated looks from every other woman that could identify with the situation after details trickled out, and shakes of the head from fellas that had gone through the same thing at one point or another in their lifetime. Well, Mom followed Ronnie, and Mrs. Parker followed Mom, followed by Mr. Parker and my Dad.

Snow and Jinx, who had been somewhere sharing a romantic moment, entered the room precisely at the wrong time. When Ronnie went to get Keith, Ni Ni, K.P., and Kiyy trooped with her. One of the girls saw them coming out of the corner of her eye, and not wanting to be ambushed again, she quickly got up. The other girls, thinking it was definitely on now, got up too and charged. Can you say "free for all?" It looked like it was gonna be ugly for a few seconds, but some quick-thinking adults wedged a wall quick fast, and though battle lines had been drawn, nobody could cross them. Mom, Mrs. Parker, and her co-worker tried to sort things amid the yelling and screaming. Mrs. Parker, trying to calm one of the girls, gently placed her hand on the girl to try and reason with her. The girl whipped away from Mrs. Parker's hand and pushed her, yelling, "Don't touch me, lady! You don't know me!"

Thank God, I was right near K.P., because I grabbed her just as she was starting to make her charge. I held her, kicking and screaming.

I whispered to her, "Not here, not here."

The adults had a pretty good wall going and K.P. couldn't have gotten to her anyway. But that didn't stop her from trying. I know I saved that girl's life, because if I hadn't turned my head, I wouldn't have seen Jinx coming like a runaway train. I still can't believe she was moving that fast in those heels. Tends to prove to me that when you react on pure emotion, mixed in with some good ol' fashioned adrenaline, not thinking about your actions or supposed limitations, you can amaze your damn self! Jinx was running slightly slanted with her hand low and slightly behind her back.

Instantly I knew it was trouble, because for one, I had taught her the stance, and two, I knew what she was holding. Snow told me later that all Jinx saw was somebody push her mother, and she just snapped. He went on to say that he had never seen that look before on her face. She let go of his hand and dropped her bag, but not before pulling out this big 007 knife. Snow admitted (and I still chuckle at this), that he was startled when she pulled away from him, dropped her bag, and flicked open this huge knife, all in one motion! *He* didn't even know that she carried it.

Now I don't know where you're from, but in Brooklyn … back in the day … a 007 (Double 0-7 for the uneducated), was the weapon of choice. Of course, now it's the "nine" … millimeter, that is. It's called a 007 because the blade alone is actually seven inches! Ladies, did you know that the average length of a man's penis is five inches? That's not flaccid, either … Just an obscure detail that I thought some of you would find interesting. ;-) The knife was originally mine, and I gave it to Jinx after she continually harassed me for it. I am not, I tell you, an accessory to the mayhem … (well, maybe sort of). It was oiled to perfection. I could flick it out from a number of different angles. Jinx became intrigued with it when I used to play around with her and K.P., walking like a madman, pulling it out, the knife, that is… you should be used to me, by now, :-/ threatening to cut their hair. Yes, it was *that* sharp (thanks to a sharpening stone). More than a few people actually knew how sharp that knife was, 'cause they had felt it ... and not by choice, either! But this girl was about to catch a bad one.

I let go of K.P. and raced around the human wall. Jinx was coming hard one way, and I was coming hard the other. We were definitely on a collision course, if I could get to her. I felt her going by me as I stretched out my left arm and tried to cup her around her waist. Luckily for me, Jinx weighs about a buck o' five (figuratively speaking, of course), and I had had my bowl of "Wheaties" that morning, so I was able to bring her in to me. But as she screeched to a halt, her forward momentum caused her to leave her feet. In a "jack-knife" position, she stretched her arms to grab at the girl, and before I could snatch her back, she swung that knife.

Don't mean to switch gears, but I just thought about this. You know that Michael Jordan commercial where Michael makes a move around this guy and time seems to become suspended? Everyone stops what they're doing, there's some opera vocals in the background, no one's moving, water is overflowing from a faucet? You know which one I'm talking about, right? Then as he goes around this guy, everything switches to slow motion as he goes up for his dunk, and just before his dunk goes in, we speed back to live action and time as we know it?

Now you know what I'm talking about, right? Well, every time I see that commercial, I think about this episode with Jinx.

Jinx swung that knife and I swear it felt like time had stood still. The girl had a French roll hairstyle. Those of you that don't know what it is are just gonna have to ask somebody. Personally, I don't like the hairstyle, but that's another matter. I've been told that hair is added sometimes to make the hairstyle appear taller and fuller. At any rate, that knife came down through the top of that French roll like somebody was slicing butter! I'm not joking, either! … It was suspended animation as I watched the hair float sing song to the ground. I kid you not! … *Yes,* I'm telling you the truth! … Even with all that gel! … I'm telling y'all … there's mad witnesses that can co-sign.

Snow reached us and grabbed Jinx. I let go of her waist and quickly went for the knife. I was not trying to get sliced, accidental or not! Jinx was spitting fury, screaming that she was gonna get the girl, no matter how long it took, and that nobody puts their hands on her mother and stays around to talk about it! It really took some effort to get Jinx's little ass (well, it's not little, but you know what I mean), :-/ out of that room. Just in case you're wondering (as I'm sure a few of you are), a freed K.P. did try and get to the girl again, but was held back. You thought I was gonna leave you hanging, didn't ya? Aaah! Don't say nothing, just shake your head and smile. :-) … You're welcome.

To sum everything up, no charges were filed, but let's just say Mrs. Parker's family or friends wouldn't be invited to any more Christmas parties at her job any time soon … or any function at her job, for that matter. When I say that, I'm for real. That was the deal. The family and friends were barred from any job functions.

Oh, as an aside (like I was really gonna forget to tell you this), K.P. and Jinx got to the girl a couple of weeks later, just as I told K.P. she would. If we had been in the street, I wouldn't have held K.P. back, but I felt at the party, the situation called for a little decorum. But I had already told myself that I was gonna get the 411 on homegirl, anyway. What ever happened to "respect your elders?" See, once the lights came on and people started adjusting their eyes, I was immediately recognized by some cats that knew the girls. Honestly, I hadn't realized that the Wolfpack had this much reach back then, but one thing about Brooklyn is that peeps stayed informed as to the happenings. They recognized me from an incident (one of many, I suppose), that happened in Bed Stuy. I didn't get the chance to solicit the info at all. They volunteered it, and I simply passed it on to interested people (K.P. and Jinx). They, in turn, whipped that girl's ass. Justice? Perhaps not as society knows it, but that's the code of the streets (*You know my Steez* ... Apologies to Gangstarr).

Since I started down memory lane, I guess I could lace you with a few more gems. Guess it depends on your perspective. These stories aren't meant to glorify. I'm just telling you what I've been through. I alluded to this incident that happened in the Bedford Stuyvesant section of Brooklyn. I grew up there. Went to P.S. 305 on Madison Street between Marcy and Tompkins, down the block from the original Boys and Girls High School, which is now off of Fulton Street. Back then, though, it was called "Boys High," and it was an "all boys" school. We had since moved from the area, but you know how you always go back to visit your old stomping grounds? Well, maybe you don't (those not in the know read "neighborhood" and ask somebody). Brooklyn used to have gangs, not like LA, of course. But still gangs, nevertheless. When I was growing up, Bed Stuy was home to "The Outlaws," "The Tomahawks," and "The JollyStompers." I hope I'm not dating myself.

:-) Years after the meltdown of these gangs in Brooklyn … "crews," "posses," and "massives" crept into existence (at least in East Flatbush). A popular one was "The Deceptacons," named after a cartoon. Many tried to label "The Wolfpack" in with these groups, but I didn't. We never started nothing, but we damn sure finished it.

I was close to entering my second decade when the "Outlaws," "Tomahawks," and the "JollyStompers" were around (please don't quote me on it, though). I didn't know nothing about territories and boundaries or nothing like that. Hey, I was little. It seemed that where I lived was considered "Outlaw" turf. I had an older cousin named Cisco who lived in Marcy Projects and was running with the "JollyStompers." The "Outlaws" found out we were related after one of them robbed me in the church bathroom. That's right, the church bathroom … for a quarter. Pulled out a switchblade, and I experienced real fear for the first time. I did not like the feeling, and I pull that from the memory banks every once in a while, when I need to. My cousin noticed I was in the bathroom a little too long and came to see what was keeping me. He walked in on the "Outlaw" holding the knife and me shaking. Cisco peeped the situation immediately, took the knife from the "Outlaw" and stabbed him.

Subsequently, my cousin got arrested because the "Outlaw" said that Cisco tried to rob *him*, and the stupid ass cops believed him, too! I had to testify at his trial as to what happened.

My cousin got off, but that wasn't good enough for him. He had missed out on the war going on between the two gangs, plus he wanted revenge against the "Outlaw" that had him in jail all the time leading up to the trial. Cisco died in a "rumble" in the schoolyard of P.S. 305. The way I heard it on the street was that he had stabbed the same "Outlaw" again that he was after, but in the process, he had gotten himself stabbed. My parents felt that things were getting too wild around there, so we moved. I didn't find out the real reason that we moved until years later. Word on the street, which got back to my parents, was that the "Outlaws" were after me for my testimony against their gang member and the stabbing of that member (even though I had nothing to do with his stabbing).

Fast forward some years, and the gangs had deteriorated. I had begun hanging out in the park in my new neighborhood, and started consorting with folks my mama wouldn't have wanted me to be with. Mind you, I wasn't participating in their dirt, but I wasn't leaving the scene either. I would also travel back to my old neighborhood (no one knew that either), to hang with Donovan. Donovan and I went to 305 together until I moved. Now, *he* was the man in the neighborhood.

Donovan was short, but very stocky, and dark skinned. The whites of his eyes were yellow, perhaps from all the weed he smoked, I don't know. Or maybe it was the reflection of all the gold teeth he had in his mouth. Anyway, Donovan and I would meet at the park benches of 305, sometimes with some of his boys, sometimes with a couple of mine, or both. One day I was there with one of my boys who had met this girl at the park the last time we trooped over. Donovan was there with his peeps, puffing. Everyone was getting open on this new thing of smoking the weed in a cigar wrapper. What's commonly known today as a "blunt." I experimented once or twice growing up, but it never did anything for me. Never got high, so I couldn't see what the big deal was. Some of you might be sayin' that I must have never had the good stuff. Trust me when I say that I did. Wherever the best stuff was being grown and imported, I had access to it (and unlike the President... I did inhale). :-/ Donovan and his family were experts. But that's neither here nor there.

I will say this, though. I used to guzzle some 40's. Old English 800. Had some recently, for old time's sake … ya know … nostalgia … I can't believe I used to drink that *gasoline!* The taste for it now is definitely not there. Like Chuck D, from Public Enemy, used to say … "Poison for the Ghetto." Hopefully the light bulb will go off in your head as it did for me when it comes to the malt liquor. As a friend of mine so aptly put it, "You don't see no white people drinking that shit! … They drinking Budweiser n' shit!" Think about *that* …

Anyway, we were holding court in the schoolyard with those that were drinking, drinking, and those that were smoking, smoking. Donovan passed me a nickel bag and a cigar. I split the cigar open (fingernail, no razor), emptied the tobacco, and replaced the contents with the nickel bag. Basically, I skilled a Philly. My wrap game was tight back then. :-/ Some crows cawed above us in the trees. I think it was three? They had just returned from killing and feasting on a couple of rats. We saw it happen. Their hunt game was something to watch. They'd caw sometimes to see if they could scare some rats out of hiding places. Other times, they'd appear out of no where and pick them off. Their hide and seek game was on point. Donovan used to always wax poetic about the majesty of crows. On and on, how smart they were, how they remembered faces, they did this, how they did that. How *he* was just like them, how *they* were just like him. He believed crows were magical, able to fly through various realms, magical, mystical and spiritual. In fact, one time, Donovan shot this dude because he thought the guy was clowning him when the dude asked him if he believed in unicorns too! Now that I think about it, crows seemed to follow him around, at least it seemed that way to me. One crow, two crows, sometimes three or more. But then again, when Donovan wasn't around crows seemed to be around me too, away from my house, whenever I noticed them.

I used to think this was why I dreamt about them. Cause I saw them a lot when I was younger? The reason they were waking me up every morning, now? They remembered me from back then. Don't blame me, blame Donovan! How long do crows live for? Are you confused enough, yet?

The caws continued above us. This guy walks by and is looking at me. He did look familiar, but I couldn't place him. Automatically, when somebody looks at you in Brooklyn rather boldly with they head cocked to the side, you take notice. But when somebody walks by you and then returns and walks by you again, antennas go up immediately if you've got any street smarts whatsoever. We were seated on top of the benches, our feet where our butts should have been. The guy stopped in front of us, interrupting our good time with his mere presence. Everyone stopped and looked at him like he was buggin'.

"Don't I know you?" he offered, nodding his head upward in my direction.

"Me? I don't think so, ma' man."

"Yeah, I know you … I *know* you," he went on.

Donovan, who is not the most patient guy, sucked his teeth real hard and sneered at dude.

"G'wan wit dat foolishness, ras'claat. Ya knowum star, whappenin' 'ere?"

It all happened at the same time. It clicked, and I realized who it was just as he pulled out the gun. It was the "Outlaw" who I had testified against. Here it is, the first time a gun is waved in my face (the first of a few times, I might add), and I'm as calm as Drew Barrymore taking off her shirt. I guess I didn't have time to be afraid. I remembered the last time I felt fear (at the same guy's hands, no less), and call me stupid, I wasn't going through that again. The bench cleared, but I didn't move. And to his credit (not that I would have blamed him if he had jetted), neither did Profit (the guy that came with me), nor Donovan, for that matter. The simple fact that we didn't run must have weighed on the guy's mind, but when I started talking to Profit, ignoring the "Outlaw," like he wasn't even there … Money started buggin' …

"Yo, Prof?"

I think I startled Profit, because he looked at me funny. But I think that seeing me calm in a sense reassured him. Of what? … I don't know. But he went with it and answered me.

"Yeah, Que … what's up, yo?"

I looked around, started to speak, and then took a deep breath and a long pause. I looked at Donovan. I looked at Profit, and finally, I looked straight into the barrel of the gun the "Outlaw" was holding (Warning! … Do not try this at home). I rubbed underneath my chin and chuckled.

"You trippin' … What the fuck is so funny!?!" the "Outlaw" snapped as he moved closer.

I purposely ignored him and looked at Profit. Call me crazy, but I figured if this was my time, I was going out on my terms. I know, I know … big words now, huh? But anybody that was there that day can tell you how calm I was … almost like I didn't really care … Almost.

"When an *E.F.* Hummer speaks … people listen!"

That line made me a ghetto superstar, but I ain't proud of it. True, it was a takeoff of that E.F. Hutton commercial, but it ID'd my area, plus it let heads know that we didn't play that up in East Flatbush (if you haven't figured it out yet, a gun was called a "Hummer" up in my area).

"What!?!" the "Outlaw" growled.

What happened next was straight out of a James Bond movie. I sprung from the bench and landed to the side of him. I grabbed his wrist, hitting a pressure point, so he'd release the gun. Then I took the gun from him and flipped him on his back, with the gun pointed at his head (thank God for Mama, and her insistence on those Karate lessons). :-)

"I said … *When an East Flatbush Hummer speaks, people listen!*"

With that, I fired the gun.

The blue flash exploded as the bullet skidded off the pavement. The "Outlaw" felt for his head, and realized that it was still intact. I guess he thought the sweat that started pouring down his face was actually blood.

"See what I mean? ... I got your undivided attention, don't I?"

I was calm up until that point. Now I looked at him and kicked him in the head. Profit got up and joined me, followed by Donovan. Everybody that had initially ran came out of hiding and helped in whipping that ass. After getting in my fill of licks, I gave the gun to Donovan. I didn't want it.

I turned my back and walked a few yards away to take a deep breath as they continued to whip that ass. Then I heard the shot ... followed by another one. Someone was running toward us, spitting bullets. We high tailed it outta there with Donovan returning fire. Profit followed me, and we made it to Donovan's house. Donovan eventually caught up. The rest of his crew had gone wherever. We sat upstairs with Donovan amped from firing all those bullets. Profit and Donovan re-lived my exploits. I really didn't find anything praiseworthy about the whole situation, but they weren't trying to hear that. After my first few words, I just shut up and let them trip. Well, with Donovan and his boys talking in Bed Stuy and Profit speaking all over the E.F., I suddenly had a name for myself that I didn't really want. But it's been helpful at times since.

Profit hit me with the news first, but I didn't believe him. After I thought about it though, I should have actually known already … after hearing the crows, I mean. But hindsight is 20-20, and I didn't know then what I know now about them. The "Outlaw" was dead. Apparently, when Donovan fired back at the guy shooting at us, Donovan shot the "Outlaw." To hear Donovan tell it later, he meant to do it. And I believed him too. Not even a hint of remorse (talk about ice water in the veins …). Of course, all that bravado would eventually catch up to him …

A guard pushed through the hospital swing doors, stood there a second, and then motioned for Marlon to proceed through. Yep … definitely looked like stitches. Marlon had gotten a bit pummeled. :-/

Mrs. Parker and K.P. had already claimed dibbs on Marlon, but K.P. got first crack as mom gave way to daughter in this instance. The guard thought about running interference, but I guess that look from K.P. towards him as she approached made him think better of it!

Marlon tried to hug K.P. Now the old K.P. might have melted at this gesture, but A.B.H. K.P.

(After Being Hit) wasn't having it. She pushed his arms away and demanded to know what he was doing there. Marlon tried to explain that he had heard about Darren, and was concerned about him and K.P. I guess we all thought it, but K.P. said it. K.P. told Marlon that he was full of it because he never liked Darren in the first place. Marlon tried to add that he was concerned because it involved the family, and that he loved her. K.P. put her hand up to cut him off … you know, stop sign! She told him that he wasn't welcome here because she still hadn't forgotten what had happened, and that if he needed a reminder, think about Ken Griffey, Jr., or what just happened to him.

He glanced over at Jinx and me. Later, Jinx and I both said that we hoped he would look at us wrong, roll his eyes, look cross at us, anything … to give us the excuse we wanted to jump on that ass again. But he didn't.

Mrs. Parker came over and asked Marlon what was going on. Marlon looked at K.P., K.P. looked at Marlon, Marlon looked at Mrs. Parker, Mrs. Parker looked at Marlon, Mrs. Parker looked at K.P., K.P. looked at Marlon … and we all looked at them. :-/ Marlon figured that he better not say anything to Mrs. Parker about what had happened with K.P.

He did speak to her and tell her that he hoped her son was all right, and that he hoped that he would get the chance to explain, but now was not the time nor place for it. With that, he excused himself. He tried to touch K.P. on the cheek, but she turned her head. Marlon turned, walked out of the hospital, and wasn't seen again.

Darren died at 2:46 a.m., Wednesday morning. He never regained consciousness. The bullet wound in his chest caused his left lung to collapse. Apparently, the shock brought on cardiac arrest and Darren succumbed.

Damn! I couldn't believe I was going through this again! The Parker women were all alone now! The sight of all three of them huddled together, holding each other, tears flowing, was enough to make a grown man cry. I turned my back to face the window (draw your own conclusions).

I've lived a semi-charmed kind of life. Looking at Darren lying in that casket … that could've been me on a couple of occasions. Hell, some may say it should've been me. The ride back from the gravesite was quiet as you would imagine. Everyone was immersed in their own thoughts. I started thinking about my near-death experiences. I guess death does that to you. Of course, sometimes you don't get a chance to reflect. So I'm lucky, I guess. Of course I'm lucky. Most of us tend to take life for granted until something hits too close to home. I've been shot, shot at, stabbed, clubbed and even poisoned … yeah, you read that right … poisoned! The moral of this little anecdote? Take time to reflect on the little things. Okay … sermon over.

I volunteered to spend the night over at the Parker household. It wasn't talked about … but there was some concern for their safety. It was actually my dad's idea to stay, although I had thought about it. Mrs. Parker finally relented, her rationale being the sooner they all got used to the idea that there would be no man in the house, the better. I don't wish that kind of pain on anyone!

I tried to sleep, but I'm a night owl, and insomnia pervades my soul. Had said good night to the women of the house hours ago, so I laid up on the sofa flicking through TV channels. I could have pulled out the sofa bed, but I just didn't feel like it. They all slept in Mrs. Parker's room that night, and I had been invited to join them, but I declined. I tried to lighten the moment by telling them that I wouldn't get any sleep lying in a king sized bed with three beautiful women … might not be responsible for my actions. Mrs. Parker, of all people, suggested that I might enjoy myself. This drew incredulous sideway glances from K.P. and Jinx, and an angelic smirk from Mrs. Parker. For a moment, laughter eased the pain of the day as I was being escorted (now reluctantly), out of the room by K.P. and Jinx … even though I offered to sleep on the floor. :-)

I heard some rustling upstairs, and I turned to look at the stairway. Coming down the stairs was Mrs. Parker. But it was Mrs. Parker as I had never seen her before. She had her hair down, she was barefoot, and she had on a peach camisole nightie. And I'm sorry … I know that this sequence we're in calls for tact, but I gotta say this … Mrs. Parker is slammin'! Call me "typical male," whatever! I always knew that Mrs. Parker had a figure, but seeing her so … so free … fellas, let's just say that you had to be there! And ladies, you're not gonna like this, but I figure that I'm in the dog house right now anyway, for lack of compassion, so I might as well go the distance.

Mrs. Parker noticed me about halfway down the stairs, and looked genuinely surprised when she gasped. She quickly covered up, and retreated back upstairs, returning with a robe. Now I believe that she *was* surprised to see me. She probably forgot that I was even down there, and with everything that happened that day, I wouldn't blame her. But that little egotistical voice that I try to suppress whispered that she knew I was down there. I know … I'm demented. There's no rhyme or reason for the male thought process, except to say that we can turn any thought into a sexual deviation. And everyone wants us, even if it's just a figment of our imaginations. Fellas, I just took one for the cause. Sorry ladies, had to go there! Just remember this though, others think it … I say it. So if I'm penalized for that, so be it. Hey, I never said I was perfect. I just understand the grand scheme a little better than the next man. :-/

"I'm sorry, Gregory. Didn't mean to give you a peep show." She turned a small light onto its lowest setting and looked at me … "Are you blushing?"

Totally taken aback … I'm like … abada, abada … tongue tied … almost embarrassed. I didn't know what to say. What? … You put Pam Grier to shame?

"Ah … no need to apologize … It's your house …"

She smiled as if I was tonic for her ego.

"No, I couldn't sleep, so I decided to make myself some hot chocolate. I forgot that you were down here."

"I ain't mad at ya … It's not like I'm supposed to be down here."

"It's not like I'm supposed to be walking around like this either," she chuckled. "But since you didn't turn and run for the hills … I guess that's a good thing … if you even saw anything. Did you see anything that you liked, Gregory? … Gregory?"

Mrs. Parker knew she was making me a little uncomfortable, and she was enjoying it … at my expense, even! She was flirting with me, and I'll be damned if it didn't make her sexier!!! Aaggghhhh! God rest Mr. Parker's soul … I thought about it … only for a split second, but I did. C'mon … can you blame me? That egotistical voice was sayin', "Yo, son? You could have a triple play … keep it all in the family, dun … Que, you could win, 'cause you bigger than Harold Washington!" (Apologies to Eddie Murphy). "Or Marion Berry!" "Or Bill Clinton!" :-/

And of course the voice of rationale was like, "This is exactly why Oprah Winfrey has the ratings that she does! Then you will turn around and say that she hath playa hateth against thee!"

The egotistical voice countered, "Oprah's last year. It's all about Jerry Springer, son! He averages a fight a day! Just think, all three could be fightin' over you, son! Jerry's ratings would go through the roof, and he'd be eternally grateful to *you!*"

The voice of rationale played trump, "Of course, I don't have to remind thee of a certain young lady's name ..."

Okay, I came crashing back to earth, but a brother can fantasize, can't he? It's crazy what goes on in my head, ain't it?

"Gregory? ..."

"Yes, Mrs. Parker?"

"What were you thinking about?"

I looked down at the floor trying to hide a smirk.

"Nothing, Mrs. Parker."

"*Gregory?*"

"Mrs. Parker ... I'm sayin' ... I was just ... um ... ah ... If your daughters look like you do now when they get older ... they're gonna be lucky."

Thank God for "smooth." Like I was really gonna tell her, "I was thinking how it would be to "hit that," Mrs. Parker."

She looked at me as if to say ... "Okay, we'll play it your way, but we both know that's not what you were really thinking."

"You're too kind, Gregory. What a wonderful thing to say about me." She laughed and continued,

"I'm sorry. I'm being bad … flirting with you like this. I forgot how much fun flirting can be …"

"And how torturous … " I muttered under my breath.

"Thank you. I needed that," she continued, oblivious to my muttering. "It reminded me of times when I flirted with Eugene, and how uncomfortable it made him, sometimes."

"I'm sorry. That's the last thing I'm trying to do, Mrs. Parker, make you think about Mr. Parker …"

"No, no … I need this therapy. Your eyes reminded me of his. They speak without saying a word. He used to try and hide it, but I could feel his eyes undressing me. His eyes would caress me, and it was such an incredible feeling. Your eyes had that same look and feel, and it was funny seeing you try and hide it. It's nice to know that I still have that 'rock your world' appeal."

Well, I'll be damned again! You know what I'm thinking, right? If you don't, I suggest you go back and just re-read from the beginning until you figure it out. Damn … I couldn't even look in Mrs. Parker's direction.

"I've noticed how Jinx always flirts with you, and K.P. has told me what you've said about me. I just figured I would have a little fun, too."

"Yeah, but you didn't play fair ... you had knowledge that I didn't know you had ... you had an unfair advantage." (Didn't I sound just like a kid?)

"Women's prerogative, Gregory. We only let you know what we want you to know. Remember that. Although love makes us reveal things sometimes that we don't even realize we're revealing until the words are out of our mouths. Eugene did that to me. Ah, well ... I have a taste for hot chocolate, would *you* like some?"

"I see where Jinx gets it from, that subtle devious innocence."

"Both of my girls have it, one just lets you see it more than the other ... Think about *that!*"

"Are you trying to tell me something, Mrs. Parker?"

"Nothing that you don't already know, Gregory. Let me get that hot chocolate started."

She returned with her hot chocolate and sat down next to me. I sat up and pulled the blanket I had covering me just below the waist. Part of it was because I had on boxers underneath, and the other part was I didn't want Floyd pulling off any surprises ... ya know ... getting nosy an' tings. I got self-control, but we weren't taking any chances.

"Gregory, can I ask you a question? You may not want to answer it, but I'd really like to know."

The loins began tingling … Mind over matter, mind over matter.

"Sure."

"What happened with Katrina and Marlon?"

"Aw, Mrs. Parker," I said, a little deflated (no pun intended). :-/ " … I'd like to tell you … but … but it's not my story to tell …"

"Gregory, you understand that whatever we talk about tonight or anytime for that matter, stays between you and I?"

"I do … but it's still not my story to tell. I'm sure that when the time is right, you'll know about it."

"But I'm her mother and I only have her best interest at heart." "I understand that too … but I'd be betraying a confidence. Let me just say this, though. You would have been proud of her."

"Oh?"

"Oh, yeah."

"I guess that's somewhat reassuring …"

We sat in silence for a few minutes. Then, just as suddenly as silence had engulfed us, it was broken by Mrs. Parker, who began reminiscing about Mr. Parker. The reminiscing soon took on a comparison between Mr. Parker and Snow.

"Luther was a lot like Eugene when Eugene was growing up."

"Naw, Mr. Parker?"

"Oh yes! Ask your mother to tell you about Mr. Parker. Tell her I said it's okay. :-) Yes Gregory, my Eugene was a terror. Worse than Luther. Pat tried to keep him away from me for a long time, but he wore her down.

"My mother and Mr. Parker didn't get along?"

"No, it wasn't that. She just saw Eugene as nothing but trouble for me. But like I said, he wore her down. Not to mention that she turned out to be totally wrong about him. Eugene ran the neighborhood, and soon after we started going out, Pat and I were afforded celebrity … well, I should say notoriety status. To make a long story short, let's just say that I helped shape Mr. Parker into the loving husband with three beautiful children."

Go figure! I would have never pictured Mr. Parker to be a hoodlum. That's like night and day from the man that I knew. But I guess some things begin to make sense now. I can understand now why Mr. Parker was so open minded with Snow and Jinx. Mrs. Parker went on to say how Mr. Parker flipped after Jinx brought Snow home and they both eventually found out what Snow was into.

She reminded Mr. Parker that he used to be the same way, and look how he turned out. He allowed Jinx and Snow to exist because he didn't want Jinx seeing Snow behind their backs, but he constantly reminded Mrs. Parker about a haunting fear. Mr. Parker never trusted Snow to be like he was in the long run. Was that the uniqueness of individuality or straight up father's intuition? Interesting.

I asked Mrs. Parker what she thought Mr. Parker meant by that. She answered without hesitation that Mr. Parker always predicted Snow's death.

"I'm worried about Jinx, Gregory. The anniversary of Luther's death is coming around soon. With that, and her brother's murder …"

"Jinx is tough, Mrs. Parker. She can get through it."

"Gregory, I think I have talked myself sleepy, along with this hot chocolate. I'm going to go back to bed now. Will you be okay?"

"Yes, ma'am, I'll be fine … Mrs. Parker?"

"Yes."

"I know it may be hard, but I pray you have pleasant dreams."

"Thank you for caring enough to say that, Gregory. I pray that I do too … Goodnight."

Mrs. Parker retreated upstairs, leaving me to think about the things that had been said. I wondered about Jinx also. I made a mental note to call Profit, and even though it had been a long time since the last time we spoke, our doors were always open to each other. And if my uneasy feelings were any indication, I'd be cashing in on another favor owed to me real soon. If there were any pluses that came with who and what I used to be, it would be that I'm owed a lot of favors from different individuals. Most shady, all very savvy. I have rarely cashed in, but it's just good to know that they're there on reserve.

I turned onto my back with my hands behind my head and looked up at the ceiling. One of those infomercials was selling something touted as the best ever. I began to think about the third anniversary of Luther Little's death. I felt a chill, not because I was cold, though. The chill is normal around this time of year, especially when I replay the circumstances surrounding Snow's death …

Jinx had spent the night at my place. She does that when she needs to clear her head. More times than not, it's usually after a fight with Snow. I almost didn't let her stay because tonight was the night it was all supposed to go down, but I didn't want to arouse any suspicions, so I just told her I had to go out.

"You've got free reign of the place until I get back, Jinx. No riff raff up in this piece, either."

"Que… I'll be waiting for you under the covers."

"Maybe your sister is right after all these years … I should just do you and get it over with!"

"I don't know why you keep fronting like you got will power or something. You know you want this!"

"Kindly refrain from quoting my girl, thank you."

"Please! Janet's stuff cannot be as good as this! Besides, I'm here … where *she* at?"

"See … why you gotta go there, Jinx? But that's good though. That's why I can turn yo' ass down, with statements like that."

"You only hurting yourself."

"Oh … Agony! … Aaa … go … ny!"

Suddenly, Jinx's mood changed dramatically.

"Que?"

"Yeah?"

"Do you really have to go out tonight? … All jokes aside." I looked at her and her face read, "All jokes aside."

"Wha … Why are you asking me that? Where'd that come from?"

"I got a bad feeling. I don't know what it is, but you've been on my mind. I wish you wouldn't go out tonight."

Ah damn, this was great. Just what I needed to hear. The last time this happened, I got shot! Did I heed the warnings? Noooooooooo! My mother and my sisters warned me about going out on one particular night. They said that *they* had a bad feeling. Would you have listened? I didn't think so. Oh yeah, sure, one or two of you might have, as *you* say, but I have my doubts. Well, if that wasn't enough for my ass, Casino and I had stopped by these girls' house that same night whom we had recently met. They asked us what we had planned for the night, and we told them that we were going to "Love Peoples," this reggae spot near Prospect Park. Brooklyn heads know the spot. Every week somebody was getting shot up there. Huh? What was that? Shut up, man! *Of course I should have known better than to go*, but I was younger, and when you're young, you think you're invincible. You never think that it's gonna happen to you, especially since I was "Street Wise Willie." Psst … *anyway*.

Well, the girls reiterated what my mom and my sisters had felt (mind you, Mom and my sisters didn't know we were going to this club), and they wanted us to stay with them. We laughed. Hint-and-a-half for that ass Number Three: We had gone to the club a number of times before, and I had never, ever gotten a parking spot directly in front of the club. That night I did. We had plans of pumping my sound system outside after the club closed to attract the ladies (fellas, you know … and more than a few of you ladies know, too). We entered the vestibule and promptly got searched with those hand-held metal detectors (I always hated that). Then, on top of that, the hand frisk body search was administered by some guy who took so-called authority a little too serious.

Inside, the music was pumping (rub a dub stylee), and the night seemed full of possibilities. Honeys was acting right, showing brothers some love … not to mention a whole lotta "back." :-/ Went over to the bar later, after a couple of dances, and that's when the atmosphere started to change. This guy was at the bar trying to talk to this girl. But she was trying not to hear it. She told him she wasn't interested and wanted to be left alone. The guy was either too drunk to care or his ego wouldn't allow him to be brushed off. He persisted in his conversation. Finally, she yelled at him to get away from her with a few expletives thrown in for emphasis and good measure.

Then he made that mistake. You know which one, right? Yep, you got it! He called her a "bitch." She picked up her drink and threw it into his face. Technical Merit and Presentation definitely warranted a 9.5, but she lost points because two people on the side caught the remnants of her drink. :-/ The guy, stunned for a second, answered by smacking her in the face. She left the bar and so did he.

But she returned with her boyfriend, who was heated, no doubt. The eyes had been adjusting to the dimly lit area, but there was no mistaking the fact that the boyfriend reached toward his waistline and produced a black 9 millimeter Glock handgun.

He had a crazed look in his eyes as he yelled clearly through the blaring music,

"Blood Fiah! Mi fillup dat Bloodclaat da hit up m'gyal she!"

He let two fly off into the ceiling. Why did I turn around in the dark and see, like a revelation, everybody in the club pull out a gun!?! Was I the only one who went through the search at the door!?!

And why did the kid standing next to me make like a magician and suddenly make a sawed off shotgun appear out of nowhere, when he wasn't even wearing a coat!?!

The music stopped, the lights went out, and the screaming started. Suddenly … *clap, clap* … the sounds of gunfire erupted in the club. My first instinct was to stay low, give my eyes a chance to adjust to the pitch darkness. I had made my way to the nearest corner when I saw the first gun pulled. The club had one exit, the one we entered, and a downstairs everyone was trying to reach.

Meanwhile, blue flashes were showing themselves like a laser exhibit, never in the same place twice. My eyes adjusted to the dark, and I wished that they hadn't. I saw two people get shot point blank, then a girl running in my direction caught a bullet and fell down in front of me. I realized that the gunfire was making its way over to where I was crouched. The stairway was jammed with people falling over each other and down the stairs. It got worse when one gunman ran in that direction, firing at someone with the other person returning the fire. The D.J. booth was locked shut with people trying to climb up into it and others banging on the enclosure below. I knew that if I stayed in my spot any longer,

I was surely gonna get shot. I looked at the doorway and saw an opening. I made a mad dash toward the entrance. I heard gunfire hit the wall behind me as I realized that people were just shooting at whatever happened to move! I made it to the door, but they were trying to close it shut. I yelled at them that I had to get out and summoned all of my strength to bust open the door from their grasp. I busted through the door and ran outside directly into crossfire! It seemed that there was a gun fight going on outside of the club as well and the doors were being shut to keep it out there. I stumbled onto the scene just as they were closing the doors.

I ran into the crossfire and started to turn my head to look back at the club doors being shut closed, and suddenly I was blinded by a blue flash. The next thing I knew I was on the ground, looking up at two guys firing at each other. One suddenly pointed his gun at me and I scrambled to dive under a Jeep Cherokee. The bullets echoed off the pavement, and I kid you not, I swear I dove under that car and out the other side in one motion! I came out from under the other side of that car and hightailed it outta there, running at least two blocks before I turned to look back! I stayed away until I heard sirens, and it was only then that I went back to the club. That scene was not pretty. Paramedics were tending to people on the sidewalk and the street, other paramedics were running in and out of the club. Casino and two girls were standing to the left of the entrance with their backs turned to me. I approached them and asked Casino where he had been.

"Oh my God! Look at you, Que!" a girl we called Trini exclaimed.

I mean, damn! I admit, I probably didn't look my best at the moment, considering what I had just been through, but I'm sayin' …

"Yeah, I'll probably have to get rid of this Gucci outfit. It's got a few holes that weren't there before, and the suede shoes … I know, scuff marks aren't in …"

"That's not funny, Que. Stop joking. You're bleeding really bad!" the other girl, Iris, said.

"Bleeding? … Who? … Me? … Where?"

"Your face, Que! You don't feel it? Above your nose, right between your eyes?" Iris said.

I reached up and wiped what I had thought was sweat pouring down my face. When I looked at my hand, it was red. Now that the brain had identified the hurt, it began to hurt really bad!

"Look at your arm, Que. It's bleeding too!" Trini chimed in.

There was two holes in the left shoulder and arm of my Gucci suit that wasn't a result of a tear. Inside the holes, if you looked closely, you could see red … the color of blood. But because my outfit was forest green, it didn't register red. It just looked wet, like I had been sweating a whole lot. That's how the front looked too. And the shoulder and arm began to hurt as well.

"Que, we got to get you to the hospital. Where are your car keys?" Iris asked.

Casino and I looked at each other as we both remembered the car at the same time. I turned around first, and we both gasped.

"Oh my God!" somebody muttered.

I had fainted! (Go figure!)

Casino is my road dog, and I always told him that if something ever happened to me, do not call my house. Call K.P. first and stay calm! Well, Casino got credit for calling K.P., but everything after that was downhill. He called K.P., but he was anything from calm. He yelled into the phone that I had gotten shot, and the ambulance was taking me to Caledonia Hospital. I know. He explained later that when I fainted suddenly, he didn't know what to make out of it. I couldn't argue with that. Well, K.P. hung up the phone and ran to her mother's room and told Mrs. Parker. Mrs. Parker knew that my mom couldn't hear the news first, because she would have a heart attack on the spot. When she called, she prayed that my father would pick up. He did. My father, for all who know him, is a cool cat. His demeanor is definitely laid back, but he was half asleep when Mrs. Parker called. Mrs. Parker didn't help matters by telling my dad that he needed to remain calm. He immediately sat up in the bed, asking her what was wrong. My mother subsequently bombarded my father with questions, and that's all she wrote. Mom started screaming, and it must have taken a half-hour for him to calm her down (I'm exaggerating). :-/

When I awoke, I was in a hospital bed, and my room was jam-packed. When the first words out of my mouth were "Where's the party and why wasn't I invited?" everyone collectively breathed a sigh of relief. My mother kissed my bandaged forehead and hugged me. I jumped in pain because of my arm. Of course, she apologized. It really was packed up in there with Mom, Dad, Ronnie, Ni Ni, Keith, Mrs. Parker, Mr. Parker ... who left work, K.P., Jinx, Snow, Darren, Casino, the two girls, Trini and Iris, Winnie, Dexter St. Jock, Temple, and some other heads that were at the club who knew me. Living testimony that the grapevine does work. And with Steven calling every five minutes from med school …

Why did the doctor make his way into the room and announce to the whole world that I was a lucky individual!?! My unconsciousness was a result of losing a lot of blood after being shot in the shoulder, arm and grazed in the forehead, and if I had turned my head a millimeter more to the right, I might not be here. Of course this was just great. My mother took that well. She started bawling. Even my father, who doesn't show any emotion in public, had a concerned look on his face as the doctor's words hit home.

Here's a little thing that I'll leave you with. I asked about my car, which incidentally had gotten shot up worse than me, and my father said,

"Don't worry about the car … the main thing is that *you're* okay."

On the surface, this may not appear to be much. But I've remembered it ever since, because while I know in my heart my Dad loves me, it was nice to actually hear the words of concern. Especially since I was a young man then (still am!) :-/ … and especially since most men are taught to downplay their emotions… which I think is a fault that hinders men later in life.

Ummph … got caught up with a story within a story. Sorry about that. I was talking about Snow, right? … And how his death came about? Well hey, it all gels anyway, so … Huh? … What did you say? You know something!?! … You have the option of putting this book down, you know that, right? And if you don't voluntarily do it, I may have to help you out real soon. So keep those attempts at snide ass remarks to your damned self. Why they always wanna test a brother? … Like I can't handle mine … Keep thinking I won't have a flashback and forget what year this is! I'm sayin' … If you consider it a threat … then so be it, son! I got hands! Do you like Mark Breland used to … Step up! No matter where this book goes, the roads lead back to me anyway, so you can kiss my ass! (_x_) All others, put an "H" on your chest and handle it! Write your own book, damn playa hater! As I was sayin' …

Jinx didn't want me to go out because she had this bad feeling. The phone rang and I answered it. The strangest thing happened. The voice on the other end was familiar, very familiar … It sent a shiver through me.

"Que? … Que? … It's a lie … Don't believe— … oh! I gotta go!" (Click)

It was a female voice that triggered something within me, but I couldn't place the voice in the two seconds of conversation that took place. I mentioned it to Jinx as an aside. The phone rang again. It was Snow confirming our meeting place. He finally figured out that I had company and couldn't really talk, so he did all of the talking. This plan had been in the works for a few months now, and its materialization was finally being realized. We knew that this "Chico Caliente" was tied to Mr. Parker's death, and Snow had finally gotten a location where he was known to frequent. One of Snow's snitches was gonna enter and get a covert photo of him and pass it to us. Snow called to tell me that there was a change of plans. He had the photo of "Chico Caliente," and we were gonna take him that night. Snow wanted me to meet him near the Lighthouse restaurant down near the water front along the Brooklyn Bridge because that's where "Chico Caliente" was at that precise moment. I suggested that we regroup and plan it better. He stressed that there may not be a better time than tonight. I reluctantly agreed to meet him near this warehouse by the restaurant.

I gathered my coat and looked at Jinx lying snug in my bed with some of my sweats on. She looked back at me uneasily, like she wanted to say something. I knew what it was and she knew that I wasn't going to listen. The phone rang again as I was leaving. I called out to Jinx to answer it and take a message or let the machine pick up. I knew she would let the machine pick up, as she always does, because as she put it, she didn't want to talk to any of the hoochies that called my crib. :-/

I got into my car and immediately realized that I forgot my backup piece. Yeah, I'm licensed to kill, but my backup isn't. You'll either figure it out or hope that I explain it later. I started to go back for it, but changed my mind. During the drive downtown, I didn't think about much … didn't want to. Maybe you can identify. During my spastic state (and I don't recommend this … you're supposed to have your mind on driving), I ran a red light. I cursed as I saw the flashing lights in the rearview. Just what I needed, a ticket. I pulled over and began the "Black man's prep," that ritual that every black father has passed down to his sons. For starters, I put the car in park, rolled down the window, and turned the engine off. I got my license and registration out of my wallet and put it on the dashboard. Silence is the rule until spoken to. I looked in my rear view mirror to see the cops I'd be dealing with. This is why no one knows how it is to be a black man (except a black man). We have to think about crap like that. White cops want to play Rambo and black cops want to play, "I'm better than you."

It actually pisses me off that I have to make a conscious effort to make sure my hands are on my own steering wheel so these white cops don't plug me on the spot. Remember this is what we go through daily. My hands are on the steering wheel, but the cops still come out, guns drawn. What's up with that? They come up cautiously on the side. I guess the big ol' stickers on my car, in plain view of their bright night light, stating where I went to undergraduate and graduate school, are a prop to fool people! I have a cop friend who defends these practices all the time. Yeah, yeah, it may be rough being a cop, and there are definitely some bad apples among us, but why is every black man guilty of something before he's innocent? I don't expect a lot of you to understand that, but there are a few that will. If you've ever had a gun pulled on you, you know it's not such a great feeling, but when you know two white cops are looking for a reason, it makes you very cautious. Let me go on record to say it may not be all white cops and it may not be all black cops, but it's enough to give everybody a bad name.

As I was typing that, I sort of had a revelation … Hmmph … that may be exactly how they feel too. Racism, perhaps? But fuck that, it's not happening to them, it's happening to me! Is that prejudice?

One tells me to put my hands outside of the door and open it slowly, while the other is shining a flashlight into the passenger side window and pointing his gun. This is alarming because I have shown no credible threat to these officers, nor have I been told why I am being ordered out of my vehicle with guns drawn on me. Another thing I hate is that "Toby" mentality, the subservient way we have to speak in a non-threatening tone of voice, and I've learned not to question immediately (i.e. "What did I do?" … "What's the problem, officer?").

I got out of the car and the officer nearest me smirked with his gun pointed at me.

"Don't-push-me-'cause-I'm-close-to-the-edge … *It's like a jungle sometimes, uh huh huh, huh huh."*

Personally, I don't think this shit is funny and I don't appreciate y'all laughing, either! I don't care if it *is* behind closed doors. I guess today they'd probably be sayin', "You like Busta Rhymes? … *Put your hands where my eyes could see!*"

He didn't even know if I liked rap, and he could have at least got the lyrics right! You feeling me?

Racist futhermucker! He followed up with, "Turn around and put your hands on the hood of that fucking car, now!"

Momentary confusion caused me to delay a split second too long as he rammed me into the side of the car and began frisking me. Meanwhile, the other is inside my car looking through shit! Mad civil rights violations, and they don't even know who I am, just my skin color. The officer frisking me feels my .45 and jumps back, yelling, "Gun! Don't move, Nigger! I swear, I'll blow your fucking head off! Put those hands up and turn slowly toward me!"

Meanwhile. the other cop has his gun trained on my head from the passenger side of the car. I attempted to speak for the first time, yelling loudly that I had a permit.

The passenger side cop rushes around and yells at me.

"Shut the fuck up. Just shut the fuck up, Nigger!"

The only thing I can say is that they didn't beat my ass right off the bat, or shoot me, as if that's something positive to say! They took my gun and had me handcuffed on my knees in front of my car door. I guess they felt it wasn't necessary to tell me what cause they had to order me out of my car since they found a gun. They weren't trying to hear what I had to say, so I felt it was time to start name dropping. This is something I really hate to do, but this situation called for it. The cop friend that I mentioned runs the police academy. And when I mentioned his name and the fact that I was sure he didn't teach them the procedures that they were using, they stopped in their tracks. In the dark, I could see red faces. Now that I had their attention, I told them that the Honorable Bruce Knight was my Godfather, and he damn sure was gonna hear all about this!

All of a sudden, I was their best friend …

"No hard feelings, right?"

"Just doing our job."

"Why didn't you tell us that at the beginning?"

Guess I was just supposed to conveniently forget all that "Nigger" stuff, huh?

My gun was promptly returned, and just out of curiosity, I asked them why they had stopped me. Their reply was going to decide what I was going to do. I was told that I looked young, and their suspicions were aroused because of the car I was driving. I got in my car and immediately wrote down the badge numbers that I had memorized, and said to myself as I drove off, "Wrong answer!"

I had been detained for at least a half hour and I started not to even go downtown, but I went, trying to control the rage of emotions that were permeating within. I was sure that the night couldn't have gotten worse. A limo pulled away from what looked like Snow's Jeep just as I drove up to the warehouse where we were supposed to meet. I got out of the car and Snow got out to meet me.

"Damn, where you been!?!" he spat.

"Yo, don't go there! I was pulled over by the cops."

His demeanor instantly changed.

"Oh man … Sorry, I know what that's like."

He wanted to go behind the warehouse where the docks were … and his men. He said he was just getting ready to call everything off. I asked him who was in the limo. He said it wasn't important and proceeded to tell me about "Chico Caliente's" whereabouts. I jumped when two big "cat rats" walked, not scurried, by our feet. We made it behind the warehouse, and just as I asked Snow to show me the picture, a gun was placed to my head.

"What the fu— …"

I didn't need to finish. I knew it was a setup. My gun was taken from me, a-gain, and suddenly the night got worse!

"Don't worry, Que, you gonna get to meet 'Chico Caliente,'" Snow offered.

I couldn't believe that Snow had betrayed me like that. There was two others besides Snow on the docks with him. Snow's cell phone rang. He seemed to be expecting a call. But it wasn't who he thought it was. It was Jinx. *My* gun was cocked to my head and a finger was placed on my lips to be quiet. I had no intention of ending my life that soon so I wasn't about to say nothing. Snow told Jinx that he couldn't talk at the moment, but he'd see her later. The conversation ended with him telling her that he loved her too.

Snow looked at me. For a moment, I thought that he didn't want to be a part of what was going down, that's what it seemed like. The phone rang again, and those thoughts disappeared as he told whoever that I was there, and it was safe to come around.

"Why?" was all I could muster up to say.

"It was either you or Jinx," Snow began. "I gotta take you out to save Jinx's life … and my own. Loyalty thing, I guess."

This motherfucker was so nonchalant with his right now, it really pissed me off. And I really thought about making a play for my gun and just going out in a blaze of glory, but I suppressed "Hood Que" and brought it back to "Intelligent Hoodlum." (Apologies to Tragedy).

"How do you know they're not still gonna kill Jinx?"

This weighed on him for a minute. A boat engine interrupted all thoughts as it came to a stop about fifty yards from the docks. The cell phone rang again, and Snow answered it.

He didn't seem to like the new arrangements … I guess he expected "Chico Caliente" to show up face-to-face. He hung up the cell phone and stepped back. He raised *my* gun and told me that it wasn't personal … just business. I've hated New Jack City ever since!

All of a sudden, we hear Snow's name being called, and he turns to look toward the sound of the voice. Three shots catch Snow in the chest as the boat roars off at the sound of gunfire. Two more take out one of Snow's men as the other stands frozen without a gun. We both stand there long enough to see *Jinx* holding a smoking gun! The guy turns to run and I lunge for my gun, which Snow has dropped, and fire at the guy, taking him out. Snow is shaking on the ground, and Jinx is walking slowly towards us. I can see her sobbing as I run toward her.

She walks past me, kneels down, and cradles Snow in her arms.

Snow is coughing up blood as he looks at her.

"Why? … Why Snow? … Why were you going to kill *Que*?"

"I did it for you, Pudding … I did it for you," he strained. "It was either him or you …"

Jinx sobbed more, then suddenly gained some composure and whispered,

"And it was either Que or you …"

That's the secret that we share.

6

———

BATTLE OF THE SEXES

Shrimp Cocktail, Crab Legs, & Sushi Style

K.P. was supposed to round out the month of sexual connotations this Saturday. Yep, another session of "Off the Hook," already. My, how time flies. :-/

I woke up on the Parker couch, thinking about that. No way K.P. was gonna do it. It has been a rough week. Of course, K.P. is not your typical person. Ah, thought I was gonna say "woman," huh? Mrs. Parker was making breakfast, and I knew what that meant. I waited for the call. Jinx was in the kitchen with her mother, and K.P. was coming down the stairs.

I fired the first missile of the day.

"Just like a bear, the smell of food will interrupt any hibernation!"

"Actually, it was the smell of your feet that broke it for *me*!"

"Oww … you trying to take me out with one shot, huh?"

"Why ain't your ass in the kitchen? … You know the routine! … Maaaaaaa, Que's up!"

"Shut up, Ho' … I was gonna get up."

Jinx, hearing K.P.'s voice, enters the room.

"Yo, dude, it's all there … Get ta steppin' … C'mon, hut, two, three, four!"

"Can I put on my clothes?"

"Here's some shorts."

K.P. threw them at me.

"Oh, y'all got it all figured out, right?"

I got up to put on the shorts. No shame in my game … I mean, it's K.P. and Jinx.

"Nice Pooh boxers, Que," Jinx smirked.

"They're even nicer inside."

Mrs. Parker walked in and I had one leg in the shorts and one leg out. I tried to put the other leg in real quick and pull up the shorts but I lost my balance. Laughter … and more laughter.

"Ha ha ha … oh—it's—soooo—funny! … Yuk yuk … ha ha."

When K.P. and Jinx ... *and* Mrs. Parker had finally finished laughing at my misfortune, I informed them that my feelings were hurt. And I was especially hurt by Mrs. Parker's laughter, because I expected it from Tweedle Dee and Tweedle Dum. Fortunately for me, I was able to fall back onto the couch, instead of the floor.

"Oh Gregory," Mrs. Parker coddled. "I'm so sorry." She kissed me on my cheek.

Hey, I know a good thing when I feel it, so I milked it.

"Another one ..."

I pouted and pointed to the other cheek, and she obliged.

"Another one ..."

I pointed to my forehead, and she laughed and obliged again. I puckered up ...

"Oh hell no!" the girls yelled and jumped on me.

"Can I move in?" I sighed.

The laughter started up again.

After the laughter, the Parker women got down to business.

"Gregory, the kitchen is all yours," Mrs. Parker said.

"Let's go, man ... I'm hungry," K.P. ordered.

"Que, I want three," Jinx barked.

I looked at them with arms crossed bewilderment.

"Y'all got some nerve … laughing at me. Pshh, y'all gonna have to come better than that!"

K.P. walked toward me and grabbed my hand.

"Oh, Que, I am famished. Would you please go into the kitchen and do what only *you* can do?"

"Que, if it wouldn't be too much trouble, I would like three?" Jinx humbly asked.

I looked at Mrs. Parker and nothing.

"Me too?" she asked astonished, pointing to herself.

I looked toward the heavens for emphasis. :-)

"Okay, okay," she laughed. "Oh Gregory … *Oh Great One.*" She lowered her head for a second, and then lifted it. "Honor my kitchen, and grace it with your presence."

K.P. busted out laughing, and I joined her. We use that "Great One" line all of the time, and obviously Mrs. Parker remembered that. That was a good one.

It has become a ritual, ever since the first time I decided to do it. Every time there's breakfast, and *I'm* in the Parker household, or wherever I'm at, whose had them, I have to make my banana pancakes, or apple, or peach. Yes, peach … don't knock it 'til you tried it. It started in Maryland actually. Casino and I had gone to the DC/Maryland/Virginia area to make the "Homecoming" circuit. We used to be "owt" (non-bruhs/lay persons read "out"), back in those days. We stayed at some Deltas' crib in Maryland whom we knew. And just to show my appreciation for them putting a roof over our heads, because we always called somebody at the last minute, usually about 3 a.m. or so, it wouldn't be a road trip if we didn't do it that way … bruhs, y'all know! I decided to make breakfast for them. I've found that it is rare for a woman not to have a supply of spices and herbs to cook with, so I went into the kitchen and started puttin' it down. Can't front, I was impressed that there was fresh fruit in the house, as well as some natural flavorings in the spice rack. Usually I'll use the flavoring, if there is no fruit, but we all know it's better with fruit. :-/

So I made banana and apple pancakes, separate … but I find they taste good together too … experiment, people! Along with the pancakes I made cheese eggs, beef sausage, and turkey bacon. The smell of food will wake anybody up. They were all pleasantly surprised, but their hair came down when they tasted the food. Made me feel good, because they had never had my cooking before, and they were raving over my banana, my apple pancakes and cheese eggs. One Delta who didn't like bananas was prompted by another to taste the banana pancakes. She did, and *she* went to get a couple! I am patting myself on the back as you read this. :-/ So whenever Que and Casino hit the area, we always had some place to stay, whether it was the Deltas, the AKAs, the Zetas, the Gamma Rhos, or some GDIs. Of course, we always had the bruhs to fall back on.

Back to reality. I've made breakfast for K.P. and Jinx when they've been over to my place, and they kind of decided for me that every time I was at their house, I *had* to make peach pancakes. They got Mrs. Parker behind it, and it's been a ritual ever since.

"Maybe, we ought'a let him move in, Mom. He could be our live-in housekeeper or something," K.P. mused. "Every time I have these pancakes, they taste better and better ... What are you putting in these things?"

I whispered in K.P.'s ear ... and she nearly choked with laughter and disgust.

"Oooo ... Mom!?! ... I'm telling, Que! ... I'm telling!"

I covered her mouth amid my laughter.

"Stop playin', K.P. ... I was just joking ... C'mon, man, shut up!"

K.P. was not to be denied.

"Ma, Que said he puts sperm in the pancakes!"

Jinx busted out laughing and started to say something, but I cut her off.

"Bite your tongue, Jinx … Damn K.P., you always trying to get a brother in trouble."

She tried fake solace with a hug.

"Naw, get away from me."

"Tome mere baby, I sorry."

"So we've been eating your kids, huh, Gregory? Is that the way I'm supposed to read this?" Mrs. Parker questioned.

The girls busted out laughing.

"See … see … wha had happened was … I … I lost my head … and um … and this, this other head … that could speak, right? The twisted head? … It like … like … it jumped in its place … and … and … dat's how it happened!"

"I'm sure your mother would be disappointed in knowing that her future grandchildren are meals. Let me call her and ask her …"

"Nooo! No! No! No! No! That's really not necessary …"

"I think Mrs. Que has a right to know, personally."

"Shut up, K.P. You gon' pay!"

Mrs. Parker went to the kitchen phone and picked up the receiver. I shook my head and mumbled, "I can't believe y'all are playin' me like this."

The next thing I know, my moms is on the other end.

"Hey girl, it's Janine. I'm doing as well as I can. Your son is making things interesting, as usual."

"As usual?" What's that supposed to mean? I started to squirm a little and put my hands in a prayer position toward Mrs. Parker. K.P. and Jinx, meanwhile, are stifling laughter.

"Oh no … no, he's not causing any problems … I don't think? … Hold on … Girls is Gregory causing trouble?"

"He tried to sneak in my room!" K.P. yelled.

"Mine too!" Jinx yelled.

I jumped toward the phone. "That's not true, Ma! They lying!"

"No, no Pat. He's too old for a whipping, ain't he? … Oh! There is something that he did this morning …"

I just sat back down. I know defeat when I see it. I'll just have to build a bridge and get over it! I know y'all are eating this up out there. But that's aight. Laugh now ... but remember ... what goes around, comes around! I'ma *be* aight!

"Do you know that your son makes the best peach pancakes? ... Yes, girl. By chance, would you happen to know what he puts in them?"

K.P. and Jinx could no longer hold the laughter back as they ran out of the kitchen. Mrs. Parker looked at me devilishly and smirked. I sat there frontin' like Joe Cool, waiting for the hammer to drop.

"Girl, we better find him a woman so that you can have some grandchildren. He keep on exerting so much energy cooking for us, he ain't gonna have none left for his wife! We gon' keep him for a while until then, though, okay? ... Chil', let me get off this phone. I'll talk to you later. Bye."

Mrs. Parker hung up the phone and laughed. I sat there thinkin' what I wouldn't give to be makin' her pay.

"I can only imagine what's going on in your mind, Gregory ... but from the look in your eyes, it's definitely not PG13," she smirked.

Damn that futha muckin' "look"! I got some work to do, yet!

"Gregory? Can you handle this?" she teased. I mean ... do you *really* think you can handle *this*?"

"You're killing me, Mrs. P …"

I got up to walk out of the kitchen and Mrs. Parker lobbed her final bomb.

"Kitchen getting too *hot* for you, Gregory?"

Fellas … it's gettin' hard … I mean, it's *really* gettin' hard. :-/ As I pushed open the kitchen door, there was laughter on both sides of it.

Everybody had decided to take the day off from work, couldn't blame them, right? Mrs. Parker went to her room and closed the door. Jinx went to take a shower. K.P. and I watched the Cartoon Network. During the *Tom & Jerry* hour, I noticed that K.P.'s mood went from spirited to sullen.

"Are you okay?"

"Actually, I'm not. Darren used to watch this all the time … "

"Why you didn't tell me to change the channel?"

"It's not like they gonna take it off the air, right? … So I gotta deal with it."

"Yo, you know you don't have to play stoic here?"

"I'm numb … I'm tired of crying … I'm tired of being strong … I'm tired of my family dying … I'm just tired!"

I moved closer to my best friend and put my arm around her, bringing her closer to me. She rested her head on my chest.

"And I'm tired of you holding me!"

I stretched my neck to look downward and sideways toward her.

"Huh?"

"I'm just kidding," she giggled.

"Oh … 'cause I'm sayin' … I could throw your rusty ass on the floor and move on …"

"Na uh, 'cause you loves me!"

"Grrrr."

She rested her head back on my chest and we watched *TopCat*.

"There is one thing that I'm getting tired of, for real."

"What's that?"

"I'm getting tired of leaning on you … I mean, every time there's drama. It's like I got all kinds of issues in my life right now … and it's not fair to burden you down with them all of the time. You got a life too, and you deserve some woman to make you happy, and I don't want you to put your life on hold to come running to me every time there's a crisis in my life … and …"

"K.P.?"

"And I just think…"

"K.P.?"

"I mean … you got things that …"

"Katrina!?!"

This startled her and she jumped up from my chest. I told her to stop rambling. I pulled her back in toward me.

"Que?"

"Yeah?"

"Are you mad at me?"

"Naw … I just wanted to get your attention, that's all."

"Good, because Katrina didn't sound right coming out of your mouth."

"Shut up, K.P."

"I'm just sayin'."

The credits for *TopCat* were rolling down the screen, so K.P. grabbed the remote and started flicking channels.

"Ms. Parker?"

"Yeah?"

"Don't worry about leaning on me, okay?" She didn't respond.

"You hear me?"

"Yeah, I hear you," she eventually forced out.

"You're not heavy …"

She sighed and I kissed her head. Jinx came down the stairs, dressed, but teary-eyed.

"Mommy's got her door locked and I think she's crying. At least that's what it sounded like. She wouldn't open the door. She said she wanted to be alone for a while."

The flood gates had opened, as now K.P. and Jinx were crying too. You like to think that even though you're human, you can accomplish a lot of things. But there are times when you get that jolt of reality, and sometimes you realize just how powerless you are. I *couldn't* take their pain away, I *couldn't* stop their tears. I *couldn't* bring Darren back, I *couldn't* bring Mr. Parker back. Don't even wet your lips. I won't speak on Snow! All I could do was be there for them. That's a lot, you might say, but a few of you out there may identify. Certain people you don't want to see go through pain, and you'd take it for them if you could … 'cause in your eyes, that's what a "true" friend would do. That's how I am, and it's killing me that I can't make the hurt and pain go away. Ladies, is that how a mother feels? An analogy that may not be pinpoint in actuality, because it's a bond between mother and child, but effective because you realize the magnitude. If so, that's the closest I'll ever come to being a mother. He's a hard one to "read" … that Gregory Que …

They kicked me out of their house in the late afternoon, assuring me that they would be all right. I left, but I gave them my best Arnold Schwarzenegger.

"I'll be baaack!"

Got in the car, turned on Janet's album "Janet" (my favorite, thus far), and pumped the beat. Eventually pulled up to a red light, and a car with two guys and two girls pulled up. They heard the music coming from my car and smirked.

The driver leaned over and pumped his stereo, drowning me out with a rap song. The girls laughed and the guys "macked." I've already said that nobody's gonna diss Janet and get away with it, let alone diss me at the same time, especially some snot-nosed wannabe "macks" trying to impress some girls (been there, done that). Yes, I took it as my civic duty to teach them a lesson.

I turned the volume up on my system and blew them away, and still had reserve left. Played like Lotto, the guy tried to turn his system up. Oops, he's realized he's at his max, and he can't touch this. Machoism Number Two: The light turned green, and he peeled off, leaving me in a cloud of smoke. My car has been through a lot, and Lord knows I take her to the max a little too often, but she always comes through. Yeah, I said "she." Guys have this love affair with their cars, so it's appropriate that the car is termed "she," but I wouldn't have gone out like R. Kelly and compared you beautiful women to a Jeep, even though I think he meant it as a compliment. Got a problem with the mentality too, huh? I think the single went Platinum, so what's that sayin'? My woman has to be top of the line, a Bentley convertible! … I'm joking! I apologize to my wife-to-be. Yeah, I know who she is, but y'all don't! … Top Five! If you think you know who it is, come to the wedding!

My car and I are the best at playing catch up. We make up ground better than anyone. So go ahead, get a head start, we'll catch you and pass you … which is what I did to that car. I waved as I drove past, and toyed with him before I honked and made him eat *my* dirt. Explain that to the girls! I know … I'm supposed to be older, the adult. I'm supposed to set the example for the youth of today. Well, guess what he learned? That age old cliché: "Don't judge a book by its cover." :-/ … And bonus, "Thy art not the one to be playethed!" :-/

I made it home and said upon entering, "Honey, I'm home." One day, somebody is gonna answer me and bug me the hell out!

I hit the answering machine to review my messages. Ronnie called. Uncle Que's girls wanted to talk to him. Uncle Que will definitely call them back. Winnie called, purring into my answering machine. We know what that means, don't we?

So like, I'm lying in Winnie's bed, right? … After the fourth round, and … I'm joking! I am not there, I'm still at home. I just thought it would be fun to do that … switch gears without warning … get your dander up … make you say, "No he didn't just drop everything and run over there again." What do you think, I'm horny? :-/ … I *can* say no. Lie next to you naked and make nary a move. Just call it a war of attrition. Listen, if you're not ready or willing to get your feelings hurt, don't make the challenge. Phone's ringing … Excuse me.

"Hello?"

"Hip Hop Hoorayyyyyy …"

"HO!!!"

"HEYYYY HOOOO!!! …"

"What's up, woman? … Miss me already?"

"Can I think about it and get back to you?"

"Forget you, K.P. What's up?"

"Just wanted to let you know what the topic is for 'Off the Hook,' Saturday…"

"Huh? … Wait, you're really gonna do it?"

"It's my turn, isn't it?"

"I just thought…"

"Don't think … just be there and bring an appetite. You'll be eating seafood, your favorite. :-/ You know the theme, so prepare for battle."

"Are you…"

"Ah, ah, ah … I'm not hearing you, Que. Just show up with your guests, if you decide to bring any … Bye bye … I got some more calls to make, okay?"

"Don't be brushing me off, Ho … I'm sayin' … Make your calls and I'll talk to you later."

"So turn off the lights and close the dooh…"

"But, for what? …"

"We don't love dem ho's!"

"Yeah … well, I'll be there on Saturday, but I'll talk to you before then. Later."

"Later."

See what I mean? Stoic ass K.P. But I guess she really needs to do this, to help take her mind off things. I mean, if she couldn't do it, she wouldn't do it … so let her do her thing. I'm curious to know what she has planned, and what she meant by "prepare for battle."

<hr>

We meet on Fridays. We eat fish ... and we talk about *you*, ladies (no puns intended).

Yes, we want all the smoke! We call ourselves "The Scholarly Gentleman Types." Really, we talk about whatever we feel like talking about, but nine times out of ten, it's the opposite sex. A lot of machismo, a little insight and perspective, and a lot of fun.

After work, we gather at Manny's, a jeweled hole-in-the-wall that serves the best fried fish in New York City. Whoever got there early commandeered our now traditional spot in the back, affectionately called "Testostezone." Again ... we want all the smoke! However now, because we show up every week, our spot in the back is roped off and reserved. The only woman that we allow back there is Carol, our waitress, and our only honorary member. She has threatened for the last two years to taint our sacred ground with females, but we counter with the beautiful tip that she always receives. Carol will even contribute to the conversation, albeit rarely ...

when she just can't bite her tongue, in the interests of womanhood, as she puts it.

One of those nights was when she overheard us taking an impromptu poll of the waitresses in Manny's that we would sleep with. She bruised egos for real that night when she came back with our food and thanked us for including her on our list. She then dropped a piece of paper on our table that had polled all of the waitresses in Manny's on who *they* would sleep with in our little circle. Guys who like to think that they got it going on were not in a good mood for the remainder of that night. Especially since there was only one guy on everybody's list (nope, wasn't me ... I got dissed). It just so happened that Gary Coleman was in the spot that night, and *he* was the guy on everybody's list! Can you believe it, that "What you talkin' 'bout, Willis" kid! I don't think it's funny. We started to jump his ass too, just for "gp" (general principle). There was a cold war for a couple of weeks with Carol, but we came to an agreement. Basically, what it all boiled down to was, "What's good for the goose is good for the gander." She wouldn't take it personal if we didn't. Soon after, we made her an honorary member. At first, she didn't know if that was such a great thing. She thought that just maybe we were trying to get back at the rest of the waitresses and make them jealous at her expense. Would we do that? ;-/ Eventually, she discarded that reasoning and we've been cool ever since.

Rick was the first one there and he was sipping on a Dos Equis when I arrived. Rick and I went to High School together, and we've managed to keep in touch throughout the years. Rick's got "soul" (if you know what I mean … someone fill them in over there).

"Your dad wouldn't be too happy knowing you're sucking down the competition, Rick."

"My dad does not have to know, does he, Woody?" he countered.

Rick's dad was Vice-President of a major Chinese Beer Import, Tsingtao (pronounced Ching Dow … go figure). Money was not an issue in Rick's family. He always downplayed the fact that his family was one of the richest and most connected in New York. His mother, an heir to the Estee Lauder empire. Rick and Casino work together for this investment firm. Rick, as a favor owed to me, helped Casino get in. Never mind that Casino couldn't get in on merit alone, even though he was more than qualified (we're not gonna re-visit that).

"I'll just keep that one in my back pocket for a rainy day."

"Bobby's gonna be a little late … had a crisis, we drew straws, and he had to stay," Rick offered.

When worlds collide … names and nicknames are thrown all over the place. Bobby is Casino. Rick interchanges the two. Rick calls me "Woody," in addition to Que, and I call him Silky Smooth, in addition to Rick. Woody is short for Hollywood, which was my nickname in High School, as was Silky Smooth for Rick.

Rick got the whole school to call me Hollywood, and I got the whole school to call him Silky Smooth. The school was a mixture of racial harmony where language barriers didn't exist. White and black slang was used as everyday language, and if it was used in the wrong context, you were corrected. Simple. White kids going, "Yo, man, that's fresh!" and black kids going, "Dude, what were you thinking!?!" Told you I was a chameleon.

We were like that one, two punch. Rick played second base, I played shortstop. I played point guard, Rick played shooting guard. I played Quarterback, Rick played Wide Receiver. Rick also played soccer … I couldn't get down with that. :-/ I earned my nickname from my flair for the spectacular, robbing people of base hits, throwing the Magic Johnson pass, marching the team down for the winning touchdown. Rick had a shooting touch like Jamal Wilkes when he played for the Lakers, silky. He made things look easy and never seemed to break a sweat, always under control ... thus the moniker.

Kenny, Armando, and Morris showed up not too long after I did. We exchanged "what ups" and took our normal positions. Carol brought Kenny his Heineken, Armando his Corona, Morris his Red Stripe, and me my Molson Black Label. This place has all of the imports! She had a Dragon Stout for Casino and asked where he was. I told her he'd be late, but I'd take his Stout.

"Feelin' kinda adventurous tonight, Que?" she chided.

"Might be your lucky night, Carol."

"Honey, I'll make you say ... 'Damn, I never ate so much buffet in my life!' ... Stick with the seafood on the menu, sweetie. 'Frisky's buffet' might be a bit too rich for you!"

The table broke up over that one, whooping and hollering. All the regulars looked toward the back as if to say, "Ah ... they're here."

"Carol, you had your opportunity ... you didn't take it ..."

"That's why I can talk, and your reputation stays intact with your boys. 'Cause if I got a hold to ya, you wouldn't want your boys to know how you acted!"

"Ah damn! What's the matter with you, Carol?" Morris interjected. "You know I'm jealous, talking like that to him."

"Morris, don't start with me. You know you're the type to come in your pants before I even reach for the zipper!"

"What time you get off tonight, Frisky?" Morris flirted.

"Same time as last Friday, same time as this Friday, same time as next Friday. You better leave it alone, Morris. If I just touch your hand right now, it's over for you. I see them veins bulging in your head. Grit those teeth. Count to ten, bring yourself down, so you won't have to excuse yourself and run to the lavatory. You live in stall Number Three, isn't it? We hear you from the ladies bathroom! Who's next!?!"

Rick made a zipper motion across his mouth and threw up his hands as a peace offering. Armando had been taking a swig of his brew and blew it out in laughter. Kenny was laughing but he was cringing at the same time, hoping that Carol didn't start busting on him. We suspected that Carol and Kenny had slept together and her digs were indirectly targeted toward him, but we couldn't prove it, and neither of them were saying. He was always flirting and coming on to her and then one day it just stopped. After hearing that, you think they had something going on too, don't ya?

Casino finally made it and we settled in for the evening. Manny, the owner, came around for his customary round of drinks on the house (we made this place hot and they love us for it). We were so loved that Manny had our section reserved even though the place did not take reservations. Carol brought Casino his Dragon Stout (I drank the initial one), and took our orders which were simply the "All you could eat fried fish/seafood buffet." Casino told Carol that she was looking tasty and asked her what she tasted like today. That was a running joke between those two. One day, Kenny was flirting with Carol and asked her what she tasted like. Carol invited him to find out on the spot. He didn't call her bluff. The next week, Casino asked Carol the same question and she gave him the same response. Casino got up from the table, got on all fours below Carol's skirt, and put his head up yonder and kissed the front of her panties. When he came out from under her and told her that she tasted like Victoria's Secret Tranquil Breezes (fellas, it's a body splash), she damn near fainted. To her credit, she quickly regained her composure and told us later that it was a good thing that he didn't find anything "fishy" about her, with her working in a seafood restaurant and things. She was told that if she hadn't tasted or smelled proper, she would have been informed (ladies, let that be a lesson to you).

Casino warned Carol not to make dares anymore, especially if they're directed at him. He went on to give me props for turning him onto recognizing and naming scents. Carol was duly impressed, and although it wasn't expressed verbally, she looked at us in a different light. Even though it was nice to be included, I hadn't done anything. Casino deserved all the credit. I was impressed that he acknowledged me. Most guys would have kept it to themselves that another guy helped them in that kind of situation. Fellas, did you catch that? Women are impressed by your knowledge of "feminine" things because it's so atypical of a man to have knowledge of these sorts of things. This is one of those things that can separate you from the next man. Use it to your benefit.

"Yo, Mondo? How was that wedding you went to last week?" Kenny asked.

We looked at Armando and waited for his reply. He went to his ex's wedding. We told him not to go because he still had a thing for her. He told us that they had slept together a week or two before the scheduled wedding (that ain't right). She called it "goodbye." I got a problem with that and I had told him so. I called her a "skank" and told him he was better off without her. He wasn't appreciative of my language toward her, but I told him that I just called them as I saw them. He told us that she did it to get back at her husband-to-be because she had caught him with a girl. What is this world coming to?

"But she still married him, Mondo … What's that say about her?" Morris spat.

Armando went on to tell us that it meant that he was satisfying her and her husband wasn't. He did her last night because she called him. Armando didn't want to marry her. That's why she went and married this other guy.

Armando owns a string of dry cleaners on the lower Eastside. Doing pretty well for himself. Ladies' man he is … part time stripper … went to school with Kenny.

"Why did you two break up in the first place?" Rick asked.

"She needed to find herself," Armando said.

We looked at each other.

"Women always gotta find themselves … They make me sick with that."

"That's 'cause they don't know what the hell they want, Que," Morris said.

"Yeah maybe some, but I suspect more than not are just running game."

I thought about the apples and oranges in my life (or lemons …), Kiyy, Lourdes, Elleana … It's a wonder that I've maintained my positive outlook on being a romantic.

"In her case, it was just an excuse to break up with me to get with this guy," Armando reasoned.

"At least you see it like that and can accept it … " Rick said.

"Please. She thought she was playing *me?* I never had no intentions of getting serious with her. She left somebody cold to be with me! Picture me going out like that!"

He gave Kenny a high five, and finished his Corona. Couldn't argue with that. Women like that give y'all a bad name. Men get their share of the blame too. But it's simple with men … you act like a tramp, you get treated like a tramp! You command respect, and men will give it to you. It may be within their own minds, and you may never get them to admit it … but you'll see it. You won't be treated like somebody that they're just trying to sleep with, and be the subject of negative round table discussions.

Ladies, get a clue! If a man knows that you're with somebody else, and he's trying to sleep with you, and he succeeds … you lose! Nine times out of ten, he's not gonna be with you. He can't trust you! Assuming the girl *wants* to be with him. Some of y'all have a guy's mentality and just tryin' to get yo's *mane*! Right? (Apologies to DJ Kool). Chris Rock says that women have the "friend" zone … well, men have a zone too! It's called the "skins" zone. Where are you with the men in your life, ladies?

Carol brought the first round of plates out and we began to chow down. Manny's brings out your side dishes, so you don't ever have to get up, and it's all you can eat also. Reminds me of this place in Virginia called "Po' Folks." They serve you too, and they have an all-you-can-eat menu as well. Manny's isn't as big, but the food blows you away. I told Manny many times that I'm gonna open a restaurant and steal his chef. Manny always responds by putting his hand into his jacket.

"Mr. Que … I am a peaceful man … but … " Manny always leaves me hanging by never finishing the sentence.

Morris was the first to switch gears and change the subject.

"Rick? What's the matter with your people? Why they always bugging?" Morris started.

"Here we go …" Casino added.

"I'm joking with you, Rick. But you need to hold classes for your peeps, man," Morris continued.

"Mo, what did we do to you today?" Rick teased.

Morris is an attorney.

"And it ain't only Rick's people either. Que, your peoples be bugging too!" Morris went on.

"What color are you again, son? By the way I peeped that cultural diversity. Subtil, tres bien."

Morris winked and nodded a smirk in my direction. ;-/

"Don't go there, Que. Don't feel like the revolution tonight, man!" Kenny mumbled.

"Know thyself Kenny and others will be forced to respect you …" Morris said.

"See, that's your problem. I don't have to force people to respect me," Kenny countered.

I looked at Kenny but didn't say a word.

"And I do? … People respect me for the things that I stand for, the way I live. They may not like it or agree with it, but since I don't misrepresent my people, they damn sure have to take me seriously," Morris said.

"Well said, Mo," Armando allowed.

"Don't patronize me man," Morris cautioned.

"Yo, I'm serious. I agree with everything you just said," Armando told him.

"Like today. I just get out of Criminal Court, and I go downstairs to get a Certificate of Disposition."

"What's that?"

He looked at me like I'm stupid, and I shrugged my shoulders.

"For everybody except Que, a Certificate of Disposition is nothing more than a final statement informing you in writing of how your case or matter was resolved."

He looked at me for approval, and upon receiving none, he continued.

"So I'm standing in line, the *Attorney's* line, and one of Rick's boys ..."

"It's all right, Mo ... you can say 'white' guy," Rick allowed.

Morris chuckled at that one.

"This *white guy* gets behind me, and after a few minutes elapses, he asks me, 'Are you an attorney? This line is for attorneys.' I looked at him and said to him, 'What gave me away ... the suit or the earring?'

... " (Morris petitioned the court to be allowed to wear an earring in court, and actually won the petition. The only stipulation was that the earring had to be a stud.)

Everybody fell out laughing, but Morris wasn't laughing.

"That's the type of ignorant shit I gotta deal with in the court system. Then he went on to say, 'I'm sorry. I just thought you might be in the wrong line and may have needed some assistance.' I let him have it then. 'So you're assuming not only that I couldn't be an attorney, but I can't read that big sign ... *right there* ... that says Attorneys Line Only? ... I think you better quit while you're ahead. Your intentions might have been sincere, but your mentality needs a lot of work."

"Whoa ... cursed him out intellectually ... I'm impressed, Morris."

"Would you have handled it differently, Que?" Morris asked.

"Nope, you handled it just like I would handle it."

"The teacher and the pupil ... how quaint," Kenny quipped.

"Shut up you phallic-less, I hope I'm satisfying the ladies wannabe!" Morris shot back.

"What?" Kenny challenged, wondering if he had heard correctly.

"Oh, I should have known you needed a dictionary! Check under phallus, and don't ask the walking dictionary sitting next to you when I turn my head, either," Morris rolled on. (:-/)

Can you say "the dozens?" Morris was coming out with both barrels loaded because Kenny had embarrassed him last week. Said his manhood was so small that fleas were rolling up on him with their girls talking about, "Check me out, now check him out! You could get with this, or you could get with *that*!"

We must have laughed for three minutes hard.

"Yo, Mo, I'd close your mouth myself, but it's not big enough for this stopper," Kenny said, grabbing his crotch.

"It's always the ones talking about how big they are who want an ocean and can't fill a puddle!" Morris observed.

"You wish you had what I got," Kenny huffed.

Morris saw Carol approaching with more food, and being the trained lawyer that he is, decided to gamble and go for the jugular.

"How big did you say you were, Kenny? Three inches flaccid, three inches, maximum blood flow?"

Kenny, who did not know Carol was standing behind him with more food, and had heard Morris' inquiry, said to Morris, "They be lining up to get this nine-inch-thick sirloin."

"*You* ... got *nine* inches of *thick* sirloin, Kenny?" Carol asked.

It was the way that Carol said it that confirmed it for me. I swear she looked like she wanted to say, "Hell, where was I!?!" To her credit, she didn't play him, but the message was caught by all who chose to catch it.

"Kenny, you had the shrimp, right?" Carol asked innocently.

The timing couldn't have been more perfect. Carol kept a straight face and handed Kenny his plate. Everybody at the table had their heads down, trying to keep that straight face, because if anybody made eye contact, the whole table was just gonna explode.

Morris stuck the dagger in further. "What? ... No jumbo shrimp tonight, Kenny?" he inquired, trying to be serious.

"Jumbo shrimp? ... Que, isn't that an oxymoron?" Carol said with her face straight, still.

"Nothing like a woman to cut you down to size!" Morris triumphed, as I nodded to Carol.

Carol left us shaking her head with an "I can't believe what I just heard" look on her face. No doubt, girlfriends were gonna hear about this one! And Morris wasn't letting up.

"Cat got your tongue, chap? Somebody knows where your 'stopper' *ain't*!?!" Morris purged, unrelenting.

"Ease up, Mo," Casino laughed.

"Hellllllllllllllllllll no, not after what I just found out!" Morris insisted.

"I don't know what you *think* you just found out, and from who, for that matter?" Kenny exclaimed.

"I don't know how everybody else read that little scene, but according to how Carol kicked it, and how it read in my book ... *the wee wee is not all it's cracked up to be be*!" Morris roared.

If there was any doubt that Morris hadn't extracted every bit of revenge that he could have from his bitter pill last week, it was erased now. *Oh! We! Howled!* For five minutes hard, fo' sho! You *know* that when you're with your boys, everything is magnified ten times. And after the steady laughter died down, everybody went in ...

"Wait, I think I got some extra inches you could use," Armando deadpanned.

"Well, there's hope for me yet! I thought the myths were true," Rick sighed.

I couldn't let the opportunity pass without throwing something in the ring. In my best Mike Tyson voice, I ranted.

"It werks, I tell ya … It werks … And so what if I wuz small? But I'm not, see! … 'Cause it werks …"

"So, Mike, what you're saying … is although your shit may be 'wee wee' instead of 'pee pee,' it *is* operational and not dysfunctional also?" Rick offered.

"Dat … dat's exackly what I'm sayin, Larry Merchant!"

"But Mike, they're saying you don't have the skills anymore, some say ya never did!" Morris egged on.

"Foreman, I know it's you saying those things about me. I'm still the biggest and baddest man on Testostezone, so drop ya drawz, man … come on … drop ya drawz … let's end this right now. I ain't no sissy … I ain't no punk!"

We took it as far as it could go, and then sat there recuperating. I think we all made our way out of there around 1 a.m. or so. I started to crash by Winnie's, but I thought about you guys, and made my way home. My answering machine greeted me with its blinking light, and I listened to my messages before hitting the sack. Callie called and said that she wanted to know how I felt inside of her, more purring from Winnie, Trini wanted me to go with her to a club so she didn't get hit on, Billie and J.C. needed to talk to me, and K.P. just wanted to be held. See the messages I get? More importantly, see how they all just wanna use me? :-/

K.P. opened the door. Now she looks good all of the time, but there are just some times that stand out and you just remember. Kodak moments. This was one of them. Your first instinct might be to think that she was all glitzed up. She had on jeans and a gold sweatshirt, and her hair was in a ponytail. No lipstick, no makeup, just au naturale. Ladies, fellas appreciate this more than you know, even though some of you have made yourselves believe that you're naked without makeup.

"What? Why are you staring at me, Que?"

"Um ... no reason."

"Well, are ya coming in?" K.P. laughs

"Yes. Yes, I am."

I walk in and K.P. closes the door.

"Thanks for calling me when you got in last night and telling me I still could have come over."

"You could have come over, ya know."

Jinx came down the stairs and I hugged her. Jinx had her hair in a ponytail too. She had on jeans and a orange oversized men's shirt with purple stripes going vertically around it.

"What are y'all trying to do to me? You know I got a fetish for ponytails … and those feeble attempts at covering those fat butts … is very lacking!"

"My butt's bigger," Jinx laughed, kissing me on the cheek (as if I needed a reminder).

"But my ponytail is longer," K.P. added, kissing me on the other cheek.

K.P. led me down into the basement behind Jinx (no pun intended), :-/ where it appeared I was the last to arrive. I was prepared for the usual suspects, and some new faces, but I wasn't prepared to see Winnie. Who invited her? I know it wasn't me, and I *know* it wasn't Dexter St. Jock. *So! … you figured out it was K.P. before I did. What do you want, a medal?* Honestly, it had never even dawned on me that they might have ever exchanged numbers. Silly me.

K.P. did the introduction thing, and I greeted the usual suspects. Kenny kept true to form and brought two women, and I had to give him his props. They were fiiiiiiiine!

Two Venezuelan twins, Lina and Pasqual.

"Damn! My eyes hurt … twice!"

My response drew some laughter after my introduction to them, and they accepted my compliment with smiles. I looked at Kenny incredulously as if to say, "How the #$%! did *you* manage to hook up with them!" As if reading my thoughts, he whispered to me quickly as we greeted that I should have hung out after Manny's.

I greeted Gillian, Trevor, Max, Casino and Temple. Max introduced me to her friend, Dana, and asked me if I remembered Dell. I did and greeted him (guess things were working out nicely for those two). Got my hug from Temple, and she introduced me to her guests, Glen and Vaughn. I finally hugged Winnie and she smiled at me as if she knew I was surprised to see her. Well hell, I was.

K.P. told me to sit down and stop grandstanding, and I informed her that she had to have me mixed up with someone else. :-/ She ran through a brief history and introduction of "Off the Hook" for those who had never been to a set before, and thanked everyone for coming out. She went on to explain that this was the last Saturday for the theme of sexual connotations and that we would play a version of Family Feud, then role reversal, and then we'd eat. She proclaimed the night "Battle of the Sexes" and told us that everything would be men vs. women.

Everybody got kind of amped, as each gender was already claiming to be the superior sex. K.P. divided the room, men on one side, and women on the other. K.P. was "host," which brought groans of bias from the men.

"How you gonna be the host? You ain't gonna be neutral!" Casino laughed.

"See ladies, they already scared … look at 'em. Ain't heard question the first and panicking," K.P. observed.

"Naw, we gon' be all right … Don't you worry about us," Trevor told her. "Bring it on."

We got in "Feud" order, and Kenny and Jinx were matched up first. They walked up to a make shift podium with a bell between them. K.P. had a board next to her made up like the Family Feud board. She had done a good job too. She had make shift envelopes in numerical order and velcro next to the envelopes. Apparently, after a correct answer was given, it would be applied to the velcro. It was colorful and she was immediately complimented by both genders. She reminded everyone again of the theme and started.

"Top five answers are on the board … Name something that men like to put in their mouths … ," K.P. began.

Kenny hit the bell first, and the men got psyched.

"Breasts," Kenny called out.

K.P. had a little synthesizer next to her and pressed a button. The sound for a correct answer came blaring through. "*Ding*." Kenny's answer was the number five answer. K.P. went to the board and pulled the number five slip out of the envelope, affixing it to the velcro.

"Yo, you kind of worked that, K.P. That was phat," Casino allowed.

K.P. looked at Jinx and asked for her answer. If you didn't know, the opponent has the opportunity to get control of the board by giving a higher answer.

"Their foot!" Jinx said, looking directly at Kenny.

K.P. pressed the button on her synthesizer. "*Ding*." K.P. looked at her card and went to the board and pulled out the velcro slip for the number one answer. The fellas were in an uproar, with me leading the way.

"Oh, hell no! Fix! You and Jinx are on some collabo kick!"

K.P. told us (but she looked directly at me), that she didn't get down like that, and nobody had seen the answers but her.

The order of the girls went, Jinx, Temple, Dana, Lina, Pasqual, Winnie, Max, and Gillian. K.P. read the question again and asked Temple for an answer.

Now if you know the game, and I'm assuming that you do ... name someone who hasn't seen "Family Feud?" ... see what I did there? :-/ You know that when you get the top answer, your team gets the chance to clear the board. However, every wrong answer gets a strike and you get three strikes. After your third strike, the other team gets one shot to steal the points that were initially gathered. Got that?

"Cigars," Temple said.

Damn, another correct answer. Cigarettes/ Cigars was the number two answer. She moved onto Dana. Dana looked a bit bewildered as K.P. cautioned her that she had three seconds.

"Um, um ... tongue!" she blurted out just as K.P. was about to hit a button on her synthesizer.

"I like the way she thinks!" Casino called out.

The fellas laughed, and the ladies smirked.

"Typical … " Max called back.

K.P. looked at her card and hit a button … *"Errnt."* K.P. informed them that that was their first strike. The fellas cheered.

"Yo, that's all right, Dana. It would have been on my list!" Casino offered.

"Woof woof," Temple barked.

"Till the day I die," Casino and I chanted in unison.

"Quiet, before I call the pound and tell them I got some strays for them to come pick up!" K.P. said.

She asked Nina for her answer.

"Ding … just because," Vaughn whispered. "'Cause there can't be nothing wrong with that!"

"Word to Mother!" Glen whispered back. "Ding and ding again … Yo, um Kenny? That's his name, right?"

Glen got Kenny's attention.

"Yo, I just wanna shake your hand … you win! Not once, but twice!" Glen volunteered within Kenny's earshot.

Dell shot a side glance in Max's direction and quickly shook his head in agreement. Kenny basked in all the attention, then acknowledged Glen with an "I got it going on, don't I!?!" smile and nod.

"Fingers?" Lina said.

"To the bone!" Glen offered out of the side of his mouth to Vaughn.

K.P. hit her synthesizer … *"Errnt,"* indicating another incorrect answer … Strike two.

"That's not true, Lina … I *love* fingers!" Kenny grinned seductively.

"Turn up the degrees … turn up the degrees!" Gillian snickered.

K.P. moved on to Pasqual, repeating the question and asking her for an answer.

"The vagina," Pasqual replied confidently.

"Not in America, honey!" Winnie shot back.

The girls showed their agreement with some high fives. The fellas? We all stood there with our mouths open.

"Whatever the answer is, Pasqual, I'll *definitely* eat to that!" Kenny declared before anybody could close their mouths.

"Greediness and his desire for the spotlight will be his downfall, you watch," Winnie told Maxine.

"She said 'vagina' in public … and with feeling … what a woman! I think I just came in my pants!" Casino gasped.

Pasqual's answer was incorrect, :-/ which meant that the ladies had three strikes. We had an opportunity to steal the points if we could come up with a correct answer. We quickly huddled. A few answers were thrown around. My answer of "gum" or "candy" and Trevor's answer of a "toothpick" seemed the most plausible.

K.P. asked Kenny what our answer would be. I started to say something when Kenny practically ran to the first spot before the game began, but I let it go. I wish I had said something. These are the times when I want to kick Kenny's ass ... when he tries to hog the spotlight. Instead of going with our agreed upon answer of "toothpick," Kenny decides to go on his own and picks "fruit."

"That's not the answer you supposed to give!" we damn near shouted in unison.

"Told you ..." Winnie winked at Max.

K.P. looked at her card and pressed a button ... *"Errnt."* The ladies cheered. K.P. told them that they had taken the points. Kenny, meanwhile, tried to explain that he thought "fruit" was a better answer. It didn't help matters when K.P. revealed the remaining answers and "toothpick" was among them ... not to mention "gum!"

K.P. called for the next players, which happened to be Temple and Glen. They shook hands and got into "Feud" position.

"Top six answers are on the board … What part of a woman's anatomy do men notice first?" K.P. asked.

Temple hit the bell first. Her answer, "hair," was the number three answer. K.P. asked Glen for an answer to take control of the board. Glen's answer of "breasts" (go figure), was number five. The women had control again. She asked Winnie for her answer.

"The eyes," Winnie offered.

K.P. looked at her card, looked at Winnie as if she was genuinely surprised, and hit the *"Ding"* button. She proceeded to pull out the number one answer.

"What?!?" Dell began. "The *eyes* are number one!?!"

"Is there a problem with that, Dell?" Maxine challenged.

Uh oh … choose your words wisely, my friend! I looked at Dell and he quickly regained himself. Whew!

"Naw, I don't have a problem with the answer … I was just wondering who's the authority? Where did you get your answers, K.P.?"

"What does it matter?" Gillian asked.

"It matters to the extent that I'm just curious, that's all … What? … I don't have a right to know where this info is coming from?" Dell reasoned.

"I don't have a problem telling you that, Dell. Most of the information is from my head, some from books."

She paused, then said nonchalantly, "And this last question I got from 'Pop Up Video.'"

Pandemonium broke out. The men threw their hands up in disgust. The women cackled like hens (yeah … I said it). Winnie confessed to K.P. that she had seen that particular episode … come to think of it … I had too!

Suddenly, I had a revelation. Believing that I knew how K.P. was thinking, I gathered the guys in for a huddle. I told them that I thought that K.P. was making the questions appear sexual, but that the answers, at least the top answers, were not. I bet she figured that we guys would salivate over the apparent sexual nature of the questions … sexual connotations! She would include the no-brainers to hook us in, but bank on the fact that we wouldn't be able to get our minds out of the gutter to get the top answers. What a weasel! I got your number, honey!

K.P. restored order, informing the masses that it was her "Off the Hook" and those that didn't like it could get the hell out. The games went on. :-/ K.P. moved to Max and asked for her answer.

"Feet," Maxine said.

"And she got some pretty ones too!" Dell told us.

That's a smart man, right there. Getting back on Max's good side with such a public display (cha-ching). She tried to hide the smile, but couldn't. Max's answer was a winner too, it was number four. K.P. moved to Gillian. Gillian shocked us when she said that Trevor would answer for her.

"Oh hell no I won't!" Trevor cried.

Gillian was willing to bet that Trevor would get her answer right. Gillian offered that if Trevor got it wrong, she would personally wait hand and foot on all the fellas that night. K.P. brought Trevor a pen and some paper, and he wrote his answer down after initially refusing to be a part of this. The fellas encouraged him to get it wrong, but I told them they were wasting their breath. If Gillian showed that much faith to go out on a limb like that? ... There ain't no way in hell that Trevor is gonna get that answer wrong. Trevor folded his answer and gave it to K.P., K.P. then asked Gillian for her answer, which she had written down as well.

"Read my answer as written, K.P. Don't try to get me in no trouble," Trevor warned.

"You're no fun, Trevor," Maxine laughed.

"You don't live with her, Max," Trevor countered.

That comment by Trevor basically summed it all up. There would never be a winner to the Battle of the Sexes because there was too much interaction with the adversary! :-/

K.P. unveiled Trevor's answer and looked at Trevor with the biggest of smirks. She then looked at Gillian's answer and hit the *"Ding"* button. The women were impressed and clapped. The men were secretly impressed as well, but more relieved that the male gender did not take a hit. K.P. revealed the number two answer of "lips."

"He better not have gotten it wrong," Gillian began. "He told me that my lips were the first thing that he noticed about me."

It was now on Jinx. If she could give a correct answer, the ladies would clear the board. I tried to rattle Jinx. But she wasn't having it.

"You tryin' to rattle *me*, Que? That's like you writing a book titled 'I married Janet Jackson!' Ain't happenin'!"

The room fell out in laughter.

"Why y'all laughing at that!?! That's not even funny! Hey! It could happen! I could marry Janet! Don't laugh at that!"

Jinx looked at me, and simply deaded me with, "Que … you're not going to be able to *doit!*" (Apologies to Double X Posse).

The laughter just intensified, and I just put the "H" on my chest until it finally died down.

K.P. looked at her sister and asked for her answer. Jinx smiled and then looked toward us. She turned and pointed. I could only smirk as Jinx rubbed it in by lifting the back of her shirt for us to see. All the fellas took it as a free peek at Jinx's butt. I took it as the proper masterful innuendo it was meant to be: "kiss my ass, losers."

"Butt," she replied.

"And a nice one it is," Glen mumbled.

K.P. hit her button as she put the number six answer on the board. By taking these points, the women were halfway to the winning total of 300. K.P. called Dana and Trevor, who were next in line.

"Dollar values are doubled for this final round, so listen up … Top nine answers are on the board … Name an oxymoron."

"Wait! What!?! … Hold up! What's that got to do with your theme?"

"Not a damn thing, Que. I figured I'd flip the script just once, in case somebody thought there was a pattern in my questioning." :-/

I mouthed an expletive to her, and she blew me a kiss.

"At least let those that don't know what it is, find out!"

"Fair enough."

She pulled out a dictionary with a tab marked where the definition was listed and let those who wanted to look up the meaning do so (if *you* wanna know the definition, you know what to do). I whispered quickly to Casino concerning some strategy, and how K.P. figured she was one step ahead of me, and he nodded in agreement. Maybe we'd luck out and her strategy would blow up in her face. K.P. retrieved the dictionary, and began to repeat the question. Before she could finish stating "Name," Dana just beat Trevor to the bell.

"Honest Lawyer," Dana replied.

K.P. looked at her card and hit a button … *"Ding."*

"You gotta be kidding!"

"What was that, Que?"

I waved my hand at K.P. as she placed the number eight answer in its proper position.

She looked at Trevor for an answer.

"Dry Ice," Trevor said.

We cheered because Trevor's answer was not only a good answer, it was the number three answer, which gave us control of the board. Our destiny was in our own hands. The order of the guys was Kenny, Glen, Trevor, Vaughn, Me, Casino and Dell. K.P. asked Vaughn for his answer. He hesitated as if he was contemplating. K.P. reminded him that he had three seconds.

"Deafening silence," Vaughn said.

K.P. didn't even bother to look at her card. She shook her head, smirking … *"Errnt."*

"What'd you think I was stupid? I was gonna show you the dictionary with that as an example and then include it? You deserve that strike, Vaughn!"

The girls laughed at Vaughn, and I just shook my head. Obviously he didn't know who he was dealing with … but come on! My nieces or nephews wouldn't even have fallen for that!

It was my turn, as K.P. called for my answer. I muttered to myself about wiping that damn smirk off of her face. Mind games. What would she do? Do I give an obvious answer? Or do I gamble? I decided to gamble and hope that my partners could think of some obvious answers, while I tried to think of some not-so-obvious oxymora. Is there really such a thing?

"Constant change."

K.P. chuckled and looked at her card. The ladies murmured. Then she pressed a button ... *"Ding."* I exhaled aloud ... my answer was number seven.

"Nice answer, Que ... " Winnie said, ever the observant one, picking up on the mind game *tete-a-tete* between K.P. and myself.

K.P. allowed a smile my way, acknowledging my answer, and moved to Casino.

"Sweet tart," Casino offered.

The ladies seemed to like that answer as they all nodded in agreement. *"Ding."* It was the number two answer. K.P. looked at the ladies with surprise (like she was impressed with our efforts, thus far), as she went to Dell for his answer. Dell's answer of "curved line" impressed even me! It was number six. The fellas seemed to be on a roll as K.P. approached Kenny for his answer. This was crucial. Luck was on our side, because nobody had said the one obvious answer known to at least three of us. If Kenny says anything other than what he'd better say, I'm gonna have to be restrained. It's not rocket science ... all he has to do is think back to last night and put that ego aside!

"Jumbo shrimp," Kenny says looking down toward my direction with a sheepish grin.

Casino started to laugh and I nudged him. I gave thumbs up to Kenny as he nodded. Kenny smiled broadly when it was revealed that his answer was the number one answer. Next up was Glen.

"Light Heavyweight," Glen said.

K.P. looked at her card and pressed a button … *"Errnt."* Strike two.

"Good answer, though," K.P. told him.

We had come back around to Trevor, and we were still alive. K.P. waited for an answer.

"Government Intelligence," Trevor smirked.

"That's the truth," Temple said as the ladies seemed to be rooting us on.

Trevor had come through again. His answer was number five. Vaughn was up next. Hopefully he had learned from his mistake. The ladies didn't think so as they huddled up to come up with an answer for a steal, and the game. K.P. waited on Vaughn.

"White Chocolate," Vaughn uttered.

I thought it was a good answer, but was it on the board? K.P. looked at her card, and that damn smirk showed up again on her face. My head went down as she hit a button … *"Ding."* We exploded with high fives as K.P. put up the number four answer. There was just one more answer to complete the board, and it was number nine. How ironic is it that it falls on my shoulders? But I wouldn't have it any other way. The ladies tried to rattle me as I tried to get inside my best friend's brain. What would she do? If this is between the two of us, then she would try and think of something that would bother me for years to come. I racked my brain, and I didn't even hear her repeat the question. All I heard was her telling me that I had three seconds. The answer smacked me in the face, as I smiled … It had to be …

"Biggie Smalls!"

The girls huddled because they figured I was wrong, and the fellas didn't seem to be too confident with my answer. But I had my eyes locked on K.P. as her eyes gave me my due and hit that button … *"Ding."* We had won the game.

The ladies were stunned, and the fellas took a few seconds for everything to register. Then the swagger returned, and all of the bravado, as the women called us "lucky." K.P. returned from putting away the "Family Feud" stuff and then explained the role reversal. She told us that we would have ten minutes to portray the opposite sex in any manner we wanted.

Sample: "Eh, yo, I be knockin' em out, son! … Honeys be going to sleep after I finish blessin' em!" Winnie began.

"Please, son … I broke Shorty's back last night … the whole building heard her!" Jinx countered, grabbing the crotch of her pants for emphasis.

"He not hitting that right … now if *I* got to it? … She be actin' right, son, dat's my word. She'd be catchin' the 'Sushi style' for real, yo," K.P. added.

"I ain't drive all the way over there just to talk!" Max said, pounding her fist in her hand.

"What!?! You stoopid, yo … You put out for dinner *and* a movie and just got a kiss on the cheek!?! … You would have been better off just shaking her hand!" Gillian said. :-/

"Meda, you go down on 'em?" Lina asked.

"Estas loco, hijo!?! … Picture me going down on her? … But she *gotta* do me!" Pasqual said.

"*Regular* size? … Psst! Magnums … strictly Magnums, dunn … What is you buggin'?" Temple said.

"I just wanna put it in for a minute," Dana pleaded.

That was a sample of their ten minutes. They came off a little bit, but we had our turn.

"That's a weave, girl … Trust me, I know … Ain't nothing hers," Trevor kicked off.

"I *know* I took your pants off, but I just wanna cuddle … I'm *not* a tease," Vaughn said.

"Uh uhh … I said I didn't mind if you did it to *me*, I never said I was gonna do *you*," Glen said.

"Stop, I said! … Wh … Why did you stop? … I didn't mean *STOP!*" Kenny said.

"I love you, but I can't handle '*us*' right now … I need space … It was never my intention to hurt you," Casino started.

"I gotta find myself … I don't wanna appear selfish, so I don't want you to wait for me while I go through this, okay? … But I do value your friendship," I followed.

"Ah, by the way, I'm getting back with my ex," Dell finished up.

"Y'all ain't even right, that's not how it goes at all with needing space." Winnie looked at us, shaking her head.

"Yeah, yeah, yeah," Kenny chimed in. "Whatever you say."

Winnie ignored him. Surprised? … I was. Temple's response during role reversal jarred my memory to last night's debated question, and I decided to pose it to the ladies. After all, the forum seemed appropriate. :-/

"There's a debate going on among some scholarly gentleman types, and I was curious as to your response to a debated question."

"Scholarly gentleman types? ... Is that right?" K.P. quipped.

I caught Casino and Kenny smirk out of the corner of my eye as they didn't think I'd have the guts to ask the question. You would think they'd know me by now!

"I'm straight up serious, so I would appreciate if y'all would be too."

"What's the question?" they asked in unison.

"What would you rather have ... a thick penis that could not reach your G spot? ... Or a skinny one that could? ... No variations, please."

I was met with some blank stares. I chuckled to myself at the shock value.

"Come on, I'm serious. Answer it only if you want to, then."

Pasqual spoke first, and everyone immediately took notice (i.e. the men). :-/

"Thickness or length? I would go with thickness because I enjoy the sensation of feeling the throbbing pulsating rhythm of him moving in and out of me.

I guess it's like men like a woman to be rather tight because they feel it better … same principal," she concluded. (Whoa!)

"Obviously, you've never had someone hit that spot," Jinx began. (O-kay!) "Thick may fill me up, but it couldn't satisfy *me*. Give me skinny that could."

"That is not true," Pasqual countered. "It is my preference … Besides, there is more than one way to hit that spot."

"Bet you change your tune if someone gets there that knows what they're doing … and can reach it," Jinx offered.

"I've been blessed to have had the best of both worlds … combined," Winnie acknowledged. "But since I'm given the choices of thick that couldn't and skinny that could… I must agree wholeheartedly with Jinx. The inability to hit the G spot is something that has caused many women to walk away in disgust."

"I'm very sensitive along my walls, and I love the sensation too … Give me thick," Max offered.

Dell strained to keep a straight, non-committal face. :-/ The debate raged on with the majority that answered opting for skinny that could while the minority argued for thick that couldn't. Ladies, does the answer depend on whether you've had your G spot tickled? Or is that not a factor, as the minority argues?

"See what you started, Que!?!" K.P. said.

"Jumbo shrimp vs. crab legs, hmmm!?!" Winnie asked out loud, prompting a host of laughter as K.P. made the cattle call for grub.

The spread consisted of oysters (appetizers for the libido), :-/ fried and broiled Whiting, jumbo shrimp, :-/ crab legs, clams, scallops wrapped in bacon, and sushi … along with an array of side dishes. I am a seafood lover, literally. :-/

7

SUDDENLY

Orange you cute!?! … Nice hat!

Kiyy!!!
"Oh My God!" K.P. exclaims.

"Oh my God, Kiyler!" I mutter aloud as Kiyy falls into my arms, bloodied.

Looking at Kiyy in my arms jarred memories that I had suppressed into the dark recesses of my mind. My brain went into a cataclysmic state as the images overflowed from my memory banks onto the inner screen that only I could see …

We met on a Saturday. The sun was out, the birds were chirping. The sounds of laughter and fun were in the air. I was sitting on a boardwalk rail at Coney Island with Dex eating a Nathan's famous with sauerkraut. Kenny ("Dex/Dexter St. Jock/Kenny" … sorry I interchange them without thought), was eating his favorite, frog legs. I can't explain it, he's weird, but he's my friend. (lol) I don't think they taste like chicken, like most people tend to say. But I tried them after some prodding from him and they taste aight. Anyway, we were there people watching, okay … girl watching, listening to music blaring from the speakers of one of the shops on the boardwalk. I remember it plainly. Billy Ocean's "Suddenly" suddenly came on. :-/ We looked at each other like "What the fuck! Where did that come from?" They were just jamming and all of a sudden … slow jam. I'm just sayin'.

About a minute or so into the song, she walked by. She had two little kids with her (found out later it was her brother and sister), and she was wearing shorts and an orange halter top. Her hair was puffy from curling, but she had a lot of it (all hers), with movie star sunglasses on top of her head. I always wondered why she was not wearing the sunglasses, but then she turned toward me and the sunlight captured her eyes at just the right angle, and the color of her eyes mesmerized me. She was lanky, about 5'6" or 5'7", brown-skinned. We caught eyes for a moment and that was that (Apologies to L.L.). As she walked by with her siblings, I looked at Kenny and his eyes were glued on a Puerto Rican girl with tiny cutoff jean shorts and an even tinier t-shirt defying laws of man, nature, and gravity. She had to be a magician getting into that gear with her assets. I was getting ready to say something to Kenny who had jumped off the rail and was headed in the direction of his eye's delight when, out the corner of my eye, I saw Kiyy's brother drop his hot wheels car. I jumped off the rail, picked it up, and ran up to them.

"Excuse me. He dropped this back there."

I handed her the car. It was an orange mustang with a purple stripe around it. She looked at him.

"See, that's why I told you to put it in your pocket. Eating ice cream and trying to hold it at the same time!"

She shook her head, and her little sister giggled.

"Thank you," she said.

I knelt down and said to the little brother, "I understand, little man. I had one like this too and didn't want to lose it. What kind of ice cream are you eating?"

"Chocolate."

"My favorite," I replied.

I looked at the little girl and asked her what she was eating.

"Chocolate chip."

"*My* favorite," Kiyy replied.

I looked up from my kneeled position and could not help but see that orange halter on the way up.

Kiyy smiled and continued, "Orange you cute!?! ... Nice hat!"

"Yeah, thanks."

"Kiyy, you should be wearing it. It matches your top!" the little sister exclaimed.

I was wearing an orange kangol bucket hat with an orange and blue short set, white shell toe Adidas with blue stripes, and fat orange shoe laces. (Wow!) (lol)

"Kiyy? That is an interesting name."

"It's short for Kiyler," Kiyy explained.

"That's even more interesting," I said, probably a lot flirty with a look to match.

"What's your name?" the little sister asked.

"Sidney!" Kiyy admonished.

"No, it's okay. My name is Gregory, but everyone calls me by my last name, which is Que."

"Like the letter Q?" Sidney blurted.

Kiyy turned her head to stifle a laugh.

"Yup, just like that!" I said.

"Cool," the brother chimed in.

We all looked at each other and laughed. It was the only other words he spoke through the whole exchange.

"We need to get going," Kiyy suddenly said.

I stood up and looked at her. She smiled, and it melted me.

"Yeah, take care," was all I could muster.

I think she was surprised when I did not ask for her number. Hell, I was surprised I did not ask for her number. It was a good space and it was an innocent exchange that felt nice. In hindsight, I was glad I did not ruin that moment. I watched them walk away as Kenny came up to me showing me a piece of paper with the number of the girl he went to talk to.

"I know you got her number, right Que?"

"Naw, I didn't," I mumbled, suddenly realizing the magnitude.

"What!?! Go get it! What's wrong with you?" Kenny scolded.

I said nothing as we both watched them walk away with Billy Ocean's ending blaring over the boardwalk, "You wake up … Suddenly, you're in loooooooooove … Ooooo, Ooo, ooooooo-ooooo … Ooooooooooooooooo." (Not apologizing Billy Ocean! Damn you!)

I thought about the girl with the orange halter top periodically throughout the summer. Walking to the corner store, break dancing at a block party, sitting on the park bench drinking an orange quarter water (you know the hand size plastic drink that you stuck your thumb through the top to open that cost twenty-five cents). Random really. Of course, when I told Kenny about my thoughts, his response was typically male best friend like, "That was stupid, my dude!" In his crude way, I had to admit he was right. Eventually I moved on, chalking it up to a lost opportunity on my part.

As the summer came to an end and school loomed, Kenny and I hit Delancey Street for Sheepskins, with the matching hats, of course, Pitkin Av for sneakers, and Fulton Street and the Albee Square Mall for the funky fresh back-to-school gear! And you know this, man! And if we couldn't find it in Brooklyn, there was always Jamaica Av in Queens, 125th and 145th Street, Uptown (Harlem, for the uneducated), or Gun Hill Rd. in the Bx (Bronx). Ironically, none of the gear I bought had any orange in it. Guess it was just a summer fling. (lol) *Yeah you're right, that was a phase I needed to dead.* Aight, knock it off, you got one in. Don't go overboard. I'm telling you, give 'em an inch, they'll take a mile. (Hi, Mom!)

———

It's the first day of school and I'm in it to win it. *Fresh dressed like a million bucks, threw on the Bally shoes and the fly green socks. Stepped out my house, stopped short, oh no, I went back in, I forgot my Kangol!* (Apologies to Slick Rick).

I have no idea why you always wore your dopest outfit on the first day of school, but that's how it was in Brooklyn. Could look like a bum on the second day of school, but not the first day of school! It's not like you won a prize or anything. Just the unofficial title of best dressed. Hey, we had goals back then, simple ones, but goals just the same. Our high school was one of the first to stop with uniforms. Most of the other Catholic schools followed suit thereafter.

The beginning of my junior year in high school. The beginning of the takeover! Remember Rick, right? Silky Smooth? That was the year we took over Bishop Walding sports. Well, to kick off the school year, the sports department had a yearly back-to-school fundraiser. This year was a fair with rides and the whole nine yards in the school parking lot the first weekend of school. Rick and I saw each other and greeted with hugs and signature handshakes. He had on a letterman's jacket. He lettered in soccer. I lettered in baseball.

"Woody!" he yelled. "Holly-woooooooood!"

"Silky Smooth in the house!"

"Where's your jacket, dude!"

"I'll have it on tomorrow, my mellow, my ace!"

"Really, dude? … Oh right, right, first day of school! I'm true to it too, Que, I ain't forget!"

I laughed. Rick was my man. We traded language and culture at Walding, and I tell you, everyone was better for it. And yes, white kids in Brooklyn came to school wearing their dopest outfit as well for the first day of school.

"Check out the mock neck and the Sergio Valentes', Que! First day stylin' with the Patrick Ewings!"

I simulated touching him and burning my finger.

"Sizzling, my dude!"

Just then, another black kid walked by, looked me up and down, and nodded approval on my attire, and then nodded at Rick slyly.

"Looking good, Slick Rick! Dat's dat Silky Smooth!"

"My man!" Rick responded, exchanging fist pounds with the kid.

"Que, let's go check out the freshmen."

"Done. Let's go!"

It had been a tradition of ours to go check out the freshmen girls since Rick and I hit it off at our freshman orientation. Rick had on his letterman jacket, and we saw firsthand what kind of chick magnet a letterman jacket was our freshman year. We had just gotten to the auditorium and the freshmen had just been let out of assembly. We were standing by the staircase when …

"Oh shit!" I muttered.

"What happened, Que?"

"Rick, I'll be right back."

I walked away from Rick and toward the middle of the room.

"Orange you cute with that orange flower in your hair."

The two girls and guy standing there looked at me like I was crazy, but the third girl turned around and smiled. It was Kiyy!

"Nice hat," she said.

I smiled back and whispered, "Thank you, God!" to myself.

I had on a forest green Tropic 504 Kangol hat (Ventair), tilted to the side, matching designer shirt and pants set, with Ballys to match. Not wasting a second, I went for mine.

"There's a fair here on school grounds this weekend. I'd love to escort you."

Ugh! I'd love to escort you!?! Not one of my smoothest moments or lines. But it was enough! Corny as it was. Take note, fellas! It was sincere and came across that way to her.

"I'd love to have you escort me," she replied.

I really couldn't tell if she was mocking me or not at that moment. I asked her later on, and she said she was really flattered. Said it showed I had manners. She told me six months later that during her freshman orientation, some of the monitors were talking amongst themselves about the cute guy who everyone thought was going to be the starting quarterback at school that year. She saw a picture of me from the team last year. I was the backup QB. She said she got excited because she wished she had asked me for my number, and here I was going to the same school! But after hearing that, she did not think I'd be interested in her because there would be so many girls fawning (her word), over me.

"Really? Okay, here's my number. We can decide on Saturday or Sunday, okay?"

"Why not both days?" she countered.

I looked at her with one eye brow raised. Gambling that this girl is not tryin' to play me, I said, "Why not both days? Good to see you again, Kiyy."

"You too, Que," she giggled like a school girl. Well, she was, wasn't she? :-)

I handed her my number and walked back toward Rick who was still at the staircase. As I walked away, one of the girls, who later turned out to be Pam, mumbled within earshot, "Was *that* Mr. Orange Kangol?"

I turned back slightly to see Kiyy nodding with a big kool-aid smile. I was high-fiving and hugging myself, jumping and yelling in my mind as I reached Rick. He saw the smile on my face and said to me, "You just met Mrs. Que, didn't you?"

I carried Kiyy to the couch while K.P. went and got the first aid kit from my bathroom. She brought wash cloths and proceeded to wipe the dried blood from Kiyy and clean her wounds.

"Que, we need to get her to the hospital! She's got head wounds!"

"No hospitals," Kiyy whispered. "He'll have people looking for me there."

"He? Who's he?" I asked, trying to remain calm.

"Carlos," she said softly. "Carlos." And then she lost consciousness.

"Hat or no hat?" I asked my sister Ronnie.

It was Saturday morning and I was trying to decide what to wear. I couldn't ever remember being nervous about a girl before, and Ronnie noticed it as well.

"Who is this girl that has my brother attempting fashion? Is that 'Hi Karate' in your hand? Damn, you serious, huh?" she joked.

"Ha ha. This is Lagerfeld. Seriously, hat or no hat?"

"No hat. Let her see your waves and your whole face. If she stays and doesn't run, you good!"

"You're not funny, Ronnie."

"Nina Simone! Come look at your brother!"

"What are you doing!?! I'm not on display."

"Yes, you are," Ni Ni said, walking into the room. "We got reps in this neighborhood. You can't go out when it matters, especially with a girl, without our approval! What are you wearing?"

I pointed to the bed, and Ni Ni looked at Ronnie, and Ronnie looked at Ni Ni. Then they both busted out laughing. This was a normal occurrence in my life.

"What is wrong with that?" I asked.

Ni Ni walked to my closet and pulled out some clothes.

"You're not going to hang with your boys. You're going on a date. Do you really like this girl or what? Trust us. You want her to be proud to be on your arm, not cringing."

"Ain't no 'Que don't know how to present himself on a date' in this house," Ronnie preached. "Do I need to get 'Pat' involved in this?"

"Ronnie, if Mommy hear you calling her 'Pat,' that really ain't gonna matter no more. And I resent that you think my clothes will cause anyone to cringe," I said.

Ni Ni and Ronnie looked at each other again like they shared some secret joke and laughed again.

"It's not your clothes, it's the occasion you choose to wear them," Ronnie said.

"I'm not wearing no V-neck."

"Oh yeah, you like crew necks. Okay, we can switch that up," Ni Ni agrees.

So I put on the clothes and stand before them, feeling like a real-life Ken doll that they are dressing while they banter back and forth.

"I don't like that color on him. Take it off and put this one on."

"Those pants are too long, they don't break right. What about these?"

After fifteen minutes of changing, they agree on a sweater and pants.

"Can I wear my Clark Wallabees?"

After debate, this is conceded.

"There is still something missing," Ni Ni says.

"I got it!" Ronnie says, running to the closet.

She returns with a blazer and tells me to put it on.

"Oh hell no! That's too much! What are you doing to me!?! I'm not going to Mt. Sinai Baptist Church!" I exclaimed.

"You're right, Ronnie. That sets it off! Put it on, Que!"

I put on the blazer and look in the mirror.

"Dapper Dan ain't got nothing on us!" Ronnie says, high fiving Ni Ni.

I had to admit, it did add a touch of *je ne sais quoi*.

"Why the blazer?"

"You're gonna thank us when … what's her name?"

"Kiyy. Kiyler. Kiyy for short."

They look at each other but don't laugh this time.

Ni Ni continues, "You're gonna thank us when 'Kiyy' feigns being cold, and you can take that blazer off and put it around her shoulders. At that moment, she's gonna be your girl!"

"Bingo," Ronnie nods.

Back then I was a snotty nosed, wet behind the ears kid who didn't really appreciate the genius of my younger sisters. The beginning of romanticism for me.

"Hat or no hat?"

"No hat!" they say together, look at each other and laugh.

They done good.

For September, the weather was warm, about seventy-five degrees that day. The sun was out, the birds were chirping (I done heard that ish somewhere before …). Kiyy and I had spoken every day since the first day of school. My plan was to pick her up, take her to lunch, and then spend the rest of the day with her, ending at the fair. I arrived at her house and rang the bell. I swallowed hard as the door opened, and a lady whom I assumed was her mother opened the door.

"Hi, I'm Gregory. Nice to meet you."

"Hi, I'm Kiyy's Aunt Carol."

She looked me up and down and yelled to the back, "Chil', he's cute. You did good!"

I could hear Kiyy in the background as she muttered "Oh my God!" and then she groaned, *"Aunt Carol!"*

Then I heard another voice tell Aunt Carol, "Carol, let that boy in!"

Aunt Carol stepped aside and ushered me in. I walked into the house and turned into the living room where Kiyy's mother sat braiding Sidney's hair.

"Hi, 'Q'!" Sidney beamed.

I smiled and said hello back to Sidney. I walked up to Kiyy's mother and introduced myself.

"Aren't we dressed to the nines? You look nice, Mr. Que."

Wearing a camel-colored blazer, blue cable knitted crew neck sweater, with navy-blue cuffed trousers, topped off with my camel-suede Wallabees, I cleaned up nicely.

"Thank you." (one for the Que sisters!)

Kiyy's brother was playing with his hot wheels cars and seemed oblivious to me being there.

"Hey, little man," I called out.

"Brandon, you don't hear him speaking to you?"

It was more like an order than a question (raise your hand if you can relate). Brandon looked up from his cars and said hi. At least I now knew what his name was. (lol)

As if right on cue (no pun intended), before things could get awkward, Kiyy walked into the room. She was wearing a yellow and orange flowered sun dress with sandals (orange polish on the fingernails, and the toenails of pretty feet), and had her hair in a braided ponytail that touched the middle of her back. She had stud earrings on and a necklace with a gold "K." She looked like the girl next door to the girl next door. She was beautiful. And I told her so.

"Wow! You look beautiful!"

I was snapped back into reality by her mother.

"Mr. Que? I'ma need a cell phone number to reach you, an address where you live, your mother's first name and home phone number, no hanky panky with my daughter, and Kiyler needs to be back in this house no later than 9:00 … *p.m.* Are we clear?"

"Hanky Panky, Martha? How about no sex in any form or fashion?" Aunt Carol chimed in.

"Oh my God!" Kiyy muttered.

"I know Mr. Que understands clearly. Isn't that right?" Kiyy's mother cautioned, looking over her glasses.

"Yes, ma'am," I said as I proceeded to provide all the information Kiyy's mother requested.

After posting bail for Kiyy's accompaniment, and sealing all documents signed by me with my blood, we left the house and made our way to my car. :-/ Before the days of electronic door locks, I used my key to open the passenger side door and helped Kiyy into the seat. As I closed the door, she smiled at me and I made my way over to the driver's side door. Kiyy reached over the seat and unlocked the door for me. Yep, this girl is a keeper!

"Sorry for what happened inside, Que, my family can be a bit too much," Kiyy said, touching my arm as I put my seatbelt on.

"I got off easy," I said, looking directly into her eyes. "I'd have surely given my right arm, leg, and a bag of M&M's to get you out of that house!"

"Wow! Only one bag of M&M's!?! ... I gotta figure out how to get you to come back here."

"I don't think that's gonna be a problem for you," I said as I started the car and pulled off.

Where does a high school kid take a girl that he really likes on a classy date when he is trying to impress her? Now I love White Castle, and when my sisters asked me where I was taking Kiyy to eat, they gagged in horror when I said I was thinking about White Castle.

"No? Burger King? Blimpie's?"

They just looked at me with disgust, like they had disowned me.

"I was thinking Tad's actually."

My sisters looked at each other. I *know* they didn't see that one coming! Tad's Steaks was an assembly line low-budget chain type of restaurant that sold steaks back then for $3.99 with side dishes included (baked potato and salad). They carved a nice niche for working families that allowed for a family night out at a very decent price.

"Okay, we need to meet this girl a.s.a.p.!" Ronnie declared. "Who are you?"

Ni Ni reached up and put her palm on my forehead. "No, he doesn't have a fever. You came up with that one on your own?" she asked.

"Yepper!"

"I don't know," Ni Ni continued skeptically. "But it's a good choice. Nice call."

She gives me a high five. Ronnie gives me a high five after I tell them the day I have planned for Kiyy.

"Are you adventurous, Kiyy?"

"Depends ..."

"Okay, would you be adventurous with *me* for today?"

"Smooth" dude! How could she say no to that!?! She couldn't.

"I will ... with *you*. What are *we* doing?" (I'm putty!)

"First order of business is to park this car."

I parked near the New Lots train station in East New York, Brooklyn. I led her to the train station. She looked puzzled, but didn't protest.

"I want to show you off to the N-Y-C!" I proclaimed.

Kiyy sparkled in the sunlight on the train platform and then blushed. The train came and we boarded, heading to Manhattan. As we sat down, she slid her arm in between mine and held it. "Pride" is all I can say. At that moment, I felt a tremendous amount of pride. I just wanted to protect her and make her happy. What was happening to me? :-/ We rode in silence for a few stops, reveling in our own thoughts when she pinched me.

"What was that for?"

"That was for not asking for my number and depriving me this moment all summer!"

It was love.

We exited the #3 train at 42nd Street, walked across the platform, and got the #1 train to 48th Street. We got off there and went to street level. Times Square! If you've never been, you have to come and experience it once in your lifetime. Of course, it has changed over the years, but New Yorkers have been fortunate enough to see the changes, good and bad. The Tad's we went to was on the corner of 50th Street and 7th Ave. I didn't know if Kiyy had ever been, nor whether she would even be impressed, but I was excited to share this moment with her.

"Do you like steak?" I prayed.

"Wow, taking a chance, Mr. Que. All week we never talked about food, and what I liked and did not like," she admonished. "I could be a vegetarian."

"I know," I mumbled, suddenly feeling my insides tighten. How could I not ask that over a week's worth of conversation? Ugh!

"But I'm not! I love steak!" she beamed. "I'm happy we're here."

With that, we entered Tad's.

"Carlos!" I muttered louder than I intended to K.P. She looked just as stunned as I did hearing the name, and the implication from Kiyy that he was behind what happened to her.

"Que! We need to do something. She's still bleeding! We're not doctors! We don't know the extent of her injuries! We don't know anything! She could even die!"

That snapped me out of my trance.

"Steven! I'll call Steven!"

I dialed Steven and yelled into the phone when he picked up.

"Tell me you're at the hospital!"

"What? Que? What's wrong with you!?!" Steven yelled back.

"I need you to come to my house right now!" I demanded. "Please bring your medical bag and your surgeon stuff!"

"Que, you need to tell me what's going on right now!"

"I will. I will. But you gotta come now, and you can't tell anyone that you're coming!"

"Okay, now I am officially worried Que! Are you in trouble? Did you get shot again? Stabbed?"

"I'm with K.P. Please come now!"

"K.P.!?!" Steven gasped. "Oh my God! I'm on my way!" He hung up the phone before I could clear up that K.P. was okay. And I take the blame for insinuating that.

———

I carried the tray with both of our steak dishes with sides, and Kiyler carried the drinks (she insisted). We sat down in a booth and I grabbed her hand, saying "grace." I saw her smile with my eyes halfway closed as I began, and she followed my "Amen" with her own. I just can't shake this warm and fuzzy feeling I'm getting being around her. Damn. Then we dug in. Fellas, you know how you get concerned spending money on a girl and she barely touches her plate? Yes, we've all been there. But every once in a few, you run across an exception. Kiyy was not a "dainty" eater. Can you say money well spent? Of course men aren't supposed to think like that, but we do.

"How is your steak?" I asked, taking a sip of my Welch's grape soda. Another reason I loved this place! One of the few public places that served my favorite soda!

"It's good. How is yours?"

"Better with you here!" Again, corny, but effective!

"Is that right? Sounds like game."

I grabbed her hand and looked into her eyes.

"Look into my eyes. You tell me if it's game?" (Cha-ching!)

Steven called me from his car, and I cleared up that K.P. was okay and that it was Kiyy. His "Oh my God!" stood firm when he found out it was Kiyy, and I explained what some of her injuries looked like.

"Kiyler! As in 'love of your life' Kiyler!?!"

"Bro, please! Hurry."

"Clean rags to stop the bleeding, gentle but firm, got it? And ice to stop the swelling. I'll be there as soon as I can!"

I looked at Kiyy, still lying in my arms. The archives had opened as soon as I laid eyes on her. I looked up at K.P. She had already gotten ice.

We sat there about an hour before I noticed the time.

"Whoa, we need to go!"

I jumped up and extended my hand to her. She grabbed her pocketbook (okay I'm showing my age and southern roots), I mean purse, and we were off to the next adventure.

We walked through Times Square back down to 42nd Street instead of taking the #1 train, holding hands and taking in the sights. I was wise enough at this time to take mental images as we walked, to store in the mind's archives. Her smile, her braided ponytail (with the small orange ribbon tied at the end), swinging as she laughed with a slight tilt of her head, the way her sun dress flowed as we walked, her soft hand as I held it tight, showing her orange fingernails, her eyes. Sleepy looking, but vibrant ... Bedroom eyes.

"Where to now, Captain?" Kiyy asked.

"Aye matey, I got my good eye on you! But I'm not quite convinced yet that you're true to this adventure?"

"Oh no, Captain, I am!" she gushed.

"Arrr, well, we will…" I never got to finish that sentence. She grabbed my face and kissed me on my lips.

"I hope that helps make up your mind, Captain. I'll sail the seven seas to see this adventure through!" (I got nothing!)

I stood there numb on the street, trying desperately to remember the sequence of events that just happened (mind blown like "explosion"). I wasn't prepared. I could not recall the softness of her lips. I was the deer caught in headlights! I couldn't remember what I said. Was it witty? Where were we headed now? What street are we on now? Get it together brother man, right now! Okay, after "spazzing" out for however long I did, I recovered to get us on the 42nd Street crosstown bus to 12th Ave. (Westside Hwy).

"Did you mean that about sailing the seven seas to see this adventure through?"

"I most certainly did."

"Well, then prepare your swashbuckling for the Circle Line!" I shrugged. "It's the best I could do."

Kiyy laughed and playfully punched my arm.

"It's not Gilligan's Island…" I stated.

"… But it's still a three-hour tour!" she finished, laughing.

The Circle Line was a three-hour boat sightseeing tour around the island of Manhattan. It's changed now, but then it included all of the sites around Manhattan, including the skyline and its iconic building, the Empire State Building, the World Trade Center, the Statute of Liberty, the Bridges, including the George Washington, Gracie Mansion, Yankee Stadium, Grant's Tomb, the USS Intrepid, and many more. I actually don't know how long it is now, but I do know they have broken the tour up into different cruises now. Nostalgia.

I presented our tickets and we boarded the ship. We went to the top deck and looked out at the water. Kiyy spread her arms and tilted her head upward to absorb the rays of the sun. I looked at her. I tried to be conscious enough where I was not caught staring. But I failed.

"What are you thinking about? And be honest, Que," she asked, catching me staring at her.

Damn, I had never been asked to be honest about what I was thinking, and now actually contemplate sharing inner most thoughts. But it was Kiyy asking, and she was really starting to get a hold on me (Apologies to Smokey Robinson & the Miracles).

"Honestly?" I squirmed, hoping for a reprieve.

"Honestly," she replied sternly.

I swallowed hard and jumped in head first. :-/

"I was thinking I could look at you all day, not get tired, and hope the day never ends."

As God is my witness, that was the thought. What? *I really don't care if you believe me or not, son!* But what you're *not* gonna do, is ruin this moment. *Should I be happy that you're still reading?* Somebody really needs to "escort" dude out of here before I start wilin' out.

"Wow, that didn't sound like game," she replied.

She turned and looked at me, and her look came across a little puzzled from her end. I looked at her and kissed her. Our first real kiss. I was ready … and I remember everything about it. I let everything go in that kiss—doubt, fear, anxiety … problems of the world today (Apologies to The Fearless Four). The kiss ended and Kiyy backed away from me, staring at me in bewilderment.

"What did you do to me? I got chills and … and look at my arms! … gggoose bumps!"

I looked and she did, literally, not figuratively. I immediately took my jacket off and placed it around her shoulders. She looked at me and whatever was going on internally for her at that moment, drifted away, and she succumbed to what I had succumbed to, without either of us knowing exactly what it was.

Steven arrived and damn near busted through the door! "Where is she!?!" he bellowed.

I had carried her to my bedroom and had laid her on my bed. K.P. and I pointed to the bedroom and Steven rushed in. For the next few minutes, Steven probed and assessed. "She needs to be in a hospital! Why isn't she in a hospital!?!"

"Before she went unconscious, she said no hospitals," I whispered with a lowered head.

"I don't give a fuck what she said! She needs to be in a hospital!" Steven roared.

Now y'all don't know the magnitude of Steven's outburst, but K.P. and I do. Steven doesn't curse, not even "gosh darn it!" So ... yeah! Now we're all fucked up!

"Steven, someone may have beat her, and would probably be looking for her in the hospital. It sounds like her life is in danger," K.P. began.

"Then call the fucking police department! What is wrong with you guys!?!"

"Bro, something's not right. There's more going on that we don't know yet. We could be putting her life in danger, and not realize it by putting her in a public hospital. Do you know any private facilities or people off the books that you trust?"

"Do you know what you're asking me to do!?! I took a medical oath!"

I could only hang my head in shame. I couldn't look at him.

"Call 911, Que. Now! I know a private security firm that I trust that I can get to watch her around the clock. It must be reported to the police. Do it now! She's got broken bones, internal injuries, and possible traumatic brain injury! I-*can-not*-help-her-*here!*"

I made the call.

<hr>

We both looked at each other a little sad when the boat docked. Honestly, three hours felt like fifteen minutes. She was still wearing my blazer around her shoulders when I helped her off the boat.

"That was really nice, Que, and whatever happens, we'll always have these memories. I'll never forget it," Kiyy said, as she handed me my blazer.

I almost allowed anxiety to creep in and ask what she meant by "whatever happens," but I didn't. I took in the moment and hugged her on the pier.

"Me too ... me too, Kiyy," I responded softly.

It was about five after five, and I figured we should head back to Brooklyn, get the car, and head to the fair. As we walked to the train station, we passed a Haagen Dazs ice cream cart, and I asked if she wanted ice cream. She nodded and I headed to the cart.

"One scoop or two?"

"One."

I returned with two cones. I handed her one scoop of chocolate chip, and Greedy got two scoops of chocolate.

"I see you remembered," she motioned coyly to her cone.

"I remembered that orange halter top too!" I muttered under my breath, nodding to her comment.

She busted out laughing and pinched me.

"That's not what you're supposed to say!"

"Well, I'm sorry, I guess this ice cream must have some truth serum in it or something," I rationalized.

"I see I'm gonna have to watch you with both of my good eyes, Captain!" she smirked.

"You might matey, you might!"

We got on the train and headed back to Brooklyn. The train ride back was relatively quiet.

I replayed the day in my head and even though there was still day to go, I mused to myself, *Today was a good day!* (Apologies to Ice Cube). We got off the train at New Lots and retrieved the car. Yes, my Brooklyn peoples, it was still there. An old Datsun 280ZX! Remember those? I thought it was a hoopty, back then. Of course it's a classic now. At that time, nobody wanted that car except a high school kid that was happy to be driving.

"To the fair?" I asked, not too convincing.

Of course she picked up on it and responded, "Where would *you* like to go?"

Was that bait? Was she baiting me? That was a little too sexy to be so casual. In fact, a lot sexy! This onion's got a lot of layers! Take a deep breath, my friend, and choose your next words very wisely.

"We should probably go to the fair. I did tell your mom that's where we were going."

She looked at me with a mischievous sparkle in her eye that said to me, "Okay, we can play it like that." If she continues this innocent sexy thing … stick a fork in me … I'm done. I gotta say though I'm really liking her, and I can only hope I've made a good impression on her.

We drove to the school. There was no parking close by, but I finally found something two to three blocks away. I parked the car. I decided right then it was now or never. I had been thinking about this since the train ride, and I needed to act before I lost my nerve. Heart be still!

"Kiyy, before we get out the car, there's something I want to ask you?"

"Okay, Que, what is it?" she replied as she turned toward me in her seat.

"I've really enjoyed today. Being with you, the train rides, Tad's, the boat, everything. I really like you. I want you to be my girl. I think we …"

She "shushed" me and put a finger to my lips. Damn Que! You played yourself! It's too soon! Why did I do that!?! You just fucked it up! I felt knots in my stomach and prepared myself for the letdown.

"I was your girl when you put your jacket over my shoulders." (Drops the mic!)

***

The paramedics came. Steven briefed them, telling them he was a doctor, and her apparent injuries, also mentioning his medical opinion on internal injuries. He pulled one of the paramedics to the side and whispered something I could not hear, but it got the attention of the paramedic. He also told them what hospital to take her to. They took over. They set up their gurney, gave her an IV, and rushed her to their ambulance. As they left the apartment, Steven pulled me to the side.

"Are you okay to make phone calls?"

I nodded.

"The less I know, the better. I'll meet you at the hospital and make sure she gets hospital security, until you can get the private outfit there. Your call is expected."

He handed me a card. He looked at K.P. and hugged her.

"I thought it was you, sweetie. I'm glad you're okay."

K.P. hugged him back and nodded. Steven left for the hospital.

I looked at K.P. She still looked stunned. She looked at me.

"What are you waiting for? Go! You can call the security place on your way."

I took a step and stopped. I turned toward K.P. and she had her back to me. I walked to her, turned her around, and saw silent tears streaming down her face. Too many emotions, too many thoughts.

"I—I'm sorry," was all I could mutter. "I realize this is so selfish, especially after …"

She stopped me, placing a finger on my lips.

"Go shower, change your clothes, and I'll get my coat."

<hr>

Que and Kiyler sitting in a tree, K-I-S-S-I-N-G. First comes love, then comes marriage, then comes a baby in a baby carriage! I think you get the idea. Love at first sight, puppy love, High School love, pure, untainted, unrealistic, unsustainable love. But who thinks about that in the moment? That pride thing was back as we walked from the car to the fair. Kiyy was now my girl. Hard to describe the feeling, but whatever, the best feeling in your life was as a teenager, draw from that.

We got to the admission booth, paid the cover, and walked into the parking lot. The fair was in full swing. There was a Ferris wheel, merry-go-round, and swirl-a-whirl. There were concession stands with hamburgers, hotdogs, popcorn, funnel cake, cotton candy and shaved ices. There was an area for eating, and there was an area with a DJ for dancing. There were booths with games to win prizes and stuffed animals. There were clowns walking around, entertaining. Was that Coach Flanagan dressed as a clown!?!

"I think that's the football coach," I told Kiyy as we walked past, holding hands, as Clown/Coach Flanagan looked at us.

Coach wasn't the only one looking at us either. Our coming out party turned more than a few heads. Just to make sure it was clear that I knew the clown was in fact Coach Flanagan, he barked, "Practice tomorrow 5:30 a.m … sharp, G.Que!"

Kiyy was amused by that.

"G.Que!" Kiyy gushed.

I attempted to quash any cute nuances.

"It's how he refers to all of us, Kiyy. First initial, last name."

"But you're the only one named G.Que!" she chided.

"The gift and the curse."

"I bet it's more gift right now than curse."

Couldn't argue with that as I squeezed her hand.

"Although it might be a curse for me, judging by the looks I'm getting from your fan club!" she continued.

I hadn't noticed anyone other than Kiyy (and Coach). Ain't that how it's supposed to be? Women for the most part notice everything. Of course, I digress.

"Do you wanna get on a ride? Get some popcorn? Cotton candy?"

"So you're gonna ignore what I said or just not address it?"

Uh oh. Better get Maaco!

"Sorry, they don't matter Kiyy. I'm with you. I wasn't trying to ignore it, it's just a non-issue for me."

"It's not just 'you' anymore, though, remember that."

I looked at her. She was absolutely right.

"Okay. I *will* remember that. Do the looks bother you, Kiyy?"

"The looks will never bother me. The touching will be monitored and dealt with appropriately though."

"Did I sign on with a fighter?"

"I'm from Brooklyn. I handles mine. Don't worry though, I'll employ diplomacy before beat down," she laughed.

And right on cue (no pun intended), two girls walked up to us.

"Hello, Mr. Hollywood. I guess it is true!" Aubrey began.

Kiyy looked at me and repeated, "Mr. Hollywood?"

"'Hollywood' is the nickname Rick gave me. The school calls me that," I mumbled.

"Aww, don't be embarrassed, Hollywood, or is it Mr. Hollywood, if you're nasty?" Kiyy laughed. (Apologies, Janet).

Aubrey was captain of the cheerleading squad and girlfriend of Rick. The other girl, Brittany, also a cheerleader, tagged along just to be nosy.

"What's that, Aubrey?"

"That you did meet Mrs. Que!"

Aubrey extended her hand to Kiyy and introduced herself. Kiyy looked amused and returned the greeting.

"Or is it Mrs. Hollywood?" Brittany asked with unmistakable sarcasm.

We both ignored Brittany. Frivolous beef…we "never mind" that! (Apologies to Mason Betha).

"This is Rick's girlfriend."

"The guy you were with first day of school?"

"Yeah, that's my man."

"You haven't introduced her to Rick yet?" Brittany pried. "I'm Brittany. Are you interested in cheerleading, Kiyler?"

"Can't say that I am yet? This is my first year."

"Well, just as well," Brittany replied casually. "Freshman typically don't make the squad anyway."

"It is just as well," Kiyy replied dryly. "Between Alvin Ailey, school, and Mr. Que here, I think my plate's pretty full."

Aubrey turned her head to hide her giggle, and whispered out the side of her mouth.

"I like her, Que."

"Nice meeting you, Kiyler." Aubrey waved as she nudged Brittany away.

We stood there and watched them walk away.

"I think you're gonna be just fine here, Kiyy."

"Oh you had doubts?" she laughed.

The ride to the hospital was pretty much in silence. I mean, what could possibly be said at this time? I can't even imagine what is going on in K.P.'s mind.

"Que, you need to call the security place," K.P. reminded.

Well, I think you all know what I meant.

"I'm calling now."

I called the security place, and they were expecting my call, just as Steven said. I went over particulars and agreed to meet at the hospital Kiyy was being taken to.

"Are you in contact with any of her relatives, Que?" K.P. asked. "Somebody needs to know, don't you think?"

"Probably so, but I only remember where her mom used to live. I don't even know if she still lives there. But if I go there out of the blue, and somebody is watching her house and sees me, I could lead them to her."

"For that matter, Que, you don't know if someone will be watching *your* house."

"That's true too. I'm really at a disadvantage right now. Need to talk to Kiyy and find out more."

"Please don't take this the wrong way, Que, but is this really your concern now?"

"Coming from you, I'm not taking it the wrong way. But until I at least hear her side, I'm gonna concern myself. Do you understand that?"

"I understand it, but I don't like it. I just have a bad feeling that this is bigger than either of us think."

We pulled up to the hospital, and I headed to the parking garage and pulled into a spot.

"I shouldn't have brought you, K.P."

"Why not?"

"Because of what you just said. I'm dragging you into something you don't have to be a part of."

"I'm in it because you're in it, Que. And you need to know that I …"

She paused, letting her sentence linger, like she was pondering whether to finish it.

"I'm here for you … no matter what happens."

There just weren't enough hours in the day. I didn't want to leave her. We stayed at the fair until around 8 p.m. I wanted to make sure that Kiyy was back home before 9 p.m, as I said she would. Rick found us at the merry-go-round, and I formally introduced him to Kiyy. He, in turn, gave her a brief history lesson in the "legend" of Woody, as he called it. I just decided I couldn't be embarrassed any further than that, and just put the "H" on my chest. I also introduced her to anyone else that came up to us, excluding her friends Pam and Carlos, whom we saw at a concession stand.

"Pleased to meet you," I said to both as I shook their hands.

"Where is Monie?" Kiyy asked.

"Monie" is Simone.

"She couldn't get out today, but she'll be here tomorrow. Are you coming out with us tomorrow, Kiyler?" Carlos asked.

Kiyy looked at me.

"We will," Kiyy said.

"Cool," Pam said.

At the same time Carlos uttered,

"We?"

Pam nudged him, and he continued,

"—should all hang out! That will be cool!"

"We'll see you guys tomorrow," Kiyy exclaimed as she led me away from the awkward ending.

We walked out of the fair and toward my car holding hands. Upon getting to the car, Kiyy handed me my blazer from around her shoulders. As the evening came, it got cooler, and I placed the blazer around her shoulders before we got on the Ferris wheel. It smelled of her perfume. Found out later on, she wore "Red." I've remembered the name and smell ever since. I opened the car door and she got in.

"I really don't want to take you home."

"Really?" she said with that innocent tone, but not so innocent look to match.

"Really."

"We should spend the next ten minutes kissing. It won't be so agonizing then when we're parked in front of my house, and you're wanting to kiss me, but nervous about my mom seeing us. I'll stay with you until 8:58 p.m. and run into the house before 9 p.m."

"Wait, it sounds like you ain't new to this?" I swallowed, suddenly wondering how innocent my new girlfriend actually was.

"Calm your nerves. You have a virtuous young lady. I've been replaying these moments in my mind for years. I owe you a pinch because you've taken two minutes from me."

"Brains, beauty, and body!"

"You been checking me out?"

"I've had dreams about that anatomy!"

She looked at me with those doe-like, devilishly innocent bedroom eyes.

"We might be able to make those dreams to be reality!"

Yaaaa … this one right here? …

"You are dangerous Kiyler Pardee."

"I promise to use all of my powers on you for good, Gregory Que."

She looked at me and then whispered, "Six minutes Dougie Fresh …"

I didn't let her finish (Apologies to Doug E. Fresh on her behalf).

We kissed for the next six minutes.

———————

Kiyy was initially checked in as a Jane Doe because she did not have any id on her person. After I told the admittance person her name was "Brenda Joseph," she was admitted under that name. I know, I know. But would you have told them her real name under the circumstances? K.P. looked at me, but did not say a word. We were told "Brenda" was being prepped for emergency surgery for a gunshot wound and head injuries, and what floor to go to wait.

"What!?!" I yelled.

"Gunshot!?!" K.P. yelled, at the exact same time.

"Yes," was the reply from the admittance person.

We rushed to the fifth floor, and the nurses' station.

"Ki—I mean Brenda Joseph?" I asked.

"She's in surgery," the nurse at the station said. "It will be a while. Are you next of kin?"

I looked at K.P.

"Uh no … ex-boyfriend."

"Okay, the police have been notified and are gonna want to speak to someone. Can you get in contact with parents, relatives, etc?"

"Um no. We've been broken up for a while. I can speak to the police when they get here though."

We went to the waiting area.

"What are you gonna tell the police, Que? You're gonna tell them her name is 'Brenda Joseph?'"

"No I'm not. I'm gonna tell *them* the truth. Hopefully they will understand the situation and keep it under wraps, at least until they can talk to Kiyy."

"Kodak moment. You trusting Po Po?"

"I know."

Just then, I heard my name being called, and we turn to see a gentleman in a suit and a bowtie with wire rim glasses, looking straight out of the Nation of Islam.

"That's not inconspicuous," I said under my breath for K.P. to hear. "That's me," I called to him.

We met halfway and shook hands. He introduced himself as Tariq Shabazz Mohammed. I introduced K.P. He explained to me that he has worked with the hospital before, and there would be two persons assigned to Kiyy's room. One outside and one inside. I would need to provide a list of non-hospital personnel that would be approved to enter Kiyy's room. I explained to him that Kiyy was admitted under an alias "Brenda Joseph," and that her real name was Kiyler Pardee. He said it was common, and it would not be a problem.

"My guys are inconspicuous, ordinary looking that blend in, and are trained for all possibilities," Tariq added. I'll introduce you to them. He called them over.

Honestly with everything going on, I probably wouldn't have noticed them anyway, but even I wasn't ready for two white guys!

"This is Jack, and this is Daniel."

"These guys were here when we got here," K.P. whispered to me. "One was reading the paper over there, and the other was listening to music over there. Ordinary is right, I just thought they were waiting …"

She never finished her sentence.

"Your brother is a good man, which is why we are here, and will be for as long as you need us. You can always reach me at this number, but Jack and Daniel are more than equipped to handle any requests and situation. I trust 'two' are satisfactory at this time, but more can be added depending on the threat."

"I think we're good, Mr. Mohammed," I said.

"Tariq, please."

"Tariq … What about payment?"

"It's been handled."

"What?"

"Everything has been taken care of."

"I—ah, okay Tariq, thank you very much," I uttered as K.P. nudged me with a thank you of her own.

"I've also taken the liberty of contacting police that we work with in this precinct to come and interview you. They will ask the questions that they need to ask, but will be discreet about the endeavor."

"Okay, thank you, Tariq."

"I hope all goes well for your friend."

With that he was gone. Jack and Daniel took over and asked me about a list. I got a piece of paper and put myself and K.P. on it.

"You want me on the list?"

"You in it, right? … That's what you said, right? Or was that just for show?"

She punched my arm.

"You're gonna have a hard time getting rid of me."

We reached her house at 8:50 p.m. Ten minutes until the ball ends. Well, actually eight by Kiyy's count. I parked in front of her door and unbuckled my seatbelt. You'll never guess what came on the radio driving her home. Yeah, ya will ... That's right, "Suddenly" by Billy Ocean.

"That's our song!" we both exclaimed upon hearing it.

We then discussed it.

"You heard that song playing too when we met?" I asked.

"Yes, and when I got home too. I just identified it with you," Kiyy said.

"Yeah, me too."

"Then it is officially *our* song," Kiyy proclaimed.

And then angelic voices sang, "Ahhhh ... aaahhh!"

"I don't want the day to end, either," Kiyy confessed. "I've enjoyed everything, and I mean everything that we've done today. I'm really happy that you want to be with me, and I just want to make you happy."

"I am happy, Kiyy. Can't say I've ever been happier. I've never told anyone that I want to share everything with them, but I am telling you that."

We both looked at the dashboard clock, and it read 8:57 p.m. I kissed her longer than a peck, and then turned away muttering,

"Be gon' 'fore I set mine eye 'pon thee forth right and succumb to wit thy charm!"

"Not sure if that is Shakespearean or biblical, but I'm gone."

She laughed as she kissed me one last time before getting out of the car. She moved so fast I didn't react fast enough to get out and open the door for her.

"Sorry," she called out as she ran up the stairs. "I don't want you to see my gown turn to rags! Goodnight, honey!"

"Good night, my love," I whispered as she closed the door with seconds to spare.

Kiyy was in surgery for five-and-a-half hours. For moments at a time, I thought she was going to die. Not because I got updates or anything, just pessimistic thoughts. Life does that to you. Sometimes you brace yourself for the worst instead of thinking for the best. I can only talk about me, though. Your experience could very well be different, jovial even.

Steven did the surgery. I was a little surprised to see him when he came out, but just as relieved to know Kiyy was in good, well, great hands.

"The surgery went well. The bullet was removed, internal hemorrhaging and injuries contained. She sustained two broken ribs and a broken left arm.

We'll do an MRI in a few days to check soft tissue and affected organs. As for the head injuries, we had to wait for swelling to go down before we could close those wounds. Neurology looked at her. CAT scan showed there were no injuries to the brain itself, but we cannot say with certainty as yet that the blunt force trauma she sustained won't translate to TBI, traumatic brain injury."

It was a lot to take in, but all I could focus on was that Steven didn't tell me about the gunshot at the house. I know it's petty.

"Whoa! Put an 'H' on your chest and handle it. You know law, I know medicine and I know trauma and how it affects people. Don't you ever tell me how to do my job!" Steven scolded me, when I threw that at him. I totally deserved that.

"Really, Que!?!" K.P. spat, "Steven probably just saved her life, and that is the first thing out of your mouth!?!"

K.P walked away. Yeah, I deserved all of that and more. But Steven didn't pile on.

"Que, neither you nor K.P. were in any state to hear the worst at that time. Kiyy lost a lot of blood, and was dangerously close to expiring before the paramedics got her to their ambulance. The paramedics on scene probably deserve more credit than I do for saving her life. They stabilized her vitals and kept her alive. We were waiting for her arrival and she went from the ambulance to surgery."

"Steven, I'm really sorry," I began.

"I know, Que. Irrational is what I deal with."

"Damn irrational?"

Steven just looked at me.

"Okay. When can Kiyy have visitors?"

"She will be groggy coming off of the anesthesia, and adjusting to the medicine she is on, so I'd say tomorrow afternoon would be a good start."

"Oh Steven, I'ma need you to wait right there for a minute as I reclaim the chunk of ass that K.P. just chewed out, so you can sew it back on."

Steven threw his hands up like "My name is Bennett, and I'm not in it!" and smirked as I walked toward K.P. sitting by herself. I noticed Jack and Daniel were no longer with us as well. They knew where Kiyy was gonna be before we did, clearly.

"I need to apologize to you, K.P. That guy back there was an asshole."

"Apologizing to me? I don't need an apology. You need to apologize to Steven."

"I did. But I owe you one as well. I made you upset with me, and I never want that to happen. So I apologize for that."

"You don't owe me an apology. I probably owe you one. I took my frustration out on you."

"Frustration? What do you mean?"

"Can we talk about this another time? I mean, if we need to? What else did Steven say?"

"Um, sure. K.P., it's been a long night. Steven thinks Kiyy should rest. We can leave."

"I was gonna take a cab. Change and get ready for work. You're not staying?"

"I mean with Kiyy coming off anesthesia and adjusting to medication, I'd just be watching her sleep. I need to go home, clean-up, change, process. This is a lot."

"Process. Yeah, tell me about it."

"K.P., what's wrong?"

"What's wrong? Your ex. The love of your life has just re-introduced herself in a most unconventional way, Que. She almost died in your home. The past is back again. There are so many unanswered questions that you never got answered that are gonna re-open wounds. There are memories that will re-surface, if they haven't already, and it's gonna affect you again."

"I get that, K.P. But why are you talking to me like that?"

"Because you don't see what's going to happen, Que?"

"You think I'm gonna fall for her again?"

"I do, and it changes everything."

"Changes everything? What are you talking about?"

"Did you forget what was happening before the doorbell rang?"

We're now at the root of K.P's ire, I think. And I understand. I get it. Do *you* get it? Oh, you saw it way before I did, huh?

"No, of course not, K.P. I—"

"Please Que, please don't say anything right now. I can't. I can't right now."

I grabbed K.P. and hugged her. She did not melt in my arms as she has done in the past. She remained tight. She pulled away from me.

"I'm sorry, Que. I need to get home."

"I'll take you."

"No, please. I need to be by myself right now. You used the word 'process.' That's actually a good word for right now."

"K.P., please …"

She turned and left.

———

The ride home was lonely. As I drove, I replayed the events that had occurred in my mind. I smiled. Kiyy did that. I got home, said hello to the parents, and went upstairs to my room. My sisters came into my room, of course, to find out how everything went. My recap pleased them, especially the part about putting the blazer over Kiyy's shoulders and her response. They warned me not to "eff" this up (as if). They also wanted to know when they were gonna meet Kiyy. I ordered them out and got in the shower. Thought about getting a snack before I went to bed, and the phone rang. It was Kiyy.

"I just wanted to say thank you again for a great day," she said.

"I was going to call you as soon as I got into bed."

"Without me?" she pouted.

"Not if I had my way."

"I wanted to call you as soon as you pulled away from my house, but I wanted to make sure you got home safe."

"I could have talked to you."

"Not with what I wanted to say, you would have crashed," she uttered seductively.

"Kind of confident there, huh?"

She went into another mode and whispered to me what she wanted to do with me, and "Floyd" sprang up like a cobra, dancing to the inflections of her voice. No control whatsoever.

If she had said, "Cum," I honestly can't say it wouldn't have happened.

"Are you hard? I know you are," she cooed.

Of course I was. But I had to turn the tables with my own spin on seduction. What I was about to attempt would separate me from the next man. It would culminate my status from pupil to student to master of seduction. My mistress would be proud. Just for clarification purposes, "mistress" used here is the feminine word for "master." See? That dictionary still comes in handy, huh? Thanks again, Mom!

Anyways, her name was Breeze, and you'd never guess her ancestry from her nickname. But everyone in Brooklyn grew up with a nickname, whether you were "brown, yellow, Puerto Rican or Haitian" … or "Black or White" (Apologies to Phife Dawg & Michael Jackson). Her "government issued" was Bree Zen, a fine ass seventeen-year-old Asian, very talented in the ways of the Far East, who took my virginity at eleven, and mentored me for five years in those ways. I am aware that a few statutory rape laws might have been violated back then and affirmative defenses might not have been plausible. I mean, Breeze took her teachings seriously, physically and mentally. Did I mention she was very talented? How about fine? She made me take an oath that I would attempt this technique three times in my lifetime. Once to become a master. Upon perfecting this technique, and elevating my spirit to master, I would pass it to one person of my choosing, employing the same teachings, techniques, and oath. Finally I am to use the final instance for my wife. I'm serious as a heart attack. All I can say further about this technique is that the goal is to reach the subconscious consciously, which you may pick up on. I've also made it very easy to pick up the elements it involves. The missing link is the story that ties everything together. Breeze, if you're reading this, two down, one to go.

"Are you lying down?"

"Yes."

"What are you wearing?"

"A tank top."

"Are you wearing panties?"

"I am."

"What color are they?"

"What color do you think they are?" she teased.

"I need you to promise me something, okay?"

"Okay."

"No matter how intense the next few minutes get, promise not to touch yourself."

"Really? You're gonna make me want to touch myself?" she challenged.

"You sound skeptical? All I ask is that you keep an open mind."

"Okay, I promise."

"Close your eyes and picture only what you hear from the sound of my voice. Are your eyes closed?"

"Yes."

"Do you see anything?"

"No."

"Do you feel anything?"

"No."

"Do you hear anything besides my voice?"

"No."

"Do you smell anything?"

"No."

"Do you taste anything?"

"No."

"What's your favorite fruit?"

"Mango."

"Picture me in the kitchen. I am cutting up your favorite into rectangular cubes. Can you see the shape? Sweet … juicy … mango. Can you see me cutting up your favorite fruit, mango, into rectangular cubes?"

"Yes."

"I want to feed one to you. Can I feed one to you?"

"Yes."

"I've put a cube in my mouth. It is sweet, it is juicy. I want you to take a bite from the cube in my mouth. But you cannot touch me, okay?"

"Okay."

"Come closer to me and take a bite. Did you take a bite?"

"Yes."

"You didn't touch me, right?"

"No."

"Did you taste the mango?"

"Yes."

"I don't believe you."

"I did."

"What did it taste like?"

"It tasted sweet … and juicy. Wait, what just happened there?"

"I need you to focus back on the sound of my voice, okay?"

"Okay."

"I'm lying next to you. Really close, but we are not touching. I'm whispering to you, just like this. I feel warmth coming from your body. Your body is very warm. I have nothing on. You have on a tank top and orange panties. Can you picture that?"

"Yes."

"Are you picturing that?"

"I am."

"I move to your neck and inhale, just like this. You're wearing my favorite perfume, Red. You know what it smells like, right? Can you smell it?"

"Yes."

"Can you picture me, inhaling the scent from your neck without touching you?"

"Yes."

"Do you know what that smell makes me want to do?"

"No."

"It makes me want to touch you, to caress you, to feel your warm skin. If I told you I was going to touch you right now, do you think your body would tingle from anticipation?"

"I don't know."

"My finger tips are inches away from your right breast."

"Oh my G— … my body is tingling!"

"Stop tingling."

"Que, what are you doing to me?"

"Did your body stop tingling?"

"Yes. How are you doing this?"

"I need you to continue to focus on my voice, okay?"

"Okay."

"Your skin is still warm, right?"

"Yes."

"I can see moisture on your neck, from your warmth. Can you see that?"

"Yes."

"There is moisture on your chest between your breasts. It is warm from your body heating it. There is a drop glistening in the middle of your chest, right between your breasts. I want to touch it. But it moves on its own. Do you feel the droplet moving down between your breasts?"

"Oh my God! Yes!"

"Relax. It is okay. Continue to focus on my voice, okay?"

"O-okay."

"I want you to picture a faucet. The faucet is dripping. Dripping water. The water is dripping onto your chest, between your breasts. It is a slow steady drip. Are you picturing that, right now?"

"Yes."

"The moisture continues to form on your breasts as I take off your tank top. Can you help me take off your tank top?"

Before Kiyy can comprehend what is happening, she instinctively reaches for her tank top to remove it when she realizes she has just taken off her tank top! As Kiyy told me later on, it was as if her mind was no longer in control of her body. Yep!

"I begin to blow softly on your breasts. Can you feel me blowing softly on your breasts? Can you feel my breath on your nipples?"

"Yes."

"I want my breath to cool you. Do you feel coolness when I do that?"

"Yes."

"Do you want me to stop?"

"No."

"I don't want to stop. I'm blowing softly down your body. Can you see that?"

"Yes."

"I just stopped around your navel. I'm blowing on your navel? Can you feel that?"

"Yes."

"Do you like the tone of my voice?"

"Yes."

"Does it relax you?"

"Yes."

"Are you relaxed?"

"Yes."

I proceeded to tell her a story over the phone. The particulars of this story will remain with the interested parties. That means "she" and "me." Let's just say it was a special story that ended in orgasmic pleasure for Kiyy, without me touching her or her touching herself, to her amazement, and my relief. :-) This is where the origins of Double Stuff and Juicy Fruit began. Other words that became part of our lexicon included "drip, drip, drip" and "Niagara Falls."

The Sexual Intellectual is-the-mixer
For Honeys whose G spots needs an elixir
Warning! To keep me off that behind
Don't ever let me step inside of your mind
My verbal stimulation gives mental intoxication
The physical interpretation is orgasmic sensations.

Just in case the "lyrical" skills didn't resonate with you before. :-/

The ride home was lonely. As I drove, I replayed the events that occurred in my mind. I smiled. K.P. did that. Always putting other people above herself. Always having my back. The peanut butter to my chocolate, the nougat to my Three Musketeers, the milk to my Nestlé's Quik.

My best friend. I don't want you to think I'm totally oblivious to K.P. She embodies the 3B's, she is fun to be around, and there is definitely something "more than friendsish" that is going on between us. But that's just it. There is something great with us that I don't want to lose. I can absolutely tell K.P. anything, and not feel that she will judge me. Even tonight, I didn't think she judged me, although she certainly could have. Am I being naïve to think that won't change in a relationship? That I will lose that? Yes, it absolutely is selfish. K.P. is selfless, I am not always selfless. I wouldn't want her to change. Being in a relationship changes people, even if they try their hardest not to change. I don't blame you if you feel it sounds like excuses. I think I'm being selfless in this situation. Yes, even after I just said three lines above that I was being selfish. Confusion is always a willing dance partner. And K.P. is absolutely right that Kiyy coming back brings everything back, and changes everything. I'm gun shy again, and K.P. is probably the unfortunate beneficiary. Don't judge me.

I park my car, take notice of my surroundings, mostly to see if anyone is scoping me or my place. Satisfied that I'm not being watched, I go into the crib. There are bloody towels on the floor, bloody sheets on my bed, bloody clothes in my bathroom, and bloody memories in my head. I get a big hefty bag, pull the sheets and pillowcases off the bed. The mattress pad has blood soaked through. I pull it off, the mattress is blood free, and I get the spare mattress pad (ironically, a spare that K.P. made me buy). I grab a linen set and fix the bed. I look for blood on the hardwood floors, and see none. I walk to the door and then to my couch, and still see no blood on the hardwood floors. What the hell? How could that be? Kiyy was bleeding something fierce when she came here. Out the corner of my eye, I see my mop bucket and mop with a jug of disinfectant outside my guest bathroom. Then it hit me.

While I was changing out of my bloody clothes and showering to go to the hospital, K.P. mopped my floors and cleaned my leather sofa. Damn, phenomenal woman is she. I also noticed with the bloody towels were her bloody clothes. Yes, K.P. and Jinx have clothes here. I put everything in the Hefty bag and cleaned the floor where the bloody items were. I then decided to take a shower before trying to get some sleep. It was about 7:30 in the morning when the hot water hit my skin.

After showering, I went to the kitchen and made myself a breakfast sandwich before ending up in the bed. You know I couldn't sleep, right? I looked at the clock, it said 8:30 a.m. Ugh! I decided to call K.P. to see if she made it to work okay. K.P. runs her own computer software company. I know, right!?! KPKP, K. Parker Komputer Programming. To my surprise, I was told by her secretary that she took the day off. Okay. Thought about calling her cell, but decided just to give her space. Ugh! Can't believe I just used that term!

Is it too early for wine? A shot of JD? Of course not! I live alone. The one rule in this household right now is that there are no rules! So I pop out of bed and head to my bar. I decided on JD, but not a shot. I like my Jack Daniels chilled. Pulled the bottle out of the mini fridge under my bar, and poured a double shot into a glass. Slow your roll, people. I'm gonna nurse this JD, and not down a double shot before 9 a.m. (lol) Settled in on the leather sectional and turned on the T.V. After sifting through two hundred plus channels, I concluded that cable T.V. was a scam because there wasn't one thing on that I wanted to see. Settled on Sportscenter. The Lakers beat the Clippers in pre-season, the Mets were targeting potential free agents, and the Steelers were on a bye week. The doorbell rang as I took a swig of the good stuff. The clock said 8:46 a.m.

"Who the hell is this? Paging me at 5:46 in the morning, crack of dawn n' now I'm yawnin'..." (Apologies to Biggie). You get the idea. The bell rang again.

"Aight, I'm coming!"

I open the door ... and I see ... K.P.!

She jumps on me and starts kissing me!

I barely had a chance to close the door. The glass of JD I was holding splashes all over both of us.

"K.P! What the ... !?!"

I didn't get to finish the sentence. She stopped me by covering my mouth and motioning with a zipper movement. She stepped back from me, took off her coat, and dropped it on the floor. She was wearing nothing under the coat! She rushed me and started taking off my clothes, kissing me at the same time. Suddenly, I just let go. Everything I felt for this woman erupted with passion! I picked her up and carried her to the bed. But she wasn't having any of that. She jumped up, reversed positions, and pushed me onto the bed. She got on top of me and stopped for a second. She looked into my eyes and made sure I was looking into hers. She lowered her head and kissed me passionately. I was consumed. We made love. I need to repeat that. We … made … love! The next two hours were pure bliss! I put everything to the side, concentrating only on K.P. I lost myself in her. How I was able to concentrate and lose myself in K.P. was a testament to the kind of woman she is, and how I feel about her. Nothing mattered except her at that moment. Unfiltered passion, unfiltered emotion … unfiltered love?

Guys … I'ma talk to you for just a second. We all have our top five orgasms, and the women that caused them hold a special place in our hearts and minds. And you know what orgasm I'm talking about. For most of us, it's a rare one. The one where you feel like your insides around the lower abdomen are gushing out of that little slit in your penis, long after the semen has stopped. If you could bottle that feeling, trust me when I say there would be no more crime in the world! Well, maybe just to get that bottle. :-/ Women, I trust you have an orgasm like that as well, a little harder to achieve because you got like nine waves to get through to get there, but when you do … it is a spiritual feeling, and you will never forget it. Just imagine if you both reach that plateau at the same time!?! K.P. and I do not have to imagine.

We laid in the bed next to each other, not touching, not wanting to touch at that moment. K.P. was being hit with systematic spasms it seemed every seven seconds, and I was catching a spasm every seventeen seconds. The look on my face was a combination of shock and amazement. The look on K.P.'s face was the realization of gratification and perfection.

After several minutes from what I thought was my last spasm, I spoke.

"What got into you, woman?"

"You got into me."

"I mean yes, but what caused this? This is totally out of character for you."

"Maybe that's the point. Maybe I needed to get your attention."

"You've always had my attention, K.P."

"No. I haven't. But I might now."

"Okay, you and I don't usually do riddles, K.P."

"I had a long talk with my mother when I left you at the hospital. I told her about Marlon, what was about to happen between us, I—"

"Wait … What!?! You told your mother what?"

"I told my mother that I was going to sleep with you, but then Kiyy showed up and— ..."

"Whoa! W-what did she say?"

"She said nothing, but I could tell she wasn't surprised."

"About Marlon, or about us?"

"About us, Que. I told her about what happened to Kiyy, I told her about my fears, what I wanted out of my life, what I wanted for my life. She let me talk, and I told her everything I was feeling. When I finished, she hugged me, and said a few things, but one thing resonated more than anything else."

"What was that?"

"Basically, she said that if I was sure of what I wanted, it was not wrong, and in this case, to go for what my heart wants, because the heart wants what the heart wants, 'consequences be damned.' But she also told me to remember that you still have to deal with the consequences of the heart, after everything is said and done. And now I have to deal with the consequences."

"The consequences of sleeping with me?"

"No. The consequences of love. I told my mother I was in love with you."

8

THE CACKLING OF
THE CROWS

It all makes sense

They know something I don't, and they revel in the knowledge that I can't decipher their language. I've missed the signs, even when I expect the unexpected. The future remains a mystery to me. The past remains a mystery to me. The present remains a mystery to me. They used to caw. They just cackle now. The cackling of the crows.

I first took notice of the crows at Mr. Parker's burial site. I gave them no special significance. Crows have long been associated in some form or fashion with death. Whether folklore, legend, mythology, or mysticism, in many cultures, the crow served as an intermediary between life and death. What caught my eye was that there were so many (about eight), perched in trees above his grave site. They were not vocal at all. They just watched. Recalling it over the years has now given it an eerie significance, a mysterious unknown that begs for translation. One I may never get.

When I returned home after Mr. Parker's funeral, one crow sat in a tree in front of my house, cawing. I looked at the bird as I got out of my car and I swear it was looking directly at me as it cawed. How can you not take notice of that? I believe the same bird perched itself outside of my bedroom window and cawed periodically. Leaving and returning for the rest of the day. For the last ten years, various numbers of crows have shown up expectantly and unexpectantly. It's become tortuous. By the way, did you know that a group of crows is called a "murder" of crows? :-/

I have theorized at various times that their message has been a warning, good fortune, or a blessing, or clairvoyance, letting me know about impending death, or even that the crow could be my spirit animal. I am just as lost as I was back then.

Reading and research is supposed to provide clarity, but it has done the opposite. It has added cloudiness, uncertainty, and confusion.

I've read that crows symbolize change and I need to look beyond myself and get out of my comfort zone, think outside of the box.

I've read that crows live in an abyss, messengers with knowledge of magic and unseen forces all around us, able to see the past, present and future at the same time.

I've read that the crow's color represents creation, where new comes into fruition. Black has always been synonymous with evil, death, and darkness, negative traits attributed by mankind. Yet here, it is beautiful.

I've read that crow caws come in distinct cadence and meaning, a complex language indecipherable to humans, because crows are not only intelligent, but also deceptive. I've also read that crows take great pride in that deception, building false nests to detract predators, being keenly aware of what they know and you don't. For me that might explain their caws turning to cackling over the years.

I've read that crows on average live about 10 years, but can live up to 30 years in captivity.

Like Aesop's fable, "The Crow and the Pitcher," the crow shows you to use the means and ingenuity you have and implement it in an atypical manner to achieve your aims. Remember, a crow dying of thirst finds a pitcher that has a little water left in it. The crow cannot stick his head in the pitcher to get to the water. After thinking, the crow picks up a pebble with its beak and drops it into the pitcher. The crow continues this action over and over again, eventually lifting the level of the water to a point where he can stick his bill in and drink. The moral of the story is that you can accomplish an insurmountable task with small cumulative actions.

I mentioned earlier that I first took notice of the crows at Mr. Parker's grave site. In fact, that is the time when I decided there was meaning in their showing up and subsequent cawing at me. But there have been numerous occasions where the crows have appeared and I thought nothing of it. Remember when I mentioned in high school about coming down and talking to Carlos about Kiyy? There was a crow cawing at me before I went to meet up with everyone that day. There was a crow sitting on a branch near the Dunkin' Donuts Kiyy and I went to when we broke up. The day I met Kiyy, there were a couple of crows that greeted me with caws as I got back home. There were two crows near the dock when Kiyy and I went on the Circle Line.

Of course these instances could very well all just be coincidence. Or there could be meaning attached to them as I have now chosen to believe. I would not be mad at you if you decided I was being paranoid. But there have been other instances, as well. The day Snow died, the day I got shot. The day I met Winnie, the first time K.P. and I kissed. And finally, the day Kiyy showed up while I was with K.P. Every instance after Snow, the crows seemed to cackle as opposed to cawing. I realize I am at risk here of readers thinking that I should be seeing a psychiatrist or psychologist. Everyone should be good identifying which one is appropriate here, correct? Sorry I had to ask. Well, I'm good. Thanks for your concern. :-/ But I am the one waking up to crows every morning. There is a reason, even if I have not figured it out yet. Just for the wise-ass (_Ô v Ô_) out there, I do not live near corn fields, or areas where crows are traditionally known to congregate.

What have these crows been trying to tell me? Well, if hindsight is 20-20, then there have been obvious warnings about danger, impending death, and perhaps bad luck. But what about the times I was with Kiyy? Those were good times, happy times. Or with K.P. The same, good times, happy times. Even Winnie, I dare say our first meeting was good times and happy times. :-/ So what were the crows trying to tell me there?

I am assuming that you are buying into this, agreeing that there is some message delivered here. I mean, you have no choice really if you're riding with me to the end of this book. But I do see the potential for this to turn readers off. But again, it's my book. Were the crows alerting me to a change in my life? Each of these young ladies effectuated change in my life, so that is possible. Is it also possible that the crows could have been warning me that if I continued on with whatever actions I was undertaking at the time with these ladies, there could be disappointment? The only one I see that course was with Kiyy. Unless I include not getting into a relationship with K.P. into the equation because I didn't want to be disappointed? And this reasoning can certainly apply to the day I got shot.

If you couldn't grasp the confusion before, I'm pretty sure most of you are on the bandwagon now. And now that I've got you scratching your head, I'm gonna let those thoughts ponder and perhaps torment you as they have me (probably not, but wishful thinking nonetheless).

<hr>

I didn't want to go out, but I had been putting Morris off for a while, and I just couldn't use the excuse of "girl problems" just for him to throw reconfigured Jay Z at me. "I got ninety-nine problems *and* a bitch *is* one. Aw, poor baby!" (Apologies to the ladies. Not too sure that Jay Z deserves an apology here). Anyways, nobody, especially Morris, is going to feel sorry for my blueprint in regards to the ladies. The gift and the curse (Apologies to Jay Z, here). See what I did there … lol.

Morris picked me up and we headed to the club of his choice.

"Come on, Que. You know girls always travel with 'they friend,'" Morris proclaimed.

He put fingers in the air and bent them twice to insinuate quotations for emphasis.

"Drinks on you, son," I retorted.

"Man, you could meet Mrs. Que tonight!"

Hmmph, if he only knew. So we're at this club called "Mystic Crow" in the Meatpacking district (I kid you not). I have to admit, there are some "bad" honeys up in this piece—all races, nationalities, and origins. Talking bottles and models and all of that (Apologies to Jagged Edge). The music is bumping, and the atmosphere is "throw your hands in the air" like. On any other night, I'd be out there with Morris on the hunt, but instead, I chilled (Apologies to Oran "Juice" Jones). Morris is ballin' with his bottle of Cristal, but he did get me a double Jack, so I'm content. We'd been at the club for a good two hours. Morris is throwin' bass at honeys, they throwin' back midrange :-/ (Apologies to the Diabolical Biz Markie). But it's all good. Morris takes a time out and checks on me.

"I'm good, fam."

"Yo, if I find a doobie with a friend, don't let me down, Que."

"I got you, man."

A fine young lady looks like she is making a bee line to us. Morris notices and alerts me with a not-so-subtle elbow. She walks up and says, "Excuse me," looking at me. "My name is Mandie. Do you have a girlfriend?"

"Yeeah," I muster, not wanting to lie, but "flirt" is always on automatic, and I hear myself saying, so as not to be rude, "But if I didn't, you could get it."

"*You* could still get it," she replied rather boldly.

The boys (meaning Morris and I), look at each other, and I quickly try to deflect, "Let me introduce you to my mans n'nem."

"He's cute, but I'm interested in you."

"Why?" I stammered a little uncomfortably.

"I've been watching you. Clearly this is not your scene, and the only reason you're here is because your 'mans n'nem' needed a wing man. Girls have been trying to get your attention all night, and either you're oblivious to it or just don't care— ... "

"Or gay," Morris interjected jealously.

Mandie gave Morris the "fool look" and continued, " ... The curiosity turned into attraction, and the attraction turned into desire."

We looked at each other again and Morris mumbled, "That's either the sexiest ish I ever heard, or the mackest ... or both!"

"Wow, Mandie, you are beautiful, and certainly bold, but my heart does belong to another."

"And she's a lucky woman."

With that, Mandie strutted off with Morris in hot pursuit to pick up the pieces for himself.

All I heard on the ride home was Morris rehashing the club scene, each time embellishing a little more than the last time. Adding curse words to punctuate.

"Heart belongs to another? Motherfucker, who got your heart!?! Tell me that, okay!?! One of the baddest women in the club! ... Hell, on earth! Comes up to yo' ass! ... *Yo' ass!* ... Puts the pussy in yo' hands! Yo' 'single' ass! At least, the last time I checked! Unless you show me a ring right now, mankind is frowning on this one, Que!"

"But you got her number, Morris."

This just made him more upset.

"Negro, please! Look how hard I had to work just to get a motherfuckin' number!?! I feel like sloppy seconds, and you ain't even hit it! And why she didn't have a friend!?! What was she doing there by herself!?!"

"But you will Morris. She—"

"Stop talking, Que. Just stop talking."

I just took the "L." My life was complicated enough with the women and events that had taken place within the last forty-eight hours. Why would Morris care about that? He wouldn't. Guys just care about getting theirs when they are in that mode. Morris kicked me out of his car and vowed that the "guys" were gonna hear about this one the next Friday we were at Manny's.

I went into the crib and sat on my sectional. But I remembered that my clothes probably smelled like cigarette smoke. I got up and went to take them off, hang 'em up outside to air out, and jumped in the shower. Got in bed and sleep did not come easy. In fact, as soon as I felt like I fell asleep, the phone rang.

It was after 10 a.m. This was not gonna be an easy-like Sunday morning (Apologies to the Commodores). It was Steven. He basically asked me why I hadn't been back to the hospital and that Kiyy was alert and asking for me. I told him that I was on my way.

After my bombshell night with K.P., can you understand my reluctance to go to see Kiyy? Yes? No? Bueller? Of course I was going. But on top of K.P. being right about rehashing everything, there is that new wrinkle, my feelings for K.P. I mean, what should that matter with Kiyy? We were broken up. She made her choice, it wasn't me. So what did I really need answers to? What did I need answers for? My ego? Well, there is the question of why Kiyy showed up at my place, and how she even knew where I lived … etc. etc. etc. While I don't know what's gonna happen or how seeing her will affect me, I know I need to get this over with. I couldn't ignore the crow cackling outside my window if I wanted to. So to the hospital I go.

Kiyy (Brenda Joseph), had been moved to a secure wing of the hospital. I had to get a pass as well as show my id in the lobby and the floor that she was on. After confirmation, I was buzzed onto the floor where I was directed to the nurses station. After checking in yet again, I was directed to her room where I saw Jack and Daniel conversing. Upon greeting me, I was updated that there had been no unusual activity to date. I thanked them, took a deep breath and walked into the room. K.P. was sitting in a chair across from Kiyy! They appeared to be talking, or Kiyy was talking and K.P. was listening. Whatever Kiyy said seemed to unsettle K.P. She had a stunned look on her face. I don't know what the look on my face said, but I prayed it was non-committal to any surprised expression. K.P. turned and gave what looked to me like bewilderment in her expression and Kiyy smiled when she saw me.

"Hi," was all I could muster.

"Hi," both replied back.

Okay, I certainly didn't expect to see K.P. here without me. Did you? It's not like these two were enemies or anything. They knew each other. And I did put K.P. on the list. So why was I feeling very uneasy? Because of this suddenly unpredictable K.P., that's why! The way K.P. was looking at me reminded me of the crow that knows something that I do not. She got out of the chair. The difference was she didn't appear to be reveling in the fact, like the crow would.

"I'm gonna leave and let you two talk."

"You don't have to leave, K.P.," I said.

"Yeah I do. You really need to hear what she has to say, okay? Call me later."

I don't know how I'm feeling about this "all business" K.P. But I do need to remind myself that change has occurred. Damn crows got me thinking 'bout everything!

"Okay," I replied.

I really wanted to follow K.P. into the hallway and get answers, but I did not. I looked at Kiyy. She had an orange bandana tied onto her head. I wanted to be mad. I couldn't.

"Orange you cute with your bandana."

"I gotta say 'no hat,' instead of 'nice hat,'" she replied, remembering our exchanges of the past. "They had to shave my head, and I didn't want you to see me looking like a punk rocker. I look bad enough as it is."

"Yeah, grew out of the hat thing, I guess. How are you feeling?"

"I'm sore, but Steven says I'm on the road to recovery. Actually, he said I'm lucky to be alive. Can you imagine my surprise when I saw your brother walk into my hospital room as my doctor?"

"Yeah, that's Steven, pulling no punches. He operated on you."

"He told me, and he told me what you did. Thank you, Que."

"Well, can you imagine my surprise when you show up to my door 'ex' many years (pun intended), later, in the condition you were in? What happened? You said Carlos did this to you. Was that true? What's going on, Kiyy?"

You're not gonna believe this one. Carlos comes from a family of drug dealers. The Vistalind Cartel. Yes, the *Vistalind* Cartel. The Bolivian drug cartel that had the national baseball team killed because they lost to Cuba. Is anyone else alarmed by this? Especially since soccer is way more popular in Bolivia than baseball? Aside from the obvious, of course!

Carlos' father and uncles run a vast empire that includes the United States. Carlos was sent to America as Carlos Vista when his father discovered he was gay. So no one ever suspected any connection. I'm not sure and Kiyy is not sure if it was a banishment or not. But his father and all uncles except one stopped contact with him. His mother remained in Bolivia, but traveled to see him. Carlos stayed with an aunt in Brooklyn, the husband being the uncle that remained in contact, and coincidentally was the loosest cannon in the Vistalind Cartel: Manuel Vistalind, notorious in his own right for allegedly orchestrating the takeover of many parts of New York City and Miami using rats as soldiers and torturers … no, actual rats. Dude is no joke. It's folklore in New York City how he allegedly (and yes, I am going to continually use the term "allegedly"), cut out a rival's eyes and fed them to rats. Then he placed rats where the eyes used to be and the rats ate through the eye sockets and into the rival's head. Did I mention that the rival was still alive!?! Of course, there are the usual murder, racketeering and trafficking allegations attached to his name.

Well, remember when I talked with Pam and she said Carlos viewed taking Kiyy from me as an opportunity? If he could make it seem that he took the most popular guy's girl in the school, it would kill all those rumors about him being gay? Well, there was certainly truth to that, but also far more to it. Carlos made it known to Kiyy who his family was. He used it to threaten Kiyy into breaking up with me. He told her he would get his Uncle Manuel to kill me unless she broke up with me, and went out with him! Kiyy, knowing very well who his uncle was, as did the world, and what he allegedly was capable of, took those threats seriously, and broke up with me to protect me. Manuel moved to Long Island and has a compound out there where Carlos stayed. He made Kiyy go with him, and she has been there since high school. The Brooklyn home was turned into a haven. Another bombshell, Manuel was killed, but no one knows it. Everyone believes he went into hiding after his name was linked to assassination attempts on a U.S. senator and the governor of New York. Carlos, who apparently was being groomed as Manuel's successor, killed Manuel after Manuel killed Carlos' lover. And no one knows Carlos is the killer, except Kiyy, and now me (and now you). Carlos has been running things since. And no one knows what really happened.

"No one knows what I just told you, Que. No one knows that Manuel is dead and that Carlos killed him!"

My head is spinning. But there was more.

"I never stopped loving you, Que. I loved you then, I love you now!"

And more.

"I told K.P. everything that happened, except what happened with Manuel. She came here to tell me not to try and come back into your life, that I was just gonna hurt you again. So I had to tell her. I told her I have always loved you, and still do. She is a good friend to you, Que. I think she was going to say something to me, but then you walked in. And she didn't."

"It looked like whatever you said to her stunned her," I pointed out.

"I'm sure it did," she replied. "I remember our breakup, and it hurt me so much to hurt you. For months all I could see was the pained look on your face. Carlos made sure I was aware that people were watching me and if I did anything to alert you or not break up with you, you'd be killed on the spot."

"How did you get away? How did you know where I lived?"

"Donovan."

"Donovan!"

Donovan ran most of New York and then Manuel arrived. From what I heard, there was an attempt to merge initially. But Donovan wasn't made that way. "Wan t'all dem glory" was one of his favorite sayings, which seemed to mean that he wanted it all. "Nuh romp wid mi, star" was another which I translated to be the equivalent of me saying, "Don't fuck with me!" Being around Donovan long enough allowed me to catch bits and pieces of Patwah, but I usually ended up just nodding.

This was a long time from the school yards of P.S. 305. I remember the last time I saw Donovan, I was in law school. I had come back to Brooklyn for Spring Break. There was a Roti spot on Rockaway Pkwy on the same block as the "L" train station. It wasn't Ali's on Utica Ave. (Ali's conch is slammin'), but it was good enough. I parked down the block and crossed the street walking toward the spot. About fifty yards away, I see Donovan walk out of the spot and up the block a little toward the "L" train station. He stopped right before the pizzeria and answered his phone. As I walked up to him, his back was turned. As I reached up to tap him on the shoulder, something made him turn around. He looked at me, and then the expression on his face suddenly changed.

"Nuh!" he yelled behind me.

As I turned to look around to see what Donovan was reacting to, I came face-to-face with the barrel of the gun that was placed to the back of my head. Out of nowhere, this guy suddenly appeared and was going to take me out, no questions asked! There was no patwah in Donovan's voice this time. Just a Jamaican accent speaking words he was sure I could understand.

"Que! You cannot walk up on me!"

"I just wanted to say hi," I stammered, shook.

"Listen star, times, dey not the same anymore! Mi different now."

What he was telling me was that he was now a drug kingpin and everyday could be his last because there was always somebody plotting his downfall. He was surrounded by bodyguards with instructions to take out anyone that walks up on him that they don't know.

"Nuh safe ti bi 'round mi yard, Que. Manuel Vistalind 'im warrin' mi."

"*Manuel Vistalind?*"

"Bloodclaat settum mi spot! Tryin' ti take mi territory, Que!"

"Holy shit! You big-time, Donovan!"

He flashed the gold teeth I remembered and nodded.

"Big mon ting," he agreed.

He asked about my mom. He always liked her. She always let him know that she entrusted him to watch my back. He'd always reply back, "Got tem, Mrs. Que!"

"Don't tell Moms 'bout dis, Que!"

"No worries, fam."

"Respect, sire."

With that, he was gone, and that was the last time I'd see him. But it wasn't the last time he was seen.

"The last time I saw Donovan, he said he was beefing with Manuel Vistalind, and that was at least five years ago. Damn. Donovan was holding it down!"

"Listening to Manuel over time, I learned that Donovan controlled most of Brooklyn, and all of the major water thruways there, a portion of Queens, a piece of Harlem and the Bronx. Manuel really wanted Canarsie Pier among other Brooklyn spots that Donovan controlled."

"Donovan's spots all over New York were by the water?"

"Yes. Manuel saw how Donovan was moving product in by water and he knew if he took that from Donovan, he could take his whole business."

"So you said you got away because of Donovan. How?"

"Manuel has wanted Donovan's spots for years," Kiyy began. "He had started grooming Carlos to get into the business. Manuel wanted Carlos to arrange a sit-down with Donovan to get a read on him, but he wasn't sure who could broker the meet. By chance, I was with Carlos one day and he got a call from Manuel to meet at the house in Brooklyn. When we got there, Manuel introduced Carlos to Snow, and told Carlos he'd be in charge of Snow and his territory from then on."

"*Snow?*"

"Yes, Luther Little, Que. It was there that Snow and I saw each other but didn't say anything."

"He never said nothing to you?"

"I mean, no, not really. There was one thing which I thought was weird, though. He complained to me a couple times that he didn't know why Carlos picked an alias to call and text him as 'Josie.' And wouldn't change it. Said it was causing him grief. I can only think he meant Jinx. He was still going out with her, yes?"

"Yeah, he was."

"But since Carlos was now calling the shots, there was nothing he could do about it."

"Damn, this is deep. Manuel took over Snow's operation!"

"Manuel was behind the attempted hit on Jinx—"

" … That took Mr. Parker, instead."

"Yes. That is when Snow offered you as a truce to get them off of Jinx. Manuel wasn't interested in that—"

" … But Carlos was all over it!"

"You can still finish my sentences." Kiyy blushed.

I hadn't even thought about it, but it was still automatic.

"Um, yeah I guess some things don't change," I replied, looking toward the floor.

Suddenly it hit me!

"It was you! It was you who called my cell phone and abruptly hung up!"

Kiyy looked at me and nodded.

"Yes. Carlos had Snow call you to set up a meet. A fight between one of Snow's people and Carlo's people caused them both to momentarily leave the room. Snow left his phone and I grabbed it, hit redial, and had to hang up before I could say more."

"Why didn't Snow out you?"

"I guess he didn't know how he wanted to play the cards when he first saw me. But Manuel trying to take out Jinx shook him, and I guess he just went for broke. I heard he got killed."

"Yeah he did."

"Carlos told Manuel that you did it."

"He deserved to die."

Maybe one day I'll tell Kiyy the truth, but that is a conversation for another day. And Jinx would have some say in whether I did or not.

"Manuel wasn't happy that Carlos let personal feelings get in the way of family business. And I believe that changed their relationship."

"Really?"

"Yes. Manuel started questioning all of Carlos' decisions, including his personal ones."

"What did that mean?"

"When Manuel found out that Carlos had a lover, he questioned why I was even there."

"He did?"

"Yeah. Manuel referred to me as 'La Coño Culo Fina.'"

"Whoa. Manuel called you 'Fine ass pussy?'"

"Yes. I don't think Carlos liked it. Manuel always threw it in his face. And Carlos always threw it in my face."

"Did Manuel ever touch you?"

"No. He loved his wife."

"Did you ever sleep with Carlos?"

She looked directly at me. "I *never* slept with anyone except you."

I couldn't return her look.

"Snow's last act before getting killed was setting up a sit-down between Manuel and Donovan."

"Snow knew Donovan? Scratch that. I guess being in the same line of business, their paths eventually crossed."

"Darren knew Donovan."

"Darren who?"

"Darren Parker."

"Darren Parker!?!"

"Yes. Darren was the common link between Snow and Donovan. Darren was the one that put together the sit-down. Donovan told Darren that Manuel killed his father, and Darren asked for Donovan's help in getting Manuel after Snow kept balking. The sit-down was to be Darren's set-up and revenge on Manuel."

"Holy shit!"

"But Donovan never went through with the sit-down after hearing that Snow was killed. And then Darren got killed when it was discovered who he actually was."

"Who killed Darren?"

"Carlos, upon Manuel's orders."

"Then how did you and Donovan connect?"

"Fast forward years later. A chance meeting at the Lighthouse restaurant under the Brooklyn Bridge. Carlos was apparently with his lover, and Manuel took pity on me and invited me to go to dinner with he and his wife, Camila."

"Wow."

"Yeah. Even the most notorious drug dealers, at least the smart ones, need to take care of home."

"How did his wife treat you, especially with what he called you?"

"I don't think his wife knew that, and if she did, it didn't affect our relationship. She was cordial and never mean to me. I don't know what she knew about the circumstances with me and Carlos, except I was never to leave the grounds unaccompanied. So there's that."

"That's enough, I guess, to look the other way, as she probably was used to doing."

"Yeah, well, we were at the restaurant. It was packed, but at some point Donovan sees me from across the room. I didn't see him. He was there with a girl. He and the girl come up to the table. 'Whappened lil' Robin? Whappened ta dem girl Kiyler, she?'"

"Oh my God. You speak Jamaican Patwah. He still called you 'lil Robin?'"

"Yes, and I still don't know why?"

"He thought robins were pretty little birds," I laughed.

"Well, that was anticlimactic. I got up to hug Donovan, and he introduced me to the girl he was with. I looked at Manuel and he had a puzzled look on his face. And right then I said to myself, 'Oh shit! This is not good.' Donovan reaches out his hand to Manuel and says, 'Donovan, star,' at the same time Manuel returns the extension of his hand to Donovan and says 'Manuel, señor.'"

"Oh, shit is right. What happened?"

"Their hands stayed clasped together for a moment before it registered who the other actually was. They both looked taken aback before they regained composure."

"'How do you know my sister-in law?' Manuel lied."

"'Kiyler? Raised up both pon di yard, wi',' Donovan lied right back."

"Were their bodyguards in the restaurant?"

"Manuel's were outside. He did it that way for Camila. I didn't know if Donovan's were inside until later. But Manuel always travels with two guns."

"Yeah, I don't remember Donovan ever not being strapped."

"Well, the girl that was with Donovan, her name was Priscilla, and she announced that she was going to go to the bathroom. I announced I would go too. Camila, I think, was torn. She knew she should have gone to the bathroom with us, but she sensed the sudden tension with Manuel and decided to stay with him, even though Manuel insisted she go."

"'Cause stuff happens in the women's bathroom!"

"You learned your lessons well, Que. You remember your sister, Keith, and those girls, don't you? We get in the bathroom, and I say to Priscilla, 'I need Donovan's help to get out of here. I'm being held against my will!' Priscilla looked at me and whipped out her cell phone, texting something to Donovan furiously. Priscilla says to me, 'We need to get out of the bathroom fast so it's not suspicious!'"

"Priscilla was on point!"

"Yes, she was! God Bless Priscilla!"

"This is some James Bond shit!"

"That's not it. But what happens next is. We get back to the table. I don't know what's been said, but everyone is smiling—"

" ... Plotting and waiting to see what the next man is gonna do."

Kiyy shakes her head. "You and that term 'the next man' ... sheesh!"

"'Cause you gotta stay ahead of 'the next man' in this one life we got to live."

"Yeah, hold that thought, love. Donovan is looking at his phone. Manuel asks if everything is all right. Donovan responds, 'E'ry ting irie, star. An' oh, bi di way, di one Kiyler? She cum wit mi, bumboclaat!' He pressed a button on his phone and everyone's phones in the restaurant started chiming. Guns came from everywhere pointed at Manuel, the front door, everybody that wasn't in Donovan's crew. Donovan owned the restaurant!"

"Donovan owned the Lighthouse!?!"

"Donovan owned the Lighthouse! No one knew it though. He told me later a shell company controlled by him operated it. Manuel's guns were taken from him, the gun in Camila's purse that I didn't even know she had was taken from her, and Donovan said to me, 'Walk, gyal ... walk wit mi.' And I walked with him out of the restaurant. That was two years ago."

"*What?* Well, where have you been? Why didn't you come and tell me what happened then?"

"Donovan was protecting me. I had to go into hiding. The first place they were going to look was you. Donovan said I needed to wait this thing out before I could go to you. Until Manuel, Carlos, and maybe the whole Vistalind Cartel were dead."

"Why am I still alive then?"

"Donovan, Que. Donovan was protecting you."

"What?"

"Que, there's so much more. Manuel was turning the city upside down to find me. I was constantly being moved. Manuel made it his mission in life to hunt Donovan down too, not only because he outmaneuvered him, and embarrassed him, but because at that very moment in the restaurant, Donovan took over Manuel's Staten Island ports."

"Wow. Played him."

"Donovan immediately put people on my mother, your mother. He always talked good about Mrs. Que."

"My mother?"

"Yes, your mother, father, and family has been under Donovan's watch for the last two years, as well as you."

"Ronnie's in Atlanta."

"I know. She's being looked after, along with her kids and Keith. Keith has somebody on the road with him, and doesn't even know it besides his bodyguard."

"How? I haven't seen anyone?"

"Because you weren't looking for anyone until now. And you still won't know, until I tell you. Donovan used to take me by your house after I told him what happened. He had a tinted bulletproof Navigator. I saw you once."

"Why didn't Donovan come to me?"

"Because you were bait, Que."

"Damn, I been out of the game for so long … of course I was!"

"Yes, you were."

"This whole thing is like fiction!"

"I know it's been a lot, but I got more to tell you, and you're not gonna like the next one."

"Donovan gave me a cell phone that only I knew of. His number was the only one programmed in it—"

"No Kiyy … No!"

I got up for the first time in more than two hours sitting in that chair.

"It rang. And—"

"No Kiyy! Stop!"

"And I answered it—"

"Dammit … No! No! No!"

"It wasn't Donovan."

Yes … Donovan. If you haven't figured it out by now, *Donovan* was the rival whose eyes Manuel fed to the rats, and all the rest.

"It was Manuel."

I broke down. I cried right there in front of Kiyy. I can't thank him. I can't tell him I'm sorry. Damn.

After a few minutes, I composed myself and Kiyy reluctantly continued.

"They were already looking at your house but it intensified over the next year after Donovan disappeared. Profit took over from Donovan after we found out Manuel finally got to him."

"Profit! I could see it, though, yeah." (As you guys can attest from my past.) "Fuckin' rats," I muttered.

"Yeah, but Donovan was never worried about the rats, like everyone else was."

"Why not?"

"Since Manuel was prone to use rats to help take over territories and torture people. Donovan came up with an answer."

"Oh my God! … Crows!"

"How did you know that?"

"It all makes sense! Donovan was obsessed with crows. He used to say they were black, small, and powerful, just like him. We'd laugh. But he'd always end it with 'But they don't rock gold teeth like me star,' in his Jamaican accent. He thought of them as good luck charms, good omens. 'Dey pose magic, Que,' he'd say. He believed all the superstitions."

"Crows are big birds, Que!"

"Yeah, tell that to Donovan," I quipped.

"Donovan always said crows are very intelligent and had great memory. They could detect evil or danger, and could be trained to recognize faces that portrayed such. He had a whole … what do you call it, Que?"

"Murder? A group is called a 'murder' of crows."

"No … roost! That's what he would say. 'I got a roost a' crow, Kiyler,' he would say."

"How would you train them?"

"I don't know, Que, but he did it. I saw it. That's what I didn't think you'd believe. Donovan had crows trained to protect and alert him and others to danger. I don't know if you remember this or not. But the news reported on an influx of crows that suddenly appeared in the city and curbed the epidemic rat problem that Manuel caused."

"I do remember that."

"So Donovan was giving back to the city that raised him."

"No doubt."

So the crows have been watching over me for a few years now. But what about the times before? I thought I had the answers, but I couldn't explain the crows before, until now.

"So how long had Donovan been using crows to watch over people?"

"You're not going to believe this, Que, but Donovan told me he's had crows watching you from when you guys were young."

"What!?! Get outta here with that!"

"That's what he told me, Que, and I believed him."

I'll be damned! Them futhermuckin' crows been cackling at me my whole life. They knew something I didn't. Damn!

"If Donovan had crows protecting him, how was Manuel able to get him? And once he got him, how was Manuel able to keep the crows at bay?"

"I don't know, Que."

"Did Manuel have pets?"

"Yes. Yes, he did. He kept owls on Long Island. I always thought it was a strange choice. He also had two big hawks I remember he kept in Brooklyn, along with more owls."

"That's how, Kiyy. Manuel figured out how to fight nature with nature. Crows are natural enemies of hawks and owls. Manuel would have had to have a lot of either to keep those crows away from Donovan!"

Kiyy looked at me like she wanted to ask something. She did.

"What's a group of owls called? And hawks?"

"Seriously, Kiyy?"

"I always remembered I couldn't stump you with animal questions. I had to try," she smiled.

"I love animals. I got my parents to order me animal cards when I was little, Safari Animal or Wildlife cards or something. They would come in packs every few weeks. But each card was in color with the animal on the front and facts on the back. A lot of information about that particular animal. There were numbered divider index cards separating animals by various categories. They had plastic trays to hold the cards. I had like four trays filled with cards."

"Are you stalling, Que?"

"You wish, Kiyy. Nostalgia. I miss those cards. I think they got thrown out. A group of owls is called a 'parliament,' and a group of hawks is called a 'cast.' Take that … take that … take that!"

"Okay, Puffy, you got that."

"So how did you finally get to me?"

"I was just about to tell you. Donovan made Profit promise to continue watching everyone's back before he gave his blessing that Profit should take over if anything happened to Donovan. Once Manuel got to Donovan, he wasn't concerned with me anymore."

"How do you know that?"

"Manuel still had the phone Donovan gave me and called me. He told me he was not concerned with me anymore. When I mentioned that Carlos probably still was, Manuel told me he would take care of Carlos, and that I should hold onto this phone and call him if Carlos or anyone associated with Carlos came to me."

"You believed that?"

"I did because I was never Manuel's fight. Manuel told me a while back that he never approved of what Carlos did, but he wasn't going to interfere with it either, as long as it didn't interfere with family business."

"Until it did, and Manuel and Carlos started beefing."

"Correct. Manuel didn't have a problem with Carlos being gay, but he did have a problem with Carlos' lover."

"Do you know what it was … the problem?"

"He was a gold-digger with loose lips."

"And loose lips sink ships," we both chimed in unison.

Kiyy continued, "Well, after I got that phone call, I talked with Profit. He was reluctant to let me go to you, and he turned out to be correct. Profit wasn't as attuned to the crows as Donovan was, so he missed the signs. The crows were cawing much more than usual, in hindsight, they had to be warning of danger. Profit wanted me to wait until he could take me himself, but I had been apart from you for years, and didn't want to wait any longer. So he sent me in a car with some people. We got ambushed a few blocks from your house. Carlos' people killed everyone in the car except me. Carlos pulled me out of the car and started beating me in the street.

"Profit, uneasy about everything I guess, showed up shortly in the bulletproof Navigator. Did you know it had slots for automatic weapons? The slots fit just the nozzle and could swivel. I'm sorry, I was always amazed by the detail of that car. But Donovan did say it saved lives on more than one occasion. Anyway, the bullets started whizzing from the Navigator and I got up to run. Carlos must have shot me when I got up to run. I never felt anything. I hid in your neighbor's bushes for at least a half hour. Carlos drove by your house twice looking for me. When his car turned the corner the second time, that's when I ran to your house."

"Adrenaline, Kiyy. That helped you get to my house, and probably helped save you."

"I guess. Maybe I'll ask Steven about that."

"Is Carlos dead?"

"No, I got a call on the phone as I hid trying to get to your house. It was Carlos taunting me. He told me that Manuel was dead, that he killed him, and he was going to kill me. I didn't believe him, so I called Camila on a burner phone that Donovan and later Profit made me carry also. She wasn't going to take my call at first, but I told her I heard that Manuel was dead, and I wanted to offer condolences. At first, she denied he was dead. She said he was in hiding. But I guess it was too much for her and she broke down and told me that Carlos' lover shot Manuel, and Carlos killed his lover, asking me to keep it all secret."

"But you said Carlos killed Manuel because Manuel killed Carlos' lover, didn't you?"

"Yes. Carlos lied to everyone."

"So you can't prove it!?"

"Yes, I can. The phone Donovan gave me has an automatic recording mechanism that he showed me. The phone was programmed to record anyone's voice that was not Donovan's. Carlos' confession is on that phone, along with Manuel's pledge to leave me alone. And since I knew what the phone did, I never said anything that would incriminate me or Donovan."

"God Bless Donovan," I muttered. "Crows, technology? I hardly knew the man, it seems!"

"But I'm a believer in those crows, Que. And I think Profit is now too."

"It's just pretty ingenious to use the crows in the way he did. But what happens now? Donovan's gone. Who trains the crows now?"

"I don't know. The crows Donovan trained were trained to respond to Profit as well. But I don't know if Donovan taught Profit the secrets to train crows."

"This whole thing is crazy."

"Que? Do you know where my clothes and things are when they brought me into the hospital?"

"They cut up most of your clothes to treat you, but gave me a bag with stuff. I haven't looked."

"You should, as soon as possible. I had the phone with me."

"You had a phone in your hand when you got to my house."

"That's it. You need to put it in a secure place as soon as possible, okay?"

"I'll put it in my safe."

I listened to her talk for close to three hours. I had no clue that anything like this could have happened. This woman sacrificed herself to save my life. My homie gave his life to protect me.

"You told all of this to K.P.?"

"Yes. Everything except Manuel, Carlos, and the phone."

"I had no clue, Kiyy. I can't say, 'Why didn't you tell me?' I can't say, 'Why didn't you go to the police?' I can't say anything, except thank you. And that doesn't even sound right, compared to what you've been through."

"You have to know that I never stopped loving you, Que. It's important that you understand that. I know I hurt you. I don't know what's been going on in your life these ten plus years. I don't know if you're married, got children, or anything. I don't see a ring. But it is important to me that you understand and hear me when I say, 'I never stopped loving you.' My love for you, and knowing you were safe, kept me going. Carlos tortured me by constantly telling me he was going to kill you himself or have his uncle kill you, even though I did as he asked. I begged him to spare your life many, many times, and many nights, exhaustion from crying put me to sleep."

"I understand now, Kiyy. I didn't then. It's been years of hurt and pain that I thought were all caused by you. This is so much to take in."

"I didn't know if I'd ever see you again. I didn't know how you would react if I ever saw you. But I prepared myself that you might not ever hear the truth from me. I prepared myself that you might not feel the same way about me that you did. I prepared myself that this might not go the way I wanted it to. But I'm at peace that I've been able to see you and finally tell you the truth."

Kiyy's pain medication had dripped into her IV a while ago. The medicine is designed to make her sleepy. She fought hard to finish telling me everything she wanted me to know before she fell asleep. Her sleep looked peaceful, like she had gotten a whole lot off of her mind. I let her sleep.

I walked out of the room, and Daniel got up to go inside. I nodded as he went past me. I asked Jack if they needed anything. I was told that they didn't, and that there was no unusual activity. I updated Jack on some of the pertinent details of what Kiyy shared with me, mainly that Carlos Vista or Vistalind or "Chico Caliente" (didn't know what he was going by right now), was the primary threat. Jack said he would convey this information to Tariq, who most likely would run a report and update Daniel on what I told him. I thanked him and said goodbye.

I walked past the waiting area, and there sat K.P.!

"You've been here all this time!?!"

"Yes. I didn't know what to do, hearing what she said, and not knowing how you would react. Honestly, I don't know how to react."

"I'm numb, K.P."

"How could you not be? Do you want to go home? Get something to eat? Do you even want company?"

"Welcome back, best friend! I didn't like 'all business' K.P."

"Is that what you were calling her?" K.P. smirked.

"That effin' 'itch was probably more appropriate."

She elbowed me.

"You know I'm joking, right? Gotta be sure … a lot of changes going on here."

"What do you want to do?"

"Let's get something to eat? I could use my best friend's company right now."

"About this best friend status? …"

"I missed you, K.P."

She looked at me and realized I was serious.

"Told you you're gonna have a hard time getting rid of me … whatever happens. I'm not going anywhere!"

We went to eat. White Castle.

"She loves you, Que. She never stopped loving you."

"Do you know how bad I feel?"

"Why?"

"Because I was angry. I was hurt. And everything she did was to protect me."

"How were you supposed to know that?"

"I don't know."

"You couldn't have known it, Que."

"I feel bad."

K.P. and I wanted to part ways and give each other space for the rest of the day. We didn't want to talk about what Kiyy had conveyed to each of us just yet. But that didn't happen.

"Do you still love her? You know what, I shouldn't be asking you that yet. I'm sorry."

"I don't have a good answer for that—"

"I know you shouldn't. You just found out earth shattering news. It's not right for me to ask that. I shouldn't have asked that."

"Of course it's right for you to ask, K.P. You of all people just acquired the right to know."

"Because I told you I love you?"

"Yes."

"Well, I disagree."

"Why?"

"Well, if you love her, it doesn't matter how I feel."

"It does to me, K.P."

"I know talking about Kiyy can overlap into what is or isn't happening with us, Que—"

"What is or isn't happening?"

"I'm sorry if I'm not phrasing that correctly. I don't know how to refer to what happened between us and what it means going forward, Que. I'm not trying to be anything but respectful and supportive of what you just found out."

"Even though it affects you?"

"I don't know how it affects me yet, but yes, even though it affects me. If and when you are ready to talk about that, we can. But I certainly don't want to intertwine the two, okay?"

"Fair enough. But I thought what happened between us was beautiful."

"Beautiful? What? Who are you?"

"Seriously, K.P. It was special … And I didn't know you could move it like that!"

"See, that's what I'm used to … the uncouth, the Neanderthal!"

"Figured I threw you enough, so I should just come back home."

"I'm sorry about Donovan."

I kind of kept K.P. away from that part of my life as best I could. But worlds and people can intertwine, as that wise ol' soul just alluded to.

"Yeah, that was tough to hear. I didn't realize how big he had become."

"Why not? He was always in the news."

"Who watches the news?"

"My guess would be the people that don't read about it?"

"That's not who he was to me."

"I hear you. I guess I was always more fascinated with the fact that you two actually knew each other, and took interest in that whenever he was in the news."

"That was my man! And I'll never get to say thank you."

"You just did. Trust me, he knows. It's just wild how he was able to help Kiyy. Talk about being in the right place at the right time."

"That's true, and being in the position to help too."

"Wonder what happened to the girl in the bathroom?"

"Priscilla. I don't know. But without her, none of it jumps off."

"You ain't never lied! The whole thing is just nuts."

"It's just hard to believe."

"Wait. You don't believe her!?!"

"Yes, K.P., I do believe her. I mean it's hard to believe that she did that for me … and endured what she did for me."

"No, it's not hard to believe, Que. Wouldn't you have done the same for her?"

"I would have found another way."

"Naa-uh, Que, you don't get to do that. Same circumstance, yes or no? Would you have done the same for her?"

"Are you on her side?"

"What are you talking about, Que? There are no sides here! There's what happened and what you do because of what happened."

"This is taking another turn, K.P. I don't want to argue with you."

She pondered what I said and then added,

"You're right. I just wanted you to understand that you do things for the people you love, right or wrong, sometimes without thought. That's all."

"I know you're thinking it, K.P. Yes, I would have done it for you."

"Okay, Que, you just said you didn't want to do this!"

"I wanted you to know that."

"But that wasn't my question, Que."

"I know it wasn't, but it had to be the thought behind it."

"When have I not said to you what is on my mind, Que? When? I don't need to start tiptoeing around you because we slept together, do I!?!"

"K.P ... Whoa! I'm not saying that!"

"Maybe I should leave. Maybe I'm getting a little too sensitive right now."

She got up to leave.

"No, you can't leave like this, K.P. Please come back and sit down … please?"

She came back and sat down.

"The love of your life comes back into your life. You have no reason not to love her again, not to still love her."

"Are you trying to get me to go back to her?"

"That's the last thing I'm trying to do. You need to figure out whether you love her still. She deserves to know that."

"You deserve to know it."

"Okay, yes, I deserve to know it too. But it's not about me. It is, but it isn't. Dammit! I'm trying so hard not to have an interest in this."

"Maybe you should stop looking at it like that. You do have an interest in this, K.P. And I have a lot to think about and figure out."

"You know what I think? I think you're putting up a front for me because you don't want to hurt me."

"Or you want me to make a choice now based on logic instead of my heart?"

"But how could you not go back to her, Que? After what happened? After what she did?"

"My mind and my heart went through something too, K.P. It took a long time, but eventually I moved on."

"That sounds selfish, Que. You may not have intended it to sound that way, but it does."

"Does it?"

"I went to see her to tell her not to come back into your life to hurt you again, Que."

"I know. She told me. And that's why she told you what happened."

"I almost wish she hadn't. It was easier condemning her for what we thought she had done."

"And that's it in the nutshell. What you thought she had done. What I thought she had done."

"But she didn't do it. I mean, she did it, but the reason why trumps that, doesn't it?"

"But I went through it, regardless."

"That sounds really cold, Que."

"Maybe it does, K.P. But that's what I gotta work through."

"I didn't look at it like that."

"You couldn't, because you didn't go through the hurt and pain. I mean you shared what you could with me, but you didn't go *through* it. It didn't happen to you. Do you understand that? Does that make sense to you?"

"I hear what you're saying, Que. But you have to get past your ego and look at it from her perspective as well. The bare bones. She did what she did to save your life. She never stopped loving you. She told me that, Que.”

“I know, K.P.”

“Do you know I went there with the intention of telling her about us?”

“When I walked into the room and saw you, I kind of had that thought.”

“Yeah, well, after her telling me what she did, you can understand why I couldn’t tell her.”

“I can. And if anyone is going to tell her what happened with us, it should be me.”

“I would agree with that now, knowing what we know.”

“How are you doing with some of the other stuff she shared? Like Manuel Vistalind being responsible for the attempted hit on Jinx, your father’s death, and … and Darren’s death? I am so sorry.”

She took a deep breath and sighed, but she didn’t address that. “I didn’t know Snow tried to have you killed. Why didn’t you tell me that, Que?”

“Because what was done was done, K.P. It wasn’t going to bring Mr. Parker back, and Snow got what he deserved anyway.”

No, I was not going to betray Jinx’s confidence, not even to her sister, and my best friend.

“How did Snow die?”

"Kiyy didn't tell you?"

"She didn't say. I didn't press it."

"He got shot."

"Oh."

"Are you going to say anything to your mother? Jinx?"

"I haven't fully decided. But I'm leaning toward no right now."

"That's probably a good idea. It just brings back the whole gamut of emotions. Nothing good comes from that, I don't think."

"Probably not. Do you know how long Kiyy is gonna be in the hospital? Does she have somewhere to go?"

"I don't know. I haven't asked. We haven't talked about anything else."

"Of course. I'm sorry."

"No need to apologize for that. It's all stuff that needs to be thought of and discussed, eventually. I believe she's gonna be in the hospital for at least another week, maybe two? I have to check with Steven."

"Okay."

I got up and K.P. followed suit as we gathered ourselves to leave.

"Come hug me, Jane."

"Tarzan, what is that in your hand?"

"Your last two White Castles?"

"What am I gonna do with you?"

"Love me … Long time?"

"Don't tempt me!"

"Kiyy is back?!?" Winnie exclaimed.

"Yeah, you're gonna have to sit down for this one. And get the hard liquor!" I said, as I walked past Winnie into her place.

After eating, K.P. and I agreed that we should give each other some space for the rest of the week or until either of us couldn't stand it anymore. We wouldn't talk about any of what Kiyy told us, or anything else, or what it meant for anything else. We would just enjoy each other's company, like we used to do. At least that was the plan we agreed to. I appreciated that more than she probably knew. Anyway, after parting ways with K.P., I got a call from Winnie to see how I was doing because we hadn't talked or seen each other in a while. Trust me, sex was not on the agenda when I told her I was coming over. But before Winnie, I had to go home and lock up that phone.

"Kiyy got shot and showed up at my house. Kiyy broke up with me to save my life. Kiyy has basically been kidnapped for the last six to eight years and been in hiding at least the last two. Kiyy still loves me and never stopped loving me."

I took a breath.

"Que, stop! Hold on! Wait … What!?!"

"There's more. I slept with K.P. I think I'm in love with K.P."

Whoa. That last sentence right there surprised *me!* Where did that come from? Winnie put her glass down and stood up. She walked to her fireplace mantel and looked at me with her head tilted slightly.

"Que, I'm gonna walk back to my seat, pick up my drink, look at it, add some more liquor, ask you if you want some more liquor, and you're gonna start from the beginning, wherever that is, and tell me everything that has happened, preferably in excruciating detail. I'll order Chinese if I have to, okay?"

"Okay, Winnie."

For the next two hours, I rehashed everything that was told to me by Kiyy, minus a few things that I'm sure you know weren't included, plus I told Winnie about what happened with K.P. before and after Kiyy's arrival. When Winnie interrupted, I let her talk and answered her questions. When she was finished for the moment, I continued. It was traumatic hearing it, and it was traumatic retelling it, but also strangely therapeutic with Winnie. Maybe I thought that because she was detached from it all in my mind, but of course she wasn't. This affected her as well, in ways I hadn't even properly considered.

"Que, I can't believe this. We've been dogging Kiyy for years, and she did this!?! I owe her so many apologies. I can't even imagine what she's been through."

"Is anybody thinking about how I feel, and what I've been through?"

"Of course, Que. How do you feel?"

"How do you think I feel, Winnie? This woman sacrificed everything to save me! I feel so low."

"How could you have known, Que? You went on with life the best way you could. Yes, she made the choice, she made the sacrifice, but there is no blame here, not at all … Just unfortunate circumstances."

"And then there's K.P."

"Damn, she finally stepped her game up and this is what she gets putting herself out there, like that? Have you told K.P. how you feel about her?"

"No."

"Are you going to tell her?"

"I don't know?"

"What!?! Wait, why not!?! You just told me. You better tell her, Que! Don't be a bitch!"

"Damn, Winnie. A little compassion maybe?"

"I repeat. Don't be a bitch! Do you love her?"

"Yes. I think I do."

"Do you love Kiyy?"

"Come on, Winnie."

"Que, if you can't be honest with yourself, please be honest with me, okay?"

"Yes, Winnie. I think I still do."

"What are you going to do?"

"Ah, the million dollar question. Can I get a rain check on that for the rest of my life?"

"You know you can't, Que."

"I know, Winnie."

Winnie stood up, walked towards me, and sat down on the floor in front of where I was sitting. She grabbed my hand and held it.

"Wow. I didn't think we would end like this! We had a great run! But you know we can't be together anymore, right, Que?"

"What are you talking about, Winnie?"

"I don't belong anymore. You've got two incredible women who both love you and deserve you."

"Winnie, stop it. You are incredible too—"

"No no no, Que! Don't do that! I *am* incredible, but I don't belong in this story anymore, not like that anymore."

"Winnie, you're really kicking me to the curb!?!"

"Que, I will always love you, but we both knew I was never going to be the one. I wasn't ready for *this*, but that's life. K.P. has done what I thought she should do. But this Kiyy thing throws a wrench in everything. How can you root against that? That's love, Que! That's ride or die. Both of them are ride or die!"

"Winnie, you could have been the one and you know that."

"We met under not-so-conventional circumstances, if you remember, Que. And I never wanted children."

"Stop that, Winnie. We talked about how we met many times, and you know I never judged you for that."

"But I did, Que. Even though I came to love you … I did. I judged me. But that's okay. I will be the godmother to your children. I will be 'Aunt Winnie,' the coolest aunt on the face of the earth! Believe that! If my godchild is a girl, she's the next 'diva.' If my godchild is a boy, he's the next 'don.' I will remain always and forever your friend indeed, and be your friend in need."

I dropped to the floor beside her and she hugged me and began to weep. I held her and let her cry in my arms. More change … the end of a chapter I had to agree to.

9

TWO FOR ONE

Fate is a cruel mistress!

"You finally came to your senses, huh?"

"I guess."

"It's gonna be the best apple pie you've ever had!"

"Why you refer to it as apple pie will forever baffle me?"

"When you have some, you tell me I'm wrong, okay?"

Of course you all know I'm talking to Jinx, right? She may be forever linked with apple pie, huh? She's been forever trying to get me to try her apple pie, forever. Well, I finally gave in.

"It's just what you said it would be … apple pie."

"Told you. Nobody's is like mine. I'ma market this bitch."

Normally you'd be right if you thought Jinx was referring to what you might have thought she was referring to. But you'd be wrong this time. This time Jinx was talking about a drink she concocted. Jinx is a mad scientist. Jinx is a mixologist. Jinx is a restaurateur. Jinx owns a restaurant/bar called, what else, "Apple of my Pie." :-/ The restaurant has a pastry theme, serving quiche type dishes, meat pot pie dishes, as well as desserts. All with hints, themes or parts of various types of apples in the crusts or fillings. She went to culinary school, after bartending for years. Can't tell you what the drink has in it, she'd kill me, but it does indeed taste like "apple pie."

She had come right over when I called, and while she had an idea of why I called and asked her to come by, there was more she didn't know.

"I know why you called."

"You do?"

"K.P. probably asked you to check on me because Snow's anniversary passed recently."

"And yes, that is true, but there's some other things I want to talk to you about."

"Oh?"

"Yes."

"Yeah, your phone call didn't sound like a booty call."

"Kiyy is back."

"Your ex-girlfriend? The one that did you wrong! What do you mean, she's back? Like you guys are back together!?!"

"Slow down, Jinx. There's a lot I have to tell you."

"What could you possibly tell me that justifies what she did to you?"

I told Jinx why Kiyy broke up with me.

"Oh," Jinx whispered. "That might be some justification there."

I also told Jinx how Snow was involved, his involvement with Manuel Vistalind, and what he did.

"He stabbed you in the back for helping him! If it wasn't for you, Manuel would have killed him, instead of Luther taking out Manuel's men."

"Yeah but by me helping, there was the attempt on your life, and your father's death."

I wanted to tell her about Darren, I really did. But as you guys know, I left that to K.P. But I really wanted to tell her, especially when you read on …

"I can't believe he would tell Manuel that it was you who alerted him to Manuel's plot, and then offer you as restitution."

"He was trying to save you, Jinx."

"So he thought. He should have said something. We could have both figured it out together. How he thought killing someone that's *family* would be okay with *me* because it saved *my* life, is beyond me. He should have known how much family means to me."

"Maybe that's it Jinx. He never considered that I was *family* to you."

"Then he was stupid too."

"Trying to reconcile it over the years, maybe he was jealous?" "Jealous of what? I never looked at another man while we were together, Que."

"And I believe you, Jinx, but men see what they want to see in times of turmoil. And maybe he saw something that made him look at me as a threat to you."

"That sounds good, Que, for *your* ego and everything. And I could see why you might think that since I flirt with you. But I only had eyes for him."

"Then what changed?"

"He changed, Que. He started acting weird and secretive. Normally when people texted or called him, he told me, business or whatever. We never kept secrets. But he started getting texts and calls from this bitch named Josie, and that's when everything changed. He kept telling me it was business and nothing else. But he would never tell me what kind of business he had with a bitch named Josie!"

Wow. Fellas, there are lessons here. Secrets kill. Literally, in this case.

"Josie was an alias, Jinx. An alias that Carlos used."

"Carlos was the bitch!?!"

Oh the irony there!

"Yes. Kiyy mentioned that when she was telling me everything."

"Why would Carlos do that?"

"Possibly for wiretaps? Throw off the authorities? 'Cause he liked knowing it might cause drama? 'Cause he was weird? I don't know. Kiyy thought it was weird."

"It's a bitch move."

"Can't argue with that."

"What is that saying … 'Fate is a cruel mistress?'"

"Yes."

"Luther's decision to not come clean with me and keep this a secret, coupled with that bitch move, cost him his life."

Jinx had told me before whenever we talked about this that the only reason she was down at the pier was to confront Snow, who was supposed to be doing business, but Jinx thought he was meeting "Josie."

"I guess he couldn't tell you because the plot involved me?"

"He could have told me anything and we could have come up with an alternative plan."

"Not then. Carlos was intent on me being gone. There was no reneging there."

"I mean before that. If Luther was trying to get Manuel off me, then we could have figured something out together."

And that sentiment right there may be the reason why men fail more often than women. Women want to figure out things together. Men want to figure out things themselves.

"I wouldn't have been down there if he hadn't called back. You know I let the answering machine pick up whenever I'm here. Usually it's some silly ho' moaning about this or purring about that. (ha ha!) But it was a dude this time, and when I recognized it was Luther and then at the same time somebody in the background hands him a phone and says, 'It's Josie,' and Luther replies he's *at the pier waiting by the*

Lighthouse? Well, then you know it's about to be on and popping! I knew where you kept your back up, I got it, and headed to the pier."

"With malice aforethought."

"What?"

"Nothing. Bad humor. I didn't intend to leave my back up, and I started to go back for it, but after I got pulled over by the cops, I never went back for it because I was late."

"Well, those cops gave me time to get down there and assess the situation. Imagine my surprise when I saw *you* show up? I'm like what the fuck?"

"My plan certainly wasn't to be ambushed, that's for sure."

"I nearly screamed three times. There were big rats, and it was dark too!"

"You get props for that Jinx. Those 'cat rats' would have shook me!"

"When I saw Luther put a gun to your head, I was shocked. I don't even know why I called him? I never thought he might hear me talking and figure out I was close by. Then he hung up the phone, got another call. I'm sure I thought it was Josie, and I snapped, Que. And you know the rest."

"Yes and I will be saying 'thank you' for the rest of my life. I am eternally grateful."

Wait for it.

"Can't be that grateful because you keep turning this down," Jinx smirked.

"I didn't before but I think I have a real good reason now. Well, I think there has always been a reason."

Everyone repeat after me, "Can you say segue?" I stand up and begin a nervous pace.

"Wait, let me guess, you slept with my sister, right?" Jinx says sarcastically.

I'm dumbfounded right now, but I gather it in.

"Yes, Jinx. I did. I think I'm in love with your sister!"

Jinx's smirk disappears and she covers her mouth with her left hand. She just looks at me. Then without warning, she runs straight to me.

"Oh my God! I can't believe it! Finally!"

Wait … What!?! Jinx hugs me!

"You're okay with this?" I asked incredulously.

"Of course I am. I've always thought you two belonged together!"

"Wait … What!?!"

"Oh my God, Que! This is great!"

"Jinx, you flirted with me. How did you know that I would not get with you!?!"

"Because you would have already, Que. When you didn't, I knew you liked my sister. So it just became a game with me. I talked to her about it, and she was cool with it, mainly because she didn't think you felt that way about her. So it was funny to her."

"But what if I had, Jinx? I'm a man! We do stuff like that! Sisters, mothers, best friends, the dirty list goes on and on!"

"You are right, Que, you could have called me on a bluff, but I would not have done it. K.P. has been in love with you for a while. I knew that. I just hoped you would see it. I continued to flirt with you to show K.P. that you were indeed into her. I mean, who can turn me down?"

"Me apparently," I muttered. " ... and thank God for will power."

"Thank God for love, Que. You just needed to see it for yourself. I would have been disappointed in you if you had tried anything, and I would have told my sister, even though I knew it would hurt her. But it would have been better to know what kind of man you were than to not know. You know I'm not apologizing, right?"

See, fellas? Women always testing your character. Remember that!

"Yeah, Jinx, and I don't expect an apology from you."

"Let's call K.P. right now! I want to take you both out to celebrate. Does Mommy know?"

"Jinx, hold on. You can't call K.P. yet or tell your mother."

"Why not?"

"K.P. doesn't know."

"K.P. doesn't know what, Que?"

"She doesn't know how I feel yet."

"You haven't told her!?! Why not!?!"

Jinx stopped in her tracks. I think she figured out the answer to her question before I could answer.

"Kiyy is back! And the reason Kiyy went away is the same reason why she is back. She still loves you … and you love her still, don't you?"

"I don't know but I can't say that I don't. Once I can get past everything, I think I do."

I nodded and sat down. Jinx sat next to me, and repeated herself.

"Fate is a cruel mistress, indeed. What are you going to do?"

"Well, the fact that I told you, Jinx, builds momentum that I am going to tell K.P."

"Que, if you break her heart…"

"Jinx, I just told you I think I love your sister. Do you think I want to hurt her?"

"What I think is that if you are telling me that you are in love with two women and one of them happens to be my sister, you may not *want* to hurt her, but she could end up being hurt anyway."

Before Jinx left, I made her promise that she would not say anything to her sister until I could talk to her myself. She promised and that's all I could do with that. The bond between sisters runs deep, and I could only hope that Jinx keeps her promise to me. I told Jinx that Kiyy, and now K.P., think that I killed Snow. I asked Jinx if she was ever going to share the truth about Snow with K.P. She said she would let me know, but did not ever want me to be the one to tell her or anyone else (i.e. Kiyy). I told her I'd adhere to her wishes.

The next few days, I visited Kiyy in the hospital and talked to K.P. on the phone. The visits with Kiyy were cordial on my part, standoffish in my mind, just to see how she was doing. But she is infectious, still, and I could always feel myself gravitating toward her, like old times. Kiyy was still devilishly innocent (i.e. sexy), and still knew how to use it. The talks with K.P. were the same way, unintended, but the same result, all the same. I decided I needed to talk to

K.P. and I told her I wanted to see her. She told me she would come over after work. I told her I would order something and asked what she had a taste for? When her answer was "you," I felt a tingle in the loins that caused the slightest knee buckle. This wasn't going to be easy. Nope.

Maybe it's because I never see K.P. dressed for work. Mental note, I need to start dropping by her job or catching her right after work. She had on a knee-high, form-fitting purple dress, low v-cut in the front, black pumps, black pearl necklace, and purple amethyst stud earrings. Her hair was lightly curled, flowing past her shoulders and down her back. Fellas, she was bangin'. Ladies, she was workin' it.

"I can't let you in here looking like that!?! You wore purple! What are you doing? We talked about this. 'No sex at "Que Quarters" with K.P. until further notice!' It says so right here!"

I showed her the imaginary piece of paper I was holding. She sashayed past me and twirled so that I could get the full effect.

"How did I know you were going to call me to come over today?"

"I ain't figured that part out yet, but that's not important. You're not playing fair!"

She walked up to me and put her hand on Floyd! I jumped back.

"Who are you? Where is K.P.?"

"She's right in front of you. You're just getting a sample of 'what it would be like to be in a relationship with K.P.' Marinate on that, sweetie!"

Yo! What the fuck!?!

"Does it come with the old K.P., too?"

"Signed, sealed, delivered, she's yours!" (Apologies to Stevie Wonder on her behalf).

"Okay, go to that side of the room and sit down … right now, lady!"

She obliged and sat on my leather sectional and crossed her legs. For some reason, I had a Basic Instinct/Sharon Stone moment and knew I wouldn't be able to concentrate if I did not ask.

"You *are* wearing panties right now, right?"

She looked at me and busted out laughing. "Purple. Matching set."

"Damn."

"Que, are you shook? Come here, baby," she cooed.

"Stop it, Katrina! I need to have a serious conversation with you and you are not helping!"

"*Oh my!* He just said Katrina! It must be serious."

Fellas, she used the "Dick Enberg 'Oh my!' voice!" Ladies, look him up. This onion's got layers!

"No, you didn't just 'Dick Enberg' me!?!"

"I'm a rare commodity, if you needed a reminder, Que!" she said, all sexy-like.

Touché (remember how men view women who like sports).

"I don't, K.P. You are a grown ass woman!" (One of the top compliments a guy can ever give a girl, trust me ladies!) "You are my 3B's K.P.!" (One of the top compliments *I* can ever give out to a girl, ladies!)

She stopped and stared at me. Now that I got her attention, I jump in.

"I'm in love with you, K.P.," I stammered, looking directly at her when I finished.

I don't know what I expected. For her to get up and run into my arms? For her to sit there and start crying tears of joy? Hey, I watch a lot of TV! What I didn't expect was what she said as her first response.

"What about Kiyy?"

"Did you hear what I just said?"

"I did, Que."

"That's your response? No 'I'm happy,' 'I love you too,' or even, 'Screw you, Que!?!'"

"Que, stop it. You know I want to hear that. But I cannot get caught up in this moment yet."

"Why not?"

"Because women aren't wired that way, Que. Women don't take solace in partial victories. We want it all! I want all of you, Que. I would be crazy to think that you still don't have feelings for Kiyy or are wrestling with them, after hearing what she said."

"Have you been talking to somebody?"

"What? No. What are you talking about?"

"Did someone tell you I have feelings for Kiyy? Why would you say that?"

"Que, I haven't talked to anyone. But I'm not a dummy, either. I'm one of the few people that's ever seen you cry over this woman—"

" … Why you gotta bring that up?"

"Because it is part of what would be 'us,' Que. You and me. Me and you. I need to know where I stand in all of that. Do you understand that?"

"Then why would you want me to tell you I love you, then?"

"Because I'm a woman, Que! I want to hear that you love me. I need to hear that you love me!"

I'm having a serious "Men are from Mars, Women are from Venus" moment right now. Of course the ladies know exactly what K.P. talks about. We men are left scratching our heads.

"It sounds like you're upset."

"I am not upset, Que. I know how hard it must have been to tell me you love me and still have feelings for Kiyy."

"I never said that I still have feelings for Kiyy, K.P."

"Are we gonna do that, Que? Are you gonna really insult my intelligence right now? You need me to ask you? Okay, Que … I didn't want to do that, but okay. Do you still love Kiyy?"

Fellas, there are lessons here. K.P. tried to give me the easy way out, and I did not take it. Now I am forced to answer what neither of us wanted to be answered at this time. I am an idiot!

"K.P., we don't have to talk about Kiyy right now. I told you I am in lo—"

" … No, Que. Do you *still-love-Kiyler?*"

Wow, it's serious when you go from nickname to government name in singsong tone!

"I do have feelings for Kiyy. I think I'm still in love with her," I mumbled, bowing my head.

K.P. took a deep breath, got up, and sat in my lap, placing her head against my chest.

"I know that was hard, Que. But you needed to say it out loud. You needed to say it to me."

"You do believe me that I am in love with you, right, K.P.?"

"Yes, Que. I believe you. Have you told Kiyy about your feelings?"

"About you?"

"About me, about her, any of it?"

"No."

"You need to tell her."

"I know. She's recuperating in the hospital."

"Yes, she is, but she's stronger than you think, Que. Women are stronger than you think. She needs to know."

We meet on Fridays. We eat fish … and we talk about *you*, ladies (no puns intended).

We call ourselves "The Scholarly Gentleman Types." That's right, ladies. Morris, Kenny, Casino, Armando, Rick and yours truly are back! When we last left our heroes, Armando was dishing about his ex, and Morris was extracting revenge against Kenny, using Carol as his sidekick.

"Hello, Mr. Que!" Carol chimed at me. "I'll be right back with your Molson Triple X."

"What's up, Carol? Looking tasty as usual!"

She smiled and went off to get my suds. I sat down amongst Morris, Rick, and Casino.

"I thought for sure I'd be the last one. Where's Kenny and Armando?"

"On their way, Woody. First round on Bobby," Rick replied after taking a swig of his Dos Equis.

"Careful Rick, you might not be calling him 'Woody' after hearing about how he flaked on the 'Puddy' last weekend!" Morris quipped, taking a sip of his Red Stripe.

The table let out a big roar at the first projectile thrown out by Morris, and the folks at Manny's knew the regulars who occupied the back of the restaurant, affectionately known as "Testostezone," was in the house!

"What'd we miss?" Kenny bellowed for all to hear as he and Armando walked toward us.

Carol, sensing that the gang was all here (or hearing Kenny), brought my Molson XXX, set Kenny's Heineken on the table, and passed Armando his Corona. Before Casino could put up a hand to motion for Carol, she set another Dragon Stout in front of him. That's why Carol gets the tip she does every week. Casino could only nod and salute. Carol said she was going to start bringing out plates, unless someone wanted to change up their usual order. No takers. The "all you can eat fried fish/seafood buffet" it was, and Carol was off.

"Morris is chomping at the bit to tell you guys about the club last week," I drolled.

"Well, speak up, man! What happened?" Armando deadpanned.

And Morris was off to the races. He told everything, even that he had not "hit" Mandie yet, which surprised me. Because at "Testostezone," there is no mercy. Simply put, we are not an "endearing group." :-/

"So wait, Morris," Armando began deliberately. "You tryin' to clown *Que* 'cause he ain't a-ttempt to push up on the 'P,' but you did, and you ain't hit it yet?"

"Yo, this is wifey material," Morris countered.

"Whoa!" Rick offered.

"There ain't no wifey material in da club, Morris!" Kenny commanded, punching his fist in his hand for emphasis.

"Yo' bitch a regular bitch, you calling her 'wifey' … Que, fuck, then feed her fast food … *You* keeping her icy!" Armando rhymed! (Apologies to Fiddy).

We hollered! And just as soon as it died down, it started back up.

"Soon as he buy that wine … Que just creep up from behind … And ask her 'what your interests are'— … " Armando continued.

"Who you be with!?!" we all chimed in unison (Apologies to Biggie).

Morris was not liking how this was turning out. Carol came out with the first round of plates, saving Morris for the time being from more abuse. After Carol brought the first round of plates, Manny, the owner of the place, came by, greeted us and blessed us with his customary round of drinks.

"Bobby, what happened with that meet you had from the other night?" Rick asked.

"We meet for the first time, and she brings a girlfriend!" Casino huffed.

"There's rules for that, B," Kenny admonished.

"Trust me, son, they was administered," Casino replied.

"Rules? So you guys gonna leave me hanging?" Rick asked, looking at Kenny and Casino.

"It's like this, Rick," Armando began. "If I'm meeting a girl for the first time and she brings her girlfriend with her, I always treat the girlfriend better than the one I was there to meet."

"Why?" Rick asked, genuinely intrigued.

"Okay, you're gonna meet the girl in a public place ninety-nine percent of the time, right?" Kenny offers.

"Yeah," Rick replied.

"Then why is she bringing her girlfriend to a public place?" Casino asked Rick.

"Because she wanted to be safe? Comfortable?"

"Errnt! Wrong answer," Kenny blurted. "You're in a public place, Rick, what does she need a chaperone for? There is no good answer. Except for her to gossip and get ol' girl's opinion."

"So it's a punishment!?!" Rick inquired.

"That's why the girlfriend gets treated better. I talk to her more, give her more of my attention, laugh at her comments, and act really cordial to the one I was there to meet," Armando agrees.

"That's why all of y'all by yourself," I laughed.

"That's why I end up getting both of them because the girlfriend always slides me her number!"

"Say word, son!" Kenny says with a gesturing high five toward Armando.

"All day, every day, son!" Armando replies with a high five.

"And the girlfriend only has nice things to say about you, and the girl you were there to meet just thinks you're being polite! Two for one!" Rick declared.

Everyone laughs at Rick's quip and enlightenment from his newfound knowledge. Carol appears with more food and drink. The table eventually got quiet from eating and drinking, but there was always room for talking and I garnered the table's attention.

"Yo, I need y'all's advice. This is serious shit. No clowning, no abuse, straight up! I need serious advice."

"Damn, Que, way to bring the room down, homie," Casino managed with packed jaws.

"Kiyy is back."

It was almost like the whole restaurant stopped what they were doing. Okay, it wasn't like that, but every time I utter those words, people get quiet, look at me in disbelief, and repeat what I've just said. No different here.

"Kiyy is back!?!" they all spat in unison.

"Hold on," I cautioned.

The last time Kiyy was spoken about, she was raked over the coals, but then there was good reason (or so it was thought). I swore them to secrecy before I began, and explained why in the next sentence I said to them.

"Manuel Vistalind?" Armando whispered. "Oh shit! Que, what the fuck!?! You got the Vistalind Cartel on your back, and you just now telling us? You putting us all in danger right now!"

Everyone looked at each other. I didn't think about that. Putting them in danger. Was I not taking this as serious as I should be?

"Mondo, trust me when I say Manuel is not after me. His nephew is another story, and I'm working on that. The 'Vistalind' Cartel is not on me, just a nephew who doesn't have the same pull."

"His last name is 'Vistalind!?!'" Armando spat.

"Yes but—"

" … Then the Vistalind Cartel is on you, bro!"

Armando got up to leave. He dropped a fiddy on the table and said, "Que, you my man, but I got history with the Vistalind Cartel, and if they find out I associate with you, it's not gonna be a good look."

"I hear you, Armando. I'll let you know when it's dead."

With that, Armando was gone. I looked at the rest of the table and told them if anyone else felt like that, I would not hold it against them to leave also, if they chose.

"It's close to home for Armando, Que," Kenny offered. "His 'ex' is in the Vistalind family. Please keep that close."

"Wow! Talk about playing with fire!" Casino mumbled.

"What does Manuel Vistalind have to do with Kiyy?" Rick asked.

I realized then that I did not get a chance to explain about Kiyy, and I did so. No one touched their food while I talked. Carol came around and did a double-take.

"Is there a funeral going on here? What happened to Armando? Is everything okay?" Carol asked.

Everyone looked at me.

"Yes, Carol, everything is good. Can I have another Triple X, please?"

She asked if anyone else wanted another beer. Everyone else raised their hand. Carol looked at the table of practically full beers and left to replace them.

"So I've told you guys about Kiyy, and how I'm struggling with the feelings that have resurfaced, but there is more. I'm in love with my best friend, K.P."

Casino started choking on his food and Kenny spat out the swig of Heineken he had just taken.

They both shouted in unison, "What?"

Morris and Rick looked baffled and bewildered. Casino managed to speak independently first.

"K.P.? Que, are you serious!?!"

"Yeah, team, I am."

"Wow! What the fuck are you gonna do, kid? They both tens, you lucky motherfucker!" Kenny gasped.

"That's the dilemma, Kenny. What should I do?"

"Both are life changing, son. But the road less traveled very well could lead to the same happiness as the road already traveled."

Leave it to "Dex" to put everything into perspective.

"Did he just butcher Robert Frost, yet make sense out of it?" Rick asked incredulously.

"Smoke and mirrors, he didn't answer the question," Morris interjected.

"Actually, he did," I laughed. "In Kenny speak, he told me I can't go wrong with either one."

"Great! Now he's a savant," Morris droned.

"You can't have my life, Morris," Kenny needled.

"I can't escape this life that I'm livin'—" I began.

"... Damn you in the mix," Casino followed.

"... You in love with two women," Rick finished (Apologies to Lost Boyz).

Of course, Rick and Bobby get props for picking up on that.

"Damn, Que, now I understand why you didn't push up on Mandie. You got major issues, bro'. Two women ... you're in love with two women. Why didn't you just say something?"

"Morris, would you have wanted to hear that then? Would you have understood it then?"

"Naw, Que, you right. I wasn't tryin' to hear anything you had to say that night. Sorry bro'."

Carol came back with the brews and distributed them accordingly. She asked again if everything was okay.

"When Manny comes to me and asks if I've done anything to upset you guys, I gotta ask. Again, is everything okay?"

"Carol, it's not you," Rick said.

"It's *never* you, Carol," Morris complimented.

"Okay, if it's not me, then it's none of my business—"

" ... Wait, Carol. Have you ever been in love with two guys before?"

"No. It's hard enough loving one man!"

"I hear that," Rick managed.

"Why? Who's in love with two guys? Kenny?" Carol teased.

That broke up the uneasiness, and we all laughed.

"Never that, Carol. I promise you," Kenny huffed.

Rick looked at me and tilted his head. I shrugged.

"One of us is in love with two women," Rick offered. "Got any advice on how to handle that?"

"Is it you, Rick?" Carol asked.

Rick threw his hands up and shook his head.

"Is it you, Morris?"

"Nope."

"Is it you, Bobby?"

"Not me."

"It can't be you, Kenny?"

"You know it can't be me, Carol."

"Que? It's you? *You* are in love with two women? Wow, I didn't see that one coming!"

I briefly explained how Kiyy came back and the feelings that resurfaced, and that there was a good chance I've been in love with my best friend for years, but never acknowledged it or allowed for the possibility, until now.

"Which one can you talk to about anything?" Carol asked.

"Both of them," I responded.

"Which one's kisses affected you more?"

"Both of them."

"Which one opened your car door for you?"

"Both of them."

"Which one has surprised you with dinner, clothes, a gift?"

"Both of them."

"Which one thinks for two?"

"Both of them."

"Which one gave you the better orgasm?"

The guys chuckled.

"Both of them."

"You're lying, Que!" Carol challenged.

"They've both given me that orgasm that only guys know of!"

"Whoa!" the guys gasped in unison.

"Two for one again! That shit is real!" Kenny mumbled.

"I'm glad I'm not you," Morris offered.

"Team, on the shield, I can't call it!" Casino added.

"You got a problem, Que," Rick announced.

Everyone looked at Rick, including Carol.

"Oh. White guys can't know about that orgasm? Sorry, it's not just a 'black' thing!" Rick asserted with air quotes for emphasis.

Again, we laughed, and for the moment the mood lightened.

"Que, there is something that distinguishes the two of them. Something that you know or will come to know."

"That sounds like a long time, Carol," Morris interceded. "Sounds like he needs answers sooner than later."

"Maybe, Morris, but there is something that distinguishes the two, and Que will be able to choose when he realizes it. For his sake, and those two young ladies, I hope it *is* sooner than later."

"Thanks Carol," I said.

"Good luck with that, Que."

Carol walked away, I'm sure shaking her head inside, thinking which girlfriends she was gonna gather up and say, "I got a story to tell!" (Apologies again to Biggie).

The rest of the evening was weird. It was like I sucked the life out of Manny's, and it was a different look and feel. Everyone seemed to take their cue (no pun intended), from us. If we weren't being loud and rambunctious, the place had a different feel. The food of course, didn't change, but the atmosphere that night did. So much that Manny came around for a second visit, just to see if everything was okay.

Something he's never done in all the time we've been coming to Manny's. Guess he didn't believe Carol. Not sure if Carol knew or cared, 'cause her tip stayed the same. We parted that night with bro' hugs and words of encouragement. Me … no closer to any decision than I was before the night started.

***

Kiyy had now been in the hospital for three weeks. She was walking, eating, and Steven said she was recovering well enough that she could be discharged soon. And not a peep from Carlos. He had to be watching. I made no attempt to hide when and where I was coming and going. I needed to know what Kiyy intended to do once she was discharged. I needed to tell Kiyy about K.P. and everything else. And I needed to see Profit. It was time to cash in some chips. First stop, Profit. I didn't know exactly where Profit was, but I did have a way to contact him.

"I ain't seen that code in a minute, yo!" Profit acknowledged. "What's good, yo?"

"I honestly didn't think you'd still be carrying a pager, let alone remember my code."

"I know you heard about 'D,' yo?"

"Yeah. I need to see you 'bout that and some other 'ish.'"

"Eh yo, you coming out of retirement, yo?"

"Let's just say some things need to be dealt with."

"Ain't you a lawyer, yo?"

"Indeed. But these streets stay home to a brother," I replied, placing my right fist against my heart.

"True indeed. Let's poly, yo!"

Profit told me when and where to meet him, and we hung up. I got in my car and drove off. If you think I was driving straight to Profit, you probably never ran the streets, and definitely not the streets of New York. Street smarts is a way of life in Brooklyn.

I drove to the nearest overhead train station and parked, all the while looking to see if any cars were following me, or had pulled off to the side. Like clockwork, the rumble of the train signaled it was approaching the train station. Like somebody that ain't new to this, I timed it. You can tell how far away the train is by listening. I waited and then jumped out of my car and ran upstairs to the turnstiles, dropped my token in the slot, and bolted up the stairs. The doors of the train were open, and I darted onto the train just as the doors were closing. As the train was pulling out of the station, two guys clearly out of breath stopped and stared, as the train pulled off to the next station. I don't know if they was taggin' me or not but they ass out. (_ ω _) If you know Brooklyn like I know Brooklyn … if you get on the train at the stop I got on at before the train heads underground, it is impossible to get to the next stop by car, and just as impossible to tail somebody if you weren't expecting it because you'll never know what stop the person got off at, if they changed trains, or caught a connecting train. Brooklyn, stand up!

Profit met me up at Utica and Eastern Pkwy. He had "Presidential style" security with him, and the sidewalk cleared as we walked to his ride.

"No problems, yo?" he asked.

"If I was followed, you can shoot me 'tree time in di head, star'!" I boasted.

"Damn, I miss 'em, yo," Profit replied.

Another one of Donovan's sayings.

"Me too."

"You hungry, yo?"

"Yeah, what you getting?"

"I'm thinking Ali's. What you want, yo?"

I hadn't had Ali's in a minute. Even though I live in Brooklyn, there are some spots that you just

don't get to anymore. So I was takin' full advantage
of this!

"Conch roti and beef roti."

"Hungry, yo?"

"I never get over here much anymore, so you
know, eat one now, save one for later!"

"Why I got a taste for Now & Laters, yo?" he
laughed.

"'Cause you hear that jingle when we was little,
'Eat some now, save some for later'!"

He looked at one of his detail and said, "Four
roti, two conch, one beef, one chicken."

He looked at me.

"Welch's, yo?" he asked.

"Yessir!" I replied.

He looked back at the person taking the order.

"Two Welch's grape and a pack of sour apple
Now & Laters, yo!"

He looked at me again.

"Three Musketeers, yo?"

I smirked and nodded.

"And a Three Musketeers. And meet us at the
spot, yo!"

The assigned person was off, and we were in
the car off to the "spot."

"I was expecting the Navigator, heard a lot about it from Kiyy."

"How she doing, yo?"

"She recovering."

"I'm sorry I got there late, yo."

"It's all good, fam!"

"She was dead up about going, yo! I told her to chill for a minute, I had to take care of some business. I would take her personally. But she was like, 'I been apart from him for long enough, I can't wait no longer,' yo. I thought I sent enough fire power, but I should have put her in the Navi, 'cause it was the only bulletproof we had at the time. Now we got a few. This one included, yo."

It was a 600 Mercedes Benz sedan.

"Prof, this don't fall on you."

"I hear you, yo. But to answer you, the Navi only comes out on special occasions now. So if you see her on the street now? Best believe somebody's 'bout to catch some, yo!"

"This is gonna be a special occasion?" I hoped.

"Oh no doubt, yo!"

We arrived at the "spot" and settled in to talk logistics. Profit asked me if I knew of Manuel's death and the denials surrounding it, and I told him that Kiyy had told me. Profit filled me in on the intel he had on Manuel's spots from Donovan. When I asked, he couldn't recall if Kiyy had ever provided any more intimate intel of Manuel's operations or layout. He asked if she was well enough to ask about it.

"Let's call her," I said.

I called Kiyy at the hospital.

"Hi honey," Kiyy gleamed.

I realized right then and there I needed to tell her about K.P. and everything before this got further out of pocket.

"Hi Kiyy," I replied. "I'm with Profit."

"Really? Tell him 'hi'."

"I will. We're talking about things, and we wanted to know if you had any intel about Manuel's operations and layouts that Profit doesn't recall or know about? It would help in Profit's planning, and we need to focus on the real threat now, Carlos."

"Okay. Are you coming by?"

"Yes, later. We need to talk about a few things. Steven says you could be discharged very soon. We need to figure out the best place for you to stay until things are squared."

"I'm not staying with you? I want to stay with you!"

"Kiyy, I may not be best equipped to protect you at my place." "You want me to stay moving around like I did with Donovan, and now again with Profit?"

"I don't know, Kiyy. We need to talk about it, okay?"

"Put Profit on the phone, Que."

"What?"

"I want to speak with Profit."

I looked at the phone and then looked at Profit.

"She wants to speak to you," I said to Profit, handing him the phone.

Profit took the phone and identified himself. Kiyy spoke and Profit just listened. Then he handed the phone back to me.

"Yeah, it's me," I said to Kiyy.

"I'll see you when you get here, Que. Bye."

She hung up. If she's annoyed about *this*, then I can only imagine how the rest of it is going to go down.

"What did she say to you?" I asked Profit.

"She reminded me of the promise I made to Donovan to protect her, you, and everyone else. She reminded me of the drawings she made of the layouts of Manuel's spots. She also said she was staying with you at your place, 'so figure it out, yo,'" he chuckled. "She feisty, yo."

"Yeah, about that …"

In the midst of our planning, I told Profit about the triangle involving me, Kiyy, and K.P., and my thoughts on what to do about Carlos. He said he had wanted to take out Manuel himself for Donovan, but taking all of his spots from Carlos would be consolation. He asked me about making a choice between Kiyy and K.P. My answer to him mirrored my answer to others. He also told me he'd have my house on lockdown when Kiyy came there.

"When she comes? That ain't been decided yet, fam," I informed Profit.

He just looked at me.

"This woman talked about you every day, yo. You gonna tell her she can't stay with you?"

I looked back and just sighed. The food arrived and I tore into my conch roti and Welch's grape. After another hour, we worked through details and concluded for the day. Profit asked me if I wanted a ride back to my car. I declined. If there was someone following me, I didn't want them to be alerted that I met with Profit. He agreed. He let me know that there were a few heads watching my crib and more were on standby at an undisclosed locale near me. He thought it best if I didn't know any more than that. I agreed.

"You strapped, yo?" Profit asked.

"I keeps it heated, son. You know this!" I assured him.

I've carried every day since I was able to get my permit. It is extremely difficult to get a concealed carry permit in New York City. You can have a permit to carry in New York State and not be allowed to carry concealed in New York City without a New York City permit. Thank God for my godfather, the honorable Bruce Knight. He didn't want to initially sign my permit because of all the controversy surrounding him, but he did. He had the press sweating him, police brass, and the mayor on him because he was outspoken about institutional and systemic racism in the court system.

But what really set everyone off was his bail practices. He insisted that bail should not be used as a punishment to hold people for preventing crime. He often set bail for the poor and minorities at ridiculously low amounts, even though some were accused of violent crimes. He was traditional and believed in the presumption of innocence until proven guilty. Folk still don't believe in that edict.

In fact, Judge Knight's decisions on bail weren't that extreme compared with his colleagues, but were certainly much more scrutinized by the press and law enforcement because of his outspokenness. He tackled police brutality and was vilified for remarks he made that acquittals by white juries of white police officers just made the police more brazen in their assault and hunt of minorities. He would tell me stories about his own experiences. He got accepted to two Ivy League schools. One wanted him to attend a minority student program and take classes before the school year began, and his admittance could be revoked if his performance wasn't satisfactory to them. The other did not have those constraints, so he attended that learned institution. He lived through segregation. He was paid less than his white colleagues at a major law firm in New York City, even though he came in at the same time as they did and did the same work. He was pulled over by white cops constantly, and most knew he was a judge. He was threatened constantly, but always declined a security detail. He would say when I asked him about getting a bodyguard, "The only ones I trust with my life are me and Roscoe." Roscoe being his licensed .45 caliber automatic. He's retired now, back down south where he and my dad grew up.

I got dropped off at another train line and made my way back to my car. Knowing that once I retrieved my car, I was headed to Kiyy. As I made my way down the stairs, I noticed three things immediately:

1. A homeless man sitting near my car.
2. A Hispanic guy leaning against a light pole across the street lighting a cigarette.
3. A man and a woman arguing about who smoked up all the weed.

As I got to my car, the homeless man looked at me and said, "Don't turn around, mister. That guy across the street has been messing with your car."

"Let me buy you something to eat, over at the chicken spot over there, mister," I said loud enough to be heard by the guy across the street, as I pointed to the spot.

The guy dropped his cigarette on the ground, and a rapid fire line came straight to my car. I grabbed the homeless man and we dove further into the vacant lot where he was sitting. My car exploded within seconds after becoming a fireball! As we lay on the ground, I heard the screeching of tires as a car peeled off. Rats, cats, and others scrambled for hiding places at the sound of the explosion. I looked at my car, and then I looked at the homeless man, who I helped up.

"Thank you for watching my car all day. And thank you for saving my life."

I gave the man the other fifty dollars I had promised him on return to match the fifty I gave him initially. He smiled and thanked me. I asked him if I could get him into a shelter, help him find a job, anything to repay my debt to him. He told me I was a man of my word and that he was good. There's no price tag for saving a man's life, but I knew it damn sure warranted more than one hundred dollars. I gave him an additional four hundred dollar bills as a small token of my appreciation and told him to be safe.

Shit just got real. It made sense to me that Carlos would try and take me out here as opposed to a hospital. Too many questions and unnecessary heat brought on yourself if you try at the hospital. Nobody cares as much for an abandoned area of the hood. He knew my house was being watched. So he followed me until there was an opportunity. Manny's was out because I took the train there. Maybe I'm giving him too much credit, but better to give the punk more credit than to underestimate him. I called 911, filed a police report with officers that were nearby and heard the explosion. I didn't ask the homeless guy to give a statement. I didn't want him involved anymore or be retaliated against, since he was virtually unknown to be involved.

When I had initially drove up and parked, the homeless man was sitting on a crate. I got out of the car pretending to be on my cell phone and spoke to him with my back turned to him. I told him not to respond verbally but to just nod his head after I finished saying what I wanted him to do. I said to him if he agreed to nod and I'd make it worth his while. He nodded. I told him I was placing a fifty-dollar bill under my driver's side front tire, and there'd be another on my return, and he should retrieve it after he saw anybody run up the stairs after I did. I got out of the car, bent over to tie my shoe, placed the bill under the tire, and took off for the train station. The rest you know.

I wasn't taking any chances. I paged Profit. I hailed down a gypsy cab and told the driver to take me to the hospital. I still had to see Kiyy.

I had called Tariq Shabazz Mohammed and informed him of the latest happenings. He immediately said he would set up a perimeter around the hospital. He also asked me if I wanted protection. I declined for the moment, telling him I had it covered. He informed me that the same deal offered for Kiyy would be offered to me, taken care of and such. I told him I would get back to him about me, but I also wanted to talk about protection for Kiyy outside of the hospital, and possibly for another person as well. OK, you guys know "another person" was K.P., right? Tariq told me he would await instruction on that, but he would set up the perimeter and maintain what was already in place.

I went through hospital protection to get to the floor Kiyy (Brenda Joseph) was on and stepped off the elevator.

Steven met me by the elevator and immediately pulled me to the side.

"Are you okay?" he asked.

"What do you mean? Yeah, I'm okay."

"Stop bullshiting me, Que. Tariq speaks to me as well."

Damn, just what I needed.

"Yes, Steven. I am okay."

"What is going on? You're in real danger! Have you told Mom and Dad?"

"Steven, listen to me. You cannot say *anything* to Mom and Dad, okay? I'm handling this. If you've never trusted anything I've said before, I need you to trust me on this."

"Que, somebody tried to kill you by blowing up your car. That same person probably tried to kill Kiyler as well. Please let Tariq help. He is ex-military black ops. He is trained for this kind of thing. You are not. I know you thought you were big time running with the Wolfpack when you were younger, but this is different now, okay?"

Nothing like your older brother putting you in your place, making you feel small.

"What do you know about the Wolfpack, Steven?"

"I grew up in the neighborhood, too, Que. Just because I didn't run in those circles doesn't mean I didn't know what was going on."

"I told Tariq I would keep him informed and get back to him, is that okay?"

"No it is not okay, because you are stalling, Que."

"Please, Steven, I've never asked you for anything. I'm asking this."

"This ain't over, Que. I'm not promising anything, but I will not say anything right now."

"Thanks, Steven."

"Kiyy will be discharged in the next day or two."

I nodded as Steven walked away and I went to the nurses station. I spoke to Jack and Daniel outside of Kiyy's door, both of whom had already been briefed, and I was told by them that all was quiet, but they wanted to reassure me that they were on heightened alert from here on (whatever that protocol meant in their jargon, it sounded escalated to me). I walked in and faced Kiyy. She looked at me as I walked and sat in the chair that faced her. She asked me to come closer. I did and she kissed me.

"I'm sorry that I got annoyed with you, Que. I realize this can't be an easy situation for you. You're not supposed to be equipped to handle this situation."

"It's cool, Kiyy. I didn't think anything about it. I know you're frustrated."

She reached for my hand and held it.

"Steven says I can be discharged in the next day or so. Isn't that great?"

"Yes it is, Kiyy."

"He said I've made a remarkable recovery thus far."

"He would know, but I think you have as well, and I'm not a doctor."

"So you wanted to talk. Is it more than just about where I'm going to stay after I leave here?"

"Yes, but you'll stay with me until we can get a better handle on this."

"All I want is to be with you, Que."

"There's more, Kiyy."

"Okay, I'm listening."

"I've wrestled with how I feel, not only about you coming back, but the way you left, the reason you left, and all of that. You were my world, but you broke my heart. Of course there was a very compelling underlying reason, which you can never be faulted for by me. I will never do it. You did it to protect me. You did it to save my life. You did it because you love me. I've tried hard not to let that influence my feelings, as I've tried just as hard to not let my feelings about how you left me influence me. But I'm human, and I figured that I am looking at it from the wrong perspective. I can't and shouldn't dismiss how you made me feel, just as I shouldn't dismiss why you did what you did and how it can influence me. Loyalty and gratitude immediately come to mind. I'm sorry, I'm rambling. I still have feelings for you, Kiyy. I am still in love with you."

"But?" Kiyy asked.

"But? ... But what?" I replied.

"You went through that whole thing. I'm not gonna call it song and dance, but you could have just led with 'I still love you, Kiyy.' So there's more. There has to be more, Que."

"There is someone else, Kiyy. I'm in love with someone else as well."

"K.P.," Kiyy acknowledged.

It wasn't a question. She was very deliberate.

"Yes, Kiyy. K.P."

Kiyy looked at me and smiled.

"Two for one! I'm not surprised, Que. If I had to pick the other, it would have been her. That's who I would have wanted you with, if I could never get back to you."

"How, Kiyy? How did you know that?"

"Women's intuition, my love. I always wondered why you two were never together? How I managed to get you and she didn't?"

"We never looked at each other that way, Kiyy."

"Maybe you didn't back then, but she did. But she was never disrespectful. She never tried to influence you, she never tried to move in on you. She was your best friend. I have to admit, I figured that you two would have gotten together after I broke up with you. Fate is a cruel mistress."

If I hear that one more time … I'm just sayin'.

"I just realized how I felt about her. Ironically, right before you showed up. After you came back, she told me she was in love with me."

"Yeah, Kiyy comes back and gets a second bite of the apple. We can't have that."

"Are you being sarcastic right now?" I asked.

"Yes, I am."

"K.P. was going to tell you that when she came to the hospital, but you dropped that bomb."

"Not a bomb, just the truth, Que. I told you that day that she wanted to say something else besides not coming back into your life to hurt you. But I didn't know what it was. Now I do. Did you sleep with her?"

"Yes."

"When?"

"Does that really matter, Kiyy?"

"Yes and no. But your non-answer confirms what I believe. I don't have to tell you that you are going to have to make a choice. She's not going to like it that I'm staying with you."

"I'll deal with that. You're awfully calm about this, Kiyy."

"Que, I went through all the scenarios. I had nothing but time. This is just one of them. Remember when I said I was prepared for a number of things regarding you? That I was at peace just being able to see you?"

"Yes, I remember."

"That was true, but seeing you also made me want more. Of what we had, of what I envisioned we could become again. It was the driving force that got me through each day. It gave me hope. I decided when I saw you that I wanted us again. Not knowing what your situation was, married, children, girlfriend. I just wanted you. I wanted to be married to you, I wanted to have your children, I wanted to live happily ever after. I wanted it all!"

"Carlos tried to kill me today."

"What!?! Oh my God! Are you hurt!?! … What happened!?!"

"He's been watching the house and watching me. I wasn't sure until I got back to my car."

"Got back to your car? I don't understand."

"I went to see Profit. I drove the car to the train station in case someone was following. I ditched the car there and hopped on the train to meet Profit. I think me unwittingly doing that gave Carlos the opportunity to take me out, because he couldn't do it at the house since he figured someone was watching. When I ditched whoever was following me, it must have signaled to Carlos that I was alone and no one was watching me. When I came back to the car, this homeless man I asked to watch it, signaled to me that a guy watching from across the street tampered with my car."

"Thank God, you're all right! And thank God you thought to do that!"

"Yeah. Listen, I'm gonna bounce. Gonna talk with Profit about dealing with this Carlos thing, protecting you at my house, and some other things I gotta do."

"Are you going to see K.P?"

"I might?"

"You might?"

"Yeah, I might. I do have to speak to her to let her know you will be staying with me."

"Please don't sleep with her."

"I'ma pretend I didn't hear you say that, okay?"

"It's what women do."

"I'm gonna get seduced, is that what you're saying?"

"Women use sex as a weapon, Que."

"Is it what you would do?"

"It's not a weapon with me. It's how I feel toward you."

"Sounds like game."

Kiyy smirked. "Look into my eyes. You tell me if it's game?"

I got home, took a shower, spoke with Profit, and ordered food. K.P. wanted Chinese, so I ordered from our favorite spot. When the usual delivery guy did not show up, I answered my door with the gun cocked. Paranoid? I think not. Behind the Vistalind name, Carlos is still a punk! Straight up pussy. Showed his true colors, I'ma yank up his skirt (Apologies to Smif n' Wesson).

You might think, *Well, he done tried to take you out, that ain't a punk move.* I would say to all of you thinking like that, "You're not from the streets." A respected move in the streets is walking up to someone and pulling the trigger. For him not to do it himself is a punk ass move. I realize that my rationale is straight ghetto, but if you ain't never been to the ghetto, don't ever come to the ghetto, 'cause you wouldn't understand the ghetto ... so stay the fuck outta the ghetto! (Apologies to Naughty by Nature). He's straight up perpetrating the fraud in these streets.

I moved away from that line of thinking and turned on the TV as I waited for K.P. to arrive. I wasn't looking forward to this conversation. She was gonna be upset and probably have good reason to be so. I flipped channels and stopped on Channel 47. Remember Telemundo? My mother and I watched

Lucha Libre (Spanish wrestling), when I was little, and she used to watch Spanish soap operas, but she didn't know Spanish to my knowledge. God bless her heart! This soap happened to be in English, and nostalgia got the better of me for a minute:

"I believe in you, Renaldo."

"I'm glad that you do, Manuela. But I need you to believe in 'us.'"

"I don't know, Renaldo."

"What is it that you want, Manuela?"

You tell her, Renaldo! Okay, so I'm a sap with the soap operas. Romanticism stirs within me. <3 Renaldo has a point though. Renaldo wants her to spend the rest of her life with him, but she's flaking. I don't understand you women. What is it that you seek? You don't know, do you? It's okay, ladies … Say it with me, "I don't know." There's still hope for you. Acceptance is the first step to recovery. Those that are still in denial may need more than the Twelve-Step program to help them come to terms with their condition.

Oh, that's the doorbell. I know at least two women that do know what they want. One is at my door right now.

———————

"Why does she have to stay here, Que!?! Why did you tell her she could stay with you? That's exactly what she wanted!"

"What was I supposed to do?"

"Send her home to her mother!"

"She can't go home, K.P."

"Maybe not, but she could have gone back to where she's been the last few years!"

"Yeah, but look what she's been through? She's been through enough, hasn't she?"

"See, right there, Que. That 'subtle manipulation.' She's sitting back and letting the situation play on your emotions. Whatever she says, it's to keep it in that realm. A comment here, a plea there. And if I point it out, like I'm doing, I run the risk of being the bad one, the insensitive one, the jealous one, even the irrational one. While she gets to play 'Sweet Poly Purebred!'"

"Do you hear yourself, K.P.?"

"Do you hear me, Que? You don't know the lengths a woman will go through to get a man. You just get to experience the end results, the pleasures. Not the treachery, not the debauchery, not the low down gritty and grimy!" (Apologies to Onyx on her behalf).

"She asked me not to sleep with you."

"Do you know why, Que?"

"Why?"

"Because it makes her come off as frail and vulnerable. And it makes you feel like Underdog coming to save the day. Meanwhile, she is plotting how she is going to seduce you, and maybe even make it seem like it was your idea."

"Is that what you would do?"

"You damn right, Que! And if you asked her the same question and you got a different answer, she's lying! It's what any woman that loves a man would do. Use any and all means necessary. You're still my best friend, and I hope I can still talk to you that way. You may not look at it this way, but this is now a competition, Que. Kiyy knows about me and is not stepping aside. With her staying here now, she gets to see you every day, using wile and subtle charm to work her way back into your soul. I think I'm gonna start calling her 'Halo' or 'Natasha!'"

"Sounds like you're saying I can't see if I'm being manipulated, K.P.?"

"No, Que, I am giving you credit. You can recognize game. But can you distinguish game from Kiyy? You loved a different woman back then. She's not the same person you fell in love with. She's changed. That's not a good or bad thing, just life. She's been away from you for ten years."

"How do you know she's changed?"

"Please don't get upset with me. Just think about what I've said and watch out for signs. That's all. She'd like nothing more than for me to continue to try and explain what is happening, get both of us frustrated and upset with each other while she stays angelic."

"I don't see what you see, K.P."

"I know you don't, baby. I am not trying to be condescending, but women see things that the male ego doesn't allow men to see. Whenever a woman that cares about a man tries to point it out, the man's ego gets in the way because he thinks he should have seen exactly what the woman sees, but it is impossible. It's just how men and women are wired. I just need you to trust what I've said to be true. And that is hard for men to do."

This is one of those times when a woman's intellect is sexy as hell! The emotion just engulfed me. I grabbed K.P. and kissed her. She responded back with passion to match. Our clothes flew off in every direction and we were in my bed. She let out a gasp as I entered her. I'd never felt as hard and as big as I did at that moment. She took all of me and gave it back stroke for stroke. Hard, fast, slow, grinding, our bodies synced to whatever rhythms manifested. We changed positions, we focused on specific body parts in harmonious symmetry, just to end up eventually how we started, driving our euphonic composition to a climaxing crescendo.

10

ABADDON

Wash, Rinse, Repeat

Your first love is your purest love. Every heartbreak and relationship after that, you love a little less. But what happens when the person that broke your heart so that you love a little less is that same person that comes back into your life and rekindles the fire that stoked your heart in the first place? Kiyy is everything that I wanted … until I knew what I wanted. Does that make sense to you? She was the standard. Everyone after got compared to her. Is she still everything that I want, now that I'm older and presumably know what I want in a woman?

Kiyy was discharged from the hospital today. She didn't want a wheelchair or any assistance. She wanted to walk out of the hospital on her own. She said that if Carlos was watching her, she wanted him to see that he didn't break her. I admired that about Kiyy, her resolve. Steven and a team of doctors had done final examinations and cleared her. She was given instructions for her recovery. She was told she was free to partake in any activity but not to over exert herself. Why the doctors looked at me when this was said is beyond me. Kiyy, of course, thought it was funny.

You would have thought Kiyy was a celebrity with the escort she required to the car. Jack and Daniel stood on either side of us, and hospital security personnel flanked her front and back. Tariq had the area scoped like secret service detail and personally crafted the travel route from the hospital to my home. Tariq again reminded me of his offer and I declined. Steven wasn't going to be happy, but I believed Profit and I had things under control. The Navigator was waiting to transport us from the hospital to my home and Profit had my home on lockdown as he promised.

I made sure the house was stocked with all of Kiyy's favorites and a few of mine. Tariq and his team rode in cars in front and behind the Navigator with Tariq leading the way. All was quiet as we made the trip to my house.

I hadn't heard from K.P. today, but that was to be expected because she wasn't happy with Kiyy staying with me. But we talked things through after our meeting of the minds (don't act like you don't know what I'm referring to), and she understands. The plan was to look for Carlos after Kiyy was situated at my house and deal with him. The hope was that this crisis would be taken care of in a week's time. Street justice was swift, unlike a court of law. Morally, I knew our plan was wrong, but the alternatives offered no final solutions.

Initially, diplomacy was administered. What do I mean by that? Well, I thought about what Armando had said to me that night at Manny's. As long as Carlos had the Vistalind name, the Vistalind Cartel was potentially on my back. I used a lot of favors to get to Javier Vistalind, to no avail. Javier Vistalind is the kingpin of the Vistalind Cartel and Carlos' father. But in my attempts, word somehow made its way to Tariq's channels. I did not realize how far this man's reach extended. Being ex-militia, I guess I should have seen the potential for underground connections, but I did not make the connect.

Anyway, Tariq brokered a meet with Javier himself, saying they had history. After speaking with Kiyy, we agreed to let Tariq bring a copy of the messages that Carlos left on Donovan's phone in the hopes of proposing a truce. The hope was that Tariq would convince Javier to force Carlos to stand down and leave us be. From Tariq's account, Javier was not initially persuaded by the recordings, mainly because they were unauthenticated. However, once they were, Javier was outdone with his son, and promised to deal with his issues in house. Tariq secured a promise from Javier with additional persuasion (still unknown to me), that there would be no retaliation from the Vistalind Cartel regarding Kiyy, myself, family or friends. Kiyy was discharged in the interim as we awaited confirmation from Javier that Carlos had been ordered to stand down. Tariq didn't want to take any chances until then, hence the hospital orchestration.

"Are you okay, Que?" Kiyy asked.

"I'd be better knowing Carlos is neutralized, but I'm good."

"I think it was the right thing to do, getting Carlos' father involved," Kiyy said.

"I hope so, 'cause it's certainly not the way I handle b-i, calling Daddy," I replied. "But in the meantime, the plan stays in place, understood?"

"Yes, Que. I'm not going anywhere without you, anyway. And don't second guess the way you've chosen to handle this, either."

"All the same, we need to be on the same page."

"I assume you spoke to K.P. about me staying with you?"

"Yes, I did."

"How did she take it?"

"How do you think she took it, Kiyy? She wasn't happy about it. But everything's cool."

"Everything's cool? What is that supposed to mean?"

"It means K.P. understands the situation."

"Really?"

"Kiyy, you should be concerned with recovery, shouldn't you?"

"I am concerned with recovery, Cap'n."

She finished that off with a salute, and I could only smirk at her.

"I got steaks to cook at the house, chicken, fish, potatoes, vegetables, Hawaiian Punch, two bags of Funyuns, and Chips Ahoy! to hold you down for the week, okay?"

"You got Funyuns!?!"

"Yes, Kiyy," I laughed. "I don't know why you liked those nasty things."

"It's just like Munchos, except onion flavored," she reasoned.

"I think not. But they're all yours. I got breath mints and extra toothpaste, too!" I chided.

"I can't wait to get up in your face with my oniony breath."

"Ugh."

We arrived at the house, and Tariq got out, surveying and talking on a walkie talkie. Seemed over the top, but it was appreciated nonetheless. He was taking no chances with us under his watch. I could see why he came highly recommended. Still had to quiz Steven on their connection one day, though.

We got out of the Navigator, and Kiyy was escorted into the house. I was alerted to the sound of a crow overhead with what sounded like cackling. Then suddenly five more appeared with what definitely sounded like cackling. I honestly didn't know what to make of it, but I didn't think they were spreading the gospel. It didn't sound like they were spooked because of all the new faces and activity, I just hoped they would settle down when Tariq and company left. Profit, who rode with us, spoke to his peeps and made sure instructions were understood by all.

I thanked Tariq for his assistance, and again Tariq made his offer known. If nothing else, he was consistent, if not persistent. I declined and informed him I'd be awaiting his confirmation call and had him on speed dial if I ever needed his services again. He nodded, wished peace and blessings upon us, and departed.

Profit explained that there were people that would be seen and there would be people around that were unseen. I assured him we'd be good and we should meet up in the next day or so if we hadn't heard anything from Tariq. Profit reminded me he was a phone call away, and he had me. We exchanged the "bro" handshake and hug, and he too was departed. I couldn't help but notice that the crows' cackling sounded more like cawing now. I looked around and nothing seemed unusual. I looked directly at the crows, and they looked directly at me and continued cawing.

I went into the house.

"Que, didn't you say you'd gotten a couple bags of Funyuns?"

"Yeah."

"I only see one bag, and I don't see any Chips Ahoy!"

I went to the kitchen and sure enough there was one bag of Funyuns on top of the fridge and no bag of Chips Ahoy! I looked in the frig and a Hawaiian Punch was gone, along with turkey meat and a loaf of bread.

"Looks like Prof's peeps helped themselves to some of the furnishings," Kiyy observed.

"Yeah, must have," I commented. "But that's the last time that happens."

"Are you gonna say something to Profit about that?" Kiyy asked.

"Naw, it was just food. I'll look around to make sure nothing else is missing, but I'm not inclined to say nothing to Prof."

I was peeved a bit about peeps helping themselves to my food, but they Prof's people and they are looking out for a brother, so …

"I want to take a shower, Que. Can I have a towel and wash cloth, please?"

I went and retrieved the requested items and Kiyy smiled at me.

"Did you always have this orange set, or did you just buy it for me?"

Dammit, the questions Kiyy asks always catch me in between!

"It's still your favorite color, right?"

"Yes, it is. Did you have an orange set previously or did you buy this for me?"

"Both Kiyy, okay? I bought the set a long time ago, just because."

"I'm sorry, Que. I wasn't trying to make this awkward for you, I was just curious."

"You still have that knack of asking me questions I don't expect, Kiyy."

"That's your mistake. What are you expecting? You set yourself up because you are not a mind reader. You can't possibly anticipate anything that I or probably anyone else might ask you with absolute certainty. It's lose-lose, sweetie."

"It's just you, Kiyy."

"What are you trying to hide from me? I had your heart once. Is that what you're hiding now?"

"I can't get hurt by you again, Kiyy."

"I'm not going anywhere, Que. I promise. Let go, and let me back in. We were good back then, great back then."

"We were great back then, Kiyy … back then."

"I'm glad I'm here. You'll get to see firsthand that I have no intention of ever leaving you again.

I am sorry that I hurt you, but I'd do it again if it meant saving your life. Do you understand that?"

She didn't wait around for my reply. She took the towel set and headed to the bathroom.

"There's shower caps in the bottom drawer," I called out to her.

She turned and looked at me seductively (at least that's how I read it).

"So you've had a lot of female company here or was this just for me?"

"Would you believe me if I said just for you?"

"No, but it doesn't matter, because they're all for me now, anyway."

She paused and smiled for dramatic effect, and then closed the bathroom door.

Dinner was a throwback and homage to Tad's. Grilled steaks, buttered baked potatoes, and salad. Kiyy had her Hawaiian Punch and I had my Welch's grape.

"I hope you are okay with the clothes I bought, Kiyy?"

"Thank you. They're fine. I'm glad I'm still the size you remember. :-) I will certainly have to do some shopping though, as I can't expect Profit to still have my clothes at his spots."

"I'll ask him. We didn't think about that. I don't think he would have thrown your clothes away though."

"I didn't see any lingerie. What do you expect me to wear to bed? One of your old t-shirts? Nothing? Are you trying to seduce me, Que?"

"No, Kiyy, I am not."

She gives me a pouty look.

"You can wear an old t-shirt if you'd like, or the gown or PJ's I bought for you."

"Did you seriously say 'gown,' Que? What am I, fifty now?"

"You'd be the best looking fifty year old I've seen."

Damn it, she got me relaxing. Matching her flirty remarks.

"Would I? My competition used to be just Janet Jackson, has that changed?"

"She's still competition."

"Why you still gonna have that woman getting cut? Ain't nothing changed on my end either. Let her ring your bell. She gettin' shanked!"

"You still jealous over Janet, Kiyy?"

"I ain't jealous, love. Just the facts, nothing but the facts," she laughed.

We enjoyed the laugh together, and that led to more reminiscing. The thing about nostalgia and reminiscing, it brings back all the good memories that were associated with those times. Fellas, she was seducing me and didn't have to touch me. Then I remembered, she was versed in the ways. She learned her lessons well. I can't be mad at the student showing the teacher what she learned. I looked at my phone, no call or text from K.P. I thought about calling her.

"Our first date is still my favorite. The train rides, Tad's, the ice cream, and of course, the Circle Line."

"What do you remember?"

"I remember everything. What we were wearing, what we ate, you stealing looks at me."

"I wanted to keep an eye on your sundress to make sure it didn't blow up from the wind ..."

"That might have worked for 'the next girl,' but I remember a perfect day with no wind at all," she smirked.

"Hmmph," was all I could manage with a wry smile.

"I also remember me surprising you with a kiss, and then later our first real kiss, and the kissing in the car."

"You really remember that, huh?"

"I do, Que. It was all I had to hold onto for a long time. Carlos was so mean all of the time. As I said, he constantly threatened your life, and took pleasure in the torment it caused me."

"When did he get all of this bravado? He was straight punk in high school. When I came looking for him, he was out of the country because you told Pam you told him to leave, 'cause I was coming to town."

She looked at me and slowly shook her head.

"You told Pam you told Carlos to leave the country, giving her the impression that Carlos was scared, right? But that's not true?"

"I'm sorry, it's not true. I knew Pam would tell you something so I meshed stories to tie in together. I also knew you would be on the warpath, and I did it as much to protect you because I honestly didn't know what could happen on his end. I knew what would happen on your end."

"But what about Pam saying that Carlos freaked out after our conversation?"

"I manipulated that whole conversation. I made it seem that Carlos was scared to Pam. It seemed more believable to me."

"Damn, so he never went to Bolivia for Spring Break?"

"He did. To see his mother."

"Damn, Kiyy!"

"You can't be upset with me for that, baby. I mean you can, but I wish you wouldn't."

"It's good to know the truth, Kiyy. My emotions are just gonna be my emotions, okay? Whatever they are. He's still a punk ass, and he better hope I never find him."

"Que, can we watch a movie?"

"What do you want to watch?"

"What do you think?"

I laughed. I went to find the movie in my DVD collection and put it on. I'd call K.P. in the morning.

"I can't believe you still like *Ferris Bueller's Day Off!*"

"It's a classic! Can we do a double feature? You can pick the second movie?"

"Okay."

"Wait! I gotta get a bowl of Funyuns! Do you want anything, honey?"

"Yeah, just breath mints!"

She returned and pinched me before snuggling up to me. It felt familiar. It felt like old times. It felt good. Except the crows kept cawing ... they kept cackling. They had moved from in front of the house, and perched themselves on tree limbs behind the house in my backyard facing the basement entrance. I had looked out the bay window into the backyard while Kiyy was getting her Funyuns and saw nothing, but clearly something wasn't sitting right with these crows. Ferris Bueller had ended and I picked *Usual Suspects* for our second movie. It was one of *my* favorites. I put the movie on and repositioned myself on the sectional as Kiyy returned to her comfort position against me.

While I changed DVDs, she had gone to the bathroom, brushed her teeth, and came out in one of my t-shirts. Her hair was down, and the section that was shaved for her surgery was growing in nicely... and she looked sexy as hell! No bra as far as I could tell, and she was wearing panties with the t-shirt. She snuggled up to me and casually (purposely), brushed past Floyd.

Trust me, there was nothing I could do to avoid the inevitable. I wanted her. She knew I wanted her, but she was content in letting me struggle with it. She looked at me and whispered in my ear. Her lips felt incredible against my neck as they made their way to my lips. Our lips met and years of longing flushed out of our beings. The longing in her eyes unleashed a fire within me that I had suppressed, but now found myself engulfed by it. We got up from the sectional slowly and she took my hand as I walked her back to the bedroom.

I had set up the spare bedroom for her to sleep in. But deep down, we both knew that was a front.

I picked her up in front of the bed and gently laid her down. I took off my clothes methodically as she laid there watching me with flame in her eyes. I took her panties off, took the t-shirt off, and looked at her body. Perfectly rounded breasts on her slender frame with a butt to match. Neither stitches nor a bullet wound could mar that body!

I started from the top and worked my way down, enjoying her moaning, remembering spots that elicited certain reactions. She was my masterpiece, and my tongue was the brush painting this perfect picture.

Her first climax was explosive. I didn't let her recover. I thought I could never get as hard or as big as I had gotten before, but I had and I entered her slowly at first, and then aggressively pushed all of me into her as she let out a satisfying groan. The pleasure of pain! Our bodies locked, and our rhythm was slow and deep. She grabbed me within and pulled me deeper with vice-like precision.

Her second orgasm was met with my first as we went through a history of positions. Her hunger not satisfied, she got on top and drove us both to a third and second apogee, as she collapsed on top of me. Hours of ecstasy finally caught up to us. We fell asleep.

The crows woke us up, but it was too late. Before I could react, Kiyy's naked body was pulled off of me, just as a hand covered her muffled scream. The gun was placed to my head as I lay in the bed naked. Carlos entered the bedroom. He nodded at Kiyy, then turned his attention to me.

"I started to bust in while you two were making whoopee, but I decided to let you have that one last romp before you died. The look on your face reads surprise, Gregory."

He looks me up and down and continues, "You're bigger than I thought. I can see why Kiyy was anxious to get back to you. And what the other one sees in you."

"What are you talking about, the other one?" I spat.

"Gregory, did you really think that my father was gonna stop me from killing you both? By the way, thanks for the heads up. I would have never been able to get into your place. Yes, I've been here for a couple of days now. My men thank you for the food."

The crow's cackling was warning me of danger. Carlos was already in the house when we got here. The basement is the only place he could have gotten in and been, and I assumed it had been secured and swept before we got there. How wrong I was. He had to get in during some shift or transition from Profit's people.

"What do you have against me?"

"*What do you have against me?*" Carlos mimicked. "You killed my first love!"

"What!?! I don't know what you're talking about, Carlos. I don't know anyone that you know."

"Oh you do. You knew Snow, no? But back to the matter. You were on the benches at 305 when he approached you. You shot him on the ground. You were with two other guys, one no longer with us, the other soon to be joining you."

It hit me like a freight train. He was talking about the Outlaw that got killed that approached me, Donovan, and Profit, years ago.

"The look says you remember," Carlos presumed.

"I didn't kill that guy—"

Carlos runs to me at the bed, grabs the gun from the guy holding it to my head.

"Shut up Gregory! Shut up! His name was Tito! It was you. I saw you! I saw you shoot him! I was the one shooting at you afterwards when I saw what you did!"

"I didn't shoot him, Carlos. I shot the gun, but I fired into the ground."

It didn't really matter at this point who did what. Carlos thought I did it. Donovan was dead, and Carlos wanted me and Prof to join him. Talk about a small world! It is crazy how worlds collide.

I looked at Kiyy. She was shivering.

"Can you get her some clothes? She's shivering."

Carlos looked at Kiyy. She was shivering from fear or cold, but she was still naked. Carlos snapped his fingers.

"Get the whore some clothes," he ordered.

"I'm gonna kill you," I muttered.

"What was that, Gregory? You're going to kill me? Tough talk from your side of the room there, ya think?"

"Let Kiyy go!"

"Let her go? And have her miss your final performance? She stays, as well as the other one."

"Who the fuck are you talking about!?!" I yelled.

"The one you call K.P.? Yes?"

The stunned look said everything he needed to know as the color drained from my face.

"Yes, Gregory, it was easy getting her. What night was it that she left your house? Friday? Saturday?"

"You need to let them go, Carlos! This is between me and you!"

"Says the guy that watches too much TV! They're gonna have front row seats watching you die. Although I haven't decided yet whether to let them see you get killed first or let you see them get killed first. What say you, amigo?"

"I say let's settle this like men!"

"Oh and fight it out to the death, right?" Carlos replies. "You'd like that chance wouldn't you? Too bad the odds are against that happening. You're gonna die and I'm the one who decides how it happens, comprende?"

"Carlos, take me back!" Kiyy pleaded. "Spare Que. I'll do whatever you want me to do."

"Silencio, punta!" Carlos hissed. "They'll be no deals with you or anyone else!"

"Where is K.P.!?!" I demanded.

"You see that? You beg me to spare him and he asks about the other one?"

"He asked you to let me go first, asshole!" Kiyy blurted.

"That he did, Kiyler. That he did," Carlos reasoned. "But it was before he knew about the one called K.P. Interesting, nonetheless. Who would he care about me killing more?"

"What are you gonna do, Carlos? You got in here, but you won't be able to get out!"

"Oh, but I will, Gregory. And you're gonna help me. You're going to tell whomever you need to tell that I am walking out of here with you, Kiyy, and that one called Profit? Or guess what? Can you guess? Come on, can you guess?"

"Let them go, Carlos!"

"Oh, you don't want to play along? Okay, I'll answer. The one you call K.P. dies!"

"I can't get Profit to turn himself over to you, Carlos."

"Okay, then K.P. dies. That was simple, no?"

"Why are you keeping Kiyy? Let her go!"

"No can do, hombre. Kiyler told my father that I killed my uncle. She *will* die for that!"

"She didn't do that! I did that! I have the phone!" I exclaimed.

That seemed to pique Carlos' interest.

"You have the phone?" Carlos inquired. "Where is it?"

"In a place where if either Kiyy or myself gets harmed, it gets released."

"Tell me where the phone, it is?" Carlos demanded.

"Let Kiyy and K.P. go, then we can talk about the phone!"

He pondered that for a second and then thought better of it.

"No. You will call whomever you need to call to get us out of here."

He handed me a phone. I did not take it. With the gun still in his hand, he started to run up on me again, but if there is one thing he knew from knowing me, it's that I would gladly sacrifice myself for Kiyy. Even now.

As he turned and walked toward Kiyy, he cocked the gun.

"I'm only going to say this one time, Gregory. Take the phone and make the call."

He placed the gun to Kiyy's head.

"Okay, okay, okay, Carlos. Leave Kiyy alone. I will make the call."

I took the phone and dialed a number.

"That's not the right number," I muttered. "Give me a minute to remember. He gave me a new number. What is it?"

I dialed a second time, and Kiyy looked at me. She knew I was lying. She knew I remembered Profit's number. What she didn't know is that I sent a code to Profit, and he and his people would be blowing down the door in a few.

"I called Profit's number and put in a code. He will call back."

"Call back?" Carlos uttered. "What do you mean he will call back?"

"The number I have for him is a pager."

"A pager!" Carlos bellowed. "Coño, who carries a pager in this day and age!?!"

"Can I put on my boxers?" I asked.

"What? Or should I say *Que?* Your name is so funny to me. Gregory What! Gregory *Que?* Gregory Who? Gregory Que! I crack me up, I tell you! You feel funny being naked in front of all these men, sí, Gregory? Yes, Gregory?"

Carlos looked around the room. He saw clothes thrown this way and that.

"Couldn't contain yourselves, could you? Find your clothes and get dressed, both of you."

He saw my boxers on the floor, picked them up and put them to his face, taking a prolonged whiff. He then threw them at me and took amusement in the disgust on our faces at his perversion. He watched us dress with the same amused look until he tired of it.

"We will be leaving shortly. Why hasn't he called back, Gregory?"

Before I could answer, the bedroom door swung open and gun fire burst in. Everyone hit the floor as pandemonium erupted in the bedroom. Two of Carlos' men dropped as Carlos turned his gun to the doorway. I dove for the gun of one of the fallen as Carlos trained his gun on me. I reached the gun just as Carlos reached Kiyy, and we both aimed at each other at the same time. Carlos grabbed Kiyy and put the gun to her head and used the rest of her body as his shield.

"If I die, she dies!" Carlos yelled loudly.

"Let her go!" I yelled back. "You're not getting out of here with her!"

"I am! Did you forget I have the one you call K.P., muchacho? Give me the keys to your car, now!" Carlos demanded.

I looked around the room. While the math favored us, Kiyy and K.P were indeed the wildcards. We all knew it. With my gun still aimed at Carlos,

I felt for my car keys on my dresser. More gun fire outside as Carlos looked anxiously at the door. I looked as well, expecting to see Profit and more men bust in. Men appeared in the doorway and more gunfire. It was Carlos' men. In an instant, they took out all of Profit's people in the room.

"What took you so long!?!" Carlos spat.

"We waited for him to show like you wanted. We got him when he came out of the truck."

Got him? Got who?

"Gregory, if I were you, I would lower that weapon, because it is the only chance that you get to see Kiyler, and the one you call K.P., stay alive just a little while longer!"

All of Carlos' men had their guns aimed at me. I was clearly outnumbered. I lowered the weapon and tossed it on the bed. What happened to Profit!?! He had to get my distress page.

My question was answered as two of Carlos' men brought Profit into the bedroom.

"You guys think you are so smart with your 'plans,' but I am smarter!" Carlos bragged. "Did you think I really thought you were calling, paging, this one you call Profit!?! And that he would actually call you back? Estúpido, of course I knew you were alerting him!"

We were ushered outside and ordered to get into waiting vehicles. Before I got in, I yelled at Carlos.

"Where is K.P.!?!"

Carlos looked at me and chuckled.

"All this testosterone, homie, is turning me on, I cannot lie. Don't worry, my friend. The party is just getting started. The one you call K.P. is waiting for your arrival, trust me!"

I smirked at Carlos, content with that answer, and was shoved into a van. The ride was quiet as Profit, Kiyy, and I were left with our own thoughts. Thoughts of demise, thoughts of escape, thoughts of love. It's funny how peril kind of forces thoughts on you. Thoughts you may not normally think of except in peril. But my thoughts centered around Kiyy and K.P. I looked at Kiyy. I replayed how she looked on the deck of the Circle Line on our first date. I thought about all of the great times we had together. I thought about the time I spent with Kiyy in the hospital, the time we just spent at the house, and how it made me feel. I thought about what we could be. I thought about what it would mean without her here.

I thought about K.P. I replayed how she looked when I opened the door and saw her the other day.

I thought about all the great times we had together. I thought about the time I spent with K.P. since she told me how she felt about me, and how it made me feel. I thought about what we could be. I thought about what it would mean without her here.

I loved them both. But at that moment, I decided that I loved one a little more than the other. I could make a decision. I could now choose who I wanted to spend the rest of my life with!

We arrived at a large warehouse near the water. We were driving for a while, maybe to get rid of possible tails, maybe because it took a while to get where we were going. I tried to get a bead on where we were, but I could not tell if we were still in Brooklyn or not.

We were placed in an elevator shaft and taken to the top floor of the warehouse. The space itself was open ended, not sectioned off, and it made the whole area seem huge. Large round metal beams or pillars protruded through the concrete floors up to the ceiling. There were holes in the pillars, in the concrete walls and floors.

In the middle of the warehouse was K.P., tied up against one of the beams facing two gym benches. The benches were shaped in a jack knife position.

Carlos ordered Kiyy to be tied up to a beam parallel to K.P.

K.P. managed a weak smile when she saw me. She didn't appear to be hurt, and I nodded at her.

Carlos had Profit and I strapped to each bench. Our arms were strapped onto the opposite end of the bench, as our heads and upper torso were straddled along the length of the bench, with our legs and ends straddled toward K.P. and Kiyy. It was a funny position to be in, but it became clear soon enough.

"Take their pants down!" Carlos ordered.

We both struggled to no avail as it became clearer as to the possibilities of our fates. Our bare asses and legs were extended for all to see! (_0_)

"I thought about fucking you myself," Carlos began. "It would give me pleasure and humiliate you at the same time. Especially you, Gregory. Seeing the look on your face as I'm pounding into you while the women who love you watch is oh so tempting. But I need to make you both suffer. So I decided to do something my uncle would do."

With that, he motioned and two separate cages with two rats suddenly appeared. Both K.P and Kiyy squealed in horror at the sight of the rats and what suddenly became apparent to all in the room.

Holy shit! Suddenly Donovan's face appeared as I could not help but to remember hearing about the gory details surrounding his demise. This shit just got real, if it hadn't hit you before!

"I'm gonna let this rat fuck you and eat you at the same time!" Carlos trumpeted. "Who wants to go first!?!"

I don't think there was anything that any of us could say to negotiate out of this predicament, but that didn't stop Profit from trying. I honestly can't say I blamed him.

"Whoa, yo!?!" Profit began. "If this is about territory, yo, we can come to some kind of understanding, yo!"

"You didn't fill him in, Gregory?" Carlos chided me. "This has nothing to do with territory, but if you must know, I've reacquired all the territory Donovan took from my uncle and taken all of your territory, Señor Profit. It has everything to do with your involvement with the murder of my beloved Tito!"

"Who!?!" Profit yelled. "Who the fuck is Tito, yo!?!"

"Tito is the man that you killed in the park of P.S. 305 years ago. You, Donovan, and Gregory were there!"

"I don't know what you're talking about, yo!"

As soon as Profit uttered the words, it hit him, just like it had me. He had an epiphany, and he suddenly knew exactly who and what Carlos was talking about.

"I didn't kill no Tito, yo!" Profit offered. "Who was he to you, yo? Brother?"

"You were there! I saw you! I shot at you!" Carlos roared.

"You was the guy spitting bullets running towards us, yo?" Profit gasped.

"You killed my heart. My first love! The love of my life!"

"The dude that was in the gang!?! He was gay!?!" Profit mumbles incredulously.

Not exactly what I would say at that moment, but if that's how it hits you, then that's what you might say. It clearly set Carlos off, though.

"Coño! Me da rata!" Carlos raged.

One of the cages was brought to Carlos, and he took the rat out. Even with a firm grip, it squirmed in his hand. The girls screamed as he walked toward Profit. He put the rat near Profit's asshole and the rat sniffed and got eager.

I suddenly had the most vile thought that this motherfucker had been keeping these rats hungry and feeding them nothing but human waste!

The first scream from Profit was blood curdling!

Carlos had my bench pushed back so that I got a bird's eye view of the rat's insertion and subsequent clawing into Profit's exposed hole. I closed my eyes as the last vision I saw was the rat's tail dangling out of Profit's asshole and then it disappeared. The screams were all I heard until they just stopped, and Profit's body just went limp. I don't know if he died of shock, a heart attack, or whatever the rat was doing inside of him, but that is possibly the worst way a person can die. And I was next!

Carlos clapped with delight, as even his own men squirmed uncomfortably trying to remain masculine and dignified.

"That went much better than I could have ever imagined!" Carlos squealed.

He looked at Kiyy and K.P., and then looked at me as he grabbed the other rat from its cage.

Remember when I said that you have all kinds of thoughts when peril presents itself. Thoughts of your demise, thoughts of your escape, thoughts of love? Well, I wish I could tell you I went out with thoughts of love. I can't. My last thought was trying to figure a way to prolong my fate. My thought was to excrement (yes, I just made a new verb!), onto the floor in the hope that the rat would be more interested in that than me. I'm keeping it real with you, here. I started to leave this out, but you've rode with me this far, I figure I owe you guys the truth … the good, the bad, and the ugly! Or the repulsive in this case!

Carlos moved me to within three to five feet of K.P. and Kiyy. He dangled the rat in front of my ass and let the rat sniff. He seemed to want to build up the rat's frenzy by teasing it with sniffs and pull backs.

K.P. and Kiyy screamed.

"Please, Carlos. Don't!" Kiyy yelled.

Carlos let the rat claw at me. As I felt its claws scrape my skin, I became nauseated at what was about to happen to me. This isn't how I'm supposed to go out. It can't be!

"I love you, Que!" Kiyy cried.

"Oh, isn't that romantic?" Carlos smiled. "Would the one called K.P. like to say something, the same maybe?"

K.P. looked at me and then looked at Carlos.

"He knows how I feel about him. Fuck you!" she spat at him.

No, she literally spat in his face.

"I think you'll be next. I was just going to shoot you, but you just earned your ticket!" Carlos huffed, wiping the remnants from his face with his free hand.

Carlos stepped away from her and led the dangling rat back above my insertion hole. The rat, stirred into a frenzy, was trying to bite the end of his tail that Carlos was holding to get to me. Carlos smiled at the rat's tenacity and held it high for all to see. He began to lower the rat as K.P. and Kiyy screamed for him to stop.

The first crow burst through the warehouse window at the same time a shot took out the rat that now dangled limply from Carlos' hand. The crow made a beeline straight toward Carlos and attacked him as scores of crows followed through the broken glass. The caws of the crows unsettled inhabitants of the warehouse as rats came out of hiding places in the holes of the pillars, walls, and floors, scurrying to find new hiding places, but the endless flow of crows began eagerly picking them off one by one.

The crows seemed to be cackling with glee as they scooped rats running for their mortal lives. Carlos and his people started shooting at the crows as the endless murder of crows turned their attack onto them.

It was at that time that Carlos' men started dropping! It was Tariq and a small army of ex-militia! They were taking Carlos' men out with pinpoint precision head shots!

Tariq had already made his way to me and was freeing me from my restraints. In the ensuing rat's nest, I looked at Profit. The rat that was inside of him managed to find his way back out the same way he went in. It must have gotten shook from the chaos of the crows. It stuck its head out first and retreated and then burst through, hitting the floor running. Perhaps it was poetic justice, but just as that rat looked like it was going to reach cover, a crow swooped in, landed on it and pecked it repeatedly before scooping it and flying away.

Profit was never a believer in the crows like Donovan was, but he must have released all of the crows Donovan trained before he left for my house. Those crows summoned crows near and far, and still more crows continued the S.O.S., until they all met darkening the sky and converging on the warehouse. We still don't know how Donovan trained all of those crows, but salute and thanks to Profit for trusting in Donovan and trusting that the crows would know what to do, whatever that was. It seems somewhat clear that they were trained to find and protect people, at least that's what I'm choosing to believe.

I wish I had not paged Profit the distress code we agreed upon. I can't help but take responsibility for his death. I got to live with that one, and it will bother me for the rest of my life.

"What took you so long!" I yelled at Tariq through the gunfire.

More of Carlos' men came from stairways and the elevator shaft on the opposite side of where Tariq and his men entered as the gunfight ensued.

"The tracking went dead within a block of this building. We had to search each building to find you," Tariq replied. "Then the crows showed up!"

"Thank God you *all* got here when you did," I managed.

Remember when Carlos gave me the phone? I activated tracking devices that Tariq insisted I place on Kiyy and K.P. since I would not accept his standing offer. I gave Kiyy a "K" necklace that enclosed a tracking device, and I gave K.P. a bracelet with a K.P. charm enclosed with a tracking device as well. So glad I did that! So glad Tariq was persistent!

At that moment, I saw Carlos run past us looking like he was heading for the stairway.

"Free the girls!" I yelled to Tariq as I tore after Carlos.

I caught him just before the entrance to the stairwell. Years and years of rage came out of me as I punched and punched him. He smiled at me as I continued to pound his face.

"Say good bye to your precious Kiyler, and the one you call K.P., Gregory," Carlos struggled through broken teeth, as he pressed a button that had apparently been in his hand.

"No!" I yelled as my final punch shattered Carlos' face.

The explosion rocked the building, followed by another and another. The building imploded as parts of floor crashed onto others below as parts of the building stood firm.

The first explosion separated Tariq from K.P. and Kiyy as the beams snapped, and they both plunged a floor below with Kiyy hanging on to a steel beam sticking out of the concrete and K.P. holding another a few feet away. There was a big hole that separated Tariq and his men continuing the gunfight with Carlos' remaining men. The concrete holding the steel beams that Kiyy and K.P. was holding onto was crumbling, and there was nothing to break their fall except rubble five stories below.

I made my way to the edge of the floor where the hole had been blown to see the women that I love dangling below. I surveyed the situation as quickly as I could and told them I was climbing down to save them. I determined that it was best to try and lower myself onto the slab of concrete near them so as not to unsettle it, as I might have if I had jumped down. I was about equal distance from both of them if I extended my arm and held onto a protruding steel beam. As my weight landed on the concrete slab, it shifted, and a large piece of the concrete broke off and crashed into the slab holding K.P. and Kiyy. The concrete broke in two as Kiyy and K.P. dangled on their own slab of concrete, holding onto the steel beam with both hands. The slab now looked U-shaped as they both were out of my immediate reach.

"I can't hold on much longer, Que!" Kiyy cried out.

"Que, I can't either!" K.P. labored.

"Don't you let go, Kiyler!" I yelled.

"Don't you let go, K.P.!" I yelled.

Some concrete above fell and nearly hit me as it crashed into the slab I was on and further loosened the piece wedged underneath that held K.P. and Kiyy. It jerked and they jerked with it.

The sound of gunfire and crows still echoed in the building, and I couldn't see Tariq or his men from my perch on the concrete above Kiyy and K.P.

An audience gathered. Crows eyeballed me from an exposed steel beam. And then it began. The cackling of the crows. But one crow remained silent. It continued to look at me with a slight tilt to its head. Its eyes had a yellow haze and it began a rhythmic caw. For a few seconds I thought it was cheering for me. Then just as suddenly, it stopped and I was startled out of my trance.

Kiyy suddenly started crying.

"I know you love her now, Que! Save her, save K.P!" Kiyy pleaded.

"I know you never stopped loving Kiyy, Que!" K.P. countered. "How could you!?! I was there. I saw what you went through. Save Kiyy, Que! I can't hold on."

"Don't you let go, K.P.!"

"Don't you let go, Kiyler!"

Suddenly, the slab I was on gave way and crumbled. There was nothing I could do as I tumbled onto the top of the U-shaped slab that held K.P. and Kiyy. My life suddenly flashed before my eyes as I saw my family, Winnie, my boys, friends, first kisses with Kiyy and K.P., first "I love you's," kids I would never see, and finally the woman that I envisioned spending the rest of my life with. I realized what I would have written to you in a book.

I guess it's a great time to tell you that I never got the chance to write this book. I think it would have been a best seller, probably a blockbuster movie too!

As I tumbled past them, their screams merged with the gunfire and the cackling of the crows. But what stood out for me was the cackling of the crows … they knew it all along …

As their screams echoed in the building, and I tumbled past both of them, I reached out to …

Wash, rinse, repeat.

THE END

ABOUT THE AUTHOR

Neal Sellers is a practicing attorney for over 20 years, he writes poetry, and is an accomplished song writer and music producer. A member of Omega Psi Phi Fraternity, Inc., since 1985, Neal is a cigar enthusiast, whiskey aficionado and diehard fan of the Mets, Steelers and Lakers. He has four daughters, and a granddaughter. A native of Brooklyn, New York, with southern roots, Neal makes a perfect banana pudding, and currently lives with his wife in Philadelphia, PA.